In
Bloom

Also by Eva Verde

Lives Like Mine

In Bloom

EVA VERDE

SIMON &
SCHUSTER

London · New York · Sydney · Toronto · New Delhi

First published in Great Britain by Simon & Schuster UK Ltd, 2023

Copyright © Eva Verde, 2023

The right of Eva Verde to be identified as author of this work has been
asserted in accordance with the Copyright, Designs and Patents Act, 1988.

1 3 5 7 9 10 8 6 4 2

Simon & Schuster UK Ltd
1st Floor
222 Gray's Inn Road
London WC1X 8HB

Simon & Schuster Australia, Sydney
Simon & Schuster India, New Delhi

www.simonandschuster.co.uk
www.simonandschuster.com.au
www.simonandschuster.co.in

A CIP catalogue record for this book is available from the British Library

Hardback ISBN: 978-1-3985-0287-1
eBook ISBN: 978-1-3985-0289-5
Audio ISBN: 978-1-3985-2265-7

Typeset in the UK by M Rules
Printed and Bound in the UK using 100% Renewable Electricity at
CPI Group (UK) Ltd

MIX
Paper | Supporting
responsible forestry
FSC
www.fsc.org   FSC® C171272

For Betty, my lovely, one-of-a-kind nan, who adored M&S and astrology and who'd likely keel over again if she could see me now

And for everyone who has ever known an Itsy

'Life and love are very precious when both are in full bloom.'

Louisa May Alcott, *Little Women*

Grief is a Forever Binding Thing

*It's a wickedness
how a person can take
not only one life
in a moment of hate
but screw up
so many others.*

*Destroying any future
and any peace of mind,
which to own, even once, is a privilege.*

*Just some pissflap,
who comes along on the random
and smashes something wonderful,
the shards from that act
wounding everyone around them.
That keeps on wounding,
generations to come.*

*How selfish.
How typically human.*

Moon Moon, *(Autumn 2023)*

THE DANGER OF A SINGLE STORY

Wellsend, Essex, 2023

Delph's not taken any chances by keeping her phone on. Tracking apps are not beyond Itsy, yet it's remarkable how it's only now, in the biting reality of this sad and sorry Friday afternoon, that his distrust starts to bother her.

When the nurse dispenses her meds, the fat final pill and a tiny one to stop the sickness, Delph swallows them without hesitation. This is day two of the process. Day two of the excuses. And, after today, it will be over. No more visits to this pale-yellow room that's not the least bit sunny. Everyone is kind though; she gives the place that. A rare oasis, for such suddenly delicate women – Delph included – all in the same boat here, picking up their pieces, coming undone. Trying regardless.

The nurse talks up the injection, the prevention from this

EVA VERDE

happening again, instantaneous peace of mind, and, though peace feels too much of a privilege, Delph just can't summon all she felt for her firstborn, Roche. This time around it is not the same. The small beginning in Delph's stomach doesn't feel made from any sort of love. In fact, instead of baby joy, there's been ...

Panic's an underestimation; that Delph should find herself a slip through the net statistic, one of the four per cent the contraceptive pill fails – at forty-bloody-two years old. Forty-two, when she should be beyond such accidents, what with Roche almost adult, already more together than she's ever been. After her A-levels, it's merely a matter of time until she flies the nest – as far from home as she can get, more than likely. Delph already knows Roche won't come back. Why would she – and isn't that half the problem?

There's been moral turmoil too. The underhand practicalities of arranging this off her own doorstep, then plucking an excuse from the sky, a ruse to leave town when Delph never leaves for anywhere – and is also lying, however she tries to dress it up.

The jab in Delph's bum marks the final step. A handful of leaflets. A form she quickly shoves in her bag, along with the tests. Says, 'Thank you.' Is thankful. Feels no different.

At the bus stop, a discreet stone's throw from the clinic, it begins to rain. The droplets creep beneath her mac to penetrate Delph's blouse, leaving her slick and slippery. And it's water she craves, home now to the flat, timed meticulously, so perfectly, missing Itsy heading out on his shift; as with

2

one foot in the shower, different droplets, dark as beet, hit the floor before she's the chance to lift the other into the tub. The visual shock of it brings giddy relief, like she's floating above herself, watching on. And, within the steam of the shower, it becomes only Delph again.

There were the obvious reasons for this termination, that clinical, mechanical-sounding word. Unplanned. Unexpected. Itsy finding out, then deciding it's not the end of the world – which is exactly what's kept this her mistake, her error. Her secret. But then, then, there are the other reasons too. This pregnancy shone far too bright a light on all Delphine Tennyson's truths. Worse, it kept her face in the bare brunt sting of them.

Delph doesn't want a baby.

Not now. Not with Itsy. Not with anyone. Ever again.

Neither does Delph want the strange sense of hopelessness that came the moment she knew she was pregnant: the thought of more years, *more life*, tied to him.

Roche hopes her last hour of school before the weekend begins is a quiet one. It's some English/Personal Development hybrid lesson. School morale's low. Of course it is. Look at the state of the world. Roche sits up, straightening her shoulders, as from the whiteboard the teacher reads out the phrase:

'WRITE THE TRUEST SENTENCE YOU KNOW.'

'D'you want my truest thing?' Winnie Russell, the resident class pick-me asks the teacher, her huge, stencilled brows alarming and false on her delicate face. 'You can't solve evil.'

Dramatic gasps burst out around the room. 'Yeah,' she says. 'Deep, innit?'

'Who can't solve evil?' the teacher replies, some semi-distracted substitute who knows none of them. Everyone drops their eyes to study their desks or to gaze into the far corners of the classroom, because no one – other than Winnie 'verbal shits' Russell – is about to start over-revealing to this stranger, or, *even worse*, to each other: peers, who'll rip the proper piss across socials the second you make a public tit of yourself. Fact.

'No one. No one at all.' Winnie states. A stream of air hisses through her teeth as she exhales, like she's got an awful lot to say on the subject. Good. Hopefully they'll be locked in convo for the rest of the lesson.

'But what is "evil"?' the teacher probes encouragingly, and as Winnie thinks, Roche takes the opportunity to slip off into her own thoughts, gazing past the back of Winnie's head and through the classroom window that looks out onto nothing but field and sky, imagining all the ways she can fill her weekend, which, as standard for most seventeen-year-olds, should be full of fun. But for months Roche's weekends – in fact, any spare time at all – have devolved into ways of avoiding home: choosing extra shifts at the chippy, going to the Dojo, the library, down the parade, hanging about anywhere, really, even occasionally borrowing the keys to her best bitch Eden's, all to swerve the flat. And there ain't even been no Eden to chill with lately.

'All the badnesses,' Winnie says, at last. 'The wickednesses. Murders and wars and paedos.'

'Mmn-hmn. And what does evil mean to you – Rochelle, isn't it?' the teacher asks, now focused on Roche. Of all the desks to stop and come alive in front of. On a Fri-yay arvo, fuck's sakes.

'Evil's the karma that put me in here with you lot.' It gets the reaction Roche hopes for when most of the class laugh. 'And all the badnesses and wickednesses, of course.'

'And, what's the truest sentence you know?'

Roche takes a moment. 'One day we'll all be dead.'

'Well,' says the teacher, 'there's no disputing that.'

'No disputing them pervs either.' Winnie's heavy make-up can't hide the fear in her eyes. 'I swear down, they're every-where, man.'

Winnie's got more than a point. Roche knows, remembers, how her life changed at around the time she started second-ary, and her bubble of invisibility popped. How, despite the school uniform screaming otherwise, she very suddenly became the inhabitant of a woman's body, complete with a depressing self-awareness that this was now Roche's life until one day men deemed her invisible again.

In fairness, it's not her contemporaries who usually do the perving – no, it's men, *grown–ass men* who have always done the bulk of the wolf–whistling, the innuendoes and basic compliments, that they expect her to 'smile, love' and be grateful for it. No, compared to all those desperate, drooling old bastards, Roche's actual classmates are the least of her worries – more shit-scared, tbh, than anything else – she's not the 2019 Wellsend and Essex mixed martial arts champion for nothing. Roche probs won't ever be a champion again, but it doesn't matter. Learning to fight was always more important than the Olympic-sized plans that her sensei once dangled in front of her. And besides, who else would watch out for Mum while she was off living the dream, anyway?

The class debate is never-ending, tangenting into talk of pervy royals, pervy BBC presenters, pervy presidents, pervy grooming gangs and someone's pervy uncle. It. Is. Never-ending.

Worse, it's fucking depressing.

At last, the teacher speaks again. 'I've been told to mention that university decisions need finalising.' They say 'university decisions' like it's the heaven-sent antidote to Winnie's world full of badnesses. 'Assistance with UCAS forms, any questions at all, can be found in the handout I'll leave by the door. Time's ticking. But, seeing as it's Friday, let's leave today a bit early. Happy weekend, folks.'

Roche grabs her bag. Heading out, she picks up a brochure.

'Applying anywhere in particular?' the teacher asks her, friendly and connected, and quite nice, after all. Shame they won't ever teach her again.

'I've not thought much about it.' Roche glances again at the uni info, the true dream – another that she can never truly imagine. She gives the teacher a wicked grin. 'Maybe just somewhere there's no perverts would be a good start.'

Leaving school and heading off for home, Roche arrives back far too early. Dragging her heels up the landing towards the flat, she stops, her key hovering at the lock.

'That you, Ikkle Batty?' Itsy says from behind the door, and though Roche can't obvs see through it, she visualizes the scene on the other side most clearly. A smirking Itsy, manspreading in his special armchair, a pre-shift snack in the shape of a pasty or sausage roll resting on the arm of it, watching *Luther* for the bloody umpteenth time, ready to prod and pry into her personal shit that's none of his actual fucking business. 'Ikkle Batty', the inflammatory nickname that only gets said when Mum's not about, that no amount of Katas, gym training, or grand plans to escape to some far-off university can ever quench how much she'd love, love, *love* to put him flat on that poor weak back of his and slap up his stupid reptile-looking face. Roche can't even breathe properly in his presence, hates that he looks at her like he knows her – which feels both exposing and untrue. Itsy doesn't know her. And he is not her dad. Roche doubts such a statement would hurt him. Especially after yesterday.

But Roche can't, doesn't want to think of yesterday.

It takes a teenage snap decision before she's back at the lift, jabbing the buttons to take her away. She's done. Proper. Not with Mum, 'course not, but with Itsy – and there'll be no more pretending different; faking the happy everything's normal vibe when nothing is.

But where to go now?

Delph, stomping across broken glass in her mother's front lawn, for a fleeting second worries for Tyson, the tiny terrier who years back she found as a stray, then babied. Until his owners reclaimed him, anyway – her mother's version of events – after she returned from a two-day walk with only his lead.

Happy days.

Here, on the cusp of evening, back on the shittier side of the city that was once home, Delph finds she's carrying herself a little harder, notes the tension, the sudden heat in her muscles – surprising, considering. Odd, how just when she thinks she's no fight left, that she's the very worst parent in the world, the lioness inside roars from the rooftops, reminding her she's still clearly needed. Roche might be grown, but she's not at all ready to fly, especially not right into her grandmother's nest. It is a nest, in every sense of the word. Webbing, actual cobwebbing obstructs the bell, so Delph covers her hand with the sleeve of her jumper and bangs hard instead.

There's shuffling behind the door, then there she is, Mother Moon, full-on theatrical in that old gold kimono, like she's ready for performance. Reaching out, she squeezes Delph's arm, beaming ear to ear. 'Darlin'. Your girl is fucking incredible.'

'Oh, she is.' Delph stops, bites her lip. It's hard, hiding the joy any mention of Roche evokes. Harder too, not to somewhere, *somewhere*, be glad to see her mother like this. Utterly unchanged in their five years estranged. Still, very clearly, on planet Moon too. 'Let me see her.'

'I'd never stop you from seeing her,' Moon says, rather pointedly, just so Delph knows what's coming next. 'I'm not like you.'

'You did that to yourself.'

'With a little bit of help from His Highness.' Moon nods behind Delph, in the direction of Itsy, still in his car. 'Lest we forget.'

'I can't forget. That's the problem.'

'Five years.' Moon huffs. 'And not even a Christmas or birthday card.'

'And what birthday of yours did you want me to remember exactly?'

'There are four bloody seasons, Delphine Magenta. You can't go expecting me to cling to one bloody day I can't even remember.'

'But you're my mum, so what about my birthday? In fact, scrap me, Roche's birthdays . . .'

Yet, despite their silence, living opposite ends of the same sprawling town meant they'd still pass occasionally, when from the bus Delph might spot Mother Moon from a distance, pounding it up the high street with her wheelie shopper, or roaring with laughter outside the town centre post office with the same jobless crowd she remembered as a girl, when they'd fill up the house on Giro day. But to be physically present is something else. To look into her mother's eyes and be seen. Not as the person she's become in their quiet years apart, but as Delph. The original version. Amazing – and yes, comforting – that no matter how dysfunctional, Moon knows just how to trigger her, sending her sliding straight back into her old role. All the dynamics of old.

Delph pulls herself straight. Repeats. 'You did it to yourself.'

'I did,' Moon admits with a sigh. 'I did. But all the same, you're still my baby. Let me hold you.'

'For God's sakes,' says Delph. But it comes tenderly, on both sides. Mother Moon holds Delph close, before beginning the seeking that, sensing the intrusion in her thoughts, Delph pushes away. Too late.

Five years, and Delph needn't articulate anything at all. It has always been this way, that her mother could decipher the contents of her brain before Delph had figured out her own thoughts. Their unspoken confidence brings also transference – Moon now looking as though she'd been right beside Delph in that sad yellow clinic earlier, the pain plain on her face, incredible to witness, her emotions always at the mercy of whoever's in the room, feeling everyone's feelings, carrying their weights, their secrets.

Their losses.

'The sad thing was a good thing, love,' Mother Moon says, seizing both Delph's hands and the moment. Queen of the Empaths.

As the words sink in, Delph feels cleansed, absolved – almost – of all her terrible secrets. Yet it is the reminder of motherly love that comes most startling. Tonight – and just for once, mind – she is glad of their telepathy. Gladder still to be here with her mother. Not that she'd ever say it. Instead, she does let Moon hold her properly, and wrapped tight in that old cape that stinks of fags and nag champa perfume, Delph, for the first time in what seems like decades, feels safe.

'Careful, Delph,' starts Itsy. Despite his sciatica and lack of dinner, he chooses this as the moment to emerge from his car, sticking his size 11's through the mother-daughter reconnection. 'You know how this goes, love.'

'Here he is. Right on cue.' Moon, all 5 ft 10 of her, levels eyes with Itsy, her stare pinning him to the spot, as he takes not one step closer. She smiles, big and wild, enjoying his discomfort. 'Never been at ease round here, have ya?'

Itsy takes Delph's hand, which sits like a little stone within his. 'Just go and get the girl,' he says, bored already. 'None of us want to be here for any longer than we have to, trust me.'

'Trust you?' Moon tuts. 'I'd rather trust a diet of raw chicken.'

Without any need to be summoned, Roche appears next to Moon, matching her height and blanched almost as pale by the situation. With folded arms they mirror each other, their similarities striking: the wide cheek-boned faces, feline-esque against their tiny, pointed chins, eyes bright with the same ferocious look that startled Delph when Roche was first put in her arms as a baby. The little rock, for that's what Rochelle means, who saved her.

The moment Roche was born, Delph knew at once why her hopes for a boy had fallen unanswered. It would've been neither right nor healthy to raise a replacement, a son forever lost within the shadow of his ghost father. For Delph, when Sol died, her sun vanished too. But then, from the darkest grief came Roche, the raging reminder of life moving on, who once in her arms made her feel again. Who's kept her feeling all this time. Just about.

But this ... allyship. Fresh agony comes from the connection, alive and apparent, between her mother and Roche, the pain unlike the mental torture from earlier; her dull, knackered innards she should be resting.

Delph steps back from them. As if it's her turn now to be on the outside.

'Of all bloody places,' Delph tries, attempting some way – any way – in, but Roche, against a different backdrop, away from the familiarity of home, is inexplicably distant, as if she's been stolen by a mudslide, then washed up most conveniently at her nan's feet. In every sense Delph feels their galvanization, a united front she might try claiming too, if she hand-on-heart believed that Itsy wanted Roche home as much as she did.

'I ... just need to lie low for a bit.' Roche avoids Delph's eyes, like she knows what's coming next.

'Lie low – you in some sort of trouble?' To even think there's trouble, which is unquestionably Delph's fault, too wrapped up in her own dramas of late to—

'No, not like that. I just some need time out, Mum.' There is no give in Roche's voice. 'Nan said I can borrow a few bits. Plus, I've got my gym stuff.'

Nan-said-Nan-said-Nan-said.

Roche keeps her arms folded tight across her body. 'I'm staying here.'

Loneliness twists itself through Delph, taking root. 'But ... what am I going to do?' Oh, the searing need to just rest, to cradle her tummy of chemicals in bed, with Roche safe in the room next door, with her books and headphones and moods and headache-inducing array of body sprays.

The comfort from just knowing she's there.

'Time out?' Itsy mocks, nodding towards his Astra. 'Stop being a princess and get in the bloody car.'

'Speaking to her like that won't help!' Delph's voice is far louder than usual, and though she'll likely never hear the last of this, of her defiance, especially in front of her own bloody mother, Delph summons her last dregs of energy to stand her ground. 'So bloody stop it.'

Itsy kisses his teeth. 'Suit yourself.'

She should've come by herself. At least then she'd be sat down by now, sussing out the state of things from an insider's perspective or, worst case, equipping Roche for how to live with Moon, should Delph's negotiating attempts flop just as abysmally.

Because it isn't all kooky clairvoyancy. Living with Moon is a full-time job. An emotionally unforgiving, never-ending exhaustion. On the surface she seems such a fun parent: eccentric, certainly beautiful enough for the coarse, rebellious routine to be considered charming – cool even. When really—

'Please, Roche,' Delph tries again. 'Whatever this is, we can sort it. Can't we?' But Roche remains distant, fiddling with her phone. 'Roche!'

'Five minutes in this dump and she'll be begging to come home,' Itsy tells her.

'But . . .' What about Delph till then?

13

'I reckon some time apart will do us good – honestly, Mum.' Kindly said. Yet final. There is no shifting her. Roche will not be coming home today.

Accepting this is a far harder pill to swallow than those in the clinic earlier. And an act of resistance, not to smother her daughter, to demand she remains by her side. What stops Delph is lived experience. It is not for a child to fix the parent. Nor is Roche the ointment to Delph's current troubles.

She just didn't anticipate losing two babies in one day.

As Itsy heads back towards the car, Moon calls after him. 'All this must be driving you potty.' There's pure glee in her eyes, to at last be the one with the poking stick. 'Not being number one for five seconds.'

'I've looked after Delph for years.' Itsy stops in his tracks to face her. Standing tall, he trots out his treasured sentence with his shoulders back. 'Raised another man's child as my own.'

'Looked after? She might've been living again by now, if it weren't for you.'

Itsy looks Delph up and down, circling her, then gestures to her feet, which leaves her feeling tiny and pointless. 'There's no shackles on your daughter. She's free to do anything she wants. Only, she doesn't . . .' Itsy heads back along the pavement, leaning into Moon's face. 'Choose to.' He grins as Moon's smile vanishes. 'And she didn't choose you.'

'Caged birds and all that,' Roche chimes in, all of them casting Delph with their own inaccuracies, which sting all the same because they do contain a tiny grain of truth. Unflinchingly, Roche adds, 'A sickness. Ain't that right, Itsy?'

Geoffrey Pearson Jnr became Itsy when a small Roche realized how much it annoyed him. How anybody could become so triggered by a child's nickname was highly amusing, even to Delph. If only he could've shaken it off good-humouredly as a bit of kid-fun, she'd have moved on to teasing him with something else – which Roche seemed naturally compelled to do – but his outrage and vanity meant he'd forever be Itsy-Bitsy Spider, on account of his height, the long arms and legs, which, unless sitting down, he never seemed to have quite full possession of.

'When will you learn your place?' Itsy glares at Roche. 'And keep your mouth shut.'

'I keep my mouth shut over plenty, you piece of shit.'

Itsy's eyes bulge, stalking between Roche and Moon as they both stand firm, jutting out their similar chins and sending out bad vibes to their common enemy.

Delph knows, just as Itsy and the vibes do, that he's powerless here.

'Mark my words, nothing makes a mother roar louder than the love of her cubs,' Moon catcalls the retreating Itsy, claiming the pain as she always does, repurposing all Delph's shit into her own story. Is it really any wonder that Delph chose isolation instead of this woman. 'Nothing.'

'Unless that mother's you.' A savage Delph cuts her off. 'I swear to God, you best take care of her properly or I'll fucking kill you.'

There are flashes, on occasion, of Delph's smart-arse spark. Usually, they take longer to nurture.

But Delphine Tennyson is not herself.

'That smile.' Itsy starts once they're home, just the two of them, taking a mouthful of the quick supper he's made. The beans are not quite hot enough, his toast underdone, petty failures that Delph's already apologized for because she prioritized herself over his stomach, taking yet another shower, needing to cry, so hypersensitive she's now numb. 'Smirking at me, and all that mind-reading shit – woman's never not given me the creeps. And you ...' Itsy points his fork at her, as Delph slowly pads around the kitchen in her nightgown, clearing up. 'The three of you, like some witchery fuckery.'

Itsy can't comprehend how Moon knows things, any more than Delph can. Her mother has simply always been this way. To Itsy, Moon's energy is detrimental, like an iron deficiency, like he's losing his potency, which of course would be a travesty. To this day, on his night shifts, he'll avoid Moon's end of town, despite her local McDonald's being remarkably cleaner, more efficient, and ideal chill territory between fares, choosing instead the grot branch on Wellsend's outskirts.

'When I think of the drama that woman's brought to our table. *To your life.*' He shakes his head, caught between his own sufferings and pity for Delph. 'It doesn't take much to remember now, baby, does it? How she'd turn you against me. *Still trying to do it.* That fucking smile, man.' He's like the old Aesop's fable, the one about the scary lion with a thorn in his foot. All the fuss of a thorn, Itsy's minutiae of small-scale shit that he's lumped with Delph's catastrophe of actual shit.

How blessed he is to misunderstand real never-ending hurt.

'Time the girl learnt the truth about that woman, anyway.' Even now he's doing it, as he tries rearranging Delph's feelings by pretending that Roche's stay in Wellsend Grove will be her greatest lesson; dealing with her nan, the functioning addict who lives on chips. 'I give her the weekend. She'll be begging to come home, trust me.'

Those chips were gorgeous, though. As a child, Delph would often wake in the night to the plip-crack of oil at scorching temperatures. Then there she'd be, Mum, in from the pub, ready to talk all about it, who spoke to who, who's protesting what, as Delph watched her cook from the safety of the doorway, Mum's bell sleeves dancing with the fat spats, Delph's small fists sticky till they unclenched at last, when a plate of perfect chips was put in front of her, and the vision of seeing her mum gobbled up by flames receded. That steaming pile of gold. Blowing on them together. The luscious collapse of radioactive potato in her little kid mouth. Back when food was a pleasure.

'Did you and Roche have a row? Is that why she's gone?' Delph covers her face with her hands, as Itsy's fork clatters on his plate. 'I ... wouldn't be cross. I just need to know ...'

'No.' Itsy kisses his teeth. 'We did not row. What a question.'

'And I'm sorry to ask. Really, I am. I ... I just wish we could've made her listen.'

17

'When's that girl ever listened – respected me? All that non-sense about keeping quiet over plenty, when she's the one who never shuts up, all her feminist bullshit twenty-four-seven. Hating on the one man that's kept her fed and watered ...'

... Who lives and breathes to protect them. Itsy should have this lecture recorded, saved to his phone, saving him the effort, as he recollects his life of martyrdom again and again. Itsy and all his tiny thorns ...

While Delph rinses out his tin of beans, Mother Moon's words return to her: how the sad thing was a good thing, the electric strangeness of her mother in her head. As if to test them, Delph puts herself back in the clinic. Replaying the morning, frame by frame, she finds no guilt at all. And if it meant the same outcome, that she wouldn't be pregnant with Itsy's child, she'd get up and do it again tomorrow. Delph's background thoughts, her constant inner repetition mutes Itsy further, as she imagines, and not for the first time, running full pelt through the kitchen door that leads to their balcony, Delph's only sanctuary, the handkerchief garden in the sky, and tipping over the white balustrade, falling the fourteen floors that'd stop the sheer fucking anguish of failed contraceptives, surprise babies, shit mothers, runaway daughters and Itsy's many tiny thorns, for good. Fourteen floors; that'd stop the worry, stop the world, stop the past, stop the whole flaming lot. Falling puts a stop to the present too. The hurt of the here and now, still incomparable to all that's gone.

And she'd be gone too.

Softened by the Kit-Kat he eats without breaking in two, Itsy disappears for his evening wallow in the bath, and alone, Delph checks Roche's socials, closing her bedroom door without looking in.

Avoiding the tantalizing edge of the balcony, Delph touches the soil of her seedlings, finds there's little to tend to this evening. The small space groans with greenery, plants of all kinds, old and young, healthy and loved. A thin bench holds pots of new beginnings, small shoots, delicate and protected beneath a drawer from the old freezer. Gardening. One of the few good things she's kept close over the years. And Roche. Till now, anyway.

Roche. That she's not inside, in her room, lost to YouTube, makes Delph's tummy lurch in her absence. Giving in, sitting for a moment, Delph breathes, and as she wonders who she's breathing for, a voice drifts sadly from above.

'I know ... I, I know that. But what about me?' It's Geena, in the flat upstairs. *'I did everything, everything you wanted. Why don't you love me?'* She sounds adolescent, like this is first heartbreak; plaintive, desperate. *'What do you want me to do? Please. I'll change.'*

Knowing anybody else's drama will likely topple her; Delph hurries indoors and straight to bed, making herself small beneath the duvet as her thoughts linger on her friend upstairs, caught in a different sort of upset. Knowing Geena, as Delph's had the privilege of all her life, the source of her trouble is likely man-related. She'll find out what's going on when it filters through Eden, Geena's daughter and Roche's

19

forever best friend. Then Delph remembers. Her heart thumps in the darkness, abandoned and sore all over again. She won't have her live updates – not now Roche's gone.

Gone. It is the unknown duration, the indefinite edge to their parting, that keeps Delph curled tight like a little balled sock, sad to be alone. Until Itsy slips beneath the covers, keen and clean beside her, to dip his hands into her bra, the tender throb of her tits volcanic as he squeezes them. Putting Delph on her back disturbs the pad in her knickers, turning her uncharacteristically defensive, and she pushes him off, gently scooping herself back into the cotton cups. 'We can't. I've the mother of all periods.'

'Weird time for that, innit?' Itsy's lip curls, like he's caught the whiff of the rancid, perhaps a burning field of rotten calves. 'You taking your pill properly?'

Religiously. And fuck him, because look where it's got her. Slipping on her dressing gown in the cold darkness of the bathroom Delph sits on the loo, her hands shaking a little as she steels herself, avoiding the light switch. How many pads has she changed, half asleep, without thinking? Efficiently, she opens a new pad, resting it on her thigh, trembling when she finds the edge of the old.

A terrible period. This is all nothing more than a terrible period.

Itsy makes hot chocolate, with milk that he heats in a saucepan but doesn't rinse, and Delph's asleep before it's cool enough to drink.

*

THE PERCEPTIVE CHILD

Yellowhayes Hospital, Wellsend, 1968

Joy is put on her feet to climb the stairs herself, cos she's a big girl now and past being carried, but she won't climb. Joy doesn't want to follow Ma into the hospital where the screams are; up, up all the steps to see Grandma, who never speaks but stares and stares at the half-mint-half-beige wall, with its big old fireplace like a yawning mouth. Joy thinks Dad's right when he shouts at Ma that 'nut-houses' aren't places for little girls.

'Come on,' Ma says, in a giddy-up way. 'You know how happy your little face always makes her.'

But Grandma doesn't seem to remember Joy's face, or Joy's name, which has three letters, that she can write now herself. Joy doubts Grandma can even remember the colour of her own eyes, which are like empty skies these days, blank, like nothing's ever made them happy or sad or stirred any emotion at all, which ain't true, cos even if Grandma can't, Joy remembers, back when she lived in the spare room at home and was painted in proper colours.

'Half an hour, love. Thirty teeny tiny minutes,' Ma tries, with a smile that's painful – and if there's one thing Joy hates most it's seeing Ma hurt, so she lets her feet take her up to the day-room that's full of the shuffling sick people who aren't allowed their shoes. Up to Grandma, who doesn't know them anymore.

After a half-hour of Joy hiding around Ma's legs, Ma touches Joy's shoulder and says, 'Kiss your Grandma goodbye, then.'

With a big breath Joy moves towards Grandma, stopping when she spots a stray penny on the parquet, her little fingers delighting in its shininess before pressing it into Grandma's hand, that's so stiff and still it's a jolting surprise when she closes her hand around it, the coin vanishing into her fist.

The feeling hits Joy like electricity, a sensation of being watched by those barely-there eyes, and then, for a lone cogent moment, a bone finger outstretched, curling at Joy's face, the papery tip dry, so gentle. She's back.

'Take me home,' Grandma begs. 'Please.'

Even outside, as Ma bundles Joy into her coat, her eyes sore and red, Grandma's pleading words ring on repeat. 'Now.' Ma sniffs, sucking the sadness back into her body, making her neat again. 'Now that's behind us, where do you want to go?' With trembling hands, Ma ties a woollen hat like a tea cosy beneath Joy's chin. The chip shop is the child's immediate thought, but Ma looks eager to please, makes Joy push a little, reach for more, as all girls should and not feel bad about it.

'Is Grandma mad, Ma?'

'She's very tired.'

'Will she come home?' Ma's pained look means Joy doesn't push anymore. Instead, she holds Ma tight, breaking the sad spell that cloaks them with a round of funny faces. It works. Making Ma happy is a magical power that only Joy possesses.

'I know. Let's go and see the sea.' Ma parks right at the front of the pier – easily, cos it's flipping freezing – and together they walk the empty length of it, recovering from the elements in the café at its peak. Joy eats sausage and chips, leaving the beans till last, in case she gets too full and can't manage the best bits, enjoying the warmth in her belly against the chill of her cheeks, still icy from outside. Spearing her sausage on her fork, Joy's eyes meet Ma's, who for once in her mouse life looks happy.

She is like a mouse. Scuttling and scurrying. Doing everything for everyone. Always.

'Good sausage, Sausage?' Ma asks a smiling, nodding Joy. 'Hold onto that, pet.'

Hold onto what, Joy doesn't know, but she likes her mother's momentary ease all the same. Joy takes a big bite, like she's a wild animal, or a hungry dog in a cartoon, and Ma laughs and laughs until she knocks over her tea, which takes out her toasted teacake too.

'Don't cry, Ma.' Without thinking about it, Joy adds, 'Grandma will get her colours back – and her wings. I promise,' just as a waitress comes rushing over with a cloth and a fresh cup of tea.

Ma's long repeats of 'sorry-and-thank-you-and-sorry-and-thank-you' makes Joy's teeth ache, makes her bite them together. When they get home, Ma pulls on her squeaky handbrake. Says, 'Don't tell your dad about today.' Joy won't. Would rather forget the lot, anyway – apart from, of course, the sausage. And making Ma laugh.

And, soon enough, Joy's talk of wings makes sense; a real, final *full circle – Grandma will never be coming home because she has gone to the sky. To look after Grandad. At last.*

Apparently.

In the sad days ahead, Ma retells the story of Grandma's wings to anyone who'll listen, making sure to mention Joy's spiritual antenna, calling her a perceptive child. But she also adds things that Joy didn't say, because Joy never mentioned any reunion with any grandad. Yet, as Ma embellishes the tale, hunched and holding her elbows in a sort of self-hug, Joy doesn't correct her. Though it's wrong to tell fibs, Ma's new version helps her sadness a little, rather like a comfort blanket might, and if it's only a story made of hopeful thoughts and soothing words, who's it hurting, really?

There's never any mention of Grandma's wings, nor Joy's spiritual antenna, to Dad. Instead, there's lots of baby talk; stuff about 'due dates' and Joy needing to set a 'good example as a big sister'. And even though Ma's not ready, still too full of grief to sort through Grandma's room, Ma does as Dad says because that is the order of things.

'Ma!' Joy gasps, on discovering the stack of canvases, abstracts and oil paintings, all vivid and wrong in the forgotten depths of Grandma's wardrobe. 'They're alive, Ma,' she says, enjoying the strange sensation that runs through her fingers when she touches them.

Joy can't read Ma's face, nor make any sense of the strange distance in her look. 'Why don't you choose one to keep?' she says at last, and Joy chooses the painting that makes her palms tingle most. Ma props it up against the mantel with a sigh. 'What a clever grandma you had. Art runs through all of us.' But Ma's neat little cross-stitch ain't even in the same room as Grandma's paintings. The bold creativity of an empty old woman who at last got her colours back.

It's only when Dad moves Grandma's bed out and a smaller bed in, when Joy starts sleeping in her own room like a big girl, that the painting on the mantel becomes a problem. Because during the early hours, in a twist reverse of things, it is Grandma who now visits Joy.

Funny, how all Joy needed to do when she tried to picture Grandma young, was look to Ma's narrow face, the same round button eyes. And it's a bit like the bible book that Ma keeps special, the Easter story, which don't make no sense anyway, so why should Grandma's return be any more startling than gentle Jesus coming back from the dead?

'I had so much more to say,' Grandma tells Joy, sat at her bedside, night after wide-awake night, a young woman again, with her shiny, bouncy brown hair and big fur coat that might've belonged to a bear once upon a time.

'But I'm sleepy, Grandma.' Joy's never frightened, would rather it this way around than still be visiting the 'nuthouse'. It's just that listening, Joy's finding, is very, very tiring. The only difference between Jesus and Grandma – so far as Joy can decipher – is that people were pleased to see Jesus again. Grandma is too demanding, too big a presence in the back bedroom that now belongs to Joy. Perhaps her paintings were best hidden by dark coats in dark places. They were too loud. Too much to stomach.

'He's not here,' Grandma says. 'Not with me.' Joy thinks she means the grandad she's meant to be happy-ever-aftering with. 'I do as I please, these days. Tell your mother that. Set her straight.'

But all Joy manages to say to Ma is, 'Take the painting away.'

With it gone, so is Grandma. Joy's perceptiveness feels like a wild daydream.

And Ma thinks it's best that way.

2

RENEGADE IN RETROGRADE

Butterfield Estate, Wellsend Grove, 2023

Roche wakes on Nan's sofa with yesterday still turning in her gut, nervous and undigested. Last night was the proper pits. Mum's hurt is Roche's hurt, always has been. But isn't that exactly why she's got to detach, try living her own life, starting with actually just breathing. Space. No matter what, Mum will always be glued to Itsy. Roche thinks of Nan's astonished face when she'd opened the door yesterday; her amber yellow eyes crinkling as she'd smiled with happy recognition, kohled to high heaven in greenish eyeliner, an absolute autumnal colour palate of a person. *'Well, ain't you just your mum and dad all over!'* had been the very first thing she'd said, before drawing circles around Roche's eyes with her fingers, giving her a little wink. *'Apart from these.'* Their matching eyes had given Roche a similar buzz to when she and Eden had worn their hair the same back in primary, when they'd pretend to be sisters.

And so had the mention of her dad.

Her real dad.

Instinctively, Roche feels beneath her jumper, squeezing the rings she keeps on her necklace, reassured and then triggered into thinking about her other less reachable belongings, as she mentally checks off her current possessions: school stuff, phone, charger (thank heavens), bank card, sunglasses, moisturiser, lip balm, a fiver and two sanitary towels. Three, if she counts the one in her gym bag at school, which is handy because that also means a change of clothes and deodorant too. But deodorant's where the handy times end, because what the actual is she going to do without all her hair shit? The curl protective balm, her edge comb, the non-clarifying shampoo. That beautiful half tub of Pattern styling cream. No lie; half of Roche's earnings from the chippy ends up spent on her tresses. And with Roche already purposefully avoiding the damp fug of Nan's mouldy bathroom, she shudders to think of the haircare options available here.

Even the spare bedding, even after a night wrapped around her, smells stale. Mum wasn't kidding when she'd say Nan was 'domestically challenged'; in fact, *that had been putting it politely*. Roche's first sighting of Nan's gross domestic negligence had been the cat litter tray; tiny, fossilized turds on the cusp of being crushed by the towering crates of God only knows what that perilously line her hallway – the doors running off it adorned with red ribbons, tightly tied around every grubby doorknob. And candles, so many candles, everywhere – horrific, when you add in the chain smoking and consider the fire hazards.

Because in every room, on every spare inch of grubby surface, there's a foot depth of newspapers, leaflets, freebie handouts, stacks of paper – some far too bloody close to the oven. The sheer irresponsibility brings back the other thing Mum would say, which comes as clearly as if she's in Roche's actual earhole, about how she, Delph, was always, always more the parent than her mother, the self-proclaimed free spirit who went by the name of Moon.

Moon: 'Problem Nan.' Bossing it about yesterday in that dirty gold velveteen cape, complete with tassels like a shaggy bat-winged fringe, which suited her in a way it shouldn't, clash-complimenting with her hair, that flame red that looks almost fake, though Roche knows she's a natural redhead, having similar streaks through her own golden-brown hair to prove it. Roche smiles, warmed, relieved that Nan's no different to how she remembers her as a kid; striking yet chaotic, her look tied together with an air of fuck the world – absolutely no hint of the dry old granny stereotype. It's only really her neck that's the giveaway, anyway – otherwise Roche wouldn't put her at nearing sixty at all.

But most importantly, especially after witnessing how things played out last night, Roche has sussed how Nan's so much more than the person Itsy lives to disparage. At home, even without her in their lives, it was still Nan who'd emerge at the end of an argument, often the reason behind the fraught, weird, cut-with-a-knife bullshit of an atmosphere. If she puts her mind to it, focusing the gift of her memory which works like a tape recorder, Roche can even hear Itsy now, saying something standard, like: *'You know, this is all your mother's fault,'* and in the end Mum would be agreeing, sounding just like she meant it too.

So yeah, Nan's digs might need fumigating, and yes, Roche's 3b curls will undoubtedly suffer, but at least there'll be no skirting round the edges, no fence-sitting agony to put up with, no cowing down to the man of the house – because here, hallelujah, there isn't one.

And, if there's distance … Roche stops, as if worried to let her idea develop, cautious already of disappointment, the negatives she's already assembling as obstacles, when she remembers the other thing in her possession – that bundle of university info from school yesterday. It feels weeks ago, light years, that Roche was sat listening to Winnie 'verbal-shits' Russell in that classroom last lesson. Uni – it's entirely possible if she pulls her finger out. She'll always worry about Mum, it goes without saying – so, couldn't she go to uni anyway, and just continue worrying from a different location?

Roche picks up her phone, studying again the rapid-fire stream of pictures she took secretly last night when Mum rapid-fire blasted at Itsy, ffs, and when she reaches the end of the camera roll, she begins again, enjoying the feeling of seeing her mother so entirely animated. Alive, even. Because honestly, if Roche had not been there herself, she'd never have believed it. It's a bit like Mum's been in hiding, which, yeah, does makes her that little bit more interesting, but Roche's tired of trying to figure out her mother. Nan's been here, carrying on when they couldn't see each other. Missing them probably. But surviving. Given enough time, it'll be the same for Mum too.

Edinburgh would be the dream. A fresh start away from all that's rotten: domestically, socially, politically. A fresh mindset. Far enough to feel like you've got away. Yet return with ease if needs must.

As the new possibilities ignite, a notification appears on Roche's phone, lighting the screen with a picture of her and Eden sunbathing by the canal on some brazen day in the hols that burnt into the next and made the record-breaking, climate-critical heatwave that toasted Eden till her skin dazzled and shone in the factor 30 protecting her Black excellence.

EDEN: Missing me yet, bitch?
I'm missing you 🤍
ROCHE: You know it 🤍 What time you depart?

But even as Roche's typing, a screenshot arrives of Eden's itinerary, a one-stop flight from Lagos to Casablanca until finally back to grey old Gatwick. Roche prickles with expectation; three weeks too bloody long.

EDEN: Aunty Flora's freaking over the turbulence already.
Still on the fkn runway. Pray for me.

Before she can reply, in the glow of her phone light, Roche watches her nan enter the living room, with a big beaming smile. 'Tea, Angelface?'

Moon dreamt of red. Of caves and caverns and returns. Flesh sleep. She wakes with a different take on Roche staying.

'As much as I'd love you here, I think your mum needs you.' Moon places her hand on Roche's forehead, passing the morning flow onwards into the universe; hopes that some might find its way to her daughter.

And that's where Moon's hope usually falters.

But that spark – her brief return last night: Delph with all the front and all the fight. It is both sad and strange, that though she's the one still here and breathing, Delph before the sadness came is the person Moon misses more than anyone. More than even Sol himself, bless and protect him.

Heavens, what he would've made of her, Roche, his clever girl, flourishing into all her grown-up greatness. What a beauty she's become in Moon's absence. Those dear pigtail plaits now a foot-high circumference of curls, complete with the most transparent shimmer; an aura made of lights. Roche, who came here for protection – of that Moon has no doubt. Yet she's strong. Moon senses Roche's energy, that unsinkability of character that Delph never possessed, which'll surely put a stop to any similar destiny.

Because the tool might be looking older these days, but his vibe's just the same: Itsy, controlling from within, like some warped puppet master. Fifteen years together. Fifteen

years of Moon being the outsider and slowly strangled out.
But he can't be pulling every string, not if she read it right
last night – about the sad thing being a good thing. It's left
a questioning, a sense of something considerably amiss in
Delph and Itsy's relationship. A relationship that frankly was
never right, anyway.

'Come on,' she says, offering a hand for Roche to take.
'D'you want to say good morning to the most happening
superstar in the universe?' She drapes a tasselled arm, more
like a wing, around Roche and it reminds Moon of Delph
yesterday, full of the same brittle reluctance to accept the love
she'll never admit to needing. It hurts.

More so, because it is all her own doing. Moon has always
been a shitty mother.

But there was once a time when this house had brimmed
with spirit: Delph's on-the-cusp-of-it-all energy – not dissim-
ilar to Roche's now – and Sol, emerging from the shell of his
shattered start. After surviving a childhood neither stable nor
happy, Sol had at last discovered peace. Such healing love.
Even Moon, who'd not had the easiest ride either, caught the
feeling, buoyed by healthy new optimism, that all of them
were finally thriving. In bloom together.

It was that throwaway phrase, how he 'had everything
to look forward to' that knocked Moon's guts more than
anything when Sol died; how he'd barely, barely got going in
the world. Nipped in the bud before his moment. Before he
could hold his own child. Such a kind, articulate soul. Catch
your breath handsome, and so sweetly similar-looking to

her Delph. She'd said as much to Roche last night as she'd made up a temporary bed on the sofa, explaining the sandalwood too, that burns continually beneath the kitchen window for purification – and for all who have passed, who are loved. Always.

On the back doorstep, looking out on the garden, the most perfect room in the house, they drink ginger tea from big brown mugs that Roche washed before bed.

'The same moon, the same stars, wherever you are. And if that's not comfort, I don't know much about it.'

'It's really something else.' Roche's sting is absent as she smiles up at the sky. 'What did Mum mean, about all your birthdays?'

'She likes to make out it's all parties and balloons on tap.' Moon tuts. 'I just choose to celebrate the things that are beyond myself, that's all. The seasons. The universe. Mother Nature's often a far better parent than most.' And though Moon could unearth a timeline of shit to prove it, she changes the subject. 'Me and your mum would do this,' she says, though most of their doorstep tête-à-têtes would usually involve Delph plying Moon with liquids after many a messy night. Unsure of the stories Roche's been fed over the years, Moon can only imagine the kind Itsy's tried weaving in her absence.

But if Roche truly thought her that terrible, surely then she wouldn't be so keen to stay. Besides, Moon knows first-hand how the worst of traps can be disguised as happy homes.

As footloose as life is these days, doing as she fancies

whenever she likes, it's still bloody smashing to have a true, breathing human around the place. Watching Roche's face upturned to the sky, softening in step with the dawning beauty, Moon's heart lifts, and as the slow glimmer of first light pierces the horizon, there is hope.

Moon will always opt for optimism.

'Now, you can't leave this bad energy between you and your mother.'

Roche rolls her eyes. 'We've not fallen out, though.'

'That won't be how she's feeling.' Moon's eyes stay on the sky. 'She'll just be there with him in that flat, trying to work out why you've gone. Blaming herself.'

'But we all know why. We just pretend we don't.' Roche looks to her lap, sighs. 'I can't do anything today, anyway – I'm working. And so's she.'

'You what?' Moon's smoker's laughter comes out in a wheezing hiss. 'Delph unchained,' she whistles. 'Well, I'll be . . .'

'Itsy's mini-cabbing got smothered by the gig economy.'

'Losing out to Uber? Nothing to do with him being a useless bell-end, then?' Thrilled to get such a big grin from Roche, she adds, 'Look love, you can stay, of course you can. But I've got to put it right with your mother first.' Moon makes a mental plan to drop in on Delph. Uninvited, but that's the point. It's hard to disguise an atmosphere when you're caught off guard.

Sweeping back her cape, Moon reveals her bumbag, black with a fluorescent yellow peace sign, and slides out a chocolate bar. It's M&S Swiss Milk Chocolate, a fancy bar that in the old days would've been stocked near the checkouts as a last-minute temptation. 'For you.' She winks at Roche, handing it over. 'And these are mine.' From her pouch comes an amber tube of prescription tablets, and though she anticipates a reaction, Roche gives her nothing but a raised brow and a side-eye. 'For my heads,' Moon explains, tapping one into her palm, small as a sweetener tablet, in the same chalk white, that disappears with a glug of tea. She pokes out her tongue, wiggling it like a triumphant child who's at last eaten their vegetables. 'When you do speak, be sure to tell her you've seen me taking them. And don't leave it too long.'

'Seriously, d'you know something I don't?'

'Just got a feeling,' Moon says, scrunching her face at Roche's instant dismissiveness. 'And you're just like your mother. She never had any time for my feelings either.'

'Look, you've no idea what it's like there. With them. With him.'

'In which case, if you're set on staying, you'll just have to educate me.'

*

Sol Barclay

Butterfield Estate, Wellsend Grove, 1993

Delph's thirteen when Sol Barclay joins Wellsend Secondary. Each day, from a distance, she watches as he fusses the hell out of the mangy German Shepherd tied outside the Spar on his way to school, likes how the sad dog's eyes look up at him all shy and grateful when he talks to her. Delph thinks she knows what Mum means when she says it's possible to feel the warmth of someone's heart by their actions, no matter how Sol tries disguising it with top-level mischief at school.

In a bid to calm Sol's disruptive streak, he's paired with a good influence, and from the moment he and Delph are put together in bottom-set maths, everyone says they look like twins. As they grow more comfortable in each other's company, he jokes, asking her things like, 'What time's Dad picking us up from school?' Which is quite funny, because neither of them has a dad, nor any attentive parent with a set of wheels.

Happiness is the lightness in Delph's belly the first time they walk home together, and Sol buys her a Dr Pepper, putting the ring pull in her hand as he says goodbye, turning back on the constant to check her, his dimples just the sweetest, which on her own face seem babyish and stupid.

They do look alike. Delph's never been a fan of her own face, believing her reflection froglike and unfanciable, yet the more she looks at Sol, the more she thinks the more she looks at Sol, the more she thinks

he's

beautiful.

Life's tough the term Sol meets Delph. Before moving to Wellsend, he'd been without a permanent foster home for a year. As a kid, he'd been sunshine-cute, and then one day, he wasn't. Hitting puberty meant Sol was too tall, suddenly; too grown, suddenly. It grew harder to place him. Though Sol's latest family performs no end of surface good deeds, like recycling and volunteering and fostering children, Sol exists as a moody threat within the shadows of their home, either in trouble for unruly behaviour or daydreaming. Pre-empted as trouble, their non-communication brings isolation. Delph's natural kindness brings friendship. And, coming from a difficult home herself, their bond is instant.

Sol confides in Delph the change in his family dynamic whenever he leaves the room; how much lighter and more talkative they become without his presence, how he often slinks off to bed early each night, choosing one of the scruffy paperbacks from the bookcase on the landing that belong to the birth daughters, Sweet Valley High stories, soft focus princess girls, admired and treasured by devoted parents forever. He tells Delph that he wishes he could remember more about his own birth mother, more than the vague memory of a freckle-brown girl, her afro turbaned in a midnight-blue wrap, the remnant warmth of her attention, before the drugs broke her spirit and made her brain so poorly that she lost her memory. Forgetting dental appointments and non-uniform days, then school pick-ups and food shops, then getting herself dressed, till one day she forgot him entirely.

Delph understands his story so well, it's almost like listening to herself.

During the new good habit of doing their homework together after school with Neighbours on, Sol says how Delph's house feels like proper homes should; smelling of chips, with telly noise and kids at play in next door's garden. How he hopes one day he'll be a proper part of a normal scenario too. But when he tries telling her she's lucky to have a mum like she's got, Delph tells him about the time she spent three days and nights home alone. How weird friends of her mother's knocked at odd hours; how Delph had the good sense to stay silent until they went away. Their stories slip, keep coming, revealing so much more than simply who can outdo whom on the worst childhood front. Because the heart can't lie nor disguise how those three days alone spored not only terror in Delph, but a triggered memory, of being alone one unending night, as if she'd been left in her cot, crying into the darkness. But it is not the sort of memory Delph wants to ask nor remind her mother of. Not when things are good.

Because Delph's happy being ordinary, finally. Glad for the calm routine that feels normal now Mum is hers again, which is only tainted by the worry she might slip off into her moods, which always take her back to the drinking; when the good parenting weighs heavy and Mum vanishes, abandoning her. Delph hopes with all her heart that the ordinary times are here to stay – because despite the occasional tumultuousness, despite Mum being Mum, there is always, always love.

And then a new tenderness grows. Delph at last knows why she's here. Like she's just been biding her time, and everything can start now they've found each other.

The most settling, stabilising force either Delph or Sol have ever known.

Love, which forever feels a blessed privilege.

3

LIVE WERK POSE

Butterfield Estate, Wellsend Grove, 2023

Roche could weep with sheer gratitude. The laundrette. Was there ever a cleaner-sounding word? The rumble of active dryers is like a warm hygienic hug, giving off the same feels as the showers at the gym, a necessary contrast to the germ factory she's currently living in.

'You'd be proper shitting it,' Roche says, offering Eden a Hula Hoop. 'Think a mouse was gonna pop up from the springs any second.'

No exaggeration.

Just the thought of sofa mice gets Roche all longing again, not just for Mum, but for her own bed, in the clean little box room she's been forever desperate to kit out to her own taste. Itsy, like some dry lunch landowner from the feudal system, always reckoned anything on his walls was a form of vandalism. Roche's clever way around that was a wall-sized cork board, just to antagonize him, but it wasn't quite the same.

'You got your clean little boudoir back at home,' Eden says, unable to resist spitting facts. 'Mama Dee's proper lost without you too.'

'I showed you the text I sent her.' It comes out whiney and defensive, as she folds her arms. 'We're cool. She knows I'm OK.'

But Roche's not made of concrete, for God's sakes. And, if she's feeling lost, even with Eden and Nan, then Mum's lonely pangs must be flipping terrible with only Itsy for company. Perhaps she should call or do as Nan suggested and meet for a bit of breakfast – squeeze in a quick sandwich one lunchtime. It would have to be quick, mind; there's not a spare second for nothing these days, not when the blimmin' laundry's a full-time job, now she's doing it all herself.

'But she ain't OK. She don't look well, Ro. Even Mum said so – and she don't notice nothing.' Eden rolls her eyes. 'Giving out the advice like she's Ms-Metropolitan-Got-Her-Shit-Together, when she's actually been sobbing over that twat she's been seeing pretty much since she picked me up from Gatwick. *Get the Injection, babe.*' Eden mimics her mother, '*Period problems are so old-fashioned. Liberate yourself.*' She shudders. 'If I've had the trauma of listening to our mothers chatting birth control, I'm not suffering alone.'

'Well, you've killed any trying to guilt me in one perverted breath.' Forever seared onto Roche's brain are the night noises

42

through the thin walls. Itsy's heavy breathing. 'Besides, Nan said she'd drop in on Mum. So, you can stop.'

Sometimes there's a scrap of truth in those crusty old sayings, like the one Roche thinks of now, about a burden shared. She does feel lighter, having Nan support her on the worry front where Mum's concerned – a problem halved that's allowed Roche the chance to catch her breath. Despite the sofa mice anxieties, Roche won't be going back to Esplanade Point. She'd rather surrender to the house of filth, break into her savings and spend a small fortune in Wilko on cleaning shit, if it means she never need suffer the mediocre inadequacy of Itsy's company ever again.

Roche wonders if his bare walls – as uninspiring as him – helped cultivate the thinking that there was little to reach for beyond what he provided, normalizing the small, bland life Roche and her mother have led for as long as she can remember. His basic trickery almost worked, because, why else would she think that working full-time in the gym up the road would become her long-term future when school was done; set and ready to pay Itsy keep, despite being in the top percentile of student attainment without even truly trying. How she'd been set to pay that keep, willingly, because how likely is it that she'll ever be able to afford her own home? He's lobbed obstacle after obstacle, repackaged as fatherly advice, obstructing her progress, killing the uni dream years back by filling her with horror stories about student debt and juggling jobs alongside degrees, to selling kidneys on the black market, and sex on street corners.

But it's nonsense. A mindset she's evolving from, which feels impossible to return to. Other students manage with a lot less than her, so why take his negging as any kind of truth? It's not even like he went himself.

Maybe it was to keep her close and needy – which doesn't seem quite right either, because all Itsy's ever wanted was to have Mum to himself. Perhaps it's more to do with the possibility of Roche succeeding in the same world that Itsy blames everything on. The fear of being eclipsed by a kid.

Well. Too fucking late, mate.

His place might be clean, and her bed might be comfy, but it's barren space. Home should be a place to grow; to be encouraged to thrive. And Itsy might be the king of his two-bedroom castle, but his stifling tricks only ever truly worked on one person.

Who obvs wasn't bloody Roche.

There's always something very satisfying, very vindicating, about the story of someone from less than nothing who ends up conquering the universe. Ain't that why the planet adores reality telly? Roche's plans might not stretch to world domination, but she's still been dreaming, plotting, manifesting, for some time ...

And maybe this is her moment.

'Stop offering them damn crisps. D'you want beefy-smelling hair or something?' Eden sits with Roche between her knees, sectioning her hair into fours, like a hot-cross bun. 'I am Jesus of Ravenous, though. Shove one in.' Roche, reaching back to the vicinity of Eden's hungry mouth, obliges.

'You gave me two.' Eden munches happily, dropping a kiss on Roche's head. 'And that is why I love you.'

Eden sections again, twisting Roche's hair into perfect Bantu knots, as Roche checks herself in the glass door of the washing machine opposite. 'I look good. Thank you.'

'Seriously, I cannot wait to get in that salon. Get my hands on all that kit,' Eden says, watching Roche's frown through the glass door. 'What?'

'Don't you worry if we hang around here, we'll just ... I don't know, sort of ... die inside?' Roche says. 'I can't think of anything worse than ending up like my mum.'

'Harsh. If it weren't for her, I'd've known nothing but silence or kids' telly.'

'But you love kids' telly.' Roche sniffs, a little knocked to be put in her place.

'And I love your mum.' Eden chews the side of her mouth. Securing the last of Roche's hair with a band, she nudges her away. 'It's not kind, what you're doing.'

'*He's* not kind though, is he? And she just allows it.'

'You can't be blaming her for stuff she don't even know about.'

'And have you told your mum – about us?'

'Rah, no!' Even with that horrified face, Eden's beautiful. Could snap her picture now and it'd be more than good enough for a glossy magazine. From the day Roche watched her move in, carrying her small possessions up and down the landing in flamingo pink sandals, to Roche she was the most perfect girl in the world.

Eden grabs her bag, heading out of the launderette.

'Where you going?' Roche asks, cross that she sounds needy AF.

'To get my own crisps.' The door closes as she pokes her tongue at Roche through the glass.

The tumble dryer flashes that it's finished its cycle, but Roche's jeans are still damp, her hoodie nowhere close to feeling how it does when it's left on the end of her bed, when she simply slips it on without a thought to how it got there. Putting in another coin, she turns the dial, frustrated to suffer another twenty minutes in here, which might've been fun if she could only keep her mouth shut.

Folding her dry items back into her holdall, Roche thinks of the little plastic octopus in the airing cupboard back at the flat, a clean, ironed shirt draped on each tentacle for each day of the week. Now Roche's quick to keep the windows open so that Nan's smoke doesn't cling to her clothes. Nan has none of her mother's finesse – which often came in the form of a hot chocolate in her favourite mug, delivered to her room every day – and neither does she do the same hovering for interaction, which Roche rarely indulged in anyway, preferring to toy with her mother until Itsy's return when things would switch completely, in favour of her fussing over him.

But God, hasn't too much time been given to these circular resentments? All this anger, trapped within the same tender space where her hurt also lives, another emotion she resents carrying, since she can't even claim to know her dad, let alone grieve for him. All Roche knows is that if he hadn't died then

46

Itsy wouldn't be in their lives. They'd be happy and round, a proper family, without the great dent of trauma meaning Mum can never be any of those things. Living alongside heartbreak, proper, irreparable heartbreak, has been exhausting. And all the love in the world can't stop Roche wanting to escape the weight of it, this cloaking sadness she's never felt right wearing. Carrying. Owning, even.

'Look, if you're serious about applying to uni, then you're gonna be gone soon enough.' Back with her Cheetos, Eden smiles, holding Roche by her hoodie toggles. It's one of the best things about Eden, how easy-going and easily forgiving she is. 'Just leave me here to my hair, babe. And I'll leave you to your big new plans.'

But what if it happens to them too, the same as to the scores of students on the forums and podcasts Roche keeps listening to – how, once you've settled, found your place within the new dynamic on campus, relationships from back home, even good strong ones, grow distant and peculiar. What would months, terms at a time, feel like, when even Eden's famalam hols feels like a life sentence? If only Eden could come too. A new place where they could test their feelings.

And try flourishing in different soil.

Moon's sliders slap against the pavement as she heads for the bus stop, then waits with a tapping foot for the 56X, to take her from Wellsend Grove to Wellsend South, cursing all the while how she's yet to qualify for her freedom bus pass, because the fare's bloody doubled since she last made this trip, which she'd once done three times a week until, well, what good is that now, going over all that's gone and done?

The bus crawls up the high street, and despite the spring sun bringing a warmth to the day that feels like a break-through after the doldrums of March, everyone's head is down, their shoulders low, shuffling along like daybreak's broken spirits. Moon can't see one fucking smile – but what is there to smile about anyway, when each shiny new week brings fresh crisis. A societal mean streak that's more entrenched on the daily. Top to bottom division, anger, dissatisfaction. Or is this just how life's always been? Hard to fathom. Unrelenting. Disappointing. Moon won't judge, having slipped plenty of times herself, regardless of good intentions, descending into the grudge feelings, instead of gratitude, which take everything, *everything*, to claw back from. No, she's not proud to be a contributor to the collective woes of humanity, but there you go. Only human, after all – ain't that what the radio tells her?

Moon gets off at the lights, by the market. Rare that she's up this early, the air fresh on her face, the old blood pumping again. It has been too long, being this properly involved in the world. The few stalls open are sad and sparse and nothing like the old days she's thrilled are dead and gone. The flower seller's bunches aren't the best either, so she opts for a couple of trays and parks herself on a bench, twisting the blooms into a bouquet, using their stems and the string in her shop-per, which is red obviously, always red: ready to bind away the evil. Protecting those who don't even know they need protecting. As if it wasn't hell enough witnessing Itsy leach from the cracks of her grieving daughter. Perhaps it's only been worse imagining it all from a distance, still playing on without her. Till now. Though Moon's intuition is unchanged, laced with the same old doom, the feeling that Itsy's kingdom is crumbling, she senses with utter conviction.

Moon heads to the nasty fast stretch of road that a footbridge once straddled, that was high and ominous and sick-making enough, even before Sol was pushed from it. Emotions, raw, unhealing and vicious as they ever were, swamp Moon as she ties her floral offering around the lamppost nearest to the spot where Sol's on-the-cusp-of-it-all promise left him. The blooms squash and look terrible, and even though no good ever comes from the sinky mud of the past, pining over all what's gone and still sits wrong, Moon betrays herself.

And cries.

For that poor beautiful boy, now bones.

A bit later, Moon finds Delph down aisle 29, giving directions to an elderly couple searching for the outdoor lighting section, just as a woman with enormous calves in the same uniform as her daughter calls out, 'Tea at eleven, Dee?' And Delph gives her a thumbs-up.

'Surprise, surprise, Ms Nine-to-Five!' Moon blocks the end of the aisle, all jazz hands, as instant panic swamps Delph's face. 'It's all good, love – don't worry. Roche's fine.'

As Delph exhales with relief, Moon can't help feeling rather thrown at finding her girl in such an ordinary environment, communicating and capable. She is here, out in the world, and granted, it's only part-time in B&Q and not what she was born for, but she is still out of his shadow. All these mini milestones going on without Moon's knowledge. No matter that it's more a money thing than any strike for independence, Delph's growth is clear – perhaps in an even better way – without Itsy witnessing any of it.

Knowing something about her daughter that he doesn't is bliss.

'And can I put you down for that extra shift next Tuesday?' the woman with the calves calls back to her.

Delph's eyes meet her mother's. She raises her chin. 'Yeah – yes, go on. No problem.'

'You're a star. I mean it – thank the lord you got rid of that virus,' she adds. 'We were lost without you last week.'

Oh, to resist air-punching the sky! Watching the woman's retreat, Moon turns back to Delph. 'I won't keep you,' she manages, still thrown. 'Just wanted to let you know how Roche's doing. She misses you, even if the stubborn little madam won't admit it. Plus, I wanted to see you too.' Moon hesitates. 'You look ... recovered.'

'Now there's a word and a half.' For the briefest moment, Delph loses her edge, her hands fluttering at her tummy. 'You were right.' Quiet, barely audible beneath the rumbling trolleys and shop noise, Delph adds, 'About the sad, good thing.' Blinking away her tears, she pulls her topknot tight. 'Don't you dare try hugging me.'

'But you did right.' Honouring Delph's wishes, Moon doesn't hug. 'You put yourself first.'

'How's Roche, really? We've sent a few texts, but it's not . . .'
It's hard for Delph to meet her eye. 'It's not real. Not like being
face to face.' Frowning, the distance comes back, returning
Delph to neutral; unreadable to anybody but her mother.
'Please tell me you're taking your meds.'

Across the way in Kitchens, a panel of wood crashes to
the ground, becoming the centre of attention as a heft of
perfection in a tight black tee and orange apron picks it up
like it's made of air, screwing it in place for a kitchen display
called Carnaby-Buzz, gloss acid-yellow cabinets Moon bets
no one will have the bollocks to buy. Adjusting the dummy
plug sockets, recessed into his freshly assembled worktops,
he spots Delph, and holding her eye, slides to the other end
of the bench, staged as part of a real-life functioning kitchen,
where there's a candlelit setting for two, champagne flutes
and fake red roses. Picking one up, he gestures with it for
Delph to join him.

Delph smiles, dropping her eyes like this isn't exactly the
first time this utterly gorgeous young man has tried this
game, and Moon's struck again by the sense that her daughter
isn't such an entirely fragile thing.

'He's tasty.'

'Ugh – when have you ever said stuff like that?'

But he is hotter than a scotch bonnet.

'Baby, I'd be nice to anyone if it meant the back of you know
who. And yes, I am taking my meds. You're welcome to check
for yourself, though,' Moon adds breezily. 'Come round,
count my pills and build a few bridges while you're at it.'

Delph chews her lip. Takes a moment. 'Like Itsy says, a few nights away and she'll be desperate to come home.'

Moon finds herself biting her own lip; knowing what'll be most powerful here, is simplicity. 'Love, he is why she left.'

'Roche said that?'

'She didn't have to.'

'Jesus, Mum!' Delph looks around quickly, scanning for customers. 'You'll get me in trouble. Can you go, please?'

'You know, you might paint me as an imperfect mother—'

'Imperfect. Is that a joke?'

'Which is perfectly justifiable. But at least I never prioritized a man over my own daughter.'

'No, you just prioritized everything else. Including all your dirty little props ...' Delph doesn't air them in detail, but Moon is hurt enough. 'You know, it didn't have to be all horrible and distant like this. If you could've kept on the good pills and left the rest alone. If you could just have stopped being so angry for one second.' She sighs, exhausted. 'You weren't ever going to like anybody after Sol. I never even thought I would. But you didn't give Itsy a chance. He's not perfect, but deep down ...'

Deep down nothing – Moon only need think of Roche, the fury in her eyes whenever Itsy's mentioned to confirm her opinions.

'Why can't you just believe he's a good person?'

Because how can she when Roche's killer words, 'I keep my mouth shut over plenty,' play on in her thoughts? Though she's unsure of the weight and the shape of it, Moon senses a secret that surrounds Roche, enraged by the thought that Itsy might be the source.

With her hands on her hips, Delph says, 'You'll burst a blood vessel one day. It's all that fury what's sent you round the twist.'

'Round the twist? How quaint. You sound like a bloody dinosaur.' But Delph's not the only one, she thinks. You only need look around to see what's happening, same as on the bus this morning. Everyone flat and stuck by the past. A national sickness that's worse than a pandemic because it's a life choice. 'Like a boring old sideboard who forgot to have fun.'

'Boring, because I choose being settled?' Delph's eyes burn as she adds with venom, 'Safe?'

Moon's unsurprised, but the disappointment stings none-theless. 'You know, love, I hoped that something, somewhere, might've changed along the way. All I'm saying is that Itsy was the barrier between you and me, and now he's the barrier between you and your girl. Both could be fixed that simply.'

Does it ever get through? It's like he built an impenetrable wall inside Delph's brain, preventing any Itsy-related doubts to enter. A master craftsman.

'But this though,' Moon looks around the DIY superstore, and then at her girl in proud acknowledgement, 'this is a phenomenal start.'

Delph sips her tea, glad to rest her feet, but even more glad that her boss, Lin, is stuck with a complaining customer, so she has a moment to herself.

Because Moon did touch a nerve.

Of course Delph's hurt by Roche leaving, but also by Itsy's way of pretending it's a good thing, that she nods and goes along with, when the only person who'll really benefit from Roche's absence will be him.

But not yet. Delph's recovery is neither as shocking nor traumatic as she imagined, but she knows and has decided that even when the blood's gone, she'll keep rejecting Itsy's advances. Because time has passed now. Time without intimacy, which is healing in ways Delph can't explain, as though she's become her own island. Almost like she can't go back.

Yet she's not dead either.

It's not like Delph's not noticed Lenny. The effortless way he lifts shit around, building kitchens, bathrooms, doing the little mime acts whenever she walks past, pretending to be cooking, or showering, using his DIY displays as props. She knows he, Lenny, likes making her smile, enough for his games to have become repetition, enough for them to pass pleasantries in the canteen. And it's a nice little boost, if she's truthful – which she's allowed to be in her own head. Having a lightweight mate, an equally harmless admirer. A small secret thing that keeps only her warm.

The warmth bursts into a full-on blaze when a text notification from Roche fills her phone screen. Delph's on it straight away, replying: yes, see you at half past ten tomoz, Gem's Café on Thames Street 🤍💙🤍

'What is it?' Lenny slides into the chair opposite as Delph beams at her phone. 'Holiday booked? A lotto win?'

'Even better. My daughter's invited me to breakfast. I'm seeing her tomorrow.' Seeing, holding, smelling. This time apart, though tiny within the scale of their lives together, has passed so slowly that it's amazing Delph's managed to endure it. Catching herself drifting, she turns her phone to show Lenny her screensaver of Roche as a younger kid, dressed in a karate gi, a blue belt tied Rambo-style around her forehead.

'Ah, she's like you,' he says, with a grin. 'You and her dad must be mad proud.'

'Oh, Roche isn't Itsy's.' Delph puts him right. Never not ready to correct the assumption.

Once, long ago, Itsy built a bookcase and desk for Roche's ninth birthday, and Delph painted her room in 'Spring Buttercup', paint chosen from this very store. They spent the afternoon arranging her new shelves, playing libraries. For a moment that day she could've been his.

'She's been staying with my mum. I can't flipping wait to hold her.'

'Was that your mum, downstairs earlier?'

Delph closes her eyes, pictures her mother blocking the aisle; the gypsy skirt, Global Hypercolor tee and denim jacket, her crossbody bag in soft tan leather – and tassels. Always the fucking tassels. She finds herself still smiling.

'It's proper nice, seeing you happy.' Lenny looks away before glancing behind him and trying again. 'You know, I think you're—'

By standing up, Delph cuts him off quick, and with break

being over, they make their way down from the canteen to the staffroom. And though Lennox Anderson's locker is on the other side of the room to Delphine Tennyson's, he still hovers near hers. 'You here till six?'

'I am.' She pulls a miserable face. Doesn't mean it. Here is always better.

'You gonna let me walk you to your bus?' He tries, but Delph does her usual looking to the sky, flattered all the same face. Heading back to the shop floor, he calls after her. 'Is that a yes?'

Lenny waits with his bike at the staff entrance, talking to some girls about the same age as Roche.

'D'you go Taylor's?' one of them asks him, batting her giant, jet-black lashes. 'We're going later. Bring some mates? Could be a laugh.'

'I'm studying.' Lenny smiles at their disappointment, which comes in a collective *aww*. 'Yeah, I know, I'm boring.' He slaps a hand down on each of their shoulders at the same time. 'Have fun, though.' Then he notices Delph. 'Delphine Tennyson.' He pushes his bike along to catch her up. 'We walking, or d'you want a backie?' His eyes linger on her playfully, before they set on something behind him that turns Delph's stomach in a single flopping motion. She doesn't need to turn around. The quick distance Lenny puts between them confirms it.

'Delph,' Itsy calls out behind her. 'I've just come from Claudette's. Thought I'd grab you on the way.'

Itsy never visits Claudette. Out of all his sisters, she's the one he has the least to do with, her opinions regarding his decades of lapsed fathering being the biggest reason. His twin sons Victor and Adrian are twenty-five now, yet Itsy wouldn't know them if they walked right past him, which is the truth, because Delph prompting him into recognizing his own babies did indeed once happen.

'Everything all right?' Delph gets into the car as, with both hands knotted around the steering wheel, Itsy's eyes follow Lenny, now stopping to dismount at the traffic lights on the corner. With a grateful smile, Delph clicks her door shut. The action is disconnecting, a submarine removal from the work bustle of moments ago – quiet and airless. Like a fresh buried coffin, she thinks, wishing instantly she hadn't.

Leaning into the passenger seat, Itsy clicks Delph into her seatbelt with a smothering kiss. She flinches as his hand travels over her stomach; he keeps constant check on those traffic lights, but Lenny's gone.

'Been told to get myself on standby,' Itsy sniffs, shifting into vulnerability as he adjusts himself back in his seat. 'Mum's proper sick, the girls reckon this is it. Best make sure my passport ain't expired.' Sighing sadly, he starts the engine, and checking his mirror pulls out onto the street.

'Oh, love, I am sorry.' Delph puts her hands together, keeping them in her lap. It has always paid to try delaying her reactions, to slow any early claim of her emotions, before Itsy begins his rearranging, shaping her thoughts into his way of thinking. Sometimes, even in the lightest moments of fun, he'll change suddenly, taking the lightness with him in one big swallow, like a damp cloth over one of Mother Moon's potential chip pan fires that scared Delph way back when.

Even here, approaching the dual carriageway where the terrible thing happened, the place where her heart bottoms out each time they drive past it, Delph averts her eyes, pretends it doesn't occur to her, never wanting Itsy to be hurt because she's thinking, never not thinking, still caught in the profound, unwavering love for another man.

For Sol.

But it does occur to her. And it always will.

Delph breathes in, her mother suddenly all around her. Their strange umbilical tie, stretching beyond the visible and the realms of normal, from Mother Moon in her filthy little house, to Delph, spotting the lavender entwined with gypsophila, held together by red string, tied shabbily to a nearby lamppost.

Delph knows in her heart she's not the world's limpest lettuce. She's simply been subdued – at surface level anyway, like her plants: gorgeous statues of green while beneath the soil there's a frenzy of activity in motion. Subdued for the greater good, for peace, in a similar way to how she smothers down her job too, suffered as if it's for Itsy, for the benefit of a cost-of-living crisis, rather than – Roche and her balcony aside – Delph's only other source of light.

Even when she'd replied to Roche's text earlier, Delph knew she wouldn't be sharing her happiness with Itsy – just the same as right now, when she won't share the breathtaking enormity of him in another country.

Indefinitely.

'I did a bit of googling. While I was waiting for you,' he says pointedly. 'Almost a grand for a return flight to Kingston.'

'I suppose that counts me out of coming with you.' Is it possible to sound even halfway normal? 'But at least we'll still have money coming in while you're away.' Ignoring his suspicious look creeping in, Delph adds, 'One less thing for you to worry about.' Rubber fingers. Rubber toes. Rubber flipping tongue. Delph licks her lips, smiles, her words like those lumps of polystyrene that look like dehydrated marshmallows. Can he sense, just as Mother Moon can, the truth of her head before she does? 'You just focus on your mum, is all I'm saying.'

Itsy glances across at Delph. 'I'll be an orphan. Makes you think. We've got to look after ourselves. Especially now it's just us.'

Us. Meaning minus Roche. There's no ignoring the sobering fact that it is just them now; a twosome rubbing along forevermore. Delph's universe hinged on his emotions. Of course, it would be brilliant if his mother recovered, but the mental respite of some distance from Itsy feels timely. Like it's a gift.

Delph wonders if she's any decency at all, being so comfortable with her not particularly nice thoughts, but she'll live with them. Just like she can also live with the termination, as it fades, feeling less barbaric, less of a devastation, every day. Mother Moon was right. The sad thing being a good thing was true.

These recent snatches of her mother, just when Delph's needed her most, is another good thing she'll keep hidden. Mother Moon, who did the best she could, being the person she was.

The leather squeak of Itsy's coat breaks the silence when he shifts to change gear, flooring the brakes just before a red light, the shock of it shunting him and Delph forward, as a woman with a buggy snarls obscenities while crossing the road just in front of them. 'Yeah, yeah, yeah, fuck you too.' Itsy waves her out of the way, and there's silence again until he pulls up at the flat, grabbing Delph's arm when she reaches for the door handle. 'I'm gonna crack on. Money's money.'

'Don't you want dinner first?'

'Do me up a plate.' As Delph tries pulling away, Itsy holds her in place. 'You're edgy,' he says, his brown eyes black with suspicion. 'Is it that boy? I saw him you know, chancing little prick.'

As he twists the flesh at her wrist, Delph says, 'I don't even know his name, Itsy.'

'You see him back there, though? All over them young ones too.' He gives her a knowing look, before releasing her. 'I worry. People take advantage.'

Swallowing, Delph leans forward, putting her arms around his neck as she kisses him. Doing it like she means it. 'Thank you for caring. I'll find your passport.'

'That's my woman,' Itsy purrs, placated. 'And text me some flights.' He shakes his head. 'This gon' be so damned expensive.'

This time, Delph is allowed to climb out. She waves him off at the roadside, at 6.23 p.m. on a dead weekday night. In normal circumstances, she'd be dead inside too. But tomorrow, tomorrow she'll see her baby.

*

THE SMALLMANS

Tanners Grove, 1970

When Joy slips into bed beside Ma, to hold the new sister who smells of the bread shop and feels warm as toast, she begins to think of someone else before herself. If Joy's chilly, she'll rest her face against Janie's to see if she might need another blanket, and when Janie grows bigger, should Joy's tummy grumble, she always asks for a biscuit for Janie too. Ma says this is love, motherly instinct, and it's a sign of the good sort of mother Joy will be in the future. But Joy's in no rush for that; she's after a dog, any dog will do, and she's been asking and asking but Dad says the flower stall's not making nowhere near enough to contemplate another mouth to feed, then Ma goes all mousey and gives Joy the look that means not to push anymore.

Joy's eight when Ma gets sick for the first time. Illness knocks something out of her, and Ma returns from the hospital as fragile and shot to pieces as she'd been when she went in. Whenever people ask how Ma's keeping, Joy simply says, 'Nerves and exhaustion,' just like Dad had when he explained things to her and Janie. Everyone lives a tip-toe life around Ma while she rests, and as Dad dishes up dinners that come in tins, he mutters things about Ma going the same way as Grandma, which isn't funny, but must be hard, being a dad and doing all the Ma stuff too.

'Don't worry, Dad,' Joy says one dinnertime. 'Grandma said Ma's wings won't be ready for a long time yet.' It earns Joy her first smack in the mouth, which, being eight and made of air, knocks her clean from her chair. Unlike the other times she's been scolded – when Dad's quickly looked sorry for having had to tick her off at all – he stays angry, with such distain it's as if he wears a stranger's face. The look marks Joy like ink, and no matter how she tries to forget, to erase the image of Dad's distrust, it stains her soul too.

Soon, Joy's distracted by illness herself – and by her new neighbours, the first Black family down Tanners Grove. Not everyone's curious like her though, and there's been proper aggro. As Joy recovers, allowed to play out if she stays close to home, cos Ma says the whooping cough ain't contagious no more, Joy spots the local Shit-for-Brains – a lad in her class who rarely goes to school – throwing stones at who Joy thinks is the mum coming back from the shops with one of her kids. They're not big stones, not ones that'd do any serious damage, but Joy knows how sometimes it's the little things that hurt most, especially on the inside. Shit-for-Brains calls them names, looking like a dog with rabies as he puts the word dirty in front of all of them, which hurts Joy too because she's heard her dad saying similar things. Joy's certain no one's even introduced themselves to the Smallmans, yet they've already been marked as no good, 'a bad bunch', and how bloody daft's that, if you've no proof of it?

Joy admires the woman's beautiful green dress, the effort taken over her appearance, but most of all Joy admires the utter class it takes to hold that kind of dignity in the face of such scum ignorance. Her thoughts lead to a red mist, an urge to smash Shit-for-Brains into place, and an 'Oi!' comes out of her before she even knows it, a fistful of his collar as Joy peels him from his crouched firing position into standing. One good whack wipes the thuggery clean off his face, alive now with the red mist that moments before was in Joy's head. 'Miss! Missus Smallman!' Joy chases her, holding the child's dropped toy, which she's retrieved off the pavement, and Mrs Smallman turns back hard but then turns soft at the sight of her, panting and smiling and holding it out.

'Why don't you come in for a minute,' Mrs Smallman says through her made-up mouth, sounding all fancy and different, so Joy accepts. How it's the same shaped house as home, yet feels and smells nothing like it, is a madness. This house is warm for a start, full of colourful things – and noise; a house lived in properly. An old lady with her hair wrapped in a bright scarf, who Joy thinks must be the grandma, chops veg in the back room, hum-hum-humming with the sort of voice that could be pressed into a record, and Joy wonders if all Black people are natural-born singers just like the dickie birds, and if that's the case then how could this grandma be any less of a person than old Grandma Iris had been, who was white, yes, but couldn't sing for toffee. A voice straight from hell itself, Dad would say, which was harsh, but sadly true. This grandma stops what she's doing to gather the kid into her lap before continuing to chop, humming on and on.

Joy's given a drink that looks like the Ribena she only gets when she's ill like lately, that Ma makes with hot kettle water and is the best medicine, if medicine's supposed to make you warm and happy inside. Joy sips her new Ribena as she watches through the window, the sweep of joined houses, quiet in the daytime when normally, in better health, she'd be at school. This Ribena is called Sarsaparilla, and it's an altogether different taste as Joy rolls the concoction around her mouth, enjoying how the word concoction fills her head too, like she's got a new secret with this new special drink.

Just as she would with Janie at home, Joy reaches out to stroke the little boy's cheek and coo at him. She loves Janie and most other little kids, but what Joy's never liked is all the 'Mum in the making', 'Mini-Mum' comments that make her feel trapped in an apron already. But here the Smallman women just smile, likely with relief and maybe with a little bit of hope that not everyone around here is against them. Because Joy's not; she'd be happy to spend all the time in the world in this new house with the new smells enchanting her senses. Joy wants to try it all, to stuff herself with their different ways and insider knowledge that no one round here could ever try claiming as theirs anyway, cos they're all too ...

They'd say superior.

She'd say scared. Stupid, even.

The Smallman house becomes Joy's new sanctuary during the summer she started unwell, and everyone feared the worst. Repaired on their pepper soup kindness, one day Joy has the bright idea of bringing Janie to meet them too. And it's all good fun till Mouse Ma's near hysterics, as she shouts for Janie in the road outside. As people leave their houses to join the search, a big song and dance brews and none of it in a good way.

At the sight of her and Janie making their way down the Smallman's path, Ma screams out stuff about 'keeping themselves to themselves; how people are decent folk round this way, and it's high time they realized they weren't welcome,' and when Ma smothers her and Janie with panicked affection, her clammy pits too close for comfort, the sound of Mrs Smallman apologizing is simply too much, and Joy pushes Ma off and legs it back into the house and up to her room.

Even though the summer's got a little life left in it, home turns proper cold when Dad loses his spot on the market. Three generations of flower traders, smudged out like they never existed. It takes Joy time to fall in, to make sense of the new vocabulary, words like 'signing on' and 'dole money', that both Joy and Janie hoped might lead to something toy-related. Before long, Ma's back 'living on her nerves', when really it's more that Ma's living on air, never sitting at the table to eat with them, especially now there's not much in the cupboards. Never settling. Rarely smiling. Joy wonders what it might be like to live with the Smallmans. She wouldn't mind being the odd one out, because when she thinks about it, they never once made her feel it. Being part of them would be better than the idiots who go out drinking with Dad, the ones Ma calls bad influences, cos all they do is moan about the same old, week in week out; never doing a thing about it. The Smallmans come from a different pattern; they are adventurers, brave as hell, just like Joy will be when she's grown.

During Joy's first week back at school, she finds that the Smallmans have vanished. Moved, just like that, 'and good riddance too,' says everyone except her, who feels she's been robbed, like they've taken a part of her, that she's no idea how to get back. James Brown and Sly and the Family Stone just don't sound the same in her house, where even the things that were happy and stable are breaking off in parts, like unsettled ground. But through her heartache, it dawns on Joy that the Smallmans did in fact leave something behind: the confirmation that Joy's tiny corner of the planet isn't the only version of life on offer. There's more out there if she's brave enough, intrepid enough. Home don't have to mean what you're dished up and given. Home will be where Joy's heart feels safe. And someday, somewhere, there'll be a place Joy can be herself.

Just as Grandma had, Joy puts all her feelings into painting; finds creating offers a place for her emotions to go. She paints the most intricate of domestic scenes, things remembered from the Smallmans' house that she never wants to forget; the summer Joy's friends came and went, gifting the glimpse of another way.

4

KEEP ON MOVING ON

Wellsend, 2023

Delph arrives early, wanting to get to Gem's Café first, allowing herself the chance to appear at ease and established, like she's the type who catches up in coffee shops on the regular. Ordering a cappuccino, she takes a seat in the front window, keeping watch, but all too soon her neck's sore from craning at the road. It's still only 10.23 a.m. and Roche's never been early for anything – another trait shared with her grandmother. Delph's foot taps a rapid little beat beneath the table. What'll they talk about? Positive things. Work and plans and forwards.

Checking Facebook, reading the rally of messages from Itsy's fam fretting over flight prices to Jamaica, life feels suddenly fresher, like a wholly necessary through breeze has blasted on through Delph's world. She's never been alone before, not truly, and what once seemed too terrifying to contemplate is beginning to feel like a godsend.

Delph's thoughts shift when she spots Roche outside. Two men part ways as she cuts between them on the pavement, both turning in sync to look after her. They're twenty-five or so, a little scruffy and rough round the edges. The one wearing a hoodie whistles as his mate nods appreciatively, saying something Delph can't work out, and Roche turns, giving them the finger with both hands. Looping back on herself, she doesn't break stride, just smiles down at the pavement, her enormous hair bouncing around her shoulders with each step. Looking up into the café a few shops ahead, Roche spots her mum and, smiling bigger, speeds up, pulling open the door.

Rising to meet her, Delph pulls Roche into a cuddle, their instant closeness making her chest ache. She smells of the fresh chilly morning, and her Beyoncé scent that's forever triggered Delph's migraines. 'I am so happy to see you, love,' she says, her voice seeming even smaller than usual.

'Me too.' Roche rubs Delph's back before breaking away. 'Have you ordered food? I'm starving.'

Roche has a full English, while Delph picks at a jam bagel and studies her daughter, chasing the last of her fried mushrooms around her plate, her unfussy palate and keenness to eat anything and everything always heartening. Remembering how she had once loved food too is like imagining a different person; a disconnection that happened slowly in Delph at first, till she struggled to eat at all, hating restaurants especially, choosing, making the decisions. Then grew the habit of opting for starters as mains, taking big glugs of water just to move mouthfuls down her neck, hoping no one ever, ever noticed. Or doing the birdlike habit of old, tearing food up into small and swallowable bites, like she does with her bagel now.

But Roche. She sets her knife and fork together and sits back, all soft and satisfied, making Delph briefly envious. Incredible how something as simple as a full stomach can act like magic. The fry-up aside, Roche does look well. Delph will have to thank her mother properly. Perhaps even treat her.

'How have you been managing with your . . .'

'Hair? Disastrously. Thank you, Mum. For bringing all this.' Roche gestures to the tote bag of haircare and other bits from home that Delph knows she'll have missed, knowing all the same that handing them over undoubtedly adds to the time she'll spend away.

'I was going to ask how you're managing with your nan?' Delph sips her cappuccino the size of a soup bowl, caffeine palpitations already on the cards. Despite Mother Moon looking well enough yesterday, the past knows how exceptional she is at faking it, deciding that she's better off without her meds than going her own way, which is usually spiral-shaped.

'You make her sound like she's got problems.'

'She has got problems.' It's hard to picture Roche living in Moon's mess. 'Is she keeping on top of the house?' The times Delph thought about ringing one of those programmes that exploit people's hoarding troubles for a quick fix. 'Perhaps you could fight through it by pretending you're on Channel 5 and seeing it as a challenge.' Roche doesn't answer, so Delph leaves it there. 'And how's school?'

'Predicted – only predicted, mind,' Roche warns. 'Two Bs and an A.'

'A genius. And gorgeous too – how'd I manage that?' Delph squeezes Roche's hand. 'I am so proud of you.'

'I haven't got them yet.'

She's blown colder. Roche takes her hand back from beneath her mother's, and Delph returns to her drink. Needing the loo but fearing it might signal the end, Delph instead tells Roche about work. How there's a night out planned with the team in a couple of weeks.

'In the evening?' Roche asks, screwing one eye shut, studying her mother with the other. 'Not with Itsy?'

Delph laughs. It falls out happy and natural. 'Not with Itsy, no.'

'Cool.' Roche makes a fist, extending it for Delph to bump, approval emanating across the table.

'Roche, what if I said Itsy wouldn't be there, would you come home then?' Delph swallows. 'His mum. She's on her last legs.' She watches Roche raise both brows, unsurprised as she is unbothered by this news. 'I don't know how long he'll be there for.'

'Jamaica indefinitely? Without you?'

'Home alone, so it seems. Unless . . .'

'Now, don't be getting upset, Mum. I just think it's better

like this. Just for a bit.' Roche hesitates, chewing her lip, for a flash exactly like her mother. 'Nan ... well, we ... actually, wondered if you fancied dinner, maybe Monday?'

'I'd love that.' Without hesitation Delph accepts, along with their new dynamic. Because Roche does make a good point. This time apart hasn't done them any harm. Space to think, as she's discovering, might be a healthy solution all round.

'Good.' Roche smiles, winding her scarf around her neck. She scoops out her hair, flicking it free. 'I hope his mum gets better and all that, though. Not her fault she birthed an eediat.' This time it's her that initiates the hug. Squeezing Delph tight, she kisses her face. 'I am proud of you too, Mum.'

Walking home, touched by Roche's praises, Delph doesn't notice the cold so much. They both do seem happier, strangely closer than when they'd been in each other's pockets, anticipating the snap that Delph can now admit she'd felt coming. It was no real surprise Roche's tolerance finally expired, no secret that for years it's been a battle of wills against Itsy; Delph, the ever-failing mediator between them. But today. Today Roche had been proud of her – for the one thing Delph's never truly been.

Independent.

But sometimes things do happen slowly. Organically. Perhaps Delph's simply been living in shock, a dormant state of trauma, which can happen with plants the same as people if they're mistreated. Delph recalls the old oak at the front of her school that a bunch of drunk kids set fire to; how brutal it was seeing the tree so charred and lifeless on the daily, the school entrance looking like it belonged in a Tim Burton film for most of the years Delph went there. And then, after about a decade of dormancy, one spring it budded plump green pods.

Delph holds the thought in her head, understands Roche's bid for freedom more than she lets on. Because with Itsy's mind on his mother, without Delph as his constant focus, she can see most clearly how his love is also suffocation.

Same old streets, same old route, yet the air all the way back to the flat tastes new.

Good. And right.

Roche spots an old hoover, dumped by a lamppost at the top of Nan's street, a damp piece of A4 taped to its body: FOR PARTS. PLEASE TAKE, and it feels like a sign. It even has a plug attached, and though there's no suction when she tests it out, after forty minutes with a step-by-step repair expert from Cumbria on YouTube, the floor no longer feels like Roche's walking on sandpaper, which releases far more endorphins than the effort it would take to get her arse in gear regarding university.

It hadn't felt right dropping uni on Mum in the café earlier, especially when she'd finally seemed more accepting of this new living set-up, and besides, Roche can work it into the convo over dinner on Monday. The application itself will, of course, burn a hole through every procrastinating action until she completes it, but seeing as the only thing that ever truly makes her shift her bum with any sort of genius intention is a deadline, it'll wait like a ticking bomb, down to the very last minute.

Vacuum cleaning has a domino effect. Roche finds herself walking about, neatening this and that, first surprised there's a cloth in her hand, and then fully involved, sweating and shifting years and years of Nan's old shit. Because if Roche ever plans on claiming the back bedroom as hers, she'll need to do the work herself. It's not that Nan's idle, exactly – more easily distracted, mostly by her piles of paper, that any attempt to sort through it leaves her downing tools to sit cross-legged on the freshly vacced floors, engrossed in the print of old news.

A few hours with Radio 6 blasting and Nan's dumping ground begins to resemble a bedroom, and even though she's not holy, Roche sends a prayer of thanks heavenward. The single divan is in much better repair than she anticipated, with a good firm mattress too, and, flopping out on it for a moment, everything feels like progress.

There was nothing intentionally nosey in moving the mountain of bin bags obstructing the almost bare and therefore useful bookcase in the corner, just as there'd been nothing more than a passing interest when Roche first noticed the two boxes – until she clocked how they were both bound in red, that is, and downed tools herself in distraction. Two bound boxes, without any postage to show they were ever in transit. Just a label in shaky blue handwriting, addressed to a Joy Tennyson.

Roche's never known a Joy before, charmed by the simple

loveliness of the name, which must surely belong to her nan. Grabbing her phone, she snaps a picture of the boxes over to Eden, with the caption:

ROCHE: Proper Pandora's Box shit innit?

The message is seen immediately.

EDEN: You know what happened to the cat that got curious, though???? 😬
ROCHE: Not helpful …
EDEN: Probs just bank statements and shit
EDEN: Or lurve letters
EDEN: On olden days paper, like we'd make in the infants with tea bags, remember? Like Wild West wanted posters 😄
EDEN: Maybe from Mama Dee's dad?!?!?!?
EDEN: Waaaait a sec …. Mama Dee's got a dad … Why I never even thought about this?????

Roche sends another pic through to Eden, a close-up of the repetitive red binding, looped over and over the cardboard, which must've taken some patience. Roche wonders where her nan buys her string – she should bloody have shares in the place.

EDEN: Don't red mean protection?
ROCHE: I said this the other week. She told me herself

when I asked about the doorknobs.

ROCHE: And them boxes seriously bound tight . . .

EDEN: Ah man!

EDEN: 👀

Roche perches on the bed, re-scrolling Eden's messages. It's not like Mum having a dad is a new thought, it's more that the mystique around Sol, her own father, spreads so far that all other family components rarely feature. All Roche knows is that throughout her mother's childhood, and into leaving home for good, Nan never had a partner, a lover, or a stay-overnighter-er. Self-confessed romantically incapable. Which seems sad, because even in Roche's first proper relationship, she knows it's a blessing to have Eden in her life and in her heart, and she tells herself so, every damn day.

It's been time since Roche thought herself a Disney princess type, doesn't know if she's truly romantic, yet the way she feels for Eden is like she's been dipped in gold, as close to religion as she's ever had the presence to articulate; a tender sensuality between them that allows all Roche's furies to feel a little less important. And now that Roche knows love, it's scary to imagine life without it, which can't help but add precious nuance to Mum's loss as well, and everything she's kept inside.

To think Nan might never have known love saddens Roche most of all, but there must've been someone, somewhere, at some bloody point; Roche and her mother are the living, breathing proof.

Something churns at the covers near Roche's feet and for a moment it's like the bed's moving, alive perhaps with mice, or – oh my days – rats, ready to charge from the sprung innards, to consume her at last. Tiny mouths and little pink hands, tails too long to be any sort of cute. Then the bed moves properly, and out comes an enormous drone of a purr.

Two yellow eyes appear, bright in the lamplight. The arch of a black cat's back. Sterilizing that dirty old litter tray in the hall had been Roche's number one cleaning priority, yet the shock of the actual defecator gets her leaping from the bed, pressed into a corner – and not just any old corner ...

... the one with the two bound boxes.

From her hand, Roche's phone pings again.

EDEN: You know you gonna look, innit?
EDEN: I know you
EDEN: ☝

Listening first for Nan, Roche crouches, beginning to unwind the box closest to her, as the cat, collarless and therefore nameless, makes acquaintances, settling under her arm.

FAO Ms Joy Tennyson: 109b Rita Road, Wellsend Grove

Wrapped and wrapped and wrapped in red.

Tucked within an old Sainsburys carrier bag that's full of tiny painted canvases is a carefully cut out piece of magazine paper, now delicate and very, very old, which Roche handles with great care to read:

EVA VERDE

No Shit Fanzine, May 1978
Joy Tennyson – High Commendation
Rub Anything
for long enough
and it'll come off
in the wash
in your hand
even good things get
the pleasure
knocked off
the shine long gone
should you
rub anything
for long enough

Seriously? Wtf ad infinitum.

As she tries fathoming the strange little poem, a rippling
begins beneath Roche's feet, her arches humming with the
sense of something remembered, reawakened, powerful in
the way it seems to connect every particle of her, from the
physicality of the pamphlet in her hand, to what feels the very
root of her soul. And as she drops the poem, the paper – being
very old paper – disintegrates entirely. Roche rubs her socked
foot and the tiny white fragments into the carpet, releasing
a dust and the strangest notion that these fragments are like
ashes she's freed. Back into the room, into Nan's home.

And into consciousness again.

Though it really does feel like some sort of spell, it's a silly childish imagining that passes through Roche, that these boxes are somehow alive. Boxes that appear to contain the unknown history of a person not unknown to her at all, but who is part of Roche's flesh, Roche's history.

And Roche's story too.

*

IN EVERY FAMILY THERE IS A TRUTHSEEKER

Esplanade Point, 2013

Itsy would often say, while rubbing his backside, that six hours behind the wheel left his arse flatter than Delph's mother's.

Roche's eight. And offended. A similar thing happens when an old cast member Itsy once had the hots for returns to his favourite soap after a decade. 'Good God, ain't time cruel?' he'd clucked in disappointment. 'Lost all definition – and her marbles, most likely.' He'd laughed to himself, flashing his gold tooth that had dulled over the years, rather like Roche's opinion of him.

Itsy's so pampered, every day is like his birthday or Christmas, his life mirroring the festive adverts of men asleep in front of the telly while the women half kill themselves in prep of the celebrations. Mum's efforts to please him always, like his Great British comfort diet of nursery meals that swell Roche's belly, leave her docile and uncomfortable.

The plates that contained those stodge dinners were relics of the past too – belonging to his marriage. Octagonal, horrible, a floral entwining pink and green pattern, faded from two women scouring at them. One who wore a ring and the other who was only ever promised one. But Roche knew from the way Mum smiled whenever the talk of a wedding was dangled in front of her, how being Itsy's wife wasn't anything she desired, numb to his jest of honest women, and no escapes.

Roche often thinks about losing Mum. Sometimes she has night terrors that somehow always feature Itsy, his cloaking presence, the man with the longest shadow in the world, smothering her mum, smothering all that might catch into life. But maybe Roche's worries are just part of growing up – because not everything's terrible; sometimes even Roche can slip into thinking that they're just a normal family.

Normal is coming home after a successful grading with a new karate belt, twisting Itsy into getting a takeaway as a treat. But normal slides away when Mum arranges Roche for a photo, passing from happy to sad behind the lens at a speed most troubling, before – first making sure Itsy had left to collect their food – she'd pulled a Nike shoebox from behind the sink cupboard.

A Polaroid's held to Roche's face, of a man with light brown skin, black rectangular glasses, and light brown fro in canerows, full of easy confidence, as he looks at the person taking the picture. But Mum and her memories sound far away, like she's trying too hard to sell something already stale. Because Roche never can join her mother in her grief, any more than she can connect herself to this box of her father's belongings, how she came to be – even though she wouldn't exist without them. Drying her eyes, Mum kissed Roche.

'Don't think I'm sad. Taking your photo just made it clear for a moment that your dad's still with us. In you.' Roche's dad is not a secret, but she's grown knowing it's better not to mention him. And though it doesn't feel great boxing her dad back into the dark of the kitchen cupboard, she understands why that's for the best too, but it leaves her full of trapped feelings that she feels too uncomfortable to share or show.

It is only later, when Roche takes the box out herself, that its contents feel different. Without the presence of Mum's grief, the only energy before, her father's things now feel as if they belong to a real person. The thin band of gold, D and S engraved inside, makes Roche suddenly queasy; imagining how this ring once sat on her dad's alive finger, attached to the once alive hand of a breathing, loving human who's now inside another box, way underground. Flesh and blood now earth and bone.

Roche can't explain why she doesn't put the ring back. Instead, along with the photograph, she entrusts them to the best person she knows.

'Eden coming down for a pancake roll?' Itsy asked, as she returned from upstairs, his arms full of takeaway, even remembering the sweet and sour sauce for her chicken balls. And as she put the box back in the cupboard while he called Mum in for dinner, her strange gut feeling to hide the ring seemed suddenly silly.

Though was proof nonetheless; Roche's always had form. For being a curious creature.

5

Box Rooms, Boxed Thoughts

Butterfield Estate, Wellsend Grove, 2023

Moon hates admitting it, but the nightmares returned the second Roche moved into the spare. It's been hard keeping track of what leaves the house disguised as rubbish, that Moon hasn't the heart nor the words to try claiming as important. Now, most evenings, Moon hovers smoking by the back door, as Roche spreads her studies out in either her clean new bedroom or across the coffee table in the lounge, even sitting on the carpet, which isn't crumby and stained anymore, not since madam tarted up that hoover, and they hired a rug doctor with the first tarot earnings to come in since Roche set up *Moon Meditations* online.

This is the skill of the young. They fly round gadgetry without thinking, like they were born programmed. Moon won't forget how she once watched a baby, *still of crawling age,* pincer the screen of its mother's phone. Enlarging and shrinking a digital image, but unable to walk yet. Good or bad? Is it either? Is anything ever one clean, solid thing?

Online tarot is a fucking goldmine, though. Twenty quid for a basic reading, which she dictates into Roche's laptop, which turns into a document Moon calls an 'astral report', which Roche then edits and emails off. Then come the replies, from souls keen for more insight, more advice – as boosting as it is draining. Moon's energies are not as rumbunctious as in the old times, when she could read face-to-face all day long, preparing herbal spliff-shaped prescriptions as another spiritual side-hustle. But now she's weak from poor-quality sleep, even taking to napping in the afternoons – after the astral reports are completed, of course.

Tech. Baffling, that even drug dealers these days operate through Instagram. Anything and everything's available; from hardcore never quite normal again type shit, to legal marijuana, which must surely be like non-alcoholic wine, Moon thinks, but might be worth a try, because weed's the only thing – other than vodka, of course – that offers any chance of a proper night's sleep. Apparently, all that's required is a health condition to get some prescription dose CBD. Moon could certainly cook up a migraine story – this terrible head's been savaging her for days now, pain that only a bud the size of a Christmas tree could solve. Obliterate her mind and push all the dark back where it belongs.

Moon pulls her cardigan around her, holding together fists full of soft wool against her chest, against her heart, as Mister

Cat weaves himself around her calves, followed closely by Roche, trying to tempt him with a Jaffa Cake.

'Ah, so you've finally met him, then? He comes and goes as he pleases – who am I to tell him what to do?' Moon feels her own tired edginess on display, as she opens and closes cupboards, and not finding what she fancies, settles for fags for breakfast instead.

'You all right, Nan?' With a frown Roche opens a window.

'I had the dream dreams.'

'The what?'

Moon slumps next to her on their morning doorstep. Despite suffering the longest of nights, the day hasn't quite arrived. A solitary bird soars across the colourless sky, then a dash of white disruption as a plane escapes their small island. 'Delph must've told you about the dream dreams now, surely.' Mister Cat presses his body once more against Moon's ankles, and as she tickles him under the chin, he moves away, settling across Roche's bare feet.

'He likes me. He was in my room last night.'

'Course he likes you, he remembers you.'

'From when?'

With a deep old drag, Moon tells of the first peculiarity, back when Roche and Delph moved in with Itsy. Cats were uncommon in the block, and Mister Cat's arrival surprised Itsy as much as all of them. With their belongings in at last, legs exhausted because of the lift that couldn't be trusted, Mister Cat had rolled up as a latecomer, slinking along the landing, only to come face-to-face with the tiny girl that was

Roche, before stretching his body long and languid round her ankles. And there he'd stayed, lithe in downward dog as he studied Delph too – but when Itsy tried petting the creature, Mister Cat had regarded him most judgmentally, before jumping out of his reach.

'Oh, Mister Cat,' Roche laughs. 'Did you and me just become best friends?'

The second peculiarity was how Mister Cat then took to popping by. Not for food or affection – more for observation, like an Ofsted inspector, silently assessing at the back of the classroom, his yellow half-asleep eyes in an otherwise expressionless face. Loving his visits, Delph took to keeping a box of Go-Cat at the ready, but Itsy, feeling judged and slighted by the creature's disinterest in him, boxed Mister Cat up for a one-way trip to the RSPCA – until that is, Moon stepped in.

'He's been my flexible house guest ever since.' Moon takes her eyes off Mister Cat, turning them towards the closed door of the spare room. 'How are you sleeping in there?'

'Like normal.' Roche looks a little bit shifty. 'What are dream dreams, anyway?'

'Well. You've got your everyday, unremarkable dreams.' Moon taps her ash. 'And then there's the dream dreams. They're the tricky ones that have you almost believing they're real. The deep, dark powerful sleep.' The underbelly of memory and subconscious. She takes out a new fag, lighting it from the butt of the other. 'And always, always bad.'

'I don't ever dream,' Roche says, carefully. 'Well, not that I remember.'

'Lucky you. Your mother had them terrible, after ...' Open as Moon is about Sol, it is his ending that always gets stuck, that never gets any easier to say aloud. 'Sol's demise. That's what they called it, the Old Bill and the paper – not death, or murder.' She sucks on her fag like it's a lifeline. Demise. Like he'd been king of the castle, knocked from his fancy throne. Demise. Like a Wall Street millionaire, sucked down the plughole of material excess. Demise. An armoured warrior, slain unexpectedly.

Demise.

In less than a week, Sol's tragic story went from regional news headlines to the size of a match box, wrapped up neatly on page six of the local rag; death by suicide, filed as unsuspicious. The footbridge was a prime jumping spot. And besides, jumping was a neater explanation, in all its comforting, dark predictability. Crisis, care home, his string of foster placements, created easy labels that sold Sol as a poor 'fragile delinquent'. Add 'ethnic minority' and all the words melt as one, guaranteed not only to close minds but close the door on a murder case the police never gave two shits about, anyway.

'You do know that it was murder?'

Roche nods, looking down into her lap. 'Yeah.' She presses her fingers to her eyes. 'It's fucking horrible.'

'D'you know what happened to the thug who did the pushing? Wrapped his car around a tree on his twenty-first birthday.' Moon chuckles. 'Twenty-one days after Sol's funeral.'

'He killed himself?'

EVA VERDE

'Who knows. Fuck him.'

Fifteen people attended Sol's funeral. At the thug's, crowds of mourners spilled through the church doors and out onto the pavements. The town a standstill. Son of a nouveau-riche football hooligan. Leader of a flashy crew of bigots, with previous for racially motivated GBH. A crew of bigots the police had never even bothered questioning properly.

'The universe is kind sometimes. Heard his father's long gone too, now. And that's the end of their lineage. But here you still are, representing.' Moon holds her hand, for a moment almost tearful. 'He was remarkable, I promise you.' She catches Roche's eye. 'What?'

'It doesn't seem right to say. But fancy going from remarkable to Itsy.'

'Her hurt was exactly how he wormed his way in.' Lips trembling, Moon takes another drag, before crushing it out in a saucer. Delph in the gaunt phase is hard to forget, when her bones would jut sharp and noticeable through her clothes, and she walked with a permanent cower. Her girl, the kicked pup in need of a master, who let Itsy take the lead, from deciding when she could go out, to if she could ring her own bloody mother. 'Don't ever blame your mum. It's brainwashing. So clever, she doesn't even know he's done it to her. Not brainy-clever, mind. Controlling.'

'Well, he can't do much controlling from Jamaica. His mum's ill. Dying or something.'

Moon's ears can't help pricking up. 'And Delph's not going?'

'I told you, innit. Money's tight. He even tried stopping

88

me going to mixed martials, even though this club's miles cheaper than my old one – comes out of Mum's benefits, anyway. She practically begged him not to cancel the direct debit. It's why I started doing Saturdays in the chippy.' Roche twists at the rings on the chain around her neck, before Moon makes a grab for them, almost pulling Roche over, her eyes widening as she inspects them.

'Your mother swore she'd lost her ring!'

Roche sits back, a little wary. 'She did. I … I just found it again.'

'And you didn't give it back?'

It takes Roche a little while to reply. 'Itsy made her take it off.'

'Made her, what do you mean made her?'

Roche swallows. 'He just … made her take it off. Then I sort of stole it off him. Jeez, you're practically purple.' Rising, Roche pushes a glass of water into her hands. 'Here. For God's sakes, Nan.'

'That man. If I only, only had it in me …' With rage bubbling at her temples, Moon tips two of her pills into her palm, swallowing them with the water. 'After all the trouble of getting it soldered back together, too. Cost me a flipping arm and a leg.' Which had been worth every penny. To see Delph's face briefly lift when she pushed it back on after all her pregnancy swelling and the emergency C-section; its hallmark distorted by the jeweller's repair job, while the most important part, the D&S, like a necessary miracle, had remained intact. Unable to look at Roche, Moon says, 'This bloody head of mine. I'm off to bed.'

Clicking the door shut and leaning against it, Moon stretches her arms to the ceiling, making fists at the sky beyond as she screams silently, inwardly, before biting down on her hand, her mouth metallic for a moment as she pulls away, examining the smear of fresh red. The tiny indentations of teeth.

A vodka would work better. Or a big fat reefer. Because, when your hands are tied and you're flipping helpless, when you're born bearing the ignorance that the world is kind and people are good, what else is there to do but obliterate yourself?

Life always finds its way to punish, somehow.

'Roche, it's been kept so lovely,' says Eden, gazing into Nan's box like it contains actual treasure. In a way, it does. It's become a project. Halfway through so far, joining dots from all these scraps to make a patchwork jigsaw family. 'By your nan d'you reckon?'

'I don't know, y'know. Reckon it was sent by someone – that's the vibe I'm getting. Who, though?'

'I reckon maybe her mum.' Eden looks thoughtful. 'But shouldn't she be dead by now? Her parents must be, like, in their hundreds, or something.'

Roche hands a photo album to Eden, who leafs gently through it, full of the oranges and chocolate browns that date the pictures instantly.

One image is of an instantly recognizable Moon. Fine-featured and perfect, like she lived in the forest she's photographed in, as some cherished daughter of the wood nymphs, flitting apple-cheeked through the foliage on the daily, her orange hair in a thick braid, curled around her head like a fancy loaf in an artisan bread shop.

'Seriously, give the kid a red cape, and she'd have the fairy-tale shizzle down pat.'

'You gotta love a chubby kid, innit.' Eden scrunches up her face. 'Proper cute. Hey, I reckon I'll be a good mum, don't you?' Roche's never really thought about it. 'Of course, like, one day. Not yet. Obvs.' Eden adds quickly, 'Don't you want to be a mum?'

'Probably not. Kids get on my tits.'

'You are proper dry sometimes.'

Roche glances across the room to her uni brochures on the bookcase, still half full of Nan's old stuff, which although she's certain wouldn't be missed, has made no presumptions about chucking. Instead, she's simply introduced her own few bits while neatening up the rest, intentional about keeping possessions to a minimum, because, well, university, innit. The word's on repeat in her head, especially now she's officially signed up to UCAS. Even if Roche had been offered help with applying, like the handheld treatment all the pick-me earlybirds get from the teachers who like them, she'd still have refused it. Not that she needed help anyway. Applying took little more than a good morning's focus. Now all Roche needs to do is look for any potential scholarship applications, because what a difference that could make, should Roche be granted one. It would ease the monetary pressure no end.

'Look at this.' Holding up another picture, Eden trails her fingers down a teenage Moon's outfit. A floor-length dress in a bright artificial blue that clashes beautifully with her hair, up in another bread-plait twist. 'I am mad stanning her in this one.'

Until finding the album that Eden's now charmed by, there had been no youth pictures of Nan, yet it's still hard to believe that the photos were ever the living reality of her life. A pub features in so many of them, where Nan always looks shoehorned in, like a pair of well-dressed feet aching for freedom. Roche's admired the maxi dresses, the flares and seventies prints she's fond of herself, but the pictures lack the cool nostalgia of the accounts she follows on Insta. Nan's images – or Joy's at this point – hold despair. Even the act of touching the photographs feels sad. So much dark, dark wood in a bar fogged with smoke – perhaps clouded by depression too, for no one looks jovial. The word depression settles, absorbs, as Roche looks again to the pictures, studying the woman always sat next to her nan, the hollows of her face making her eyes almost invisible, like she's in her very own version of the Sunken Place. She is a hollowed creature, the sort of woman who might be described as a bundle of nerves. Her dainty port and lemon, surrounded by big mahogany pints that match the dark, dark wood, the creamy slosh of beer froth clinging to the sides of the glasses.

The Feather and Broomstick. Roche has googled, and the pub's very much still standing. She had the idea that she could go, ask around.

Ask around for what, though?

'Look at her hands, Roche.' Eden taps the pub picture, at the woman in the Sunken Place. 'Who carries herself like that?'

'Best put this away, quick. Nan's coming, I swear it.'

And Roche's right; by the time the girls scramble about to hide the box and head for the front room as if they've been watching *Escape to the Country* this whole time, they spot her heading back across the road towards the house with armfuls of yellow-stickered products, proud as.

Amazing, to be connected through the same body, the same genes – from the ghostly woman in the pub pictures with the hands like Mum, to Joy with the strong arms. To her. Rochelle Barclay. And it's fascinating.

'Budge up,' Nan says. Decanting her wares across the coffee table, she waves Roche off for some plates. 'Supper awaits.'

'If ham was a vegetable, I'd be the happiest girl in the world.' Eden pincers up a posh slice, dropping it into her mouth from a height, eyes closed and swooning, like the ham's become grapes and she's in ancient flipping Greece.

'The world would be a lot nicer,' Nan says, 'if we were all so easily pleased.'

Often it's the little things that make you the happiest. Like Nan's supermarket secret. Should she reveal it, everyone'd be at it and the game would be over, and Roche's touched she's been allowed in on the wily secret. Saturdays in M&S, just across the way, are always ripe for a visit about half an hour before closing, when there's bargains galore. Enough reduced convenience to make Nan's heart soar – Roche's too, because it's been nice having things that aren't pie, or sausage, or mash, or some other Itsy meat and dense potato classic, night after flipping night.

This evening Nan produces – along with the two packets of ham – tabbouleh, vegetable spring rolls and gooseberry fool yoghurts. With the new potatoes, mixed leaf lettuce and the radishes from the garden, it'll likely do lunch tomorrow too.

'I never succumbed to the pressures on mothers at meal-times. We all have mouths and guts and appetites, regardless of gender or spirit.' From nowhere, Nan also produces a family bag of Monster Munch and three cans of Sprite that Roche and Eden thank her for profusely. 'I have a vagina between my thighs, not drudge tattooed on my forehead.'

The girls laugh. Nan too. And for a moment – only for a moment – Roche lets herself just be, enjoying the fun of her most awesome companions.

It is only later, when Nan's dropped off in front of *Silent Witness*, after stretching out and claiming the sofa-for-one, that Roche feels confident enough to resume her box dipping. Nan's story is fast becoming all she can think about – *Who Do You Think You Are?* in box form. And, in a box within the box, addressed, stamped and posted, in an envelope softened from overhandling, Roche uncovers a letter. It's the same shaky blue writing as the box label. She swallows. A return address – and localish, too. Danes Lane. Tanners Grove.

December, 1980
Joy,

To write instead of seeing you I've no good words for. You're missed, and I'd give a kidney to hold that little angel on the way even once. Know that both of you are in my heart and in

94

every thought. Janie's knitting's going strong; your bubsie's
got enough coats and hats to do the whole maternity ward
when the time comes. I know she misses you. Maybe even more
than I do.

Here's five pounds. I can't spare more in case it's noticed,
and for what it's worth your dad misses you n'all. I know he
hasn't always been the best at showing it.

Take care of yourself and bubsie. Love Ma x

PS. Picture our shock when that Nigerian chap turned up
looking for you. Your dad never knew you'd kept in contact –
nor I, for that matter. I've enclosed his letter, which I hope you
can see hasn't been opened, though it was a mission and a half
to keep it so.

PPS. It broke my heart seeing your man shot down on telly
the other evening. Every time Imagine is on the wireless I catch
myself welling up. John meant so much to you growing up. I
hope you didn't take it too badly.

Roche's insides fill with the noisiest, most resonant of heart-
beats as she searches deeper into the box in search of the
other letter, eager to link this first solid piece of the past.

But it's not there. Not even on the third look.

'Easy, Mrs Manic.' Eden's hand arrives gently on the back
of Roche's neck as she reads the letter herself. 'Roche. This *is*
proper Miss Marple shiiit!'

Perhaps it is Eden's reaction that makes Roche feel suddenly intrusive. And guilty. This isn't a game. 'Put it back.
Come on, I want to put it away.'

'But . . .'

'No buts. Photos and poems are one thing. This feels, it all feels a bit . . . real.' Awash with the strange sicky feeling, like she's gone too far, Roche feels cheap, like she's read Nan's diary – which, by the way, she'd never do. It's a breach of privacy she's suffered herself, having lived with a nosy control freak.

'I get you,' says Eden, and Roche knows she does, but she's still unable to resist. 'Nigeria though, babe. You might be a princess too, like me.'

Eden's dad is an A-class shit, but the rest of his fam have always been a constant presence, despite her dad not being around. Every couple of years or so, Eden goes visiting some place just outside of Lagos, and every couple of years or so, Eden returns with not only the most fantastic garms, but bucketloads more confidence, an inner assurance, like she's been fed well from her roots. She's also got half-siblings that she's now old enough to keep in contact with herself, rather than relying on Mr Unreliable who made them all, which Roche privately finds rather lovely, having always been lonely herself. What a thrill, discovering new people you're connected to. The closest Roche got to anything remotely similar was on the rare occasions when Itsy's twins would visit, Victor and Adrian, quiet boys who'd slink around their mother's legs until it was time to go, and Roche would be most relieved to be an only child again.

'Mama Dee's dad. It's got to be,' Eden says, before repeating, 'Nigerian chap.'

'Leave it.' This is an overstepped boundary that could hurt. Like Roche's taken advantage, somehow. It's not nice feeling guilty towards someone who's shown her nothing but kindness. 'Let me check on her. At least.'

Silent Witness has given way to the news, some Tory bastard nemesis of Nan's now filling the screen, but even that's not disturbed the sleeping beauty, frowning and older-looking in her slumber than the lady hotfooting it across the road earlier, so full of herself, the very thing Roche loves most about her. This bold woman, so different from her mother. So needed in her life.

In both their lives.

'Still sparko.' Roche smiles to see Mister Cat cosying up with Eden, draping himself across her thigh as Eden hands Roche a well-stuffed official-looking envelope. 'Babe, I said we're done.'

'Yeah, but I think you should look at this.' Eden points at the letterhead poking from the edge. Wellsend Social Services. 'Was your mum ever in care?'

'Not Mum, no.' Roche frowns, conflicted. 'But my dad was.'

*

Daddy

Wellsend on Sea, 1983

Delph sits in an old Maclaren buggy, one with deckchair stripes and a sweaty plastic canopy that descends at the first hint of drizzle, sealing her in like a space capsule. The sky matches the concrete pavement, alive with litter and noise and purposeful crowds minding their own. Chock-tight bus shelters and stationary traffic.

'Legs beat wheels, any day of the week,' Mum says, her hair whipping about her face, giving her a wild look as she strides past the bus that won't let anyone else on. 'Look at 'em, Delph, love. Blimmin' sardines.'

Delph agrees. She and her mum are better off as they are.

A material world of trousers and skirts whizz by, till they cross the road to the middle, Mum waiting on the island barred by metal, before someone steps in front of them, blocking Delph's view of the box she likes staring at until the man inside it turns from red to green, that Mum says is a show of Delph's magic. Another step to becoming invincible.

'Getting big now, innit,' the person says.

'Yeah,' Mum replies. 'Three last week. Be school before you know it.'

'Definitely, definitely.' They make loose chat Delph doesn't understand, yet senses must be about her, from the way the man keeps looking down at her, and because her mother's voice suddenly forgets to be nice when she puts a hand on Delph's head a little bit too hard.

Then he asks, 'You taking care now, Joy?'

And it's that. You taking care. The old name. It spells intimacy. A history.

Delph thinks this man is her father.

At home, a few days later, the same man comes to visit Delph. Mum, watching from the living-room doorway, makes an awkward spectator, feeling checked up upon and full of sharp words, but what more should a stronger expect from a child but stilted interaction? Though Delph doesn't know him, he does have experience of entertaining children; knows how to comfort, change bums, rock them to sleep, having three small offspring himself, all fed and clothed with the good woman, in the true familial nest.

Once her shyness passes, Delph reaches for his face. 'My eyes,' she says, pointing at his with a chubby finger.

'Our eyes,' the man replies, and thinks he could love her.

When he leaves, Mum has Dallas to watch and a vodka, a double for her and a snowball for Delph; they pull their sofa up to the electric fire which matches her raging mood, not caring about the meter as all three bars blaze in their faces, like they've become part of the Ewings' sun-bleached Texan ranch too.

EVA VERDE

The man feels intruded upon all the way home, like he's returned wearing them both. It's a relief to reach his own front door; like crossing over – away from the little girl with his identical eyes.

In the warm front room where his family wait, the smallest runs to greet him, oblivious of the other child, the side shoot, so easily clipped out that, in time, even the very thought of her heals over. Eclipsed by legitimate children. And then forgotten.

Delphine. The baby he made with the tiger woman.

6: Part One

Tiny Wings Try

Esplanade Point, 2023

Delph's not thought of the 'Man of the House' game for years. A game she invented, roleplay where she'd become the most atrociously chauvinistic character the world had ever seen. 'Where's my dinner, woman?' she'd boom at her mother. 'It should've been on the bloody table three and a half minutes ago!' Mum would laugh as Delph's misogyny escalated, the game evolving into her adding a comedy moustache and the shirt and tie from her school uniform, following her mother around the garden, pointing out, 'You missed a bit, you got that wrong.' The game never got old, or indeed any less funny.

She doesn't know why she's remembered it now, but it's better than the strange nervousness that comes whenever she thinks of Itsy catching his flight. Jamaica: nine and a half hours, 4,500 miles away from Wellsend, Essex. Delph's checked, countlessly, as if the enormous numbers might be duping her. Unsettled doesn't quite cut it, Delph thinks, as Itsy turns over, cosying up beneath the bedcovers.

'You gonna be all right on your own?' he asks, with an arm around Delph that she snuggles into. Kissing the side of her head, his lips brush her temple. 'Up here. In your head.' He lets the words bed in, allowing her time to absorb them, and when Delph opens her mouth to reply, he speaks again. 'Cos if you don't, I don't know, feel strong enough, it might be worth calling work, explaining the family situation.' An alarm rattles his phone from the bedside table. Irritated, he reaches out to silence it. 'You might get some kind of bereavement.'

'But I've never even met your mum.' Politely disentangling her limbs from his, she heads for the bathroom, feeling better straight away for the distance.

After breakfast, Delph says, 'Once this shift's behind me, I'll shoot back here to send you off.' She's pleased how it comes out, as ordinary fact, as opposed to seeking permission. 'Another manic Monday.' But the busier the better, truly; Delph's never minded Mondays. It is the only day it ever feels like she's moving, distancing herself from all she's tied to, tied by, tied in. Tired of.

Picking up their mugs, she heads for the sink, and with her arms preoccupied, Itsy uses the opportunity to push her against the counter, her hip bone connecting awkwardly with the edge of it. Running his hands down her legs, he begins to push up her skirt. 'There's not time.' Delph uses her elbows, keeping him at a distance. 'Please. I'll be late.'

'And there was I thinking we'd have more time here, now you're not sitting about with the girl of an evening.' Itsy kisses his teeth. 'Love Islanding or Strictlying or whatever the new ting is now.' Releasing her, he adjusts himself. 'Our last day together, yet you're out. And then out you'll go again, as soon as my back's turned, gallivanting tonight.'

If gallivanting means eating a Dr Oetker pizza with her mother and daughter . . .

'Without my . . .' Delph knows he's thinking of the word permission, senses his resistance to use it. He knows what saying it out loud makes him.

Mother Moon called Itsy a bullying cunt the last time they were in the same room. In true celebratory form, on Delph's thirty-seventh birthday, she'd aimed the last of her carvery dinner at Itsy's feet. Gravy thick as custard spattered his pristine Reeboks as they'd eyeballed each other like a staring competition. All that, and the plate didn't even break.

Itsy blinks, as if remembering too. His small teeth clench, the veins at his temple pulsing between skin and skull. 'Makes me think you'd rather be anywhere but here with me, is that right?'

Delph looks away, out of the window, across the rooftops of the smaller blocks, windows glittering in the sunshine, concealing other lives. Better lives. But thoughts like that don't help anybody.

Creamy cloud does its best to hide Canary Wharf in

the very far distance, obscuring its flashing red pinnacle. Amazing what the eye can see but the feet can't reach.

'Of course not. You're right. You're totally right.' Quick to placate him, Delph clasps at her wrists, thumbs racing over the pattern of her veins. 'It's our last day.' How easy the words come, selling them both the false narrative. Habit. Operation: Preserve the Peace Without Conflict. 'I'll tell them I've got a bug. Then I'll pop to the shop. Get some bacon. Do your favourite.' If she gives today over to pleasing him then they both go off happy this evening. Yet it feels deeply shitty letting work down, especially when they were all so nice when she came back off sick leave the last time. She'd been missed, her absence noticed, which made for the loveliest, loveliest feeling. 'They weren't happy,' Delph says, putting her phone down. 'But who cares?' She wraps her arms around Itsy, a sense of despair claiming her when he cups her bottom hard, nudging her towards the bedroom. 'Today is about us.'

His skinny legs are all Delph notices as he pulls the curtains – pointless, considering they're so high in the sky – leaving a bothersome gap in his hurry between her thighs. It is hard not to tense at his touch; to instead choose to welcome it. An endurance, but is life not just one giant endurance, anyway? And though any sort of hope has always felt more like self-harm, Delph's unsure if she can stay caught in this web for the rest of her days. Here, with Itsy huffing on top of her, the collapsing old wardrobes witnessing this never-ending game of one-way fuckery.

Delph hopes with all her heart that if Sol knew what the

loss of him felt like, which made her turn herself as small and safe and insignificant as possible just to get through it, because life, fuck, life goes on, that he'd forgive her.

'You know I'd know, don't you?' Itsy whispers into her neck. 'If anyone else were to touch you.'

Impossible. Yet, still, Delph's heart seizes tight. That's how far his tentacles reach, and with his favourite one in his favourite place, it makes uneasy conversation.

Delph assures him, says how she loves him, while he has her in a way that makes belonging to him feel more like a punishment instead of a choice.

'You're mine. Don't ever, ever, ever forget.'

'I can't breathe.' It's not a lie, not an excuse, Delph realizes as her hands reach for the frantic shallows of her own breath, which brings the sensation she's about to pass out, as the room fades, swallowed by a single pinpoint of light, which shrinks into absolute darkness.

*

Before Barack

Esplanade Point, 2013

The same night the evening news announced that Obama had won his second term as president, Delph, for the first and only time, tried leaving Itsy. Roche was staying the night with her nan when Delph had packed a bag, and knowing Mother Moon's would be the first place he'd look, she'd readied herself for upstairs. To Geena. Who knows it all yet knows nothing. But she loves Delph. Geena's the only other person she can trust.

As Itsy snored on, Delph silently grabbed the essentials. Trainers, knickers, purse and phone. Toothbrush. Passport . . .

Her passport's been missing for years. Vanished after a fallout, because Delph dared speak to the same man twice during the weekly turn around Sainsburys. He'd let her overtake him in the freezer section, and when they got to the tills he made the fatal comment: 'We ought to stop meeting like this.' Innocent, predictable banter – deep as air, same as Delph's polite laughter that followed, and meant nothing. It takes two people, at the very least, to make an argument an argument, and though Itsy blew up for them both, Delph's nat-ural response was only to apologize.

It was much the same again, this time. Nothing new about his terminal jealousy, except the utter hopelessness Delph felt within her, which evolved into this panicked, split-second decision to bolt.

Welcoming Delph in without a second thought, a drink was Geena's answer, same as it would be Mother Moon's answer, as Delph realized Geena had already put her own kid-free night to good use by going out with her City workmates and getting plastered; all that beautiful autonomy she takes for granted. Bars, drinks, saying what she likes, leaving when she likes. Wearing whatever the hell she likes. Her life is her life.

'You look fantastic, Geena,' Delph says from the heart, as she smokes her way through a pack of ten that she bought that day, and should've lasted all week. 'What a life you made. You're lucky.'

'Yeah, yeah,' Geena replies. 'But I'm not, am I? I'm wearing uncomfortable clothes to show men I'm worth their interest. And I say lame-arse things that might imply I'm worth their inter-est.' Geena is always, always honest. 'Men. Misery-makers.' Taking Delph's fag, which was mostly ash, she stubbed it out. 'So, what's he done?'

But Delph has sold Itsy so well, she doesn't know where to begin. Like finding the edge on a roll of fucking Sellotape, the harder she tries to find it, the more it evades her.

There are no words.

No reasons.

And in floods the doubt.

'Can't we live together?' Geena says as she peels off her lashes,

which doesn't alter her gorgeousness. 'It'd be so much easier.
Nothing would change. I'd still go to work, only I'd come home to
nice dinners and wouldn't have to do my ironing.'

The irony. Delph couldn't help but laugh. 'Look how quick you
jumped into domestic misogyny.'

'I know. Sod it. Ain't that my problem? I know I'm too much, too
driven, too passionate, too noisy, too fucking hot to handle. I never
met anyone that could.'

Delph's kitchen-sink troubles, eclipsed by the dramas of an
actual life.

'Normal, Delph. Just someone fucking normal, is that too much
to ask for? Company. Kindness.' She looked across the lounge at
Eden's toyboxes and Lego overspill. 'A grown-up life.'

And despite the bag, despite the time of night and Delph's obvious
distress, Geena missed all the signs. 'Don't be cross,' she'd said a
little later, convinced that ringing Itsy was the right thing to do. 'He
sounded so upset on the phone.'

Geena opened the door, and Itsy filled the frame of it.

He is sorry. He is so sorry. He is always sorry.

And as he led Delph away, Geena squeezed her arm gently. With
love. 'You'll thank me in the morning.'

6: PART TWO

TINY WINGS TRIED

Esplanade Point, 2023

Itsy buys the bacon himself, as Delph repairs on her balcony. South-facing and protected, summer always comes early up on the fourteenth floor. At street level, urban nature sleeps on in the communal gardens, but up here it's already a blooming paradise. Containers packed with letterbox-red geraniums are edged with drifts of tumbling elysium. Baby toms like small sour bullets collect the sunshine between shaggy salads. Delph will sound like her mother, but it's true: plants do calm the mind.

Panic attacks during sex, now. Suffocating to be so inti-mate, needing him that close, in order to win him over, in the strange space of their relationship there's no conversation for, where rules exist in the silences between words that Delph knows to never question, has learnt well in their fifteen years how to avoid the sulking silent claustrophobic power that charges the atmosphere, making her sorry and guilty for practically nothing and absolutely everything.

But how long can he sulk, cloak her for, when he's a flight to catch?

He can't stop her visiting Roche if he's not even here to, yet it's still hard to temper her anxiety, to dispel the looming sense of disappointment when she feels his intent to her core. To fuck with her plans.

After lunch, Itsy has the idea of doing the budget. He uses Roche's old scientific calculator to pad in the week's expenses. 'Sixty-two quid to SKY?' Itsy kisses his teeth. 'Daylight robbery. Did they deduct for the day of no signal? ASOS. Fifty-three pounds and nine pence?'

'The jacket Roche had her eye on went in the sale, at last,' Delph explains. 'I've put it aside for her birthday.' Always something to be kept on your toes for.

Once she was grateful for it. The small cash budget he'd bestow at the start of the week, keeping the receipts. It was simple. One less burden, like not having to find a new job because women are 'queens of the home'. Like no longer putting Roche into childcare, because queens and their cubs, innit.

Explanations for the money she now earns. Not matching his, but her hands still fill those shelves, and her feet take her there and back – Delph's saving £3.80 a day when she walks instead of taking the bus, which he'd do well to remember, considering how he does so adore his receipts.

'We're earning, love. We're doing OK.'

'And what about Uber, all the gigs on my heels?'

Why now? Delph's tired of sixth-sensing his feelings, living by the whim of his mood. It comes again, like a wave lapping against the old feelings inside her, a reminder of all she's done so well to stifle. The sad unfurling desperation to give in. Because if it wasn't for Roche, for the thought of later ...

But contact with Roche will only continue to shrink, now Roche knows she can do it alone. There might be the odd phone call now, but they'll fritter out, into reassurances, obligatory texts, as Roche's world grows, and so will she to match it. Because she's a fearless gem of a person; hard to think Delph had any hand in her creation. If it wasn't for Roche, Delph would've checked out long ago.

Now there's this time. All this time.

To kill.

Because that's all this is.

Itsy moans about numbers, trivialities catastrophized, like Aesop's lion and his little thorns; they've enough to pay each bill and keep their hunger away. Even now, in the light of a big problem, the imminent death of his precious mother, he carries on with the pettiness. Still leaving it a week to go and see her, because the flight cost £126 less – best kept between Delph and him though, obviously. Who would he tell all this shit to, if she wasn't here? If today was the day she chose to freefall.

It's the same old: obsessing about money, the fear of having none, which itself is no triviality, but it's a tool that is also convenient, because money worries mean limited choices. Living by necessity makes life restrictive. Small. So convenient to blame money.

'Why you looking so angsty? All to make your life easier, innit. Car tax is sorted. Insurance renewal too. I even went up the dump like you'd been on at me for.' He chucks Delph under the chin affectionately. 'The old junk we hang on to, eh? Good to have a clear mind to focus on my mum. And you won't have to worry about anything while I'm gone.'

A sweat like no other spikes her pits, as it occurs to Delph that if she were to fall, to chuck herself over her own paradise, Itsy wouldn't have time to catch her.

He'd never see it coming.

It is only in the quiet of late afternoon, when Delph's getting ready to head across town, and Itsy packs his final additions, that his talk of old junk makes her seek out Sol's shoebox, tucked in the cupboard behind the kitchen sink, in the nook that you'd not know existed, unless you'd lived here forever.

Delph gropes in the dark, ever desperate, finding nothing, her panic coming in hot waves as Itsy's shadow appears in the doorway.

'Please tell me you didn't.' Delph tries to breathe, breathe all this into logic. 'Please, tell me you didn't . . .'

'The past is the past, Delph.'

'No, no, you can't've.' Because no decent human would.

'That wasn't the junk I took to the dump, Delph. No, that

was a box of pain,' Itsy overemphasizes, as if he's done her a kindness. 'Eight years and you didn't even know it was gone.'

'Eight years?' Delph's confused, cuffing snot, but it's only seconds before everything clicks in. Eight years ago was when she'd shown it to Roche, who couldn't have been less interested.

Of course it was.

Delph's not looked through Sol's belongings for years. The comfort was simply in knowing that his things were there. Because Sol's always been part of them, on the periphery of every big moment and decision. First words, first steps, first full day of school. Every good moment that has ached with the echoes of him. Yet aching helps. That throb of hurt, impossible to heal from, impossible to share, keeps him real. There's always been more comfort in the hurt than in all that comes from looking forwards.

'It's all we had.' Delph's tears splash onto the checkerboard lino. 'All Roche had.'

'And that's what I'm talking about. Me coming second to a dead boy's box of trinkets.'

On her knees, palms flat to the floor, it registers in Delph that this is symbolic. If ever an action could demonstrate the astronomical scale of how Itsy puts himself first.

But sadly – *sadly* – the glaring other side, is how Delph's facilitated that. So, what's the fucking point? What's the point of any of it?

Because here it is, happening again – this unfathomable, astronomical sense of loss.

Photos. Cards, notes and receipts, most returned to blank, ink fading in the years since the meals, outings and precious ordinariness of Sol's day-to-day purchases. The ring pulls, bottle tops, celebratory corks, each with a memory, a goodness, a story: of them. Physical symbols of his existence. Sol's ring. His jumper. Their photos. His door key.

There are no words. Delph stays hunched on all fours, little and defeated.

'Unhealthy anyway.' Itsy stretches to his full height, taking up most of the doorframe, sounding terribly self-righteous. 'All this drama, and I've got to get on a plane to say goodbye to my mother.'

Fury sprouts in her chest. She'd felt this coming. Something hefty to properly crush her with in his absence. But to take a dead man's mementos, a kid's only link to her father, and bin them so very fucking mercilessly?

There is nothing, nothing, *nothing* of Sol now, except what's in her head. Though Delph only remembers him in snapshots of memory, she forces herself to conjure his eyes, calling to mind their brown magic, the gentle fun of him. The tilted duck of his head that showed he was really listening, the touch of his hands on her swollen baby belly. Untroubled happiness, and all their beautiful naivety.

Who is this person she became, doing things to please? Consenting to keep the calm. Anything really, to avoid upsetting Itsy. Because what then? The most baffling part of all is if someone were to ask Delph what it is, what's the big bad thing he does that's kept her desperate to please him, she'd be stumped silent. Unable to explain the constant flattery, the fannying around like he's some sort of prince. And what is she? Not a princess. Not even a wife. Just an insignificant woman who wanted to hide from the world.

'You can't go out now, not looking like that,' Itsy sighs, shoving his hands in his pockets. 'They'll think I'm ...'

What? A bullying cunt?

She knows and he knows, but it's hardly news to Delph. It's just bloody awful admitting it, knowing the people she loves most have been right all along. To even think that there could've been a baby on the way.

But nothing brings clarity like a pregnancy.

'Besides.' Perfectly timed, Itsy looks out of the window, into nothing but night. 'Dusk ain't really your thing, is it?'

Delph would've risked pitch-ink skies for tonight. But he knows her fight has gone. She texts Roche, says she can't make it, offering no excuses, just sticking to Itsy's script that he prompts over her shoulder, her heart the same as that empty cupboard with no box.

Energised like a well-fed parasite, Itsy leaves Delph with the truth she can only distort for so long, that has so very little to do with Itsy at all. That Delph is abandoned. Twice over.

Roche choosing Moon.

And Sol. Who didn't choose dying.

'We'll sort this when I'm home,' Itsy offers Delph his cheek. What else to do but kiss his face and wait for his return?

As soon as he leaves, Delph switches on her phone.

ROCHE: I may as well have not been born.

At least the pain is something.

Yes, she got longer, more years alive than Sol did, but that doesn't mean much, not on the other side of things. Given enough time, Itsy, her, this flat, and every inner endurance will all be of no single consequence.

Moon looks across the lounge at Roche, sprawled over two big floor cushions, like a wildcat in its natural habitat, doing what everyone does these days: staring at gadgetry. Of course, phones have their place; Moon simply wishes Roche's wasn't permanently stuck to her hand – because a bit of cosmic snooping would be beneficial, lately. But how can she attempt to read Roche's palms when she never gets a chance to bloody see them?

Moon thinks back to the day Roche turned up on the doorstep – kid Roche evolved into womanhood, her aura colourless. Not greyscale colourless, the way Moon always saw her own mother's, but transparent, as if Roche was constructed from ozone, from life. Everything Moon longs to see again in Delphine.

But there's progress. Look at tonight, for example. Delph en-route for tea and company. Moon tries remembering the last meal they shared, just the three of them – hurts, because she can't recall it.

'Stop bloody staring.' Roche rises, looking out of the window to check for her mother again, Moon admires her ascension to the blinds. What brilliant genes. Like Delph, and Sol – and Moon too. Sixty almost, and still not gravity's bitch.

Moon is no one's bitch.

'Do you think she'll be lonely? With him gone, I mean?'

'Give her time. She'll be dancing,' Moon says, lifted by Itsy's imminent departure. 'I say gut that place, finally. Jazz the dump up. What's he gonna do about it, all them miles away?'

'Why should she though? He should get off his arse, put them muscles to use.' Flexing both arms into a muscleman pose, she kisses her biceps. 'Arms like Arnie, but them ickle-wickle spider legs. You'd think he'd try building them up to match. Twat.' Roche wears the expression of someone who knows they're right. It's a look she'll likely temper once out in the real world, where even now no one truly likes a gobby girl.

'Itsy by name, Itsy by nature. It'll do him good, running around after his mother. You know, I never got past him having five sisters. Imagine. A misogynist, with five bloody sisters.' Moon chuckles, then frowns. 'Love, she won't get here any faster with you standing there.' Falling quiet for a moment, she tries pushing away the sudden feeling that they're about to be disappointed, unsure if the negative energy from their bitching – which can happen – has anything to do with it. Karma's quick to fall out of your favour, no matter how deserved, if you become a prick too.

'How about I do your cards while we wait? Come on, just a quick spread.'

Roche looks wary. 'Why now?'

'Why not? You can focus on something else for half an hour.' Moon senses Roche hardening, from the inside out, a far better control over who she lets into her thoughts than Delph ever had, though she's not suffered any real breakage, thank the Universe.

Yet.

But balls to the maudlin – she has her granddaughter here, her other girl soon too. Moon adores how she – discovered through years of past life regression meditation, female since the beginnings of time, and always an earth sign too – can feel the vibrations of all her old selves in her soul, so infinite. How they reach like branches, connecting her to her off-spring, her offspring's offspring, who was once an egg inside of her too. Waiting to become wonderful.

Focused on the happy present, Moon dots lavender oil on both wrists, offering the tarot cards to Roche, who begins her own shuffle. 'I can't lie, and I can't tell you what you want to hear. Not everything the future holds is shiny and good,' Moon says, pointedly. 'All we need is to be free of our obsta-cles, to seek what we already know as instinct.'

'I can't lie neither,' Roche grins, handing the cards back. Moon turns them over respectfully, treating each one like an old friend. 'You're epic at this, Nan.'

'There's a big decision ahead. Don't be afraid of it.'

Roche's blank, but Moon is insistent.

'That's uni, maybe,' Roche says, brightening a little. 'I always wanted to go, you know. Perhaps become some lawyer or barrister – fight the good fight, you get me?' Moon does, smiling wide at her warrior princess, these new helping hands to right all the world's wrongs. 'But then these past few years, I've just thought, what's the point?' Roche sighs. 'I think of all the rage I'd carry if the arseholes got away with their arseholery. I don't think I could stomach it, really. I'm not after a life of always being angry. Funny innit; when I was fighting for belts, I felt my most peaceful.' Roche stops, listening as a bus turn into the road, which passes by without slowing. 'Stupid. To even think I could make a difference in the world when I'm more like a lost puppy waiting for Mummy.'

'There's nothing stupid about you. And you know it.' Moon holds her eye. 'But you're right. You can't hang about for everyone else, and neither should you live in the pursuit of righting other people's shit. You deserve your peace, *however you can find it.* And if that means going to university, then so be it. Doesn't have to be law.'

Roche frowns, pained for a moment. 'What about Mum, though?'

Putting the cards down, Moon places her hand on top of Roche's. 'Years ago, I'd volunteer on this helpline, not helping much, more just listening. Believe me when I say there's more than one Itsy in the world. Not seeing you both was never my choice, love. And believe me, I tried to fight for her.' She leans over the table, kissing the top of Roche's head. 'Some things take time. And sometimes people need to set themselves free.' Moon closes her eyes. 'But I hope, I hope with my everything, it's coming.'

'I keep getting these ... vibes. I've had them all day, in the back of my head, thinking she mightn't show.' Roche sighs. 'I'm so sick of feeling this way. Having this ... worry. I've got all this shit to read, to study for, that I need to get right, or else I'll never even get into uni anyway – but the truth is, Nan, I can't imagine it.'

Roche's unburdening has little to do with the cards – which aren't the most revealing spread in the world, but certainly aren't the most terrible – it's more an energy at work, a bond establishing between the two of them. Though it feels good, and right, and what loving normal families have from the off, there's a pull in Moon's guts, a disruption, as her thoughts again are swamped by Delph. Of wrong.

'What do you mean, love?' Moon asks, unwilling to give in to the dread. 'You're bright, you'll have your pick of universities.'

'It's not getting accepted so much. It's more me. Like, I can't ever see myself really being part of it, existing somewhere other than here and worrying about her. And I am too young to have done so much worrying.'

'You are,' Moon confirms. 'So I'll fight here so you don't have to. No matter what sort of hold that bastard thinks he's got—' Moon abruptly shuts up, watching Roche's reaction, the disappointed tears as she reads a text just arrived, which requires no psychic skills at all to fathom who it's from. 'Oh, love,' Moon says softly, as Roche cuffs her tears away.

'Why did I even think she'd come, anyway? I'm an idiot.' She pulls her feet up towards her body, crossing them at the ankle, before looking at her phone again. 'It's seven. His flight's tonight. He ain't even there to come first.'

Moon has the clearest vision of Itsy, rolling his eyes at the sight of her name as it flashes on Delph's ringing mobile, the swamping sensation of Delph's hesitation as she pretends his rolling eyes and long-assed sighs have nothing to do with her rejecting the call.

'There's an open day coming up,' Roche says, as Moon wonders if the vision was truly hers, or a fragment of Roche's memories she's been able to decipher. 'I'd thought about asking Mum, but after tonight ...'

'Love, it's not her fault.' Yet Moon feels the unravelling of their progress already, watching Roche's detachment, the self-protective wall she assembles around herself. 'It was a miracle even thinking he'd let her out on the day he's due to fly. It's his last chance to tighten his grip.'

Roche looks down to her hands in her lap. 'I've got the money. It's in my saver, from Saturday-ing in the chippy. Will – would – you come instead, Nan? To look around Edinburgh Uni with me?' Looking up, she finds Moon there already, imagining herself drifting round with the scholars; chilling on campus with a takeaway Greggs – or their Scottish equivalent, of course – listening to some impromptu feminist poetry delivered by humanity's future, the bright and hopeful youth.

Because Moon's purpose, before the Wellsend concrete sets around Roche too, is to set this precious bird free.

And Delph?

Mission impossible will have to fucking wait.

*

121

Heights

Butterfield Estate, 2004

'Have you told her?' Sol sweeps his fingers over the new roundness of Delph's tummy.

'How long have you known my mother?' Delph can't believe he's even bothered to ask it. 'She probably knew before I did.'

On Sol's eighteenth, he moved in with the Tennysons permanently. Changing his doctor, and encouraged by his housemates, he'd bombarded every building in a five-mile radius with his CV, most of them slipping it into the bin, but no matter, because one is all it takes.

An office job marks the start of a regular life, and soon he's enrolling in college. By twenty-four, Sol is fearless – unapologetic. Why should he keep to the shadows, like he did all his young life? Though it's not a surprise, it does hurt how provoked some folks become by the likes of a successful man of colour with a tongue in his head.

But Sol will never be silenced again.

This is the work of Mother Moon, the confidence she's installed in him, as is always her way. Rooting for the underdog is one thing, but it's how she goes about it that's concerning; encouraging Sol's inner chaos, stoking his rage, ever hopeful for a bite of rebellion, however she can get it. But there are no hard edges, no masculine typicality in his behaviour. Nothing about Sol stirs any echo of the bad men before. Who still exist, far too close to home.

'The world needs more fucking heroes,' she remarks, watching the news one night, where another poor darling's been found in pieces. Moon lets it hang, 'Imagine being butchered for your handbag.'

Sol would protect Delph to the end, thinks the world of her. And she him. Never a doubt of their devotion ever casts its suspicions in either of them. Their love's pure, honest as breathing and just as natural – just like this pregnancy, which wasn't some surprise because they're young and careless. Simple maths tells the world they've been inseparable for almost a decade.

New Year's Eve smelt different. The air, cold but sufferable, held sparkle; squeaky cliché feels of fresh starts and striving onwards. Beautiful hours have been spent considering names, pondering over meanings – New Year's Eve finds Delph a round and healthy eighteen weeks pregnant. Firm flutters, to first kicks; definite, yet not pronounced enough for a hand or foot to be determinable. A June baby – and what a nice name that is too.

'I'll bring you back chicken,' Sol promises. Delph's hot wings obsession consuming every thought since conception. 'I love you.'

'Have fun,' she says. 'Not too much, though.'

Last words.

They don't know.

As Delph waves Sol off with a kiss on her garden step, Mother

Moon cradles her daughter's stomach. 'A water baby. Oof.' And the baby moved in connection.

'Go on then, Mother Moon. Get your cards out.'

And the cards come out, as does the white sage; lavender oil dotted on each pale wrist, dusted with freckles. The softest wrists in the world.

'Delphine Magenta.' Moon whistles admiringly, taking a long puff on her epic joint as she closed her eyes, blissed. 'I gave you a magnificent name.' It is always a shame about the Tennyson part, but that'll be gone for good when Delph becomes Barclay. Moon herself is simply singular. Mononymous. Like Madonna, Cher, Sade and Björk, she's Moon. Ms Moon Moon to the pen pushers; deed poll still the best sixty quid she ever spent.

Great clouds of puff reach for the sky, clawing the air, like an indoor humidity, and Delph watches the smoke alarm, like she's forever watched the smoke alarm, coated in cooking fat and dust, waiting.

The red light comes, just as Moon turns the cards. Wishing she hadn't.

Sol's exit from the world is quiet. Unpleasant, but not unusual. A short life mostly in care, a pretty girlfriend in tears on the local news, clinging to her flabby-armed mother. The death of an innocent Black life is never shocking enough.

Even when it's murder.

Moon is snarling, snotty, as she bashes her hands against the police desk. Instead of following leads, investigating properly, they simply label Sol, 'The Jumper'. 'But he'd never do that! He's a kiddie

on the way. And a girl. A girl who'd die for him.' Moon keeps bang-
ing till they threaten her with a cell. 'How can I go home and tell
her you think he topped himself? What do you think that's going
to do to her?'

To them, it's a ten-a-penny tragedy but to Delph and to Moon,
it means the rawness of his death will never end. There is no one to
blame, when of course somewhere, there is.

After all the exasperating years of Mother Moon's mysticism,
it's ironic that Delph now longs for a sign of her own, that Sol's
somehow still near, but she won't ever ask her mother to make any
sort of connection. Delph will never give her that power again. And
neither can she trust her, when she vanishes after identifying Sol's
body, the devastation of seeing him hidden, his injuries too horrific
for display. Just his hands, and his lilac eyelids, the same shade as the
moons of his nails. Wrong. 'All wrong.' Moon had blabbered on, how
this shouldn't be the end of such a good new soul, not when a shitty
old soul like hers could've taken his place, her eyes liquid and red as
her hair, as though she'd been pulled from days in water. Bloated.
Broken. Because if she could've swapped places, she would've.

Three days and nights pass without a mother, and without her
soulmate. Every memory now a lone ache, a constant fear, as time
uselessly continues.

There is nothing. The world is over; both Delph and their baby
giving up in the aftermath. No kicks, no swells of movement.
Delph's body feels listless, her pain insurmountable. Exhausting.
Delph hopes when she gets the sleep she longs for, she'll never
wake again.

And it's then that she thinks about it.

Delph heads through the hall, past the pictures of her rising in age, past her mother's door, always kept ajar lest the past get stuck and smother her, the mountainous lump of her beneath the wicker headboard still both missing and missed. Then to the front door. Simply, she lifts the handle and turns the key, welcoming the cold and all its potential.

It takes twenty-three minutes to walk it. To stand where Sol stood, on the least solid ground. How could someone confront and push, knowing the fall would kill him? Six metres. His body hitting the floor flat, all at once.

Was there a final thought? How did it sound? Did Sol shout, did he call her name – perhaps his own mother's name as he lay there dying. Did he realize? Did he know? Did he think of Delph, of them, in that last flash of thinking. Of consciousness.

She could go too. Over the railings where there's no more feeling, but instead overwhelming peace. Some deep space vat of nothing. It is this that Delph imagines; all that could make her darkness permanent.

But for the kick inside.

A sharpness comes, most pronounced. Delph pulls up her jumper, stroking her stomach. Her flesh rises, jutting out before disappearing, as she traces the dark downy through line, following her baby's movements with her finger. And Delph knows.

Darkness isn't the answer.

The following morning, Moon returns home with a picture frame, which she had to bend Sol's photo to fit him into.

The most grown-up act of love that Delph ever witnessed.

7

HERO IN A SHELL SUIT

Esplanade Point, 2023

Delph's phone stays silent, Roche's 'I may as well have not been born' text acting like a full stop, the freezing outdoors now just as uncompromising. Unkind. But with her hiding place expiring, there is no more than this.

She likes it up here, despite the whipping wind running rings around the rooftop of Esplanade Point. She stands a few feet back from the edge, from the four-foot ledge separating safety from non-safety. With familiar ease at being so near to nothingness, Delph dares herself, moves a little closer, something like excitement seizes her heart. Not party-time excitement, nor any sort of happiness. But a thrill from the fragile fringes. Excitement from death's dangerous proximity.

As the sounds of the estate rumble on below, Delph looks out for a moment at the zigzag of lights, the metal shapes moving along the motorway in the distance, then down to that teasing edge, the pavement alive with people heading home, lost beneath shuffling coats and shopping bags in both directions, like she's kicked over a stone revealing a highly skilled network of worker insects. What are the chances she'd be caught and carried, stage-dive-like up the high street, instead of the black exit she imagined before when she'd almost ... Delph keeps her 'almost' with all her other inner agonies, which will vanish when she does, never again to be disturbed or recovered. That gorgeous possibility of absolute nothingness.

The people who love her already know the true Itsy, despite the good light she tried to cast him in. They know he's not the misunderstood nice guy, just as she does. Delph's unsure if even she ever truly believed it. Funny, how pregnancy snapped her out of her living coma. All that time on contraceptives, a saviour at first from the erratic periods that started at the time of the weight loss. And the worry. She's swallowed a pink pill every night for as long as she can remember; a baby never something she wanted to risk.

And doesn't that say a lot too?

Did she ever love him? Is obligation life's love story?

But Delph's already had the real love thing. She's neither naïve nor lucky enough to think she could have unparalleled happiness twice.

It's a giving-up feeling. The peaceful acceptance of slowly deadening. A tolerance to the elements, the wind now a force to be swallowed by. And a want: to sleep forever. Just slip out of the world, the same way you came in, returning to the starry nothing.

'Christ it's cold. What you doing?' Geena's voice comes from somewhere, as Delph's thoughts, like a slowing round-about, return to focus.

'Just thinking.'

'That never helps nothing, trust me.'

'I like it up here.'

'I like it up here too. Don't mean I'm hanging off the edge, though.'

Delph smiles, the cold catching in her throat, making her gasp out a little choke, which does sound a bit like she's crying, as she takes Geena's hand.

Geena's flat is like Geena. Sleek. Quality. In fluffy little slipper mules, she undulates over to a wine rack, arranged in bottles of three: red, white, rose, Prosecco. Everything is exact, how it should be. A clean freak, same as Delph, but this is uncompromisingly Geena's space, Geena's taste, and Geena unquestionably has her shit together. The tiled floors throughout look like the stars and the whole entire galaxy has been put through a blender, their shattered bits set and sparkling in what looks like white porcelain. Geena's flat is Geena's castle. Dazzling pictures of her and Eden sit about in diamante frames amidst the dove greys and chrome décor that evokes modern minds, modern thoughts, modern women.

And Delph sits in the bedazzlement of it all.

In shock, she thinks.

'How did you know?' Delph asks with a sense of déjà vu, not really wanting the flute Geena's pushed into her trembling hands. 'That I was up there.'

'Your front door.' Geena raises her brows, amused. 'Wide bloody open. You of all people know better than that.' The divide between here and their old ends has the longest tail. Forever cast as the ruffians from the bad side of town, despite Geena doing much better than most living in Esplanade Point.

It is another form of insecurity, being so utterly anchorless. Moon's old house no more the answer to home than the flat below them; Geena's polished porcelain being Delph's Artexed ceiling, swirled like whipped meringue, slowly greying but not fast enough.

'Snivelling on rooftops. He ain't even been gone five minutes.' Nearing the bottom of her glass, Geena looks to her recessed ceiling spotlights, the tips of her lashes meeting the arch of her perfect brows. Defined to an inch of their lives. Everything about her intentional, utterly magnificent. 'What I wouldn't give for loyalty. Sta-bil-i-ty.'

'Stability?'

It must come out sounding entitled, ungrateful, for Geena sniffs, shifting in her seat. 'You, my friend, don't know a good thing when you've got it.'

'It doesn't feel good,' Delph confesses, aloud and at last, and as simply as she can explain things without feeling overexposed, or like she's telling tales on Itsy. Because, despite her hurt, he still matters. Despite admitting the truth to her heart. That they are over. 'We don't feel good. Lately, I mean.'

'Well perhaps that ain't entirely his fault.' Geena looks Delph up and down, first critically and then like she's eyeing her up for a project. 'What I mean is, we all need to make the best of ourselves.' Which is easy to say, when you're special and beyond good-looking yourself.

'Working's changed things.' Delph twiddles her bubbles. 'You'll laugh, but at first it was like tasting fresh air. Like I was almost . . . me again. Me.' Drinking, she sighs. 'Almost. You'd think I should've learnt not to hope for too much.'

Hope. Hoping for something; anything. If there's more to this, more out there, beyond the familiar. Beyond Itsy. It makes her soul heavy, how she's given him so much power over all that she is. How her thoughts, decisions, tastes and experiences can completely change at his choosing. If he's disapproving. Who is Delph, really? And if she is just a shell, a puppet forever dictated to by Itsy's needs, what's really the point of her at all?

Doesn't it always come back to that point?

'So, B&Q's been giving you these big revelations, and now you want to do an Ian Beale and shuffle off all broken in your dressing gown?'

Shuffle away; sever and separate entirely.

'You know, all you really need is a night out.' It's Geena's rescue remedy for everything. Always. 'I don't care if his mum's dying, you think he's tucked up at 8 p.m. in Kingston?' She roars with laughter, slapping Delph on the leg. 'Come on!'

'I can't.' It's not something Delph's ever liked. To be out in the proper night. Doesn't like how the blackout vulnerability makes her remember being left home alone as a kid. The fun times of no mum and no electric.

'You know I'd look after you, right?' Geena suddenly sits upright, stroking her caramel ponytail, as sleek and high shine as J-Lo's. 'You can stop me wasting all this hotness on any further fuckeries,' she says, before her mouth tightens. 'Jerome went back to wifey.'

'Jerome?' Who must've been the reason for the tears last month, but Delph can't place him.

'And there was I thinking Eden told her downstairs mummy everything,' Geena says, doing nothing to hide the flare of envy over their relationship. 'Funny, innit, chasing love.' She nods at Eden's picture, first-year secondary. 'I'm glad she don't seem bothered. Or interested. Long may it continue. Shit-stain men. Most of them, anyway.'

It's years since Eden came downstairs to Delph, emotional and barefoot in her emoji pyjamas, Geena having shut her out of the flat. Almost a week of hostility passed before Geena knocked to make peace, after a mate raised the point about her current beau's dating history – how all his exes were also the mothers of pre-teen girls. That perhaps she should've believed Eden's discomfort, instead of feeling threatened by his interest in her thirteen-year-old daughter. She'd taken them all to Pizza Express, their meal for four on Geena, part of her apology. Delph remembers hoping Geena wouldn't notice her pile of crusts, the rest of the pizza hidden beneath under a napkin, as she'd banged on about men belonging to the past tense and how it was just her and Eden now, as she'd made eyes at the waiter, leaning back in her chair, pushing her chest out. A real-life wildlife documentary, where the budget wouldn't allow exotic travel, and they'd had to make do with the mating signals of Great British Humans instead.

Eden's mum became Eden's mum again after that. Eden always gets remembered when the shit-stains wash out; flourishing when she becomes her mother's focus.

'I'd never dream of telling you how to live your life. All I'm saying is, you'd be foolish to even think about chucking it all away.' She looks at Delph pointedly, making her feel for a moment that Geena's seen right through to the truth of her. 'Because, what if he stopped trying to win you back? Then the rug would really be gone from under you. What then – moving in with your nutcase mother?'

Delph resents the nutcase comment, but lets it pass. She turns, glass in hand to the big window, the urban sprawl, never-ending. 'Don't you get tired?'

As she shrugs, pouring herself more Prosecco, it's evident that Geena isn't tired yet. In her leather pants, high-waisted, smooth and enticing, Delph's as admiring of her curves as she had been watching her change for PE all those years ago. If anyone's a nutcase it's Geena; that she's literally no idea of how incredible she is, owning her own shit – or to even think that Itsy's absence is the true source of Delph's misery.

Odd, how Delph must never even smile at another man, yet Itsy can freely admire women at his choosing. Even Geena's not immune. Itsy's hardly handy, but he could always change a plug or unblock a sink at the drop of a hat for Geena. Delph had never felt threatened, nor truly understood jealousy, until it became the daily battle to temper Itsy's.

Geena and Eden's move to Esplanade Point, two years after Delph and Roche's, was uncanny. And it was also the perfect set-up for Itsy, who never minded their new neighbour popping in for tea – until Geena started asking him to babysit, so that she and Delph could go up town and 'recapture their youth', something Delph rejected even more than he did.

'That reminds me. I found something.' Geena's up, rummaging in a drawer. 'Was mad as hell the day this was taken, I remember.' She hands Delph an old photo, of her, Geena and another girl who moved away just before they joined secondary. Roisin, Delph remembers. They're in the adventure playground on Butterfield. Hanging upside down on the swings, aged about ten, looking like proper little shits. 'Could've killed you when you turned up in that same fucking shell suit.'

Delph smiles, tracing their baby faces. 'You still sound cross about it.'

'Remember them? So comfy. They're making a comeback, you know. This time I'll have a wardrobe full of 'em, instead of the one on offer in Woolworths. Woolworths,' she says again, briefly looking like the little match girl, peering through a window into a better world.

'Mama Dee!' In a hair bonnet and oversized tee, Eden emerges from her room, startling Delph.

'Hello, lovely.' Delph pulls herself straight, patting the spot on the sofa beside her. What she wouldn't give to have Roche home like this.

'You look a bit ... Is everything okay?' Eden looks from Delph to Geena, questioningly. As normal as it is to see Delph, it's most unusual to see Delph outside her home. 'Just my time of the month,' Delph smiles, a stock response to such a horrible fucking day, dreading to think of the state of her.

'I told you, get the injection,' Geena interrupts. 'Liberate yourself.'

What would Geena say if Delph told her the truth, that the most liberating week of all is when the blood comes. It's a holiday, a mini break from wandering hands and permanent availability. Because look where that got her.

'Not long till your gig.' Delph changes the subject, picking up on the inner cringe going on beside her. 'You and Roche decided if you're staying up there?'

'Doubt it. Central London is serious p's. Roche said about a hostel, but who wants to share a bathroom when we can be back here in an hour anyway?' Catching herself, Eden cringes on the outside too. 'I didn't mean—'

'Darlin', I know you didn't. Besides, me and Roche, we're all right.' Were. Till Itsy's games knocked the shit out of their progress. Something hot braces Delph, that again feels like fury. 'And if things weren't, that'd be for us to sort, so you never need worry about it.'

It feels the right time to leave them. Only 11.49 p.m., yet it feels a witching hour. What a long, awful day.

But still not the worst she's ever had.

Hugging Eden, rather than asking her to ferry long begging messages, she settles for the most important one instead. 'Will you tell Roche that I love her?'

*

Always Look at the Home First

Tanners Grove, 1976

Joy grows fast; is nicknamed 'Stringbean' when she shoots upwards, easily the tallest in her year at secondary. Another thing that grows alongside Joy is frustration, which implodes within her, like a big bang. And all because of a poem.

Other than a new school, nothing else changes. Rather, it cements into the same, as Joy ticks off in her head every milestone occasion that brings her a little closer to being grown enough to leave Wellsend. Because it's hard to be herself around here; lonely too, when everyone thinks being big and caring about nature makes her the biggest spanner on earth. Cos she's got no friends, really – except Janie, of course, who loves their forest walks as much as she does, deep in the gorgeous quiet they've always liked escaping to. Outdoor life is best, because home is Dad's domain. In contrast to their Mouse Ma, Dad is king of his jungle. His way is the only way.

All beast.

Joy's already too gobby, especially for a girl. When Dad says, how 'it'll be her mouth that gets her in trouble', his words feel so much of a threat that she turns her voice onto paper instead, which opens a whole new escape hatch for her feelings – just like the painting used to.

Joy's thirteen when she comes third in the Friends of the Earth young poet competition:

> *HUMANS*
> *stealing beauty*
> *left me a sad world*
> *despite all*
> *you were given*
> *HOW SHAMEFUL*

Ma does sausage and chips, Joy's favourite tea, to celebrate, and treats her to a new frock from the Freemans catalogue that'll take Ma twenty weeks to pay off, which she's mentioned twenty-odd times too. Joy chose the dress herself, liked its description, a 'demure maxi dress' that covers her completely. Puff sleeves and broderie anglaise, made in the same blue as the garden hydrangeas, a colour Ma calls 'striking', especially against Joy's hair, which grows like the picture in the big artsy library books she can't borrow: Botticelli's Birth of Venus. *As they eat, Ma says – not for the first time – how Joy's 'grown into a proper beauty', adding quietly, and almost prayerlike, 'one day she'll have her pick'.*

Joy's filled with awkwardness, thinks of the Saturday mornings Ma takes her and Janie breakfast in bed; bacon and egg bloomers, with mugs of sweet tea – the only time she disobeys Dad, who says that it'll spoil them. 'One day they'll be doing all this for someone else,' is always Ma's gentle reply, as she travels round the house like a whisper, never not waiting on him first. 'They might as well make the most of it.' Ma means because Joy and Janie are girls. But times are a-changing, and Joy will show her.

'I don't want to pick anyone, Ma,' Joy says, unable to stop herself.

'Course not. You don't even like picking flowers,' Ma says, 'but you won't have a choice in the matter.'

'But I do have a choice. Girls do these days.' Joy speaks for Janie too; a born-again mouse, who she must fight for as well.

She won't marry. Just like Grandma was, Joy's a creative – only she won't go the same way, won't allow herself to be worn through by courting and settling. Because it's 1976, and there's more beyond this repetition, of sad men playing at kings, ruling nothing worth mentioning. Marriage was Ma's way, just as it had been Grandma's, and her mother's, her mother's mother – and so back it goes forever, a maternal chain-gang of wedding bands.

'I warned you, Angela, didn't I? I said this is what'd come of her thinking she's a cut above, winning …' Dad clears his throat for effect and full mockery: 'Poetry Contests.' As Joy's face burns, she wishes with all her might that she could become like another red-headed girl, Carrie White, and use her mind to fling every sharp object in the house through her father. He senses her rage anyway, because he pushes Joy's face down into her plate, holding it firm in the leftover food mush of humiliation that stains her new dress.

For Ma, this is a catastrophe. She drags Joy to the sink, wailing how she's 'not even started paying for it', sponging and blotting the fabric first pale then transparent, as Joy burns with shame, and

Dad sits back watching them like it's a Sunday night sitcom, till Ma proclaims it 'ruined' before taking to her bed.

The next morning in Home Economics, Joy's teacher hands out worksheets, images of a messy working kitchen, asking the class to circle all the hazards they can find. The picture wears the heading: 'Most Dangers Are Found in the Home', and Joy understands completely. There's no need to turn the pain into a picture or a poem; she has found the words necessary to explain her situation.

And she won't forget them.

8

WATERFRONT SUNSET

Wellsend, 2023

'Roche speaking, can I take your FreshFry order please?' Roche will never understand people. Why still ring, when they could just, like, Just Eat?

As she takes down the order, she looks up, acknowledging the man jingling the bell as he comes through the door. Her most regular, regular. Two cod suppers every Saturday since she started. He'll have a bag from the offy next door too; an Echo Falls label just visible through the blue carrier. An expectancy in his footsteps, hope in his eyes. He never rings, and it's always the same. Him in a clean shirt, facial hair on point, properly still looking after himself, and probably about Nan's age, now that she thinks about it.

Fuck. Roche feels shit all over again, rising inside her like a wave of polluted seawater, clean eclipsing all the mum stuff. If she's truly honest with herself, Roche knew she should've listened to her gut, that it was inevitable that Mum would let her down anyway – so no, this other shitty feeling stems not from Mum at all but from the horrid guilt that's come from going back on her word and back to snooping. But the box is too much of a temptation, sat there in the corner, like a half-finished story. And a distraction so very needed, too, because it has helped Roche stop thinking of Mum's sad eyes reading her 'I may as well have not been born' text, still probably wondering if she'll ever call.

Almost

I waited,
he said
he'd come
he was serious
and we'd show them.
And I waited,
at the window
and the street outside
stayed empty
as my heart
full of hope
became empty too
Joy Tennyson 17 (and a bit)

For Roche, Joy's poem is memorized, scorched in, and it hurts. Found in a pale blue jotter, which began as a school exercise book and became scrap for lists and scribbled reminders, and this, another of Joy's small poems, two pages from the back.

Joy is Nan, Nan is Joy. Roche's certain. But why did she want to escape her name; to become Moon? And why hasn't Roche been more curious about Nan's reinvention? More curious about her? Roche can't deny how she finds her grandmother fascinating. There are so many traits, both physical and characteristic, that she shares with this free-thinking spark of a person. And perhaps Roche would've grown curious sooner, should Nan have been in their lives, but five years apart and you can't help but begin making up your own story. Life moves quick, and when you're a kid the past is boring as hell. Hard to connect with. Irrelevant.

Good as Nan's been, Roche can't ignore the worry, the haunted look she's got of late. Nor can she ignore the nightly pacing, and the disruption. Roche can't do life on less than eight hours' sleep. It just ain't possible.

It also gets Roche wondering what Nan's pills are actually for. What is her condition – if she has one, which she must if she needs meds to manage it? Mental health perhaps, because Moon is physical health personified, brick shit statuesque, smoking AND vaping since Roche suggested cutting out old-fashioned cigarettes and their unnecessary chemicals. But Nan doesn't seem able to do anything by half. All of her goes into everything, so now, instead of dropping the cigs and opting for cleaner vaping, she's enjoying both. Roche watches her consumption, nothing like Mum's off and on habit that's almost like a supportive friend. No, Nan commands the smoke into her body, like she's its master, needing only herself.

But the man. Yeah, Roche focuses back on her customer, heading her way in his fresh shirt. In his carrier bag there'll be Ferrero's too, or whatever cut-above chocolate deals the offy's got going on that week.

He always looks so happy, performing the ritual of putting his order in with Roche, as he's doing now: 'Regular cod and chips twice, mushy peas and a curry sauce, please.' Raising his shoulders in sync with his brows, he adds, 'S&V on both.'

Nan could have this. A man bringing her supper on a Saturday night. Love. It's not too late. And the 'romantically incapable' line simply isn't true. The poem proves it.

So, who was he – the man who kept her waiting, who broke her heart? First love? True love? A grandfather?

And how will Roche ever know, without clean out asking?

'Twenty pounds thirty, please. Be about . . .' Roche looks at the fryers behind her, to Mo, the boss, who gives her a little nod of acknowledgement. 'Ten minutes.'

A contactless connection, then he sits on the small bench to wait his ten minutes out patiently, gazing through the glass at the comings and goings of early evening seafront activity. A little smile on his face. A man content with his lot. Like everything the week might've thrown at him has been worth getting here, to this moment. Saturday night. Going home to eat chips with someone he loves.

The most beautiful thing in the world.

On the sly, Roche takes out her phone, a softness all about her as she first smiles at the summer screensaver of her and Eden. And then she types.

*

RESCUES

Wellsend, 2005

One doctor claims that Delph's loss of appetite is a response to her grief. Since Sol died, she can't get anything past her throat, which seems shrunk and strange and altogether older than the rest of her. She is never hungry, nor peckish, nor craves anything specific. Asexual to food, Mother Moon jokes, without joking. Delph's only prompt is to eat when baby Rochelle eats. A few nibbles here and there, sharing a Farley's rusk, as it grows harder to part her lips, not only for sustenance, but to smile. To speak.

Another doctor says three years is more than enough for the pregnancy hormones to settle. He prods and pries for different causes, but his manner is cold, and Delph doesn't feel like explaining again. She's found her own small saviours anyway, in the big cardigans that hide her, and by running errands early, to the shops or the playgroup before returning home to the enormous relief of being cushioned again. Safe. Until her thoughts wander back to the darkness, with nothing to break the spell.

Road accidents are a regular way to die. Tragic and terrible, but not unusual. Out like a light on a dual carriageway, pram wheels and car wheels in a bang and gone accident. Yet still Delph takes her chances, safer with the wind on her face from the lorries whipping off the slip road than facing that mean little underpass, all the lurking and pouncing in the rat runs beneath her feet. The ammonia piss that blows her senses – what must it be like for Rochelle in the buggy, so much closer to the ground?

One day, the road is cordoned off. As the underpass waits to swallow them, a man jogs along to catch up with Delph, lifting Rochelle's buggy down the stairs. So helpful. A true BFG.

'You're a lifesaver,' Delph says, and manages a smile. 'Much appreciated.'

'Geoffrey,' says Geoffrey, with a hand on his chest. 'And who's this?' Dropping to his haunches, he shakes Rochelle's hand. 'How do you do, young lady?'

Rochelle looks up warily, but seeing Delph smiling, smiles too, as the thought's dredged again, of how Delph's misery might manifest in her new daughter, who must always remain fearless. 'This is Rochelle. I'm Delphine – Delph. It's a terrible place to cross.'

'Tell me about it – but best you be careful. Roads are one thing; you got the alkies and junkies down here, no place for a baby.' *And Geoffrey must notice she's wary, because he adds,* 'I see you. Coming home from my shift some days. They need green men putting in, or a zebra.'

'Like that'll ever happen,' Delph says, in the same politicized manner her mother would. 'It's the only way to toddler group. And she does love it,' *she explains, as Roche claps her fat hands together.*

'Got two myself. Twins. Though since my Mrs left, I don't see 'em as much as I'd like.'

'Sorry to hear that.' Delph waves to a passing woman with a kid, heading in her direction. 'Well, thanks again.'

'You're most welcome,' he says, watching her as she goes, and calls after her. 'Have a very lovely day.'

Enter Geoffrey Pearson. Adored by five sisters and a kind doting mum, made an envious man of his father, who disappeared soon after he was born. Geoffrey, who grew fast into a little prince, yet beyond his fan club at home, the real world came like lime juice on chapped lips. That he was not the centre of anyone else's universe shocked him, and on leaving school with mediocre results, it was another shock how no one rushed to employ him either. But instead of adapting to the world, Geoffrey found ways to elevate and set himself apart from it. Joblessness sounds altogether different when you're self-employed, when being without work becomes the fault of the economy, rather than his alone. Everything's malleable if you can keep coasting through on minimum effort, apart from his style, of course, being Mr High Maintenance. The groomed perfection of Boys II Men, despite dying in the nineties, Geoffrey considers cutting-edge trendy, forevermore. But no matter, he's a strong seven on the handsomeness scale, and thanks to a lifetime spent listening to his family of only women, he has all the chat and charm too.

Confident girls he never bothers with; those types could be offered the earth and still be unhappy; usually far more interested in themselves than fawning over him. When out on the pull, Geoffrey knows to approach the shy friend, or the girl with her shoulders down, those in need of a brief parachute, grateful for a saviour. Ever beholden.

Back in the day, each morning before school, should Mother Moon be coherent, she'd warn of the 'roads and pervs' along the journey. There's always danger.

Roads, at least, are indiscriminate.

There was nothing romantic on Delph's part when Geoffrey began stopping to pick her up, saving her and Roche from the fate of fresh road-death statistics. He was just a nice man with two kiddie car seats in the back. A family man.

Children. God, children. Victor and Adrian. Siring such healthy, good-looking boys – especially in one hit – was impressive, yet the effort, the sheer fucking cost of them, the fact that his wife Beverley never even noticed Geoffrey since they came along, was quite another.

As Geoffrey left the wholesome family-man impression on Delph, he formed his own of her. Sweet. So very, very hurt. Tiny. Beautiful. Her sheer fragility stirred something – not exactly menacing; more, protective. The kid seemed quiet enough too. And besides, girls are different anyway. It's almost as if they've been waiting for him to save them. Because there's no doubt. Delph needs him.

Some men take a beautiful girl and hide her away from the rest of the world.

9

The Cavernous Future

Wellsend South, 2023

Delph knew she'd become the shadow creature, the ever-shrinking woman of her mother's feminist fables, the night of Geena's Prosecco intervention – the night Delph said she was fine, then returned to her flat only to press her face to the floor and wish with all her being that she'd never have to get up again.

On the lino floor of her little square kitchen, alone in its clean bleach spick and span, with not a put-off chore or a single thing to do, Delph remained in the worst of hells. And as her mind flitted between the blank room and her inner carnage, she'd wondered if this was not already a sort of death.

Again, it took one small intervention to take her away from the edge. No different from normal, as she simply continued to go through the motions, and anyway, what else had she been doing all her life? Running the bath to brimming danger, and using an old gift set of Roche's, Delph emerged smelling of someone else entirely, leaving oily hoops reminiscent of Itsy's own bath time detrius, which regardless would still be her job to remove.

Then she dressed and came here. Where no one knows about any of it. B&Q is all bright artificial light and chat about last night's telly, pointing old dears in the direction of the plant section, where Delph thinks she'd quite like to work. And, in that small forward-looking thought, comes a glimmer of good.

It's just gone eleven when Lin relieves Delph from the till. And as she gathers her bits from beneath the checkout, Delph wishes she'd done it years ago – got back out in the world instead of coddling inside the flat, further evidence that her mother had a point about shrinking women, after all. She'd talk of them like they were folk tales, mentioning more than once her own grandmother's warnings from the other side, the advice not to marry, nor fade within an empty man's ego, the story of her own life, from a fierce artist's temperament to unrecoverable catatonia.

With Delph's excellent memory, a sensitivity that has meant it's possible to relive moments in perfect recollection, she remembers an old story of Mother Moon's, categorized with the same lucid precision. The tale goes, that as Moon and her grandmother queued beneath the stripy awning of a butcher's shop, through the window was a man in a death apron, pushing hulks of flesh through a metal device, which came out the other end as mottled worms.

'That's how little girls who talk to strangers end up.'

'Who are strangers?'

'Bad men.'

Throughout Delph's childhood, Moon filled her with tales of shrinking women, as grim as the Grimms would like it, but it was only really when Lin had asked how Delph wanted to receive her wages, when she first accepted this job, when Delph saw the prejudgment registering in Lin's eyes as she'd produced the bank details with Geoffrey Pearson's name on, that she remembered, and it felt like the actual shrinking woman was tapping her on the shoulder.

Or looking back at her in the mirror.

The same would happen when Cindy Lauper's classic came on the radio, Moon growing angsty in anticipation of the one line she'd shout almost maniacally, believing it.

'I want to be the one who walks in the sun.'

Is stacking shelves walking in the sun, though? Is walking in the sun that panicking moment when the shop gets so busy Delph's swallowed and present again? It's been three months. Three months of twenty-five-hour weeks, shifting up to thirty-five should this probationary period be satisfactory.

Satisfactory. Lin gets professional for a full five seconds when she invites Delph for 'a quick chat'. They sit in a side room off the warehouse, freezing their tits off from a through draught, as the lorries unpack their deliveries just outside. Without a word, just a big smiling face, Lin passes a permanent passcard to Delph, her picture already attached to it.

'Welcome to the fam, man,' Lin says. 'If you're happy, so are we – and up to thirty-five hours too, like we discussed.'

Delph beams properly, probably for the first time since her café breakfast with Roche, as she claims her new pass, feeling truly like she's part of something. 'Thank you.'

'Thank *you*. Seriously, if we could just clone you now. Them kids down there, honestly, they do not stop talking.' She rolls her eyes, not really bothered. 'How long was it since your last job?'

'We moved over this way fifteen years ago. God – fifteen years.'

'Lucky bitch.' Lin pushes some papers across for Delph's attention. Sipping her mochaccino from a flimsy machine cup, she clocks the cubic zirconia on Delph's wedding finger. 'Your man must be doing all right, innit?'

'Not lately.' Absolutely not lately, in all the ways.

Itsy's obsession, his endless questions about whose bones Delph would one day lie next to in a cemetery, his insistence that she be buried next to him, instead of her first love, meant she no longer wore the ring that meant the world. It was handed over, replaced with this nothingness, as meaningful as the glass it was made from, and just as transparent. Because there were never any serious plans to get married, nor any Will to set out their dying wishes. Just his word, his instruction, which has always been enough. Itsy. Master and commander. Of everything.

But not of Delph's thoughts. Not anymore.

Not now the wind's changed.

'My bank details, they're not up to date.' Delph chews the inside of her mouth. 'I'll bring them in tomorrow, if that's all right.'

'Well, you best. Payday's Wednesday. Now, did I tell you what happened at Parent's Evening? I swear, I could've killed—' Back in flow, Lin takes the papers back, shuffling them like she's on the news at ten, gobby as the Saturday till kids, who Delph bets never handed over someone else's bank deets when they got their jobs because they had their own bloody accounts for their own bloody money. Even when Roche started at FreshFry's, every penny of her earnings stayed hers.

Roche has neither acknowledged nor returned her mother's messages, but if Delph's honest, she's a little tired of Roche's judgyness. In fact, she's a little bit tired of everybody telling her what to do and how to think. Because when, if she really thought about it, was the last time that she pleased herself?

Later, Delph asks to duck off early, to catch Metrobank while it's still open and set up a new account. In her name only. It takes the earth for Delph to sit herself at the clerk's desk, almost trembling as she hands over her ID, like she's a criminal, guilty for wanting access to her own earnings, for considering her own bloody wants.

Truth? Delph wants to be alone for a bit. To try out having things her way, just for once. Isn't it better to scrub her own oily ring from the bath, protecting her own fucking energy? The bank stuff is easily organized; a new account ready to receive her permanent thirty-five-hour wages; a new card dispensed, which Itsy will never touch.

And it's a feat.

Glad to be home, Delph clears the fridge of everything she hates, without considering waste or Itsy's housekeeping budget. There's nothing she fancies anyway, so instead of dinner she watches Instagram make-up tutorials with a bowl of cornflakes, enjoying a brief back and forth with a woman in the comments from Dundee, also flying solo on an early weekday evening.

And when she looks at the clock, and finds it's past eight o'clock, the despair she felt up on the roof feels almost as if it belongs to somebody else.

Almost. But she got through twenty-four hours. All by herself.

Similar simple days alone pass – then one day, while Delph's on the balcony tending her plants, with Capital Xtra for company, it seems like magic, like a sign, when she notices a plant that she'd almost given up on starting to emerge.

Itsy said she'd never be able to grow it. *'Look at the space they need,'* he told the telly, told Monty Don, straddling his planted asparagus in a ditch the size of a field. *'Beyond you, love.'* It was Itsy's delivery, the mockery of the gardening that gave her such pleasure, that made Delph quietly go about her research, learning that container-grown asparagus, though difficult, was entirely possible in small spaces.

Her asparagus fern nest foliage is almost two years old, yet it is only today that there's the beginnings of what looks like a true spear.

'That's not how you do it, Delph. That's not right. What do you know?'

'Beyond you, love.'

Delph totally gets – expects – to be challenged by Roche, endures it because she made her – and isn't being difficult standard teenage shit, anyway? But Delph did not make Itsy. Always so quick to dismiss all she says, unwilling to discuss, to open his mind, preferring instead the trusted sameness of her doing everything for him, sweet as a nut in his comfortable routine, forever with the final say.

Does Itsy really know more than she does? Delph doubts it. So why should he have any more claim on the world than her? Perhaps she's finally channelling her mother; done with the male assumption that they know everything. Thinking of Itsy, thousands of miles away, the idea that he has any sort of hold, any sort of anything at all, seems ridiculous.

Yet with each text notification, Delph's confidence wobbles.

ITSY: No change. Meds have proper shrunk her. She's tiny.
ITSY: Hopeful of a little more time.

Delph begins typing back, when he sends through a quote he's screenshotted:

YOU ARE MY DEEPEST LOVE
YOU ARE MY FRIEND
YOU ARE THE BEST OF ME
ITSY: Missing you like MAD.
ITSY: Makes me realize.

Delph hovers over her touch screen, unsure of the right response. Knows she must, that her online status will be all he's staring at as he wills her into replying.

She settles for just a love heart, the minimum necessary to keep the shit turning. Can't stomach sending a red one, so chooses a white one instead. Sent, she puts her phone down, his distance becoming ever more the blessing.

Asparagus growing was never about a bountiful harvest. All Delph ever wanted was a single spear, just to prove him wrong.

And now it looks like she's got it. Her phone vibrates again, and because it might be Roche, she does check it, though on seeing Itsy's name, the phone's placed face down. And ignored.

*

Homespun Fun

Tanners Grove, 1978

'*Everyone says you can't be a punk AND into reggae, but people need to wise up,*' Joy says. '*Imagine, vanilla's your sworn thing, and you go around turning your nose up at all the other deliciousness available till the end of time. No wonder everyone's broken. Why do we always have to put our whole selves into this box or that box. What if I don't belong in any box?*' It comes in one stream of high-as-fuck narrative, as Joy relights a spliff longer than her longest finger. It smells thick, comforting, and more than anything Joy loves how her thoughts begin separating into categories called don't care and couldn't give any less of a shit. And then Joy's smiling. '*Nothing grown natural is an evil, no matter what The Man says.*'

'*Imagine never having rum and raisin,*' Janie says, thirteen years old and kissing the sky too. '*Or tutti frutti.*'

'*No one fucking likes tutti frutti.*' Joy puffs and passes, happy to share the green, but the green alone. Janie doesn't need to know about the other drugs at the parties like the one they've just been to, *their newest way of avoiding home and Dad's heavy hands, and his never-ending stare, which hooks into Joy in the same way that all the other men look at her.*

It was when Ma got carted off for another rest in Yellowhayes Psychiatric, this time on the chronic ward, that the changes at home came quickly. Joy, who never wanted the ring or the man or the world of drudge, got the lot anyway. At sixteen years old, who needs regular school when there's cooking, cleaning and other wifely duties, now she's become Ma's supple replacement.

Janie still believes in Joy's magic, though. Joy just wishes it was the type that could actually do stuff. Like in comic books, where she could melt the face off their dad with x-ray eyes. Turn him to dust.

At least Dad can't hurt Janie. She's too fragile, not like Joy who is buxom and capable and built for male attention. 'What's the time?' Joy will never wear a watch.

'Time we sped up. He'll be coming from the pub any—'

It's like fate, as their tall father turns the corner, doing that drag drunk shuffle, no different from the alkies who barricade themselves in boxes down by the canal. He trips, veering into a neighbour's privet, as coins spill from his pocket, tinkling onto the pavement. Though he swoops to retrieve them, it's half-arsed, and patting his pocket for his key, shuffles on, right past them.

From their hiding place, on the other side of the hedge, Janie reaches out through the sparse bottom branches, grabbing at the coins like some Victorian street urchin might, her arms silvery with the scars of the terrible habit she never will talk about. It puts pain in Joy's eyes, so Janie gives her a shove, pulling the little half bottle of voddie from her bag, as if she's giving it a peep show. 'Dropped

*over three quid, enough for another bottle. Git. All that moaning
how skint we are, yet for booze ...' She's right, because there always
seems to be enough money for the pub, the nights spent socializing
with Dad's factory mates and their concrete boots, weighted by
years of shit circumstances that are always someone else's fault. Joy
remembers Ma innocently mentioning how Bev the Avon lady's
better half had got himself a new job in sales – that came with a car –
and Dad sneered, rather enviously, 'When's it my turn, Angela?',
even though Bev's husband had a failed market stall too, but chose
an evening course at community college instead of evenings in The
Feather & Broomstick.*

*'Probably afford a bit more of this too.' Janie twiddles the joint in
Joy's face. 'Bunk off up the allotments?' But Joy wouldn't feel right
going up there. She wouldn't want to see their plot, the small corner
assigned to her and Janie to take care of years back; a memory that
feels more like a daydream, like it's almost too good to belong to her;
when they had their own little kit to share, fork and trowel, each
with a fold-up chair just like King Dad's; before the booze came and
the darkness settled on him and ruined it all.*

*These days, the idea of Dad as a good man is like believing in
Father Christmas. A really fucking stupid, deeply immature idea.*

'Quick, make a wish on the silver.'

*Janie presses the coin to her lips. 'Pray they do a swap. Ma gets
better and he takes a turn. A bad one.' Her eyes burn into Joy's. 'So
he don't come visiting you no more.'*

*A year later, Joy's at secretarial school. There's a hopelessness about
her, but the vodka and ganja allow the happier, more confident,*

creative girl inside an outlet, a way of forgetting the troubles that lately have bled into the cracks of life beyond home, like Mouse Mum's lipstick bled from all her decades sucking on Menthols, the constant habit Joy now emulates. Joy loves and hates Ma, hates the weakness, the fact she's sure her mother knows, must know, about what happens on the nights she pops her Valium, and Dad pretends to drop off in front of the news, his night breath already setting in as he begins his silent ascent up the stairs, choosing Joy's room, where she's fake sleeping, lain out as coldly porcelain as she looks. Like a doll. With just as much autonomy.

Escapes come in flashes. Nights out. Drinking most recklessly. Booze Britain's always been a thing. Dad does it in his male way that's normal and never questioned, getting blottoed down the local, and Joy does it under disco lights. Nights that always seem to end in fights, because Joy sees, sees and sees what's going on – can't resist calling it out when she clocks them taking advantage, blokes on the prowl as their nights tail into increasing want, splintering off to hunt alone, just as the girly groups begin dissipating too. Joy's fury spores from the predatory acts of the man zoning in on the lone woman who can't find her coat, whose legs are bandy, as uncoordinated as her thoughts.

One night, Lion Dad's in waiting, parked behind the disco to collect his drunk daughter, who stumbles through the doors and out onto her knees. He rushes to her aid, scraping her off the pavement as Joy screams the quiet street down, for him to take his hands off her, her short dress rising as she's manhandled into the car. Closing her into the passenger side, he warns through the glass to sit still. Joy does as she's told, can't run in these bloody wedges anyway, and her knees pissing blood, so if he chops her into a million pieces at least there'll be evidence. That she was here and bleeding in his shitty little vehicle. Climbing in, and closing his own door, Dad begins screaming too. He screams her silent, till Joy's covering her ears, feels his words on her face that she's numb to, words that vibrate nonetheless, as their loathing sinks beneath her skin. His hand locks, a half-handcuff on her leg, so high she knows what'll be next and she wishes to fuck that he'd just get on with it.

Rest in pieces.

Yet the night delivers a twist. Maybe it's the pill Joy quickly swallows, what it's made from she's unsure, but it's loose in her bag like a blessing, because who knows what's in store for her at home. Ma's in one hospital and Janie's in another; she's cut herself, says she doesn't remember how. The bony haunted girl who was once her happy sister is safer in the hospital than with the razors and the compass she keeps in the tin beneath her mattress.

In her room, where she knew he'd end up, Dad's eyes fix instead on Joy's ouija, near her bed, as Joy's eyes fix on him, curious of how his entire demeanor's changing, the way the board seems to shield her; how the skin above his lip that's sore from shaving now prickles before her very eyes. Joy rests her fingers, calm on top of the glass, adding to his nervousness, as he shifts from foot to foot. 'Stop that.' His same old noise lacks clout, and he knows it. 'You'll end up like your granny. Give it here.'

In no rush at all, Joy does as she's told. Placing the glass sideways, she rolls it towards him, comes to a stop at his parted feet. From feared to fearing, Joy thinks, as her father looks down, and the glass suddenly, inexplicably, shatters across the floor, too delayed to be explainable. Logical.

And, by the powers of the universe, Joy's protected.

10

TEMPORARY LIBERTINE

London, 2023

Roche and Eden aren't even out of Fenchurch Street Station when there's an—

'Oi, darlin?' It comes from a dapper guy with locs, city dressed but not remotely conforming. He focuses straight on Eden. 'You are very beautiful, my darlin', you know that?'

It comes, natural as: Roche's arm around her shoulder, vexed proper as she flicks her eyes up and down this opportunist. 'She is. And I do know that.'

Dapper takes a step back, taking in the pair of them, in utter admiration. 'Well then, may I scrap that, only to say that you are by far,' – he points a finger to the sky, as if acknowledging, thanking God for such greatness – 'by far, the finest-looking lesbians I've ever seen.'

He goes off, likely back to some skyscraper office, leaving Eden smiling and Roche still frowning.

'What you cross for? We *are* fine.'

'I know. But we're not here for him and his perv approval.'

'He wasn't pervin'. He was being friendly.' Eden smooths it all in her nice, nice way she's got. 'Take the compliment, he was a harmless hunk. Think if the world was full of hims.'

'Sometimes, y'know . . .' Roche bristles, shaking her head, not done with the vexations.

'Sometimes what? You know I am all about you. Don't mean I don't like looking at hims, though,' she adds cheekily.

Roche can't work out if she's miffed because she's jealous, or because Eden's taste roams vast. Boys are totally fine; Roche's not like Nan, for God's sakes, with an actual signed picture of the actress who played the original Miss Havisham in the depths of her secret box, casting everyone with a dinkle as a wrong-un. Roche just knows, like she knows she'll always need to piss, that it'll always be girls for her.

'It's 2023.' Eden's on a roll now. 'Why on earth would you shut the door on anyone? And really, what's gender anyway? Everyone should just, like, fancy who they fancy. Forget about all that genitals shit. You'd think by now someone might've thought up a groovier word for genitals, though,' she adds, buying up half the station kiosk of its overpriced chocolate.

'There's a bloody Tesco Extra over there, fam.'

'But look at that massive road to cross. I ain't risking my life. Plus, I'm not taking one step further until you eat this fucking Mars Bar. I mean it; you, hunger and Google Maps is a recipe from hell.'

And she might be right, because Roche's not even halfway through her Mars and the sugar's hitting already, easing her into almost-placid, this trip feeling like an adventure again and not an inconvenience.

'Told you,' Eden says, vindicated. 'After you then, bitch. Head for the District line.'

They've saved for this. Concerts are expensive; staying overnight in London and doing food and the whole shebang is expensive. But shit, if you're not seeing Little Simz at the Roundhouse, Camden, who even are you?

Bags are dropped, snacks scoffed and channels flicked through before they're showering, dressing up, making up their faces, a synchronicity with each other in the way they've had since they were small. Then they are lost, vibing, part of the collective, the cool collective. It's belonging. It's youth and it's freedom, and it's theirs for the claiming.

Roche puts her arms around Eden, and pressing her forehead against hers, kisses her, publicly, properly. Smiling against each other's lips. 'I really fucking love you.'

Eden can't hear her. It doesn't matter.

On their way back to the hotel, they stop at off a food stall, stuffing their faces with vegan pizza and a pitcher of beer that Eden flips out at because, 'Can you believe it's three times the price of the cocktails you get down at the bingo. But London, innit. Not Wellsend. You're paying for the privilege.'

It is a privilege, being swallowed by some rare fun, parking up all the madnessess of her family. 'It feels like we're on holiday. A forty-minute train journey and it's like I've had a brain transplant.' Roche looking questioningly at Eden. 'What?'

'Ah, I just forget what you look like when you're smiling.' Eden reaches across the table to squeeze her hands. 'I know you've a lot on, and granted, a lot of it is fucking weird ...'

'Let's not, please.' Nan's paintings of some family called the Smallmans continue to run through her thoughts, unsettling Roche in a way that the poetry and old photos haven't. Maybe it's the kid perspective; that some small person projected all their longings into the strange tiny pictures, the names of each family member carefully written on the back of the portraits. The names she can't forget: Derek, Clyde, Angelica, Rose and Kingsley.

Roche shakes her head, shakes it off, smiles again – the rare thing she does, that makes all the difference because her frown lines are too real for comfort, and criminal, considering she's still three months off turning eighteen. 'Remember when we'd play that game – pretending we'd hatched out of nowhere? Belonged nowhere. No memories. No history. Like aliens.'

'Hatchlings,' Eden laughs, remembering. 'Yeah. Just turning up on the estate, all bewildered like. Pretending we didn't know where nothing was, or how to turn taps and shit. I'm sure I did a whole day of pretending I didn't know who Mum was.'

'I loved that game.' Roche shakes herself again, as if she's shaking herself free of her own familial baggage, like a shaggy wet dog might after a swim. Her phone vibrates, and she casts her eyes heavenwards. 'Who d'you reckon – Nan or spam?'

But it's a university admissions email. A pending acceptance on the proviso of further criteria. From Edinburgh. Wordlessly, she turns the phone to Eden, watching as the liquid she's sipping through a straw comes to a standstill.

'It's like, spitting distance from real.' Considering it's all they've talked about lately, the thought of going feels brand new again, and suddenly unsettling. Eden, pale beneath her contouring, looks as if she might've caught the feeling too. 'You're my fucking world, Ro. You always have been.'

Edinburgh makes three pending acceptances, subject to smashing her subjects, of course. Edinburgh, Birmingham and Brighton. It is spitting distance. Spectacularly scary.

But good.

'I'd really, really love to say come with me, that somehow we'll manage.' Roche grabs Edens hands across the table. 'But I don't want to manage anymore. And I don't want to be childish. I really, really fucking love you. But also, I really, really fucking need this.'

'I know,' Eden says simply. 'I'll just really, really fucking miss you.' She kisses each of Roche's hands, her stamp from the concert, smudged now into nothingness. 'I tell you something though, we're already waaay better at all this emotional shit than our mums.'

'Indirectly the very best of role models.'

'To Mums. And Nans – Happy Birthday, Gran – sorry Little

Simz was more enticing than your party.' They knock their glasses together, still holding hands. 'We'll be all right, you know. At least, out of all the things you do have to worry about, I'm not one of them. Now. Back to business. How splendiferous was Simbi looking tonight?'

Roche tips her head back, smiling into the sky at the memory of her lyrical hero, catches a reefer from somewhere behind her that piques not an inch of interest. Living with Nan lately, the gradual reintroduction of her most treasured habit – which was hardly worth mentioning when Roche first moved in, but is sitting a bit strange lately now that weed's the first thing she's reaching for on waking – means it doesn't hold the same appeal as it used to, when she and Eden would do their long walks that took them out of the concrete and into some green, where it's true a little of the devil's lettuce had been shared between them – nature meeting nature, and all that.

Experimenting, Roche had once pinched a cigarette off her mother. Geena caught them taking pulls in turns on the roof of Esplanade Point when she and Eden were about thirteen, and after properly losing her shit, made Eden smoke a pack of ten, one straight after the other. Eden, yakking all over the place, couldn't get past three, sick for three days solid, a day of puking for each fag, which did the trick, because aversion tactics are a madness.

'Simbi was, if I may say, the finest-looking girl I've ever seen ...' Roche mimics Dapper with the locs from earlier, making Eden crease up, which then makes her crease up, and feels as if the universe is at last giving her permission to live her own life. Like she can vaguely hear the door ahead unlocking.

Suddenly it doesn't matter that things are broken. Roche knows, without any need for gut feeling, that she hasn't had a hand in any of it, that their damage, her mum's, her dad's, was all someone else's doing. And is past tense. What good is it to carry what can't be changed? What Roche can change is to start doing the best for herself. My Life, like Mary J B sings on Mum's many, many albums, her duetting along like a boss, yet never listening to the words. Yes, one best thing for Roche, without doubt, is Edinburgh University.

And the other best thing is sat right here. Best friend. Best person. Blessed love.

*

HOPELESSLY DEVOTED

Wellsend Wellness Centre, 2006

'Take yourself off in your head. Go on. Should you feel any panic, if it all gets too much, retreat into your safe space.' Grief counsellors have all the best death hacks, enough pearls of wisdom to string a thousand necklaces, and so does Delph's third shrink, Dr Kahn. 'Where is your safe space, Delphine?'

It is the place she can't return to, not now she's sad and empty. The old bright eyes and energy belongs to the girl before, who'd rush for the morning train in her Nikes and hair rollers, who could paint perfect cat-eye flicks and make up her face, regardless of a packed and moving carriage, as she headed for work at a London department store.

Delph loved her red suit, the red lips she'd pair with it. Looking like a flight attendant, a Virgin Atlantic type, with all the charm of a trolley dolly too. Delph's everybody's-friend sweetness suited a make-up counter, perfect for the role of cosmetics consultant, as she always knew she would be. Yes, Delph's safe space is back behind her counter, assured yet approachable, every bit the French Laboratoires representative, like she'd done it all her life.

But then life ended. And she is here. Grief counselling. Clinging to crumbs, to anything at all, that might help settle and soothe.

Nothing will. That happy, happy girl she once was has gone.

Besides, Delph already knows what Dr Kahn will suggest, the techniques; from breathing exercises, to filling an imaginary box with her worries, to getting a pet – the perfect solution, considering she's currently coping with Rochelle's terrible twos, and still living with Mother Moon, who never truly evolved from her own tantrum phases.

'It's vital to keep connected to the world,' Dr Kahn says gently. 'Staying social. Sometimes a new friendship can be the breath of fresh air we need – a tonic against the loneliness grief brings.'

'I've not slept since he passed.' Delph remembers the quiet reve-lation in the small treatment room, which always felt more private than it was. 'Never had any greys before, neither. Now I look like I'm the one who died.' A newly widowed customer, whose worried, generous children had gifted a voucher, was how their friendship started. A fortnight later, around the same time as her first appoint-ment, the lady reappeared, pointing to her eyes before stretching them upwards, as she pushed her face into Delph's eyeline.

'Sleep's no better, but this stuff's working miracles.'

Sheila indeed looked less puffy, her hands a little steadier, the same as her voice, though the unsure tremble was never far away, emotion only ever round the corner, ready to wash clean the begin-nings of normality she'd slowly but surely tried resurrecting – at least until the sadness rushed in again. The never-ending ebb and flow of total desolation.

Delph had thought there'd be years – fifty, at least – before she mirrored Sheila's sadness.

Every few weeks she'd pop in, sometimes buying, sometimes not, sometimes bringing her small granddaughter, a dear pixie-looking child with a wonky fringe and hot, high-colour cheeks from teething. Delph wonders if, in her absence from her counter, she's been missed by Sheila. Or if she's just another loss, barely registering in the vast annihilation of grief that she herself is now swallowed by too.

'New faces, the introduction of a pet.' Delph feels herself compressing, when Dr Kahn adds, 'OK. Enough on your plate already – I get it. But perhaps someone at playgroup, someone unconnected ...' Dr Kahn clasps her hands together, a neat line appearing between her brows, as Delph reminds herself that she's only trying to help. 'I read something, a quote. I can't recall where from. It said something like: grief is love with nowhere to go.' Dr Kahn sighs. 'Beautiful.'

But Delph does have an outlet. What else is Rochelle if she's not a new face, a new person to channel all her love into. But it doesn't work like that.

Rochelle is a permanent reminder.

Geoffrey's a new face. Unconnected. Getting to know him, as she slowly has, lessens her everyday pressures. Always there, never expecting – even picking her and Rochelle up from their own front door to take them to playgroup, even though he lives all the way across town.

All the way across town also sounds appealing. As does how he looks after her; the temporary relief when she's in his company and feels protected. Cocooned. Something solid against the return *of the turbulence Delph remembers well as a child. Stability, which Mother Moon's forever found impossible to provide.*

Perhaps Dr Kahn has a point.

Next to her bundle of notes, a spider plant also shares Dr Kahn's desk. The leaves, each rusted tip, sigh over the edge of the pot. Dr Kahn nods to the carafe of water on a side table. 'Shall we water it?' she asks. 'It. We need a name.' Stroking the leaves in a soundless gesture, she looks up, her eyes interested as Delph, now focused on the plant, hopes it hadn't been left to deteriorate for her benefit; another trickery of a technique, albeit a new one. 'We could call it Delphine, help it along together. I wonder where you both could be after our six sessions?' From a drawer, Dr Kahn takes out four biros, placing them one by one on her clipboard, their lids pointing towards Delph like arrows. Blue, green, then a black and a red pen. 'Let's start with an exercise, perhaps. Save on the talking,' she says. 'Choose any pen. It doesn't matter.'

But it does. She'll analyse, assuming some internal knowledge that Delph will offer unwittingly, already knowing to avoid the green pen – mad people write in green. She remembers the stories of her artist great-grandmother who, before her catatonia, refused to make her bed and left lights on in the daytime; wonders if she was also partial to a green biro.

The red pen's also a no-no. A sure sign of anger or defiance. Warning or bloodlust. Slowly, Delph selects the blue. There are too many dark, dark thoughts to even consider the black pen.

Dr Kahn begins writing, but Delph can't crane to read what she's put. She's not that type of person. Never rude. Nor pushy.

Dr Kahn holds the pad up.

I DON'T GIVE TWO SHITS WHAT PEN YOU CHOOSE.

She smiles out from behind the pad. 'Look, I know. Therapy. I get it. But I promise, Delphine, it is only to get to know you – to understand. So I can help you. And you can be happy again.'

Impossible, when happiness is in the ground, in the memories that've become dreams, as Delph questions their reality, now they are only hers, only playing in her head, wearing thin, and distant, but never any less devastating. Happiness, happening but once, like fucking Halley's Comet and just as short-lived.

But then Rochelle, now awake in the buggy next to Delph. The timely reminder of why she's here and why she keeps on trying.

Lifting her onto her lap, and using her blue pen of choice, Delph writes two letters in the very centre of the page.

OK.

She shows them to Dr Kahn, who smiles, as if she's single-handedly saved the NHS.

Who might help, after all.

11

ONE DAY IN YOUR LIFE

Wellsend, 2023

Delph expects swamping nostalgia, as if the moment she walks into their old haunt, through those old wooden pub doors, *the same doors*, with the frosted glass, engraved with ancient ships at sea, she'll feel like she's wearing iron cuffs that'll slowly send her sinking as if she's in quicksand, down through the burgundy carpet and the floorboards, varnished even darker now, to the stony little cellar below, with the damp floor and the smell of wet earth, colder than cold. Delph knows it's there because she worked a few shifts here back in the day, when she fancied herself as Tiffany, the barmaid in EastEnders, and was saving for a wedding ... So many, many ghosts.

But Delph's not remembering the sad stuff for once, but all that was once her; who she was and what she liked, stuff

176

she's not thought about for years. How she now goes to bed at eight with no intention of sleeping; with her own thoughts instead of a book for disguise or to hide behind. She's bathing more, showering less; valuing the time it takes to fill the tub and to bob about in the bubbles as a luxury. Why, even on the way home from work the other day, she bought one of those organic ten-of-your-five-a-day posh soups, which she had to season the shit out of to get it to taste of anything at all, but she enjoyed nonetheless. She even had the idea that she could try making her own soup. Delph's supper had satisfied, hitting a spot specially selected for her taste and not the tins and overprocessed meals that kept Itsy happy.

Kept.

The flat without his presence feels like rot that's drying out. It helps that the evenings continue to grow lighter, the earth warmer, as life – like Delph's asparagus – trembles into waking beneath the soil. This gearing up, getting ready for the new phase, to greet the changing seasons, has also worked to restore a little of Delph's bright side too, especially considering there isn't the slightest whiff of Itsy returning any time soon.

Nonetheless, his messages keep coming, demanding her instant attention, and she finds herself replying politely, the drama on the day he left unmentioned.

Geena gets served first, despite being last at the bar. 'What you having, lovely?' she asks Delph, smiling over the top of a cocktail menu. 'Cheeky Wimto? Sex on the Beach?'

'It's only lunchtime. And we are only actually here for

177

bingo.' How Delph loathes the word *actually* – almost as much as she loathes the way she sounds. A dry lunch has-been, who's past tense. But she's not. Can feel she's not. Can feel the way her eyes are flicking round the room, enjoying for once the presence of other people, lost in their own jovial little bubbles, ducking in here for a bit of lunchtime fun. It is lovely, warming, to think similar set-ups are going on all over the place, for the social and the hopeful. It is only fucking bingo, but the energy is good. Delph feels good.

'Wimto's on me.' Delph slips her new Metrobank card from a shoulder bag she found in Roche's room.

'Second thoughts, that blue WKD'll wreck my veneers.' Geena scans the menu again. 'We'll go for a pitcher of The Godfather.'

'We will,' says Delph, handing over her card, and with a pitcher she's struggling to carry, they head to their reserved table.

'This *is* wicked,' Geena says, 'just like the old days. Mad to think we're now saying shit like "in the old days" when we are still so utterly delectable.'

'Speak for yourself,' Delph says, discovering her Godfather. Not disliking it.

'You know, you are so boring, sat there all effortlessly thin, and what – pickled in time, is it?'

'Thank you, I think.'

'It's your shit brows, Delphine. No offence, but they make you look about ten.'

Delph laughs with Geena, her quick wit just like Eden's.

Strange, how Delph fell into the habit of resisting their closeness when she's known her for longer than almost anyone. Geena, one of the few people who remembers it all, because she was there. A wave of emotion sweeps in, filling her eyes before she knows it. 'I don't much like to look in the mirror these days.'

'Now that is a shame. I tell Eden about your eyes, them mad flicks – Winehouse before Winehouse.' Geena smiles, remembering. 'And that course you took – in the West End. We were all chronic jealous. Jobs like that though, you do it for the love of it. You must. Bending round someone's face all day would bloody kill my back. I'm very comfortable in my sit-down job, thank you very much.'

'Good. Because it's made you very comfortable. Your flat's gorgeous.'

Geena beams, happier than Delph's seen her for months, and makes her think maybe this is doing them both good, getting out and about together. If Mother Moon could see her now, she'd laugh her head off. Though she never was a fan of Geena's. Delph can't for the life of her remember why.

'I think I might try persuading Itsy to redecorate.'

'How is he, his mum – any news?'

'We WhatsApp; he said she seems fine. Like she's just really pleased to have all her kids there. It's nice.' It is more than nice. For all of them. 'Itsy looks very hot.'

'Very decent,' Geena corrects. 'I think hot's pushing it.'

'I meant sweltering in bloody thirty-two-degree heat. You know, you can't ever tell him that. He already loves you swooning over him.'

'Never bothers you, does it? Never bothered you with Sol either. But then, he was always yours. No doubt. Hey, cheers.' She looks at Delph as if she wouldn't want to be anywhere else. 'Happy us day.'

Delph smiles back, clinking her glass. 'And thank you. For thinking—for inviting me.'

Delph would be lying if she said her first thought when the doorbell rang earlier hadn't been Roche. The hope was real, but Roche having a key's also real and so the hope was fleeting. Instead, there was Geena, so gorgeously casual, inviting her to bingo, all enthusiasm, like they'd planned on hooking up like this weeks ago. She'd given her ten minutes, wouldn't take no for an answer, and so Delph, being Delph, did as she was told.

As the room darkens, Geena grins across the table, lifting her cocktail glass in the air. 'Cheers, fam.'

As the celebrity caller appears on a satellite link-up, the table just in front of them responds most animatedly, the pair of old ducks seeming almost to pre-empt the banter, like they know all the ropes. Delph enjoys watching them; the table just across the way too – a mixed group of seventy-plussers, having shedloads of fun on a Friday lunchtime. One of the old boys calls over about them being teenagers, and sets her and Geena off laughing again, in this strange little moment she's invented all by herself, that's called living.

Fucking hell. Delph could almost, almost cry, because it isn't much really, sitting with some old school mate in the battered old bingo hall that used to be a club that used to be a pub.

But it's hers.

It's new memories.

'I'm going to get another jug, and some food?' Delph suggests, before the next game begins: a regional hook-up; three grand at stake.

'I warn you, don't be expecting no Jamie O here, babe. I'll have a cheese, tomato and onion toastie – and dirty fries. Why break the habit of a lifetime,' she adds cheekily, waving some notes at Delph. 'But this is my shout.'

Ten minutes later and still not served, Delph's giggling with Nora and Rose, the ducks from the table in front, serious bingo OGs both wearing tent dresses, crocs and half their body weight in gold.

'Every morning, we walk that seafront, rain or shine.'

'Put our feet in.'

'Breeve in deep. Cos you gotta breeve in deep, girl, to know you're livin'.' Nora, dressed in pink, squeezes Delph's hand, the moment feeling like something lifted straight from her mother's handbook for the occult. 'Don't. Die. Wondering.' She even looks like Mother Moon; much older but with the same wide face, the knowing, knowing eyes.

'I love that,' says Geena, joining their group. She puts an arm around Delph, 'Should be a tattoo, or something.'

They win nothing, but to Delph she's won everything. And when the dark foyer opens into daytime, it's as if she's been in a bunker for decades, as both women instantly shield their eyes from the sun.

Seized by spontaneity, Delph grabs Geena's hand, and once

across the road, they hurtle down the stony beach together, pulling off their trainers and socks, Geena keeping hold of hers because they're Limited Edition Air Forces, 'and you know there's chancers round here, babe – we were once them.'

'Close your eyes,' Delph orders, as the freezing waves lap round their ankles, leaving behind the froth that'll leave its salty tidemark. 'Breeve in deep, girl.' Eyes closed, she smiles. *Don't die wondering.*

What's next? Delph thinks. What's next for me?

She remembers them back in the day, the after-school hurry to hit the beach the second the sun showed its face, the lot of them teenage and inseparable, all navy ties and blazers, in the thick of their animated circle. Delph breathes deep, as the afternoon sun fills her mouth like a sweet treat as she reminisces, always easier to do with her eyes closed. First the angles of Sol before memory colours in the rest of him; elbows and knees compact as he'd sit crablike at the water's edge. She forgets he was tall. The light brown canerows, black-framed glasses ...

'Shit, what's the time? Got to get preening. It's Gran's eighty-first. She's hired decks.' Inspired, she slaps Delph's bum. 'Come? Oh, come on – so many olds, you know half of them anyway. Could even swerve past your mum's first.'

And at the word Mum, Delph's sunny Sol memories are gone. She blows a raspberry, rolls her eyes.

'Is she still proper ... ?' Geena makes cross eyes, twiddling a finger at her temple, that old ignorant universal signal for madness, which would irritate Delph far more if she hadn't twigged how being in the sudden sunshine and drinking most of their two Godfather pitchers might be the real reason for Geena's loss of eyeball control.

'She's well, actually. Her and Roche seem to have hit it off, so ...' Delph is clipped, suddenly tight, mirroring the vibes she'd got off Geena when she'd referred to her as Eden's downstairs mummy. It's not nice. 'I miss her. So much.'

'Enjoy the peace. I like that they're growing, off doing their own shit – like the gig in Camden. Wouldn't you just kill to swap places? To do it again?'

Delph thinks about it but doesn't answer.

'Roche, she sort of ... saved you in a way, didn't she? Gave you purpose?' Geena swallows. 'Well, when I had Eden, I felt like she'd clipped my wings. Total opposite of you, fam, and if I'm honest, there's been times that I felt proper resentful. You and Roche, it's so natural. It ain't like that with us.'

'All you do is love them.'

'And I do. And sometimes I don't.' She looks Delph dead in the eye. 'You think I'm wicked, don't you? But it's like I'm being stolen from, permanently. Like there's never enough time. Yeah, like I'm time's victim. And it's slowly eating me, till I'm just ... irrelevant.' Looking at Delph, she checks herself, begins putting on her trainers. 'I don't even know what I'm saying.'

'I'll come back with you.'

'Stay put.' Geena leans down, ruffling Delph's hair affectionately. 'You look right at home.'

As Geena heads back towards the pavement, Delph trails

her hands across the pebbles, looking out at the sea. She's sat here a thousand times, but rarely on her own. Avoiding herself, such has been the desperation to fill every second rather than face what's inside of her, too vast, too painful to navigate. Because what would she find there? Better off learning how to clean the oven handles via YouTube. Obsessing over seed catalogues.

Delph thinks maybe she's been afraid of herself.

Sitting here, she's just as afraid. Her smallness, and, if she truly admits it, confronts herself properly, even Itsy's controlling has played a part in her strange little comfort zone, the fog of repetition becoming its own padded cell, a gentle place for her mind to just exist without thinking. But stepping out, pushing through the fear of the unknown other side, perhaps it's not death that waits for Delph after all, but a new phase.

Of life.

The two dears from bingo head up the beach towards her, the heavier of the two leaning most reliably on her friend's wrist, which she grips tight. 'Hello darlin',' she calls out. 'You been abandoned?'

'She had a better offer.'

'Let's hope he's handsome.' She winks. 'Now did you do as I said, soaked your feet, let them stones do their magic?'

Delph nods, climbs to her feet as the other lady squeezes her elbow, adding, 'Who needs a bloody pedicure.'

'I did. And I'll do it again too.' Delph shivers as if on cue, wishing she'd more than her cardi. 'It's getting a bit chilly. Think I'll push off home. It was so nice to meet you both.'

'We've booked another session this afternoon. It's our last one for a while, you see. I'm off for a little stay.'

'She means hospital,' corrects her friend, with an upbeat smile that feels practised.

'Well, that's too bad. I hope you're well and back to bingo soon.'

'Why don't you join us, a game for the road. You can be my lucky charm.'

'She needs all the luck she can get. Don't you, mate?' Love matches the worry in the look that exchanges between them. So much feeling in the world, in a long life. Even in a hard life there are the good moments, the brief exceptions. Delph doesn't think anything so grand as that this pair of dear souls have been magicked up just for her, yet she knows all the same that she was meant to meet them.

Knowing. These fleeting 'gut truths', her mother would call them. Perhaps another sensory part of Delph's soul waking up.

The pair are so deeply endearing that Delph doesn't even think about saying no. She just slips her arms through theirs, linking them together with her in the middle, as they rely on her to help them back up to the promenade.

They have G&Ts, Delph a lemonade. And as the lights dim again, and the celebrity caller repeats his jokes from earlier, her companions are no less enthusiastic to the banter they throw back. It has done Delph good to witness how they've built their own little version of happiness independently, beautifully.

And Delph's so floaty and tuned into the good, that it comes as a slap back to earth when Nora points out her row, shouting out, 'Bingo! Bingo! Over here! Bingo!' On her behalf. Because Delph's only gone and bloody won.

The national link-up jackpot.

Heading home, Delph walks up the high street in a daze. She stops to stare through the big glass windows of John Lewis, the make-up people buzzing around with their tools and their chat.

Going in, Delph finds herself browsing beneath the hot brilliant lights, trails her fingers along the tiny pots of Bare Minerals, tweaking the teats of the little bottles from The Ordinary, like a hi-tech apothecary, a dream world to Delph these days, which still smells so good, is still her favourite scent, the combined smell of hundreds of bottles, tested into the atmosphere, settling over clothes, the same smell as when she worked in the West End, where nothing worse than the wrong shade of foundation ever happened. A safe space. Her happy space.

A woman with white locs beams at her across a pyramid display of boxed aftershaves, dressed in a black tee, MAC written across her chest and a smile on her plum-coloured lips. 'Got a minute, darling? We've a gorgeous new eye palate I've been dying to try on someone like you.'

Delph slips into the chair. So much more theatre than back in her day, behind the false wall and white curtain. Delph watches the woman through the mirror as she chats non-stop about highlighting, contouring, and other new terminology that Delph is just discovering, thanks to YouTubers and their easy-to-follow directions. The matte look Delph remembers wearing, shine being the ultimate faux pas, expired pretty much when Delph stopped wearing make-up, the bare face still separating her from the girl who spent every second experimenting. A true artist, Mother Moon had said the day she painted her as a butterfly, had kept it on for as long as she possibly could, long after the Wellsend parade, which she'd overdressed and over-drank for as usual.

Thin brows are also so over, which is sad because Delph never had big bushy ones to begin with, and no skill on earth can create the bold look that's trending now, especially in Essex. No, Delph tells the assistant, she doesn't bother with make-up unless she's really going out, but she never stopped her skin care. Little housekeeping tricks meant it's been possible to luck out with Aldi's range, and because it did the job, Delph didn't mind scrimping.

Nonetheless, it's a long way from her red Clarins suit.

Mandy the MUA chats, and Delph happily chats back when she can, when she's not holding herself frozen while Mandy paints her lips, trying not to breathe too heavy with her so very close to her face.

Delph's so detached from her reflection, Mandy needs to nudge her into looking. 'So, what do you think?'

Delph stares and stares. At her Kardashian sculpting, the Disney princess eyes.

'The palette's on special ...' Drifting off, Mandy grabs

the fixing spray from her apron, like she's drawing pistols in the Wild West. Delph shuts her eyes as Mandy mists her up. 'There.'

'What's that you're using?' It glows, refreshes, the fine mist setting the look.

'This? Fixing spray. Magic. I can go clubbing all night and my slap don't budge an inch.'

'I'll take it,' Delph says.

'The fixing spray, or the palette?'

Delph smiles, and that too is somehow more dazzling, in her old-new made-up face. 'Everything you used – I'd like to buy please.' Despite her better nature, Delph can't stop staring, struck by the woman in the mirror, the let's-not-beat-around-the-bush-fucking-knock-out – with *seven thousand pounds* to boot, n'all. 'The brushes too.' Her hair looks wrong now, flat and tired, so she scoops it into a high bun and, praise Kelly, Michelle and Beyoncé, Delphine Tennyson is officially back in the room. A glow-up two decades too late.

But here we are.

She makes several more stops around the beauty hall. L'Occitane for hand cream, Clinique for their 7 Day Scrub, and Clarin's for the biggest-sized beauty flash balm they do.

It had always been Delph's dream to be a make-up artist; she'd always loved making up Mother Moon's face – any face, in fact, that she could get her hands on. Even Sol's, which was a good way of dictating her own, their similar length of eyelid, the right width of liner to compliment the shape in one perfect feline swoop of black, which seemed to make the brownness of their eyes more luscious than before. It set her apart, as a liquid flick has for many over the decades, Ariana Grande doing a fine job of keeping the torch of the cat-eye burning brightly, passed as a classic from generation to generation, and became her masterstroke. Delph's thing. Delph's look.

Back at the fragrances, on the way out the door, she finds her eyes naturally aligning with the cologne she once saved and saved for, before she was ever a Clarins girl. Without thinking, she sprays without restraint, her purchases dangling from her wrists, and for the first time in a long time feels more connected to herself.

Yeah, materialism; it is connection all the same.

The short walk home has Delph feeling like she's in a music video. Just ahead, some man about her age cursing over the parking ticket on his dash, clocks her and double-takes, dropping his keys on the floor with a giant grin Delph doesn't realize at first is for her. Instead of heading straight up to the flat, she pops to the shop, treating herself to a box of Maltesers. As she stands in the queue, eyeing up the wine refrigerators, she spots Geena, helping herself to a frosted bottle of rosé. Spotting her back, Geena does her own double-take.

'Er, what the fuck happened?'

'Turns out I was Nora's lucky charm,' Delph smiles. 'We played another game and won. So, I treated myself.'

'I always miss the best bits.' Overwhelmed by the big bout of FOMO, Geena notices the Maltesers, glaring at the box like it's an enemy. 'Please tell me you're not going upstairs with just them for company.'

'And Graham Norton.'

'I should've pushed you off last week.' It's clear Geena instantly regrets saying it. 'Look. It's been a great day, right? Well, why stop here? Come on, our girls are out having fun, and so should we.' She is born temptation. 'You know you want to.'

'I dread thinking what you'd be like if you were a man.'

'Babe, I'd be king.' She tilts her head, bats her lashes. 'Come on. I've an Uber on the way. I'll even schedule one for later. No walking in the dark. On my life.'

Delph self-serves her box of chocolates, as Geena rolls her eyes. 'I really thought I had you.'

'You did,' says Delph, 'but I can't go to your gran's empty-handed.'

In the Uber, Delph thinks she ought to get Geena's gran some flowers as well. 'Let's be dropped at that M&S. I can dash in there quick.'

And as they hop out, clicking across the road to the shop, Delph notices another Uber employee, this time on a bicycle, who comes to a stop right in front of them.

'Delphine Tennyson, up in my ends. You're talking the stuff of dreams, now.' It is Lenny, the scotch bonnet from work.

'Ubering as well – don't you ever sleep?' Delph asks him, as Lenny gives her that smile, which would give even the most sworn off hot flushes.

'Not if I can help it,' he says, leaving Delph empty of any sensible reply.

No words. Just connection.

'Oh my days, who's he?' Geena's head snap-swivels like the possessed, watching Lenny push off up the road. 'You almost made him crash. Poor hot youth tingaling.' She laughs, big and bold, the same girl she's always been. 'Where the hell have you been hiding?'

Behind a monster. And a ghost.

Yet neither of them, now Delph's facing herself, have ever truly been real.

12

TWO FOR JOY

Butterfield Estate, Wellsend Grove, 2023

Moon's doing her favourite, stalking the M&S local for its late-night reductions. She could be a multi-flipping-millionaire, and still nothing would give her more pleasure than a Quiche Lorraine marked down to 50p. If she'd had more babies, another girl, she'd have liked a Lorraine. It might've helped Delph, having a sidekick. Silly, when she could barely manage the one – and besides, there was no father to sire another. Or any man, for that matter. Moon jumps, startled by her own loud chuckling. Christ, is she smiling? She touches her face to check. Lord, it's true.

As Moon thinks about it, she realizes there's never been a time in her life when she wasn't first looking out for somebody else: Ma, then Janie . . .

Never had a chance to know her standalone self, never got

that moment of becoming. Her childhood shit simply mor-
phed into a different kind of child shit. Like when Delph, at
last, began sleeping through the night, and Moon would leave
her home alone to slip off to the pub.

Earlier, just the same as then, Moon had that same feeling,
the same all-encompassing need to get out, to get as high as
she could. Insomnia's a fucker, and so is the past, back bleeding into the here and now. It's becoming more about how to
facilitate the act, the correct opportunism, which is another
feeling of old.

Moon uses binoculars to spy on the shop, which though
unnecessary adds a little fun to the moment. M&S is new,
still shocking, on the corner of the road opposite. Back in
the day, it was a newsagent, housing all manner of business
pursuits; from knocking shops to drug dens, the target of
many a late-night break in; glass smashing, dogs losing the
plot and car alarm dramatics, long over with by the time the
police arrived, because it happened with regularity.

A Spar, even a Tesco Extra, would've been the more obvious choice. M&S is a jewel in the shithole, a cut above, and
all the local scrotes, herself proudly included, can now bask
in the glow of food luxury, ripe for exploration and exploitation, which not only restores balance to Moon's rage against
capitalism, but also helps salve her consumerist guilt because
despite her affection for it, M&S is a corporation, still a dent
in her moral peace. True to form, Moon's worked her naughty
habit into something more legitimate. Bargain-hunting is
wily and clever, a kick in the teeth to the system. M&S arrived

just when she needed it most, when it was getting harder to get herself to the big shops. The mental effort. All the reminders of a life Moon had not moved on from yet didn't wish to be reminded of. M&S Local was a godsend.

M&S Local loathes Moon.

Kimberly's on till duty, and the instant Moon sees her reach for her roll of yellow stickers, she downs her binoculars and puts on her shoes, before checking out Kimberly's whereabouts one last time. Bingo. Grabbing her trolley, aptly named the Jazzi shopper, Moon hot-foots it across the empty road. The automatic doors swish open with a sigh like the sound of premature irritation, which becomes a real thing when Kimberly looks up at her new customer.

'No, there aren't any hazelnut yogurts,' Miss Kimberly smarty jobsworth informs her. 'Before you ask.'

'Coronation chicken?' Moon makes hopeful prayer hands, temporarily letting go of her shopper, which clatters to the ground, and yeah it does make a racket, but no one's here but her and power-trip Kimberly, who's shielding her ears like she's under siege. Moon ignores her, drifting up the chilled section, hopeful of half-price falafel bites.

The deli bits are her favourites. These days, instead of deep-frying, Moon indulges her culinary laziness with tiny tubs of potato salads, hummus, olives and feta cubes. And veg, already prepped, chopped and ready for dishing.

The falafel dream comes true. Two packs are on offer, but Moon only takes one, knows to share the love, especially with the less fortunate, a boundary she teeters the periphery of herself. But being on the breadline's not necessarily a one-way ticket to turkey twizzlers and Type 2 diabetes – because is there actually anything more insulting than rich bastards who think that because you've got fuck all, presumably you've also got no tastebuds? Only out of touch, overprivileged twats think like that.

Same as having class. Not the socially constructed monstrosity, but the kind of classiness that comes from within, minus the odious props of money and access and man-made privilege. Moon's had friends with fuck all going for them, hopeless since the day they were born, with more charm in their big toes than all those looking-down tosspots who think class can be bought or born into. Character too. Having some and being one are also different things, and though Moon's unclear where her ranty thoughts are taking her, all she does know is that even on her Universal Credit, she is more than entitled to a hazelnut yogurt and a pea and mint falafel, thank you very much.

'You can't leave that trolley there.' Jobsworth follows her along the aisle as Moon helps herself to the reduced buttered new potatoes that come in a handy microwaveable dish that she can repurpose into a bath for the garden robin.

Taking her time picking up the Jazzi shopper, Moon makes a point of avoiding the self-serve checkout, so that Kimberly stops what she's doing, huff-shuffling herself behind her till. 'We display on the outside what we are on the inside, you know,' Moon says, as Kimberly tuts, scanning through the potatoes, falafel, corned beef, and some yum-yums – a treat for Roche and Eden when they get back tomorrow – and if she's thinking of treating them, then she really—

'That's seven pounds five pence.' Moon hands over her money, mostly coins which Kimberly reluctantly begins counting out, as if this is the most tedious time she's ever had, with the world's number one most ridiculous woman. 'You're five pence short.'

If it weren't for the pleasure she takes in saying it, Moon might be able to hold her tongue. But Kimberly's self-satisfied look tips her over the edge; she empties her empty purse, along with her bag onto the conveyor belt, where's there's not a spare coin in sight. 'I bet you're an internet troll in your spare time.' Moon storms back to the refrigerators, picking up a tray of reduced party eggs that fit within budget. She snatches up her shopping, claiming back a fifty-pence piece. 'Put your corned beef away yourself,' she calls over her shoulder.

Moon's seeing ghosts. Or beautiful apparitions. She blinks, but Delph's still there, hurrying past on the pavement in front of Moon's house, pausing in her clicky little boots when she hears her mother. 'What you doing round my ends?' Ends. Moon tries on the young chat. Quite likes it.

It's the first thing Moon notices when Delph walks in after accepting a cuppa – 'but only a quick one, mind', promising to catch that Geena girl up, who's not changed a jot, still desperate to know she's still pokable – how Delph's wings are back, those lush black sweeps framing her eyes, more perfect, more striking than even before, as if they've been in hiding, like a prize car, some classic in the dark of a musty garage, beneath a dust sheet. And then one day, some random rare day for the hell of it, they get another moment in the sun.

There's a dangerous energy about her daughter that Moon can't decipher. Whether she's the one in danger, or if it's Delph that's in danger of causing pain to another. But if the other is Itsy . . . Ooh, he must be seething over her looking like that – and it is then when Moon remembers. He's not here, but in Jamaica, with the poor ill mother.

'You look . . .'

Delph bristles, rolling her eyes.

'Well don't take a compliment, then. Just hurry past without even ducking your head in, happy to go off visiting someone else's mother but not your own . . .'

'Tell me about my daughter.' Delph ignores her, as Moon unpacks her shopping bag, realizing she's accidently picked up the meat-free party eggs, which recharges her with irritation. She takes a moment, rubbing her temples, so keen to numb the world out, despite how flipping extraordinary it is seeing Delph exactly as she's begged the universe for years and years. Delph well and together again should be more than enough. Restored, from two tiny weeks out of his shadow. Moon watches her, popping party egg after party egg into her made up face, and notes everything. Delicately dainty, but without the nervousness – and present, like Delph's back in the room, at last. 'I only know about her life through bloody Instagram. Thank God for social media, eh?'

'She's stubborn. It's a beautiful trait, isn't it?'

They smile at each other.

'I'd not realized, till I saw you side by side, how very much she resembles you.' Delph's elegant hands reach up to pat Moon's cheekbones. 'She's lucky.'

Is she? Moon loathes that she took her father's looks. How she grew for noticing, like some strawberry Barbarella. And she was glad, despite the aggro it caused, that Delph was half of something so contrasting, so polar to her own genetics. Moon thought she'd shook off the look of him, but then Roche, those cheekbones all over again, the eyes, long and turned at the corner, the same tiger eye amber too. Perhaps it's why Moon understands Roche, because she's built from the same elements, their deep fire fury matching on the inside too. That anger at the world. Defiant. Alpha. Roche will never come second to some second-rate twat trying to claim her. Ever. Snap, again.

But Delph is not like them. She didn't grow in a vat of toxic masculinity. Moon might be accepting of her many maternal incompetences, but there's no way she could ever be accused of being a meek little mouse of a mother.

Mouse Mum. Mouse Mum. Freed from its cage, the name chases round her brain.

'Are you all right, Mum?' Delph asks, kindly enough, but this is always how her soft prying starts. She'll be asking: 'You are taking your pills, aren't you?'

'We've already done this. But I'll have some of your magic beans if you're sharing. Going round in a bloody magical makeover with that girl, who come to think of it I never did trust much.' Moon's eyes narrow. 'Watch yourself.'

Delph stands, disappointed. 'I'll head off.'

'Oh, not yet . . .' Dismayed, Moon's prickliness has gone too far. 'Could you just do my eyes up, quick.' Thinking on her feet, she lies. 'I've a Zoom soon, anyway.'

'A Zoom?'

'What's so amusing about that? I'm so up on the tech these days, I'd give Bill Cosby a run for his money.'

'What the hell?' Delph frowns, disapprovingly.

'Gates. You know I meant Bill Gates. Look, it's an online meditation. Go on love, make my eyes up, like you used to.' She dashes off, returning seconds later with Roche's over-spill make-up that didn't make the cut for Camden. 'I'm sure she won't mind.' Moon reads the label of an eyeshadow. 'Revolution.' She smiles. 'I'll have some of that. And look who's come to see you.'

'Mister Cat.' Delph's face lifts at the sight of him, and as he weaves around her calves, she strokes his head, most lovingly. 'You don't look a day older.'

'Funny that.'

Delph gives her mother a look. Gives in. 'Sit down then, quick.'

Like dear spirit creature Mister Cat, time has by no means ravaged Moon either, yet she wonders if Delph feels as she touches her face, how it speeds up, if she can tell that her mother does not contain the same strength as the old days. Lack of sleep is a torture, the same as mirrors become because of it. And then the vices, and if it ain't the vices it's the voices which won't stay buried. That no amount of meditation and holistic therapy has ever helped her truly let go of. But how can anyone help when Moon's never once said aloud the truth. When she's the rage of a fucking tsunami in her soul, battling against the very existence that she's fought her whole life to contain, to distance herself from – the only true friend, her safety net of being able to turn down the shit and bask in the sheer fucking glory of feeling nothing.

It is only a matter of time.

'You're beautiful, Mum.'

'What is beauty, Delphine – what's it really? Was it beautiful when I left you in the park so I could score? Was it beautiful when I forgot to pick you up from school? Flawed as fuck, me.' Moon folds her arms. 'You, too. Not as bad. But not enough. You made a good kid, showed her the worst example.'

Delph slams the brush down. 'Er, wasn't this about you?'

'I'm not the point.'

'Well, I think we're just about done.'

Watching Delph pack away, zipping up the bag in a hurry, an ache roars through Moon, like she's caught herself fraying but can't keep a hold of the strands. 'I'm sorry, I didn't mean it. On my heart, I wish I could've prevented all of it. Meeting that parasite of a human. Suffering that kind of hurt.' She swallows. 'Of losing Sol.'

'I didn't lose him. He's not at sea or stuck down the back of the sofa. He was taken. Snuffed out.' Licking her lips, Delph can't hide their tremble. 'I best get over to Geena. Before it gets—'

'Dark. I know.'

It is on the cusp of night as they say goodbye, on the lawn with the broken glass, still not cleared up from when Delph was here the last time.

'You know what I think, Mum? That it's better to have the hurt, because otherwise I'd never have known, would I? Good love.'

With a long sigh, Moon closes her eyes. 'Praise be you know the fucking difference. Dare I ask when His Highness is returning?'

'We're not joined at the bloody hip.' So she says. 'Hey, don't try hugging me – save that for your trees in the park.' Between them there's not exactly progress, but movement. Better than the silent gulf of absence before. That neither of them truly wanted. 'Stop. I'm too old.'

'Age-smage. Load of shit. I love you.'

She watches Delph walk down the street; the light of Moon's life, who only feels safe while it's bright. Not the fault of Sol's ending at all – but hers, having left Delph alone on so many nights, when the escapes were necessary, and temptation won.

As Delph turns the corner, Moon grabs her purse.

It feels like she's swallowed her heart, when she knocks for her old hook-up, pushing three twenties through the letterbox, with a mumbled request for the green. But that's not where it ends. In the chemists, Moon details Delph's long labour, the 9lb breached baby (six-pound caesarean birth), the decades of care work on her feet (three months, failed probationary period), the back that never got better, how she's suffering the agony of another slipped disc, all while looking after her granddaughter, with no time to get to the doctors. And the mega dose co-codamol and codeine are handed over, the usual warnings dispensed about how to take them, when Moon has her own recipe, the final component a bottle of vodka. At home, she finds her old jar, nestled in hiding at the back of the oven that never gets used, and stashes the lot – apart, of course, from what she sets aside for immediate consumption.

Look now, though. She could run a masterclass on serenity. Cosy in her home-alone ganja bubble, where nothing bad can touch her ever again.

*

FORTUNE'S ALWAYS HIDING

Tanners Grove, 1980

The house party's hot, crowded to silly levels; too many people, too many thoughts, which drown and overpower Joy's own. She'll need days in her own company to get over this, wishes she had some sort of mental barrier, a way to shut out other's feelings sometimes. Joy chooses the garden instead, finds a man out there having a quiet beer, his profile turned to absorb the evening light, a profile that feels achingly familiar. From this distance, he is the most serene creation. And he must feel her watching him, because he turns and smiles.

'It's a beautiful evening,' *he says.*

'It is.' *Joy steps from the back door and onto the grass.* 'It really is.'

'The moon comes and goes, and no one truly takes her in.' *He gestures to the sky before turning to Joy properly.* 'Having the sky for company is good for the soul.' *He rises from the chair, and Joy's surprised to find that he only just reaches her shoulder.* 'You don't remember me at all, do you? Kingsley.' *Kingsley points to his smiling face.* 'Kingsley Smallman.' *Not the little boy who once dropped*

203

his toy, no, but the brother, the brief playmate a few years older than Joy. 'Small world . . .'

Kingsley's hands clasp around hers; warm and firm, beautiful too. His brown eyes twinkle in the last of the light, which settles the flutter of worry within her. 'It gets a bit much, doesn't it?' He nods at the house. 'Loud people, loud music.' As Joy sits with him, and the remains of the day slips into evening, and the smell from next door's supper wafts over and stirs their hunger, and neither of them have any drinks left, they still don't move, at all. And in the chilled dusk, warmed by Kingsley's jacket, in the company of just him and the sky and the talk of his family, Joy reckons this might just be enough happiness, after all.

It's in the stars, meant to be, all the way, into bed.

A moment. How she should've learnt.

Mouse Mum appears around the living-room doorframe, her forehead folded into tiers of worry, as she fastens and unfastens her housecoat of padded, pale blue. When it's worn through, she'll replace it with something near as dammit the same. Routine is the last remaining safety net, holding her nerves together. 'Are you sure you got the day right, love?'

'Yes, Ma,' Joy says to her mother, identical now to Grandma, thirty years sooner, but with the same vanished, depleted look.

'Maybe it's him with the day wrong, then.'

All evening, Joy refuses to leave the window. Knows the moment she takes her eyes off the street, turning back into the house, is the moment the hope is over.

Hasn't she always known that the only person she can trust is herself? Which is hard, when Joy can't even do that a lot of the time. How daft, letting fantasy cloud the obvious. Because why would Joy matter to Kingsley, when she doesn't matter to anyone. Not even Janie, or else why would she keep trying to leave her?

For weeks, Joy imagines that Kingsley might still knock; that even if he's lost her number he'll know where to find her. It's only when she sees him heading into the Wimpy, with a hugely pregnant woman with a babe already in arms, that Joy admits what's happened – and what's happening to herself. How she has tits made of fire and all Ma's cooking sends her retching unbecomingly.

Yet Joy's main thought is her father. How this shuts the door so very firmly on any great escape. She remembers the dream, of horticultural college, when she'd found the courage to ask – though it was met by her classmates with much mockery – were there courses to learn about plants? That she might be a florist, with her own always thriving flower stall, somewhere sunny and bohemian, where she'd live in flip flops and a big floppy hat, making her floral creations.

All the things Dad said, realized into reality. All that made Joy falter, like demons in waiting around every hopeful turn, obstacles gatekeeping a world brighter than Joy could ever truly be herself. He was right. Joy's world, already shrunk, shrinks further; just another second-class-working-class citizen, hands and womb tied by accident . . .

. . . and solely her problem.

13

FIRESTARTER

Butterfield Estate, Wellsend Grove, 2023

Roche's on a roll, showing Nan picture after picture. Of her, of Eden, the sights, the lock, the market; Simbi doing her thing, looking totes increds on stage – though most of them are too hazy to get the vibe from if you hadn't actually been there, and she's glad she recorded a few moments too, because there's no taking away the vibe from the voice ...

'Can you type in cures for stubborn bloody daughters while you're lost to that thing,' Nan mutters, all prickly, leaving Roche unsure if she's pleased to see her back. It's as if she and Eden have walked into a parallel universe. Nan's house, which was beginning to feel like home if she's truthful, now feels alien, like there's a strange force repelling her away, no longer a welcoming hot mess. 'I can't believe you've not spoken to her,' Moon adds crossly.

'How d'you know?' Roche stops thumbing through her London pics.

'She popped in yesterday. Didn't stay long mind, was off out with your mother, actually.' Nan offers Eden a yum-yum, which Eden, because she's polite like that, takes even though they're both full of Maccers, their last treat and all they could afford as they returned to the rainy reality of Wellsend.

'I bet I'm still in mad trouble for swerving Gran's birthday.' Picking up her bag, Eden checks her phone. 'I better be off.'

'Er, rewind, please. Mum was here?'

'She was,' states Moon. 'And you'd never have recognized her.'

'Oh. My. Days,' Eden says, nudging Roche with her phone. 'Talk about glowing up, showing up. I ain't never seen Mama Dee like this before.'

It is conflicting, how Roche goes from proud admiration to fury that Mum's not messaged since the evening she cancelled, yet here she is, with Geena's fam, sociable, partying – actually alive. That she's been here for tea and fucking yum-yums, which were probably edible yesterday, Eden still working through hers, that's become more like a brick.

And there's Mum again, this time on Geena's feed at bloody bingo – looking much more like her mother in their selfie, granted – but she's never even been to bingo, and they've been asked plenty. Why now. Why now without her? 'Who's she think she is?' says Roche, offended but not, unsure as to how she should be feeling.

'What's your problem?' Eden's confused. 'She looks

fantastic. I thought your mum cutting loose was what you always wanted?'

'Delph unchained,' chips in Moon.

'Yeah, man,' Eden laughs, high-fiving her. 'I like it.'

'I don't even know that person,' says Roche, knowing she sounds a tit.

'You sound just like His Highness,' Nan tuts, offhand, returning to the mountain of bedding she's dragged from her room to the sofa. Like a hamster would, she rearranges, making herself a fresh nook to nest down into. With her back to both girls, she sparks up, which doesn't set off the smoke alarm, vanished now Roche realizes, looking for it, just a perfectly clean circle on the kitchen ceiling. Maybe the cleanest spot in the house.

No, Nan's not herself, and Roche can't help feeling responsible because she knows in her gut that this is linked to the box of secrets, in the same certain way she knew Mum would be a no-show when she invited her to dinner. And for a moment she's swamped with immense guilt, having gaslit, left, right and bloody centre.

'Am I not allowed to criticise her, then?' Roche says, unable to leave it. 'That makes me a bully like him?' She pauses. 'I think you should take it back.'

'It stinks in here. Have either of you trod in anything?' Irritated, Nan sniffs around, even checking the fridge as they both check their trainers, hoping to find anything that might explain away this unpleasantness of feeling. Because that's how it all feels, suddenly. Like they've soured. The altered energy is visceral, yet Roche can't help but be drawn to it, hungry to know more; the opposite of Nan, allergic to her own past.

Stomping up the corridor, Nan sniffer-dogs at the bedrooms, chucking her own open, before holding back, unwilling to even set her hand on Roche's door. It is amazing to witness, but true, how it's now physically impossible for Nan to even try entering, as if some poltergeist presence repels her away.

Perhaps this is the reality of life with Nan, rather than the vague kid remembrances of her before, the bold nonconformity Roche fell for.

And maybe, maybe she should've just listened to what Mum tried telling her.

Roche looks up at the sound of Nan's voice, arriving ahead of her before she peeks her head cautiously around the door, waving Roche's overspill make-up bag but not entering the room. 'I said to your mum, "Revolution" – that's some on-point branding, right?'

And it's then that Nan notices the string, her red string, peeking out from beneath Roche's puffa coat. From her spot on the bed, Roche watches Nan's face grey as she turns her eyes from the poorly bloody hidden box to her, and then back again. Breaking her own rule, she moves across the room as if hesitant to uncover, to confirm her suspicions. It is jolting when she shoves the clothes rail, letting it wheel across the floor, before moving the coat, which reveals the string properly, loose and clearly disturbed.

'Fucking little ...' Moon trails off, beginning to shake. Proper tremors.

Pulling her feet towards her body, Roche makes herself small. Why did she leave Eden to tidy up earlier? That girl was born messy. But Roche knows it's her fault. 'I was just ... clearing up.' Unsure what to add next, Roche slowly approaches her, placing a hand on her shoulder.

'Oh, Nan. I've never felt such, such ...' Roche's voice trails off in a tremble too. But how to describe all those terrible feelings? Sadness. Fear. Desperation. Desolation. Emotions where even the creativity, the pictures and the poems, spell sadness.

'I take you in and you gut me open,' Nan spits through barred teeth, exploding real rage into Roche's face. 'What respect. What appreciation! To think I've been on your side all this time – when you ain't got the foggiest what it is to live in a proper bloody nightmare. A hell on earth homelife. With your concerts, and your clubs, and your little mate upstairs.'

'But Nan ... I told you.' Roche bites her lip.

'You told me enough to get the sympathy going. Poor lonely old bag, stuff her full of nonsense and she'll roll over for a belly rub.' Despite them being to the brim full of tears, Moon's eyes are hard. And wild.

'I never thought that. I never would.' Roche is hurt. 'I've loved being here – I love—'

'So much love that you ...' Moon grabs Roche's hands in hers, and pushing them into her stomach, drags them up, navel to throat. Flinging Roche's hands back at her in disgust, she parts her kaftan, revealing the grey marl joggers and sleep bra. 'Find what you were looking for when you dredged my guts, did you? Want another look?'

'It was the string. When you said about the red – I was . . . curious.'

'*Curious,*' Moon repeats, in a girly kid voice. She flies from the room, flinging the back door open, which hits the worktop with such ferocity the glass panel shatters into rubble. Alarmed by what's next, Roche listens to Nan's movements before she marches back in, snatching up the box, which she holds her face away from, like it contains something decayed and contagious, before taking it into the garden.

Smoke catches in Roche's nostrils.

Like a bonfire.

Before Moon has the chance to come back, Roche makes a dash for the other box, not as heavy as the last. Shunting open the window, she drops it into the evergreen just below, which doesn't hide it in the slightest, a big cardboard corner sticking out of the bush. As her heart thumps sickly, Roche manages to close the window, distancing herself just as Nan comes back.

She shifts the other bin bags. Frantically does it again. 'Where's the other one?' Face to face, there's a singularity about the way she stares into Roche, like she's beaming a torch around a darkened room, into all the corners where things might be hiding.

'What other one?' Roche says, revolted by herself. 'Perhaps, perhaps . . . I've not come across it yet—' The slap comes sharp and unexpected. Instantly chastising. Nan's hand, striking, *striking* her face. It turns her head. It literally turns her fucking

EVA VERDE

head. There's a sizzling in her fingers, a reflex tension, as
Roche fights the desire to find posture and blindly retaliate.
Roche isn't down at mixed martials. And she'd never, ever hit
her nan. Even if she struck her again.

Grabbing Roche's nail polish remover, Nan flies out again,
followed by Roche, who hovers in the background as the
mediocre bits of card that are beginning to smoke turn into
a fucking fireball that whooshes into the sky, taking Joy's
past with it.

She is mesmerizing, terrifying, as she throws handful
after handful without examination into the flames, before
dumping the whole box unceremoniously into her barbecue,
whispering inaudible words as she closes her eyes, reaching
to the sky. A piece of caught paper lands at Roche's feet and
she's quick to stamp it out.

'. . . to tell you this way, but there was just no saving her, Joy. I
hope you know and can remember, not to blame your sister for her
choices – blame me instead. For putting her through a childhood
like that . . .'

But it's pointless even trying to figure out the meaning,
this scrap of sorry on old, singed paper, which Roche has no
understanding of.

Nan's eyes glitter up into the night sky, mascara streaming,
a mythical creature, a goddess of extreme emotions – the fire
and her hair and the bottomless secrets within her, vast and
never-ending. Her own universe. If only she could call on the
powers of the earth to save her. If only Roche knew what it
was that went so wrong so she could help. Or try somehow

to make things right. Both sound flimsy. Too logical. Oh, for a logical life.

Nan is strong. Roche is stronger, yet she still lets her grandmother shake her, allowing the rage she knows isn't about her. Yet it's only when she wails, almost collapsing into Roche's arms, helpless, fragile and scared, that Roche's nerve bottoms out too.

Then the ranting. On and on and on and on; it's so hard, staying engaged, connected, keeping awake, as Nan retreads the same circular pattern around the dying flames of her cremated history. The open backdoor has allowed wafts of black smoke to enter, Nan's past not gone but redistributed, returned to the house. Tired, her arse sore from keeping her distance perched on the edge of a raised bed, Roche rises, wiggling herself loose again, before keeping to the fence, avoiding her nan as she heads back into the house.

Sweeping up the glass from the broken door, Roche feels a hand on her shoulder. Nan looks down at her, not quite serene, but . . . slack. Slack-faced, slack-limbed, like it's a miracle she's on her feet.

'Whatever you've done with that other box.' It is a different sort of haunting that moves between them. 'You best hope for all our sakes that it's safe.'

Tonight, in the strange empty hours she's rarely ever been awake to witness, it's now Roche who cannot sleep. Because if she's vague enough and sharp enough and open enough, she can just make out the silhouettes as they pass, soft-edged, human-shaped, through the jar space shadow of her bedroom door. Protectors. Ancestors.

Dangers?

Roche is more than sad and sorry; she's a little girl again. Hates that she's crying, how easily the emotions crash from being so on top of the world at her concert last night to this, so very lost, now that her hungry curiosity's been discovered. That it's over. That she's let Nan down. How stupid to think that she knew better than her mother.

To think of Mum as a kid, so vulnerable here. In the absence of anger, Roche's steeped in protectiveness. It'd be nice to see her.

To share.

This scary night.

14

BETTER THINGS

Esplanade Point, Wellsend South, 2023

Delph spends her third consecutive Saturday alone, doing the housework in her dressing gown, Queen Mary J Blige's *My Life* blaring at top volume, which makes Geena text from upstairs:

Jeez, I thought I woke up in 1996.

Her asparagus spear is now a centimetre. Strong and dark green. She blows it a kiss.

It's doing Delph good to wake up in Roche's bed, as close as she can get, though she knows she's well, having seen the pictures of both girls at their concert, so beautiful and happy – and blessed that tech gives her a window to check in from their stalemate distance. The front door buzzes, and Delph finds a mountain of ASOS packages, which until yesterday had been sitting in her favourites. She's never spent hundreds on herself before.

It's like a selfish solo Christmas as she sorts through the bags, experimenting, posing in front of the mirror. Her clothes had looked a bit . . . safe. Dull. Items she never had to think about: skinny jeans and tees, a lover of the full-length cardigan, that's felt like she's walking around in a comfort blanket. Lots of the new stuff reminds her of what she'd worn in the nineties. How are the nineties back? How's it possible to find herself in the second phase of a trend she's seen already – which surely must mean Delph's officially ancient.

But she's not feeling it. Certainly not yesterday, the kindnesses of the old crowd, the unknown newbies too. A world out there she can step right into. Untethered.

She's hungry. Once upon a time, Delph loved eggs, lived on them every single way, every single day. Even when eating was hardest, an egg was sometimes manageable. But apparently they made the flat smell, contaminating the other cups and plates; eating them not worth the aftermath of Itsy's egg-phobic grievances. The apologies. Sorry for a smell. Sorry when something's out of place. Sorry when a sugar's forgotten from a cuppa, all to avoid any upset, keeping his mood just right. Puffing him up and smoothing him out through the bossy-boots days and bossier nights. Slipping into his life and his rules unquestioningly. Glad for not having to think at all.

But eggs are what she fancies. In her new clothes, a lemon-coloured playsuit and denim jacket, paired with white Air Forces, she pulls her hair into a bun, using her new cat-eye sunglasses as a hair band, and with a proper actual spring in her trainers, grabs her bag to hit the supermarket.

Delph takes the longer route through the park, feeling clear and positive because of it. The trees are full-on green as the sun casts kaleidoscopic patterns through the leaves and onto the tarmac. A disco ball of a journey.

She buys the things she loves. Strawberry mousses, black grapes, a baguette just put out in the bakery basket, and though she's not big on bread, the smell and the warm squish of it changes her mind. Then the big free-range eggs. A box of twelve is scary, so Delph chooses the priciest six-pack. And a box of Solero lollies on offer.

At almost midday, with a huge chunk of day ahead of her, Delph cuts back through the courtyard, taking the path home beneath a shield of greenery as she stuffs her mouth with the still-warm fluff of bread, the deliciousness of it soothing all the sore rawness she'd taken as permanent.

And with each mouthful of paradise, she feels a little bit freer.

Until she's home.

'I'm an orphan.' Itsy's own boiled egg baldness has been neglected. A shadow of hair maps his head in an old man pattern. High behind the ears, missing from the crown and hairline. His posture's off too. Even the slump in the way he's holding himself is noticeable.

Delph stands with her back against the closed front door, both her throat and the flat shrinking as she swallows her bready mouthful, while he watches from the kitchen doorway. The last room they were in together before he left.

'Proper full of it she was. Then quick as dammit, gone. The girls are still there. I was getting in the way of the arrangements. Felt so useless, I left them to it.' The sad deep thrum of his voice stirs something gutting in Delph. Things buried, still too tender to think for long upon. Crossing the room to her, his sobs condense against her neck.

'Oh, love, I wish you'd said. I could've met you at the airport, I could've ...' But there are no answers. None that'll soothe, anyway. 'And there you were, thinking she was on the mend. I am sorry.'

'Loss. It's a wicked thing.' Itsy breaks away, and cuffing his nose, smiles, brows raising in response to her new-old look, but that's all the acknowledgement he gives it. 'We didn't part well, Delph.' He strokes her face. 'Crossed my mind we might've been over.'

Before Delph rushes out all the usual assurances, she catches herself. Couldn't this be her chance? Here, in this normal enough atmosphere, is a glimpse of escape. Leaving the kitchen, he comes back with a bouquet of flowers, made mostly of thirsty carnations. The price is still on the cellophane.

'People say shit, do shit. It doesn't mean anything. Not when they love each other.' His grip grows a little tighter on her arms. 'I love you, Delphine. It's why I get so ...'

'I know.' Delph treats him with gentle cotton ball hands, providing all she knows will help. Sky sports news with the window open a fraction, his giant navy mug of tea. Three pieces of Hovis white, lightly toasted and cut in triangles with a heated tin of beans, generously peppered. Two KitKats for pud. His washing on as he bathes, now fed and rested. And though she comforts, it is autopilot behaviour. Delph's heart is just not in it. But he's sad and kind – and he is trying. What else is left to do but return to their bedroom?

It doesn't even feel like her bedroom anymore.

Emerging from the bathroom in his burgundy kimono, Itsy chats words about fixing drinks, suggesting, as Delph predicted, that she might like to freshen up too.

Maybe, if they hadn't had this gap apart. Maybe, if she hadn't once known eager gentle togetherness, the short walk to their bedroom mightn't feel so destroying. She'd never known intimacy with anybody before Sol, and certainly only Itsy after. As if she learnt purely, instinctively, together, until there was Itsy's way. His prowess, the sole initiator, never allowing any sort of autonomy. Whenever Delph's heard that clapped-out phrase, lie back and think of England, she'd think how true – how she didn't fit the narrative, but it worked all the fucking same. Lie back, pretend you're doing some grand duty. For some underserving, entitled little place/penis, delete as appropriate. And does her raw throat now return by itself, or is it Itsy's hand that does it? His touch never fun nor truly exciting, which never fails to add to his keenness, the dominating edge never not missing from their coupling. Administered by him.

219

After, and naked, Delph shuts herself in the bathroom, pushing open the window. Perched on the fridge-cold toilet seat, she slowly smokes two Bensons back-to-back. Itsy might be asleep when she returns, attempts at a round two averted.

Waking in the early hours, Delph's woozy. Bursting upright, straight from sleeping, she promptly vomits down her nightshirt.

'Stay put,' Itsy says, ready to assist. 'I'll get a cloth.' He opens and closes the kitchen drawers as if he doesn't know where anything lives anymore, till at last he comes back with a tea towel, which a grateful Delph accepts, still trying to catch her breath.

'You did only have the one rum last night?' he jokes, rubbing her back, knowing she's not a big drinker. 'Or have you got something else to tell me?'

Delph flies to the bathroom, clutching at the seat as more awful retching rips through her body. Then, whatever it was is out of her. Trembling, Delph slumps against the radiator, and wiping her mouth with loo roll, kicks the door shut.

She'd have bet her own head that there was no one on the planet who could've been any more militant about taking their contraceptives than she was. And it had been the cherry on top of the shock positive test – being part of the small per cent who falls preggers while on the pill.

Brushing her teeth, Delph considers events. How awful she's felt – even the suicidal thoughts. She's always had them if she's truly honest, but never with the convincing ferocity of the other evening – and certainly never since the first time the feeling took her, which had her almost believing it was the best thing, unable to imagine going on without Sol. Delph locks the bathroom door before she switches on the shower, considering the troubling possibility that she might've been through some sort of cold turkey experience. The dreams she's had since stopping the contraceptives; the night sweats. Though it makes for uneasy thinking, she was only taking the pill, hardly high dependency medication.

Just an ineffective little pill, which Itsy was always most insistent that she take correctly, just like she'd been.

Delph feels suddenly nervous.

'Why you been sleeping in Roche's?' Itsy asks, behind the closed door. 'How is the girl, anyway?'

In the mirror, Delph watches herself brushing her teeth. 'Really well,' she says, before she finds herself adding, 'considering the company.'

Are we really back to this? Delph's wholesome ride of progress chucks her off without warning, landing her dizzy in her own strange vomit.

'Missed her more than you missed me, I'm sure,' he says, coming full circle, like being in permanent competition with Delph's daughter or Delph's dead is normal behaviour.

But not everything is about him. Climbing into the shower, Delph feels better by the second. Cleansed.

Clear again.

Not everything has come full circle. That docile acceptance of his rulings certainly needs tweaking, but there's not the usual fog eating away at the periphery of Delph's vision, that's kept her blinkered, unable to ever take much in.

Why is she suddenly so clear?

If she were in a police drama, there'd be some handy specimen container at hand to collect her puke in, before calling in the favour of a friend of a friend who works in a toxicology lab. Then she'd know for certain.

Is it too baffling a notion? That Itsy might've been medicating her, perhaps even swapping her contraceptives – contraceptives that failed – with something else?

*

HOUSEWIVES' FAVOURITE

Esplanade Point, 2016

Telly can be so revealing. Watching The One Show, *harmless early-evening talk television, it's announced that some old nineties boyband Mum once loved with a passion have regrouped, introduced by the host as 'housewives' favourites'.*

'Is that right? Housewives' favourites?' Eyeing up his on-screen rivals, Itsy had then glanced at Delph.

The truth is always hidden in the silence before Roche's mother speaks. Yet, caught in the fun, in the memory of remembering herself when this band were cool and perhaps so was she, Mum answered unthinkingly, all doe-eyed at the telly, 'That's too volatile a question for a man like you.'

Not enough time will ever pass for Roche to forget Itsy's questioning, his mental gymnastics of pretending he didn't care, when it couldn't be more obvious that he did. And watching him move so seamlessly between angry-insulted-soothing-seducing in ninety-odd seconds, a new fire was born in her.

When she'd asked for a story before bed, her mother's hesitancy stuck in Roche's head; she could tell Mum wanted nothing more than to remain in the safety of her daughter's vision. But Itsy's hand was on her back, steering her mother towards their own bedroom, with nothing kind or gentle in the gesture.

'What you mollycoddlin' the girl for? She's plenty old enough to read her own books.' Itsy kissed his teeth, looked to Roche again, a handy device at first, a prop to prove what a wholesome fatherly catch he was, who quickly became an inconvenience. Like a tiny judging police officer living under his roof, bed and board. What should've been the lounge, they made the main bedroom – an attempt at protecting Roche from the thin walls, the night sounds of the creaking bed, Itsy's heavy breathing in the room full of another version of her mother's silence.

As Roche grows out of her night terrors, she grows less inclined to be alone with Itsy. His odd, cloud-of-a-depression personality, inertia and ego make for difficult company.

'It's just the way we are, Roche. Stuck in our gender roles, I suppose,' her mother continues excusing, doing everything for him, sitting down last at mealtimes as he makes comments about how she's like a fly that can't settle. Should a condiment be forgotten, a spoon to dole them out with, she's up, fast as. Same at night, if there's a draught; if Itsy's thirsty, hungry, bored. Up she gets. Made of air. Mum of nothing. Nothing to ever hold onto.

All Roche keeps inside, she lets explode every Monday and Thursday at mixed martials, always with the same determination. A dedicated, one-track, brilliant yet absent focus, which has made every teacher and trainer question her reasons for doing it, for *choosing fighting as her passion. But Roche's medals and successes keep the questions in their heads. Questions that could cloud her potential to become their Olympian – which could be a way of escaping Estuary Essex. Home's draining, like it's holding her back. A weak mother, just like her mother's mother, Moon – a slave to the weed and the booze, without a responsible bone in her body – but at least Nan wasn't a doormat. At least there was that.*

Funny, how whenever Roche's nan enters their thoughts, it likely bodes her re-entry into their sphere, the small circle of just them that Itsy's fought to keep to himself, knowing how easily the cracks from outside influence form. Roche is a problem enough. She is teenage too soon, got too fucking bold. And mouthy. When did girls start behaving like men? Itsy's noticed, and he's looked plenty, and just don't get it; can't get to grips with Roche being a potential knockout honey, and choosing to look as she does. Shapeless sportswear – like she's a member of Run-DMC. The tight bun knot on top of her head that pulls her fierce and feline. She's none of her mother's soft features; Roche is angles, cheekbones – like the nan.

Roche is fifteen the first time a policeman drops her home with a warning. She kicks off at their front door, shaking off the limp filth hand on her shoulder. Such a try-hard rozzer. Failing. Why is it every man, instead of surprising her, confirms the belief that they're all just twats? 'It's why you're in the job, innit? No power in real life. You got to pick on underage girls defending themselves. Cos we all look so much older, so much more guilty. I couldn't possibly be pure. Or decent. Take your try-hard hands off me, you sweat.'

'Watch your mouth,' is all he says, banging on the door again, and Roche knows it won't open if Itsy's there. He'll be quivering in

some doorway, always shit scared of the police. To be fair, though . . .
'*So.*' *Police boy gives Roche the side-eye, flicking up and down the tallness of her, more kid gangly, now he's noticed and he's honest.* '*You're telling me you're under sixteen?*'

'*Should've asked that before you went manhandling me to my own front door. You should've also asked what that idiot did to deserve it.*'

'*Violence doesn't—*' *police-boy started, and Roche kissed her teeth. Yet her anger, like always, is scared anger, and she doesn't know if it's convincing. Last thing she wants is police-boy thinking she's weak. But there's been a significant tone change – and not on her part, for once. More like a teacher at their wit's end, rather than someone he was moments ago close to handcuffing.*

'*Look. Either my mum's boyfriend is HIDING.*' *She drops suddenly, to shout it through the letterbox, and in the distant kitchen Roche thinks she sees a shadow of movement, a retreat into the recesses of the room.* '*Or he's not here. Either way, I'm a fifteen-year-old girl, and you mate are in the wrong.*'

But so is she, and when the Dojo says her behaviour means she must find another club, Roche's Olympic dreams of escape are dashed.

'*Probably for the best, anyways,*' *Itsy says, like he knew all along it'd never happen.* '*Men like women to look like women, not Popeye, you get me?*' *He shakes his head like he just can't make sense of it.* '*Muscles on a Doris shouldn't even be allowed to be a ting.*'

As a backlash against his chronic sexism, Roche ups her reading diet, leaving bell hooks and Audre Lorde around the flat. '*Keep your dyke books away from me,*' *Itsy says, on the day there is no coming* back from. *The word he's chosen confirms his spying, confirms the eyes in the cracks of doors and the sense of eavesdropping that's hung heavy for far too long. Her private life is none of his business. Not that she gives a shit much, but it's Eden. She just ain't ready for the publicity.*

And, until she is, they're trapped.

Roche can't tell her mother about the names he calls her, now he's stepped up his game on the insult front, so quick to put her down. So quick to make a big deal over her sexuality, like it's a new toy he's no sign of getting bored of.

'Probably them books that done it,' he says, like an explanation's required for Roche to feel the feelings she felt since before she even fucking knew what feels were. 'Lesbians. All so angry, cos they're hungry.' He grabs a handful of bollock as he scratches his cock, far too prominent, floating loose in the baggiest of joggers. Roche thinks of covering her eyes, but then how would she know if he involved his rank genitalia with his insults . . . and good God, how many wrongs are in that sentence?

Something sparks, right at the stem of her spine, a primal warning, like back from the days of cavepeople fleeing wild beasts; fight or flight or gut truth instinct – that if it didn't happen now, something very badly wrong would happen soon, as it dawns on her that maybe Mum isn't the only person he's capable of hurting.

Just as Ms Angelou says in one of Roche's books: 'When someone shows you who they are . . .'

15

DECOUPLING POUR UN(E)

Wellsend South, 2023

Delph's always rather touched by how quickly Lenny seeks her out, how he never pries; speaking just enough for the both of them. As they wait for the canteen's snack machine to deliver Lenny his salt and vinegar, he tells Delph the same story he shares most Saturdays on their breaks together: how every big night out on the town should always start with Whitney in the shower.

'You know the order of events,' he says, knowing she now does. 'Before I get all lathered up, I'll be hooking up my playlist. Starting with a few big numbers to belt out in the shower like "Run to You", "The Greatest Love of All". Holding off on the ultimates "I Have Nothing" and "Saving All My Love for You" till I'm back, clean and flexing in the mirror, singing into my hairbrush.'

'Which is much kinder on your canerows than using it properly.' Delph nibbles her cereal bar, pleased to find it takes away her slight headache, which is more down to hunger than anything sinister, but proof that the weird vomiting spell is still far from forgotten.

Work's a relief, a separation, which sits strangely considering how fast she's fallen back into being Old Delph at home – but only on the outside. Her sickness brought a temporary return to those feelings from before, the gentle padded monotony of existing without thinking, and in hindsight – and of course, with her growing suspicions – nothing about it feels right.

Because she knows better now than to ignore her gut truth, and the nagging, nagging question: has it truly been Delph's depression, grief, her own sad mind, holding her captive all this time . . .

Or him?

Delph probes her memories for the red flags, recalling the things they ate and drank on the evening of his return, and all the other moments of opportunity where Itsy could've medicated her with something of his own choosing.

Because it would explain so much.

The notion rings wildly through her thoughts. To think it possible. To simply even think Itsy capable. It's exactly the thing her and Roche might've watched on Netflix. And Delph's done her googling; recognizing the symptoms of substance withdrawal, the dulled sense of self and strange absence of hunger – not the same sickliness as early pregnancy, yet not proper illness-illness either; the sad limp body that'd need rest and fluids and recuperation.

Now, even if it's a cup of tea, Delph's not touching anything Itsy prepares.

'There's something, I don't know, different about you. Fire in your eyes,' Lenny says, a little bolder than usual, leaning in a little closer, and though it's half on her lips to mention Itsy, to remind him of her other half, Delph doesn't want to be a half person any longer. 'Reckon I could fan them flames even bigger, you know,' he adds.

'I could be your mum, cheeky.'

'You totally couldn't.' Laughing, he begins to skim his phone. Lenny turns the screen, revealing a photo of a smiling woman with a short afro and glasses. A statement necklace of giant beads in the same satsuma shade as her jumper rest on her tits, accentuating their largeness. She's got to be sixty. 'She had us late. I'm the baby, the last chance. The reason why I'm studying more than I'm showering with my Whitney. All dreams are pinned on me.'

'Her dreams or your dreams?'

'Ooh, that's deep.' Lenny presses a hand to his chest as if injured. 'Too deep for breaktime, anyhow. We should meet up properly. Just us.'

'Your place or mine?' Delph smarts back, using a little of her out of character adrenaline. Is it Nature Valley's sugar hit? Or is it Lenny? And why can't her brain return to habit, and just be quiet for a bit, to let herself simply enjoy this man's attention. Because, much as she hates to admit it, the shadow of Itsy remains in every thought, like the dark behind the curtain. How she's his. How she'll always be his. God forbid she ever, ever forgets it.

'Oh, now we're talking.' Lenny looks dreamlike towards the ceiling, batting his lashes. They don't move, remaining thick in their perfect curl, looping back as if into his lids, as he strokes the back of his hand down Delph's arm, so gently she can barely feel it. 'I mean it. I'd love to take you out. Anywhere you wanted.'

Delph looks up, into the same block pattern of suspended ceiling. But she doesn't answer.

And Lenny doesn't push.

'If I could go anywhere,' she says, after a bit, 'it'd be to the Chelsea Flower Show. Never been properly. Just make do with the telly. I bloody love that week.'

Lenny looks at her, surprised. 'My mum likes gardening.'

'There, you see? Old birds like flowers.'

'Age is nothing, man.'

Says everyone. When they're young and it doesn't matter.

There's twenty minutes of work left, but even from the till Delph can see Itsy's Astra Estate through the shop window, though she can't make him out inside it. It's perturbing, wondering if he's there or watching her from elsewhere. Because she does feel watched.

'Thought I'd save your legs. Take you out.'

'Out?' Delph, damp from running through the rainy car park, gets into Itsy's car. He's dry, clearly been sat there all the time, looking like proper efforts been made too. 'We don't have to.' But it's hard to react negatively as he kisses her face and drives her to their local Harvester.

Itsy pulls out a chair for Delph to sit down. It silently glides through the plush ruby-coloured carpet, and she thanks him, moving herself nearer to the table. Sitting opposite, Itsy accepts a menu from the waitress. 'Can I have a pint of – sorry, love. What would you like to drink?'

Itsy studies her as she smiles into the menu. There's not a single thing that looks as if she might've been struggling without him. Neither has she that gaunt look that's always quick to present – usually the first sign she's suffering. No, she has thrived in his absence, becoming almost a stranger. The hair off her face, up in that big high bun, has done a great job of shaking off a few years, and she's wearing nothing he recognizes.

'House dry white, please.'

'I'll have the same,' Itsy says, sure to catch her eye. 'Apparently, stimulating the same taste buds at the same time creates togetherness.' He straightens his knife and fork. 'In couples.' Chuckling, he clears his throat. 'It was something like that, anyway. Some tipsy suit in the cab yesterday, chatting about reuniting with his partner – it was something along those lines.' He smiles, rubs his lips. 'Sometimes you don't realize what's in front of you. What you got. Like when you have a head cold and can't believe you ever took breathing for granted.' There is love poetry in there somewhere. 'That a new top?' He tries again.

'Er, yeah.' Delph feels a bit shifty. 'Thank you.' Her splurge is down to Geena's winning generosity after a Godfather pitcher too many. Delph will never in a million years tell him any differently.

'The mixed grill for me,' Itsy says to the waitress.

'And I'll have the chargrilled halloumi, please.'

'And how's the world of B&Q?' Itsy asks a little later, taking a sip of the dribble of wine that's been poured for him to try. He nods agreeably, the involuntary grimace suggesting a different story.

Delph talks carefully around his chosen subject, playing work as the necessary evil, as Itsy nods politely, the dappled shadows from the wall lights playing on his head, smooth and bald again now, and all the better for it – but that's where the positives end. Grieving's left him at half-mast; he's tired, sad around the eyes. Clean, but not fresh-looking. Despite all his obvious efforts.

'Cheers,' Delph says. 'This is nice.'

'So are you.' He clinks her glass. 'And, are you all right now?' Itsy's hesitant, like it's taken him till now to figure out how to approach the subject. 'After the sick thing?'

'Weird, wasn't it?' Delph offers a little shudder before smiling innocently, better at masking herself than Itsy, because he does look away – a sly glance to the right, before looking back at her. She bookmarks the moment, to think back on later. 'Maybe I should go to the doctor's.'

'You were only there five minutes ago,' he says, perhaps a little too dismissively, for he adds, 'You think it's linked, that bleeding ting and this? Because honestly if life's taught me anything lately, it's that I need you.' Reaching across the table, Itsy squeezes her hand. 'Reckon you might be pregnant?'

'You know I'm on the pill.' Delph studies him, covertly, like a Big Brother body language expert might. 'Besides, we've—'

'A little one of our own might be nice. Proof of our love. Our commitment.' For a moment he's gentle, soft-eyed, terrifically handsome, a flash of Idris about him. 'Or a wedding.'

'That's a jump.'

'I'm just thinking y'know, of something nice, something meaningful and positive after Jamaica. I think Mum would've liked that. I wish you could've met . . .'

'I know, love.' Delph keeps her voice gentle, can't help but try to comfort him. 'I think I should go back to the doctor's. In the meantime, you'll just have to cover your friend up. Getting down on one knee's one thing, but there'll be no rugrats for us.'

Itsy looks at her, embarrassed. 'I really am sorry. For chucking all your memories. For behaving the way I sometimes do.' He sighs. 'I don't know what you did, bewitched me or something. I never was a jealous man.' He takes both her hands this time, all slick sincerity, his voice full of the smoothness of old, that did lure, attract, win Delph in the end. When he seemed the most natural option. Before she knew better. 'But I do understand now. Grief. We've got a common bond.'

And even though Delph's gracious, and smiles like she

believes him, it's as though she's grown a shell, and no amount of sorry will ever crack it.

The instant they're home, he is on her, as if the flip comment about no babies sparks the return to practising for the non-event, and Delph again finds herself pandering to his desires, cancelling her own, because his wants/happiness/opinion continues to hold the most value.

What's happening between them chimes with when Delph did her back in; the two spinal discs that lost their juices, rubbing dryly at each other without any lubricated barrier to keep her moving comfortably, until they both prolapsed like felled trees, trapping a nerve she still can't spell, which ran from her hip to her foot. For months, standing had been her only source of relief – that, or dangling her heels over the top step of the hallway staircase, to elongate the muscle and break the cramp she'd often leap from her bed in pain with. Cramp so debilitating it could've floored her, could've sent her down that staircase, concrete, steep, uncompromisingly dangerous. Certainly fatal. And, somewhere in the agony, Delph found pleasure in the potential for such an accident. Life would all be over and done with, and not for a second her fault.

Because who is she, anyway? Just Itsy's small, insignificant supporting act.

He wants her. So here she is.

They're not even in the bedroom, when he tugs her top apart, his mouth on her skin consuming as he suckles her breasts; the sight of them in the hallway mirror jarring.

235

Delph impossibly passive. Her face set, not in fear exactly. But resignation.

She is a consenting adult.

She's lying to herself. Itsy twitches his brows towards the bedroom and Delph silently complies, lays beneath him, thinking of all the words that describe this.

Succumb. Submit. Surrender.

He scrambles from his clothes with a hand in her knickers, his fingers offering as much excitement as a regular flow tampon. Grabbing his wrist, Delph shakes her head. 'Kiss me,' she asks instead, a quiet request that slows his haste, a bewildered look as he does as he is told for once. But the tenderness is fleeting. Soon he is glazed, frenzied again – yet, as he objectifies, positions, exposes, nothing stirs in his pants.

'It's . . .' Delph tries, as he clamps his hand over her mouth, fingers barring her nose as he rolls his play-doh dick across her thigh, and ferocious nausea again rises from the pit of her guts to take hold of her. '. . . too much.' For a few clarifying seconds, it's like the world's gone 'Boo!' and Delph's all at once part of it; connected again, alive, sharing its breaths as she shoves at Itsy's crushing weight with all she's got.

Delph has the urge, the gut need, to run. To flee this place; race till everything aches and there's no air left in her. Past the flats, the shops, leaving behind her a blur of streetlights. To run beyond this town and all she's ever known, escaping every darkness she's forever kept too close.

Itsy rolls onto his back. Won't meet her eyes. And Delph

wonders if this is her body's way of protecting her. From him. Because her mind's not strong enough.

Not yet.

But she can't carry on like this.

Delph chooses to sleep in Roche's room, and Itsy makes no attempt to stop her. Silently, she shuts the door, and flicking on the reading spotlight looks around. Bare, but for the border of daisies Delph hand-drew and painted herself. And the pinboard. Enormous, leaning against the back wall, full of quotes and photos and all Roche's ephemeral baggage. Good baggage. Achievements. Fun.

Big capitals, enhanced by fluorescent highlighter, stand out from the chaos.

'Each time a woman stands up for herself, without knowing it possibly, without claiming it, she stands up for all women.' Maya Angelou.

Delph touches the words. Lets her fingers drift to a photograph, Roche and Eden, hanging off each other in bright yellow netball bibs, giving V signs to the camera, Roche with her mouth open, chewing gum showing.

Not giving

one shit.

16

FURY

Wellsend, 2023

Roche's biggest problem, apparently, what she's reminded of each time Mr Treason hands an essay back to her, is not presenting the flip side of the argument at least half as impressively as her opinion, her refusal to offer a fair examination of both sides.

Which mightn't sound half so bad, if it wasn't coming from him. 'A one-track brilliant mind is still an ignorant mind, Miss Barclay,' he says, all sanctimonious like. 'You may adorn your arguments with all the references in the universe – you may even be right, but that's no good if you can't present a balanced debate.'

Throughout her A-levels Roche has watched Mr Treason, how he provokes a certain bristle from a certain minority section of the classroom, while exercising his authoritative cards.

Usually, Roche would hold in her own bristle by ignoring his button-pushing condescension, but he is proper vexing her right now. She's tired. After the never-ending night with Nan, Roche's mind is not to be trusted or relied on. Today's exactly the sort of day where she might flip and regret it.

Boy, does Roche regret opening that box. Regrets even bloody looking at it, that her nosiness – because that's all it was really – has put such doubt in Nan's heart that it's even made her question Roche's love, ffs. Because she does love her nan. And never for one second did she want to hurt her. She was just too caught up to realize that Nan's life must've been so painful to deal with, that her only coping mechanism was to bind it away.

So, why keep it at all? Maybe for the same reason people keep the bullets that injured but didn't kill them. Physical proof. Of their survival.

Nan shouldn't have swung for her, though. Roche's face grimaces as she remembers not just the whack, but the reverberating stun it left . . .

'Are you with us, Miss Barclay? All your new grand plans for Edinburgh, I'd have thought you'd be trying to tie up your weaknesses.'

Treason's classroom smells of actual toilet. Or is it him who stinks – Roche never can work it out. All she knows is that fleeing after double history is like sticking her face in flowers. Treason. Weird name. No significant other. Stinks of piss and damp washing. And pot and kettle too, because debate ain't even in his vocabulary – Treason must always be right.

239

Which is why he's stood over her desk now, fully exploiting her unusually tired and quiet disposition to really ram home his verbal point.

'You mustn't presume your supporting argument is the correct one.' His face makes Roche think of a snowman, wide and undefined, his features lumps of charcoal thrown like darts at a board, slightly missing the targets. A true NPC in and out of the classroom. Forgettable. But here, during periods 4 and 5, he is King. 'Everything's debateable,' he adds smugly.

'Can't you go and have another operation, or something? Because I really miss that substitute – I can't be the only one thinking it.' Glancing around the room, Roche acknowledges her audience, noting the hungry look of potential carnage as her fellow students shift in their seats.

Treason's lips tighten into a dog's bum. 'Your attitude has grown progressively worse this past term, Miss Barclay.'

'Does it stink as much as you do?'

'How dare …' Turning pink, he chews his own mouth shut again.

'With respect, sir, some things ain't up for debate. Slavery, for example – there ain't one positive. Acid attacks. Nuclear weapons. Child Abduction. Cancer. Shall I go on, bruv?'

'You vile, facetious …' The button-pushing condescension has now officially slipped.

'Says Mr Faecal Smelling.' Roche gets several laughs, as someone behind her claps. 'Serial Killers. Adolf Hitler. What, am I supposed to write a thousand words on Adolf's evil acts, then chat some nonsense about how he was dog lover too, just for balance? What sort of logic, sir, you've got to ask yourself.' She's calm as, creating condescending bristles of her own because old Treason looks ready to pop. 'If this is education, then this is a waste of my time.'

'Yet it affords you the choice of heading off to university?'

It's the smirk. His upper-handed little side smirk.

'Troubling, what turns some people on.'

'What did you—'

Roche stands. Keeping her hands on the desk, she leans forward to stare the teacher in the face. 'I said, it is very troubling what turns some people on.'

'You disgusting—'

'And your prejudices shouldn't afflict certain members of this class.'

Roche gets a 'whoop' and a 'you tell him, sister' as a rumble of hands bang on the desk. She ain't ashamed to admit that it all feels bloody fantastic.

'I'm calling security.' If hate and outrage had a baby, it would look like Treason's face, twisted red and fucking throbbing with all that'd end his chosen vocation if he were to say it aloud. He storms to his desk, swirling back with his face still a-twitching to shake his walkie-talkie at Roche. 'I don't need to tell you how this outburst affects your future.'

'Like I'd ever ask you for a reference?' Roche says calmly, holding her fingers together in a delicate loose sort of prayer hands. 'And please know, for future reference, that it's been a real fight to stay awake in your lessons, so maybe, y'know, a refresher course might be good for you.'

But Mr Treason's not listening; he's barking words into his walkie-talkie, words that inflame, like he knows they will.

'The function, the very serious function of racism, is distraction.' Roche speaks over him, clear and beautiful. 'It keeps you from doing your work. It keeps you explaining, over and over again, your reason for being. There will always be one more thing.' She loves how the room is quiet, the focus absolutely on her, the command of every word she recites from Ms Morrison to this fool, who is quite frankly lost. Lost if he ever thinks she'll pen an essay on the positives of Empire. Twat.

He gawps like a goldfish at her roaring radiance, while the class erupts into cheers, and Treason totally loses his shit, barking at her to get out.

'Roche, babe, your plans seriously need another rethink. You know you'd make one hot as hell barrister. I was proper flushing back there.' Catching her up and checking that no one's about, Eden holds Roche's face in her hands and kisses her. 'You wiped the floor, proper. Prick.'

'Hot? Is that seriously all you think about?' Roche, so far, has kept a lid on the regret levels; there is nothing she just said to that fool of a teacher that she'd take back. Yet already she can feel how she's heading for friction; friction she'll wish she hadn't started. 'Fuck it.' Roche crumples up her face. 'I'm off, though I'm probably in for more agg from Nan the second I'm home too. *Home*. What jokes.'

'Your nan feels robbed. You went noseying without her permission.'

'It was you who didn't hide the bloody box!'

'Bitch, please.' Eden sticks her hand in Roche's face. 'Take some ownership. Because did you ever stop to think what you'd have done if you'd actually discovered something mega? Like, if you'd found out who Mama Dee's dad was – some address type ting. You were just gonna sit on that, were you – or go all investigative journo and track him down yourself? You ain't superwoman. You ain't even eighteen, fam. And it ain't like you're even talking to your hot mum.'

'Don't call her that.'

Eden shakes her head. 'I love you and everything, but babe, you are not perfect. And Racist Prick Treason does have a point – you do lack the distinct ability to ever put yourself in anybody else's shoes. You're right. You need to get away. And you need to grow up.'

'What the fuck?'

'You've people all around you who see you, but you're too busy picking holes in it all and missing the very basic point that you've a mum and a nan that love your fucking socks off. Three weeks. Three more weeks at school and we're done here. Can't you just chill for once? Because what honestly is the point of causing unnecessary fuss now?'

'Because where has being quiet ever got me?' Keeping her mouth shut to protect the people she loves has taken a monumental toll on Roche these past few months. 'I am sick

243

of being quiet. I've never caused no fuss.' Roche throws over her shoulder, spitefully: 'And I'm sick of everyone.'

Eden's face snaps into her neck, affronted. 'Oh.' She reads Roche's look, with a small hurt jut of her chin. 'That includes me.'

The worst thing is, Roche don't even mean it. She watches Eden turn on her heels, without another word or another look.

But Roche just doesn't have the room in her head, or the life skills right now, to call her back.

'In a hurry?' Mr Senior Leadership rounds the corner of the corridor, urging Roche to stop.

'Dentist, innit,' she lies, but he's an okay one – a non-threatening presence around the school, who isn't a total prick.

'I was buzzed by Mr Treason.'

'You know he's a prize penis, don't you?'

He smiles, like he does know. 'So, stop feeding the monster. Look, if you want to avoid going on report, you might want to have a think about having a little chat with the counsellor – now, don't look at me like that. What's the good in one of our brightest falling so close to the finish line?' He smiles again, encouragingly, in what Roche imagines is a dad-like sort of way.

Odd, how Roche now thinks of Itsy; the only remotely paternal time they ever spent together was when he taught her how to play poker, a distraction during the antsy build-up towards Christmas, Roche a coiled spring in human form, anticipating the celebrations. She learnt quickly, and after the first few times of Itsy pretending to lose, there was a rare light-heartedness between them as they played properly, which made Roche happy to be exactly where she was.

Until she wasn't. Because Roche can't forget the person he is.

Where does she want to be now? Where exactly does she belong?

Her adrenalin bottoms out, leaving Roche anchorless. And alone.

'I've got to go.' Roche doesn't wait for any sort of permission. 'I'll, I'll think about the counselling.' Before there's a chance to answer, Roche starts into a run, heading for the school gates.

Briefly, she contemplates the gym but has none of her kit; the early efforts of doing her own laundry having dropped considerably in Roche's priorities lately. Her phone's also tempting in her pocket, to call Mum, because Eden's right – what point is Roche even making now really, by remaining stubborn and playing with her feelings. And if this strange time apart has done anything at all, it's revealed her mother in a way Roche might've never noticed, living in the proximity they had – as a woman in her own right; a singular person who just so happened to be her mother, and also, as a kid, with a whole heap of real responsibility that she should never ever have been burdened with.

Yet neither should Roche have been. She frowns down into the pavement, as Public Enemy blasts through her headphones, filling her with energy, the rage enough for ten people. Her heart thumps along to the beat, 'Rebel Without a Pause' resonating deep in the pit of her chest. Yes, it is time to get away from other people's problems and other people's shit and invest in some shit of her own. Kiss this dump goodbye ...

Roche comes to a stop in the middle of the pavement. Across the road is Itsy's car. Shiny and clearly back in use, in the car park of McDonald's.

It's not until she's doing it, dragging her keys along the bodywork, the frenzied, jabbing denting into his bonnet, not till her headphones come loose and the car alarm's screaming, and she's being pulled off by some bulldog in a black bomber jacket, and there's blue flashing lights – and when are there ever pigs just passing?

Flat white in one hand, a hot apple pie in the other, Itsy watches through the window as Roche is walked towards a police car. Yet it is only when Itsy stays put, instead of heading over to diffuse the situation, to say something like, 'Hey, that's my crazy kind-of daughter, and I'll take it from here,' that her actions start to register.

17

The Healing

Butterfield Estate, Wellsend Grove, 2023

Moon's not expecting whoop-whoop the sound-a da police, but the bastard's knocked his siren, asserting his powerful presence, which has her up gawping out of the window in seconds. After chipping out her spliff first, of course. And as the car stops outside the house, she reaches for her stash, putting it right at the back of the oven, thanking her lucky stars that she's buying rather than growing it. Plants would be an immediate giveaway, she thinks, Febrezing the room with one hand, the other jammed on the fly spray, before turning the aerosols on herself. Even if her home doesn't smell of weed, it's highly likely she might.

It takes a moment of readjustment to forget the head-fuckery – being still wounded, and still carrying a lot of awkwardness and feelings of shame over hitting Roche – and to properly take in the sight of her in the back seat of the police car, staring out of the window straight at her, hard as nails. Scared fucking shitless, really. Guilt tingles down Moon's arms and into her fingers as she tries absorbing the poor love's nerves, but noting her own temper rising, checks herself. It is Moon's angry resistance that's got her in trouble before. That always gets her into trouble.

Moon's heckles climb like the hairs on a paranoid dog, as the policeman escorts Roche to the door. 'Can I help you?' she asks him, all nice, smoothing her hair, a hand on her soft flesh hip as they stand on her glass-crunch lawn. She is an invisible woman, a messy eccentric. Nothing to be wary of. Just a nice, mature white lady on loads of drugs. Standard practice. Standard way of life. Nothing to fucking see here.

'You're Nan?' Moon loathes the incredulity of his tone. Like it's impossible to be a multicoloured family in twenty-fucking-twenty-three. Are people still living under rocks? And when are there ever actual breathing police in the vicinity, anyway? Moon thought they evaporated at about the same time as the local station shut down. Moon knows, despite the shit she's forever had to wade through, that being white means she's lucky. Lord, how quickly she grew embarrassed of that luck. How she thought her heart knew bigotry until she had a small brown child of her own, knocking off any last remnants of a white lens.

'. . . vandalising a parked vehicle,' Moon catches, his tone monotonous and his feet too tiny to inspire any sort of fear now he's here on her doorstep. 'A car belonging to a . . .' The police officer looks down at his notebook. 'A Mr Geoffrey—'

'Itsy's car, Nan,' Roche interrupts him. 'And not half so bad as he's making it sound.' They never do listen, always prefer the versions they pluck from the sky to suit the current mood, and themselves.

God this girl, so many rough edges in her. As much as Moon wants to rub them down, she admires them. Doubts anyone would want to come up against them. Roche's young adult fearlessness makes Moon swell with pride, but she can see beneath it, the most fragile tremor. A reminder, too, that Moon's supposed to be the fucking adult in the room.

There's no getting away from the fact Moon's behaved abominably. So, she'd better get this situation sorted, begin putting things right between them quick, because the idea of returning to their estrangement, the mere thought of more years apart in conflict, inspires real anguish.

Moon clears her throat. 'Has he reported this . . . incident himself?'

'Not yet. We caught the young lady in the act. The car was unattended.'

'He wasn't in the car. But he was there, Nan. I saw him in the McDonald's window. Fucking lech.' It drops from her lips unprompted, as if her brain hasn't even had to fashion it.

'You know she isn't eighteen,' Moon tells him, though her eyes stay locked on Roche.

'Miss Barclay's made me very aware of that fact, yes. So, she's here with a warning – in a few months this would've been a very different story.' He gives Moon a godlike smile. All powerful. Deeply pathetic. 'Unless Mr Pearson makes a report, I'll leave you to discipline your granddaughter – without a caution.' He rocks his little heels back and forth, notices the crunch in the grass. 'Now. No more trouble, young lady.'

But in Moon's mind, he's vanished before he's even climbed back into his metal box and gone. Quiet now, Moon takes Roche gently indoors, and sitting her on the sofa relights her spliff with trembling hands. 'It's for me back, all right.'

'I'm not judging.'

'No? Not like your mother.'

'Mum shouldn't be the judge of anything.' Roche's eyes fill with tears. 'I miss her.'

'Well,' Moon's smoke dangles from her lip to clap her hands, 'that is a breakthrough.'

'How? When I fucking hate him. He's back, in case you hadn't guessed.'

'Oh, love.'

'So, there can't be any big breakthrough. Not with him in the way again.' She slumps back into the cushions, to stare at the ceiling. 'You know, he'd ask me all the time why I didn't have a boyfriend.' She raises her head, looking down the sofa at Moon, giving herself a double chin. 'I said I never wanted one, especially if they were anything like him.' Closing her eyes tight, she folds her arms. 'He'd get proper uppity. So bloody easy to dent his pride, yet I'd always be wary to, unless Mum was about – and that sounds weird, doesn't it?'

Roche's words bring with them an involuntary shudder,

like someone's walked over Moon's grave, bringing waves of repetition beneath her skin. And it's like Roche's cork has popped, because all that's been beneath the surface erupts into the open.

Moon's joining dots, but they're still loose, and accusations are only accusations – plus, Roche's not actually said that he's touched her. Though Moon checks herself to remember that fact, it's not as if she wasn't witness to the crawly claiming way Itsy would behave around Delph when they very first met. And it is the same feeling of unsettledness all over again.

'He's always a hungry mess around Eden's mum too. Embarrassing. The worst type of flirt when he gives her a lift and stuff, y'know.'

'Yeah, well, we all know how he loves that damsel shit.' Moon could let rip, have a proper bitching field day, but she contains it; knows this must be Roche's stage. Because Moon can tell, by the rare tears and trembling hands, that it's going to be a job for Roche to say whatever she needs to. And Moon knows also, in her gut truth, that it's imperative she does.

God, how she'd kill (preferably Itsy) for a double vodka right now. Or a bottle.

'And Eden's so polite round him. It gets on my nerves a bit. Yes, Mr Pearson. No, Mr Pearson. He don't deserve no manners.' Roche swallows. 'Sometimes ... there's things I can't even tell her. Which is hard because I tell her everything.'

Moon remembers taking them on the bus to the Lido when they were smaller, watching them jump in and out of the water all day long, their skin covered in sparkles, the sun turning them browner and browner. Eden was never any trouble, whether you took her swimming or for a turn to the corner shop for a tube of Smarties. The pair of them happy, contented little souls. 'What can't you tell her?' Moon manages, keen for air, as it dawns on her she's been holding her breath. Thumbs aching, she slices down their edges with the nail of another. She inhales, holds for five, resetting herself.

'Where do I start, Nan?' Roche sighs, and before Moon knows it, she's swiped the jar, beginning to assemble her own smoke. Expertly. 'It's more . . . more what I felt he could've done. It's hard to explain. He's caveman by default; I don't like it, but I get that. But then I started noticing how he looked at Eden.' Blushing, she rushes on. 'And of course, why wouldn't you, she's perfect – but he's like, like fucking old, man.' She hands a perfectly rolled joint to Moon, who immediately lights it off her stub to offer it back. Refusing it, Roche shakes her head. 'And she's, well . . . he's known her from small. Like me.' Taking her time, she swallows, as Moon gently takes her hand, flinching at first from the contact. 'I'm so sorry.'

Roche breathes in, sniffling, before letting it all come out, good and proper. 'The day I came here.' High-pitched and emotional, she cuffs her nose. 'I'd got home from school, even had my key in the lock and I just . . . everything inside me told me not to go in. I know, God, I know that don't make sense – and honestly, it's not like he's ever actually touched me.' At this Moon's shoulders sag. 'Same as I can't explain how I know the truth behind the act he plays for Mum – but on my life, I do.'

'Oh, baby, all of it makes all the sense in the world.' Just as Moon suspected, Roche too holds the gut truth. Their line and sensitivities continue.

Essex witches. Still being persecuted.

'It's called instinct. Don't you ever, ever ignore it.'

'What else can I do? Nothing changes anything. Not even actually leaving. So, I keep my mouth shut.' Roche sighs, defeated. 'Just like he says.' And everything remains bound by silence.

Here Moon remains, too. Still keeping her own. And for a flicker of a moment, she's glad that fucking box went up in smoke. What was it for anyway? But even without it, he's always there, monstrous as ever in her thoughts, the father she tried so hard to escape from but never can, because his behaviours seed deep and spread just as prolific in so many other men. How many rounds and reinventions will it take for the Tennyson women to heal even a little? But they are not special, and this is nothing new; the whole world hurts alongside them, both behind closed doors and on the news every bastard day, unimaginable crimes against women.

If only they were unimaginable.

Much as Moon wants to lift the lid and speak from the soul, which might go some way to explaining why she just can't ever get anything right, why her brain takes flight when things feel too much, why she's fearless but not and so she runs from being grown . . .

. . . because the growing happened too fucking soon.

Where did Joy go?

'. . . Sometimes I feel so lost, so ungrounded, I forget myself. Forget that my actions have consequences.' Roche flings her arms around Moon's neck. 'I'm so glad I got to come here. And I am so sorry I went through your things. I should've known better. And I've no excuse for that.'

It takes maturity, but Moon just about manages. 'I'd probably have done the same.' She would. And it's not difficult to see from Roche's perspective really, searching for the answers she truly desires, understanding the roots to make sense of her own growth. To make sense of herself. 'And as I said, you are welcome here, for as long as you want to stay.'

'Thank you. And thank you for forgiving me. I'm going to speak to Mum, move past this bad energy. It'd be terrible to go off to uni and still be at odds with each other.'

'Love, I guarantee that your mother, just like me, will always, always be open-armed for you.' Grabbing Roche by the shoulders, Moon looks her in the eye. 'You listened to your gut truth, and you did brilliantly. And you're more like me than you think. The good parts, anyway.'

'Oh, Nan, all your parts are good.' Roche kisses her face.

'Polluting you with this? Oh yeah, of course they are.' Moon holds aloft her ashtray; glad Roche didn't imbibe. Elders are supposed to condemn this shit, not blaze up the fucking gateway. 'And giving you a good wallop?'

'I deserved—'

'You stop that.' Moon holds her chin, makes sure Roche knows she means it. 'No one deserves that. And I am very sorry.' It is time to look forward. Forward is always better.

'We'll try again. Invite Delph to dinner. Minus that pile of wank. We could even ask Eden.'

'Yeah. Yeah, okay. Maybe not Eden, though.' For a fleeting moment, Roche looks troubled again. 'Keep it simples, yeah?'

'Simples it is. Now, I don't want you thinking about nothing but bonny Scotland, and that's an order.' It feels nice, being the grown-up. The safety net. The easer of troubles. 'Leave the rest to me.'

'Yes, Nan. I get you.'

With a raised brow, she looks down at the gone-out spliff. 'Quite a talent for rolling there, madam,' she says, ready to change the subject. For now, there'll be no more talk of the past, especially as a new, brighter light grows clearer, giving her brain cells a glow-up. Because she sees it now. Understands that she, Moon, has been The Intervention. The Protector. For one of the people she loves most in all the universe. And with that thought, her fighting spirit starts a fluttering recovery.

Moon is destiny's child, and this is all luck – where we're born, and to whom. Moon's luck's dipped and risen and troughed again, but she's found it's almost always better to look forwards. Because it's tiring, embarrassing, to still be clinging onto the same old story. The reasons for life not going the way it should've. Better suiting yourself, blocking all the bollocks with lovely green.

While weaving a little magic around her girls, of course.

18

ACTS OF RESISTANCE

Esplanade Point, Wellsend South, 2023

Delph's still suspicious, unsure how to prove anything at all, yet the hold Itsy's had, that she'd always adhered to, has evaporated into feeling as if she's about to jump out of a plane, an anticipation, as Roche's room continues to act as a sanctuary, a place of healing, a return to self. And a space to repair from him. The fracturing of their relationship, in much the same way as his absence had, makes everything gappy, airier; the claustrophobic edge of Itsy knowing her every movement feels more like a fucking fable by the day. But much headspace is needed for Delph to truly think back, to try and revisit when the real control started, to begin piecing it together.

His power. The unrelenting jealousy. And the other thing, that she'd deemed normal: his unfaltering attention. And how many years exactly, has Delph felt she was missing in action, her life blurred without meaning. Slow-mo functioning, without much feeling.

Outside Roche's room, the atmosphere's laced with the whiff of an ending. They're rubbing along so politely, Delph's built of static friction. Any sudden movement now might be biting point. Igniting point. And what then?

There'll be no putting that kind of fury away.

'You're leaving yourself vulnerable,' Itsy says this morning, scaring Delph into coming straight home instead of going out for the first time with her workmates. 'What you so set on proving your independence for? Didn't you hear about that perv the other night? Was on the local news. Some girl. Just walking home.' A rank move to use on the already traumatised. 'All they were talking about at the cab rank. You best be careful.'

Unbelievable, though, if he thinks it'll ever work again.

Plus, Delph's got the shoes now, the effortless flats that'll make her seem effortlessly stylish, the type who goes for drinks after work all the time. The flats will match her skinny jeans and new top, mustard bat-winged and off the shoulder – exactly her style. Earrings – her usual hoops, or her long ones on the bead string, which trail fluently until they graze her shoulders, stopping at the point of her hair. To impress.

Maybe.

'Perhaps you should do a test – just to make sure you ain't pg?' he tries again later, with a touch of concern, his voice warm with kindness, as he makes Delph a coffee that she won't drink. 'Can't be getting drunk if you're in the family way.'

How different life could've been, on the flip of things. How such a sad thing became her best decision. But there was never any moment, if she's honest, when she wasn't certain that the termination was absolutely the right thing. Was it not, in fact, the spark that set this off in the first place, this coming back to herself. This ... realization. Delph's growing belief that he might've been drugging her. Those small, bright-pink, innocent-looking pills, that she wished she hadn't flushed in such fury that morning of the two blue lines.

'I'm not. I know I'm not. Besides, we've not been like that since ...' Delph closes her eyes, turns her face towards the window, to the sun, as if scorching out their last proper intimacy. The marks he had to make before removing the handcuffs and leaving for Jamaica.

When life was as sunshiny as that beautiful island in his absence.

But Delph won't press pause on her life any longer.

'Haven't you some clever thesis you should be concentrating on?' Delph asks Lenny, his eyes like the bitterest chocolate, another set that could pass for her own. What is it about finding comfort in people who look like her, that brings the feeling of coming home, of understanding without explanation? The security of similarity and self-identification that a big family brings has always been absent for Delph, who instead got Mother Moon alone, the pale fiery woman who no one believed was her mother.

'You know what they say about being all work. But it's a shame there's no time for Whitney.' Lenny winks at her. 'You'll have to take me as I am. Shall we get the bus, meet the rest of them there?'

Delph hesitates. Thinks of Itsy. The threat that he might pop along to the pub and get to know her work buds himself, ignoring all the signs marking out their finish line.

'Unless, unless of course, your other half . . .'

It hangs in the air. Delph plucks at the challenge. 'You're a terrible influence,' she says, as they make their way upstairs, towards the back of the bus, dipping into the second from last row. Lenny slides in next to her, their thighs touching, and as they begin to kiss, Delph is neither sure who starts it nor why exactly now is the right time for it.

'My, aren't you the gifted one.' Delph disguises the flusters by sitting on her hands.

'I've been practising on the back of my hand for weeks, imagining you.' Lenny looks relaxed. At ease. And very, very pleased with himself.

'I've a list as tall as you of the reasons you shouldn't.'

'Oh, Delphine Tennyson,' he smiles, carefree and unbothered, like every ache and worry has melted in reverence to their sparkle. 'Instead of all that down shit, why don't you focus on the positives. Like sharing all your wisdom.'

'Oh yeah? What wisdom's that then?'

'Tell me everything,' he whispers against her mouth, 'that makes you happy.'

'I don't think you'd need any lessons for that.'

'My sister, she's out – I mean, she works. She's away with work and I'm flat-sitting. I don't suppose you . . .' He trails off. 'Do you . . . wanna come over?'

'Now?'

'I got her keys.' Lenny checks his watch, growing a little bit bashful. 'It's only early. We could hang out; I'll get you back to the pub in time for—' He stops, already not wanting to mention Itsy, or the likely fact she's on a curfew, which was only agreed to because it saved any further attempts to chip away at her evening. 'Your cab home.'

Delph thinks of Itsy's car in the place of this steamed-up back of a bus; its bright ordinariness against that silent airless box and wonders why on earth she considers resisting. Because she's had a stomach full of resisting.

The decision is made as the bus cruises past the pub – and the friends who'll get there, putting Delph and Lenny down as no-shows – transporting them instead all the way to Wellsend Grove. Butterfield Estate. Home turf for them both.

Wellsend South and Wellsend Grove reveal an imbalance between the haves and have nots. How one has the hospital, the better primary school, while the other has strings of betting shops. This journey across the city was what Delph missed most about seeing Mum. And life always felt better on the bus, letting it carry her. A chance to give Delph's legs a break and her mind a rest.

All these years without talking, as time unpreventably kept moving, because Itsy's wedge between them won.

But not forever.

A lady with a buggy dings the bell as the bus slows to stopping, Delph heading for the doors just behind Lenny, now standing on the pavement, hands on hips grinning, awaiting her descent. He takes both hands, helping her off, even though no help is really needed, and when he kisses her again, she's even less worried. She's already checked the faces of everyone on the bus for a scrap of recognition. They're safe.

'I hope tea and cheese on toast rocks your world,' Lenny tells her, as they half walk, half run, hand in hand in the stone's throw direction of his sisters – and nothing sounds more perfect.

Delph doesn't expect fireworks, vaginal explosions. She's learnt not to expect.

But she's surprised. Lenny's enthusiasm, his longing, is contagious. There's no need to kick against it, nothing to stop Delph rising to match it. No marriage to protect, no small family who'd be broken. No stern, ashamed parents or happy home she'd risk losing. Though secure, the flat has never felt like Delph's. But hurting Lenny must be avoided. This kind, gorgeous boy with a future far bigger than her. Delph doesn't want to become another Itsy.

Lenny must never regret her.

'You're beautiful, you know. Perfect.' It's all so earnest, his big eyes searching her face, before kissing her again, a trembling hesitation to start, him loosening her hair, little nibbles

261

across her mouth, chin, neck, the time he takes, patient caresses as Delph's thoughts slip like silk through her fingers.

Strange to be seduced at his sister's. With mugs of PG tips and Radio 6 low in the background. No Keith Sweat, old R&B and the dry routine of home. This is the keen, committed lovemaking that reminds Delph of the very old. But even those way back thoughts don't stick, don't sink Delph down for long, as Lenny leans back a little from her body, pulling his t-shirt off with one hand. He knows exactly what he's doing. That he's a masterpiece.

But he doesn't quite know her.

She kisses him hard, shifting herself to sit straddled across his lap. Not so dexterous as to remove her top with one hand, Delph can with her bra. His lips trace the contours of her nipples, and it is instinct when he lifts himself from the sofa to graze his crotch against hers – his hardness disorientating, as her want for him escalates.

'I'm ...' Why is it so difficult to say? 'Not on the pill.'

'That's all right. I'm a sensible, responsible man.' Lenny's hips raise again, grazing, scorching, before he stands, his jeans tent-poled as he does a little dance over to the stereo, turning the volume a fraction higher. From his jacket he retrieves a box of three condoms, cellophane intact. And his eyes don't leave hers.

Delph's skilled at creating her own climaxes. A scalding hot shower to leave her weak, then bed, immediately; Delph's fingers her personal excellence. Itsy's all about the prowess. The visual. She'd rather those unfulfilled moments than to ever dent his pride, learnt fast to make the right noises and pretend. And on the side, whenever she had any urge, she'd please herself. It's been too long coming, Delph knows, but there's not a single molecule left within her that wants a future with him. They are done, and there's freedom and fun without him – and there's Lenny, devouring her with such eagerness, she's floored, quite literally, by the attention of his tongue. No claims that pussy-eating's for fools, no dry jackhammering with dialogue designed to demean – 'feel it, take it, do you want to feel me come', where Delph would usually moan out yes, before they'd collapse in breathless unison. Glad it's done and dead inside, while he's puffed up and super proud of himself.

Faking doesn't even occur to Delph now. The stars were firmly out before he'd even stuck it in, as her stomach shudders again, knees trembling. Aftershocks from even the very thought of him. And breathing, her breathing still isn't right, hasn't yet settled, and they're all the things Itsy picks up on – and will he know in two tiny hours when he meets her outside that pub? Trying to search the contents of her head, like her mother would.

Delph, pressing her hand to her neck, finds she's boiling. Fever-hot, she licks her lips, salty and swollen, and as much as she tries putting herself back together, to hide this sudden ease, this abandon ...

She. Just. Doesn't. Want. To.

Lust is a thing that's long been dead. To initiate, to ignite desire, returns like forgotten treasure. And there is nothing,

nothing about this newfound joy that's sad or emotional; just remarkably fresh. Like a transfusion, the old seeds are washed clear as something restorative's blasted through her senses. Not love, but delight in each other, a gorgeous connection, which feels very grown-up, yet at the same time ... liberating. How admired Delph's been by this man. This gorgeous youth Lenny, with the world at his size 12s – and what a bloody marvel that is too.

And God. How dead. How dead she's been.

'You're like Sleeping Beauty,' he says, stroking her hair, as she drifts and dozes. 'I always thought that about you. Like you're removed someplace. Caught in your own world.'

How accurate. How deeply intuitive.

'What's this, then?'

'Well, that's it,' Lenny says, 'I had to hack through the forest, the mists of your thoughts. Kiss you awake.'

It is exactly what he's done.

But how now to escape her tower?

'Speed up, that's my mum's house.' Delph quickens her pace, choosing the pavement opposite Moon's as a yearning seizes at her stomach, like it wants to pull her across the road to the little house containing everything she truly loves and treasures. She makes a vow that the next thing she does will be to put things right again. With Roche and her mother.

But not like this. Not with semi-damp hair, and Lenny stuck to her.

'As a kid, I could smell the ganja before I'd even unlocked the front gate. Our house proper reeked. Of weed and the fat fryer,' Delph shares, though she doesn't know why. 'Chips were all I ate till secondary. My skin improved as I went through my teens. You think I'm joking.'

'Na, man.' Lenny smiles. Bright straight teeth. 'Just struggling to picture a mum who don't force-feed veg.'

'She had bigger worries than my diet, trust me. Inequality, Yugoslavia, Poll Tax, AIDS. You get the idea.'

'Woke before woke. She sounds cool.'

'Perhaps. At a distance.' It has always been this way. To a spectator, Moon's always the dream parent.

'What about your dad?'

'What about yours?' Delph deflects, and he holds his hands up.

'I get carried away; I do love a question, though. My dad's no longer with us. Died when I was a kid. Got nothing but good memories though, which is more than can be said for a lot of people.'

'It's how good people get to live forever,' Delph says kindly. 'I've "Father Unknown" on my birth certificate. Never met him, just had stories of a man who swept her off her feet then vanished. I don't think even she knows the truth anymore.'

'Disappeared like how? This is Wellsend, man. Impossible to disappear forever.'

But Delph knows some people do.

'It's your birthright, to know where you come from.'

'I do know, sort of. I know he died young. And I know he had another family. Not even sure if we even met properly. Hey, don't look sad.' Though Delph's touched by his compassion. 'He wasn't interested in me, so it's hardly worth tearing myself apart over, is it. Besides, this is where I really come from. I know it's not far, but I rarely get to come back.'

'Which I reckon might be a-changing, now that we're bonding.' He is built of cheekiness, fucking delicious. 'My mum won't never leave these ends. She likes the closeness, friends dropping in for tea or a moan. She knows everyone.'

'To be honest, I'd just be happier living closer to Tesco,' Delph jokes, a little bit envious. There is a lot to be said for community. Connection. 'Bags are always murder on the bus.'

'I'm gonna learn to drive once this MA's behind me. When I've got a proper job.' Stopping, he bares his teeth. 'Not that ours ain't proper jobs now.'

'It's all right, I know what you mean. Remind me what you're studying?'

'Biochemistry. Chemistry and biology,' he tells her. 'A mixture, y'know.'

'The sciences. How amazing,' Delph says, as an idea takes form in her head. 'I'm sure this'll sound odd, but I don't suppose you'd know how to go about identifying some medication – some old tablets I've found?'

'What, prescription stuff?' Lenny rubs his head. 'You thought of trying the chemist? You could speak to a pharmacist. Take the meds in and show them.'

'That's a brilliant thought.' Delph could kick herself for chucking them, that's made her doubt both herself and her suspicions. Has this pill obsession simply been blindsiding her? Because it's entirely possible those tablets were simply ineffectual. Delph's hard luck.

But then she thinks of Itsy at the Harvester. His sly eyes and questions.

Maybe Itsy, being the devious MoFo that he is, has his own source of meds to dispense at his choosing. Maybe Itsy, being Itsy, wouldn't even keep them in the flat. There are only two alternative hiding places Delph can think of: the garage, with the stuck padlock and heavy door that's mostly rust, or the other place, Itsy's actual car; his other world, the home from home travelling shell, which wouldn't be easy to search at all, with his dash cams and trickery, obsessed with security.

Delph won't let Lenny join her in waiting for Itsy. She needs time. Alone thought. To process the joy, the absolute physical joy of being spent – and, of course, to get her head straight.

'You're lovely, Lennox Anderson, Warehouse and Construction.' Folding her arms tight across her body, Delph leans into the road, squinting at an approaching car. 'But please shoot off before he clocks you.'

He takes a step back, like he knows the moment's broken. Delph sounds different – can hear it, even in herself, in preparation of becoming somebody else. Lenny distances a little, leaning against a smouldering old advert of Nicole Scherzinger with a yoghurt, the glow from the pub signage spotlighting them beautifully as the bus he needs to get home passes without stopping. He's got that youthful stubbornness. An obvious determination to hang around. Bastard curiosity.

'You know we could just chip off, right now,' Lenny says, giving her an option. 'You don't have to—'

Circular lights blind them, and she steps forwards to confirm. It is. The car slows as Itsy peers over the wheel, watching.

Still leant against Nicole, Lenny takes in everything, like he's expected to remember every detail for a test or identity parade. The car is a silver Astra, five years old, and both the dented bonnet and all along the passenger side are key-scratched quite considerably. Rosary beads in the colour and style of the Jamaican flag dangle from the rear-view mirror. Inside the car sits a man who looks like he's stepped out of one of the rerun cartoons from the eighties that Lenny's sisters would make him watch. Like a toad. A breathing Baron Greenback from Danger Mouse.

'That youth still bothering you?' Itsy dead-eyes Lenny over the steering wheel.

'Na. He's just checking I'm safe.' It sounds so ordinary that Itsy pulls away without a second glance, mumbling how that's exactly the sort of ploy muggers and rapists use to dupe their victims before mugging and raping them.

'Or both,' he warns, in the soft, gravelly way he has instead of shouting, which he knows is effective. 'So, best be careful, if you plan on more wild night things like this.'

The wildest of nights. Delph thinks of Lenny, still leant against Nicole. What he's thinking, now he's had a window into her world. Delph's so wrapped up that the car whizzes down the dual carriageway without her noticing. She doesn't make the sign of the cross or hold her breath for as long as she can stand it, which is usually till they reach the lights at the top of their turning.

And if she's honest, it barely even registers to Delph that it's proper pitch-black dark.

'Sorry, if I'm boring you,' Itsy says, feeling ignored. 'Don't let me keep you if there's somewhere else you need to be. I can always drop you round your mental mother's.' He kisses his teeth as he waits for the lights to change. 'Least there's no marriage like last time, leaving me destitute.'

Delph doesn't contest him. She just wants out. Out of the place she thought was a safety net, him guarding the door, her burly protector, who was worth putting up with, if it meant she never had to face the real world. She could hide up in her tower, pretending things like being pushed off overpasses didn't happen. But they do. They always will. Whether she's shut up on the fourteenth floor of Esplanade Point till the end of days, or not.

Because it's not done; life's not done. Nor over. Delph's not the one who's dead. So why continue to play as if she is?

'Trying to keep up with the youngs at work. Bit embarrassing.' Yes, usually, words like these would be enough to make Delph don another cardigan, scrub off the lipstick, meek and mild. But that's another feeling that's shifted. 'Ain't that your phone?' he asks, as Delph pretends not to notice. 'Bit late for chit-chat, innit?'

'Probably sales.'

'At this time of night?' His eyes narrow. 'Answer it.'

'Keep your hair on.' Delph takes a while finding her mobile, her stomach clenched. Then she sees the name. 'Roche! You all right?' Straight into mother mode. No matter they haven't spoken for three weeks and three days.

'Course,' Roche says. 'Nan and me were just wondering if you wanted to—' she stops on hearing Itsy's horn, as a car overtakes without indicating. 'You out?'

'Just heading home from some drinks with the work lot. Only the pub.'

'Only the pub,' Roche repeats. 'Look, it's time innit, we all sorted things out properly. You about tomorrow?'

Delph thinks of Lenny, the loose plan to hook up and reac-quaint. 'Course I am,' she says. 'Do you want to come home? I'll make you something nice.' But Roche is quiet. 'Roche?'

'What about at Nan's? I've study leave after lunch. Come by then – unless, of course, you need a permission slip.'

Roche just can't help herself. And to be honest, Delph doesn't blame her. 'I'll be there, love.' And she's gone. 'What are all these bottles of water for?' Delph asks Itsy, pointing to the backseat full of mineral water multipacks, changing the subject before he's the chance to wield any further fresh bullshit tactics.

'Got 'em cheap,' Itsy mutters, with a sideways glance, 'for silly cows like you who can't hold their drink.' He nods for Delph to take one. 'Go on. I don't want no vomit in here.' She reaches into the back, selecting the first in the corner of the crate as he watches her. 'Not that one.' He snatches it out of her hand. 'Some have had knocks. Lid's loose.'

Delph selects the one next to it. She doesn't need water. No alcohol's passed her lips all evening. All she needs is a shower, tea, the quiet of Roche's room.

And the most delicious dreams.

*

New Moon

Mistley, 1982

Mothers should not let you down.

It's part of the rule book, the fabric of life's truest facts. The bond. To protect and love for always. The animal kingdom uses the same language – see, we are not so changed.

But Joy thinks humans must be, when Ma stays glued to Dad, even when Janie cuts her own wrists – not in the bath, with a tap left running like in TV murder mysteries, but in front of Coronation Street. In the ad break, when Ma thought to put on the kettle, there was Janie, waxen grey, but for the darkest blood; raw holes in her beige sleeves.

Panic popped Ma from her Valium mist, enough to grab poor Janie's wrists, the guilty scissors embedded still. And as Ma wailed, Janie's eyes, slippery liquid, there but barely, lost their colour too. When the ambulance arrived, Ma knew and said, 'Please God, don't take my baby.' Over and over again, the most unforgettable sound, remembers anyone who had the sad trouble to hear Ma's cry that

*evening, when all the memories rushed before her, and the light Janie
carried emptied. And died.*

*Her parents had already broken everything when they gained
custody of Delph for six whole months, following an 'anonymous
tip' to the social, which was the kick up the arse Joy needed, realizing
Delph was her lifeline, that all the booze in the world couldn't salve
what she missed the night she came home to no baby, nor the oblit-
eration she punished herself with when they put Delph in the care
of her bigoted parents. The only palatable part was that Janie was
there. Just about. Faint like her original scars, a silvery gossamer
guardian angel.*

*It brought pain like no other, how her parents cemented the
notion of how 'unfit' Joy was – an easy label for the teenage lush
with a brown baby and no money or man in sight, with no mention
of their own unfit behaviours. Like when Dad very publicly spat in
Joy's face, at the news she was carrying a Black man's child. Anyone
with an ounce of heart could've figured out that gaining custody of
Delph was more about power than anything to do with love, and if
the social were people instead of robots, they might've deciphered the
truth behind the 'stable' mum and dad; the worms behind his eyes,
the wickedness in every part of him; but their red tape and rules
and health visitors writing in their little books will never be on Joy's
side, and she knows it.*

*So, Joy does as women have always done and gets resourceful.
When you think about witchcraft and gifts, is there anything truly
outrageous, other than riding a broomstick, that any mortal soul
couldn't achieve? Empathy, a dash of chemistry – what difference
is there really, between a recipe and a spell? Between elements and*

alchemy. Wily ingenuity, so the misunderstood might survive this unwelcoming world. Joy makes a mental potion to take her parents down; knowing their secrets, the sole trick up her sleeve.

Joy has a clean, focused mind when she meets Ma in a café, away from the front window, because what would people say if they saw them talking again, after all the scandal and shame she's caused.

'I want her back,' Joy says, before even 'hello', and Ma's heartbroken. Joy, even grown, still doesn't like to see it – but this is Mouse Mum who sides with the monster; Ma, who likely knows all. Her hands, laced around Delph's chubby midriff, tighten as Joy thinks of breastfeeding for the first time, her tit double the size of her baby's tiny head. 'She's not yours. And she ain't bloody his,' Joy says, sounding strong. 'I've got a family therapist, who knows the law.' She stops to let the words bed in. 'So best be here same time tomorrow, with Delph packed to hand over, or I'm going to the police.'

'Whatever for?' Ma laughs, so ordinarily, it's as if she really doesn't know. But Joy won't spell it out, would rather watch how Ma's face alters, like she's had a rewiring, like she feels her daughter all up in her head, when Joy says:

'You know.'

Joy has no therapist or legal connections, but she does have a job, on the new-age stall by the precinct. She's accepted a council house on the new Butterfield estate too – and there's no way Delph's not coming. 'You can unpick your meddling with the social, as well. Tell them they got it wrong,' Joy says, emboldened by her mother's panic.

Celeste, the owner of the new-age stall, holds weekly meditations. Joy tries to be healthy-minded, accepting a proper rebirth in celebration of severing ties with her parents, a phrase never heard without wincing after Janie's death. Instead of attending her funeral, there is a baptism; it is time to leave Joy behind and step into who she knows she is.

A good soul. A person undeserving of hurt.

Joy's ceremony takes place not far from another stretch of Essex estuary, in a rented cottage that backs onto miles of forest. Wearing white, anything white, from Levis to Victorian-looking nighties, to someone's old bridesmaid's dress, Joy's new crowd of new-age people venture into the woods. Forming a circle before her blessing, Joy's encouraged to speak her truth, a request which feels like prying, disconnecting Joy from her night, from the powers of Mistley's Old Knobbley tree which, until Celeste broke the moment with words, had felt a sanctuary for Joy, just as it had in the past for others like her. Joy's cross at the weak connection between her and the universe, a bond that's usually so effortless, as the moon gets lost behind endless cloud and the sky is bland without it. A non-colour, but for the silhouette of Knobbley's branches; outstanding, commanding – and a little bit frightening – if you didn't trust all they were made from, the roots tangled deep beneath her feet, ancient veins of wisdom, which you either notice, or you don't.

Even without the drink and the drugs, without their beautiful magnification of all things good, while at the same time shielding all what isn't, Joy is glad to be one of the noticers.

She doesn't need this group of sympathizers. She's simply here to be free of the past. To stop this cross-contamination of history and current circumstance fucking up any more of her future. Of Delph's future.

Life is short, Joy thinks the tree says. Live it wildly. Live it right.

Who is Joy to argue? She goes with the flow, choosing nature,

275

choosing herself instead of the crowd – another thing, which has always served her best.

Joy cannot speak her secrets. Knows she never will. It is too-long fetid; and strangely, perhaps Joy's secrets are where she finds her own strengths. Karma will fix her parents far more effectively than any day in court – this Joy believes. With all her heart.

And is it magical willfulness that gets Delph back? Or sheer bloody resourcefulness?

That night with Dad and the ouija in her box bedroom still leaves questions. Did Joy break that glass? Or was it another force, another presence in their home, borne from the bad energy and the bad feelings? People get used to the cruelest of things. Desensitized and brainwashed. And how can good people prove what's right, when the wrong-uns are never punished? When badness is all the rage, the trending currency, always.

Joy's baptismal ceremony puts her in a category she, for once, doesn't mind being defined by:

Spiritually connected and open to the universe
In touch with nature
Persecuted (mostly by threatened people)
Misunderstood
A sixth sense – of more beyond themselves
Cat fan

A witch, of sorts.

Joy opts for the things that have never let her down. Nature, the *forever forwardness of growth and rebirth. The sky and the stars and the vast freedoms of being so utterly insignificant in all of it. Joy chooses Mother Nature. Protecting the Earth is a better battle anyway. The planet deserves more than the broken folk intent on destroying it – and destroying each other. Self-made zombies, all hungry for the happy fulfillment of life Joy knows is a fabrication. But never the type to mope, Joy keeps moving forward, always. Looking up.*

Reunited with her daughter, Joy decides who she'll become. The whole of the moon. A man will never be necessary again. And she'll be enough for them both.

Until Sol came along. Changing both their lives for the better.

A boy, of all things.

19

THERAPY

Wellsend, 2023

Roche is early. She enters Pastoral, heading for the desk of Miss Chubb, who absolutely, positively does not live up to her name, until she says, 'please, call me Willow.'

'Your first name suits you more than your last,' Roche replies, because she's not sure what to say.

'You're not the first person to say that,' Willow smiles. 'Come Roche, let's find a space and have a wee chat.'

They exit through the fire door at the back of the class, onto a small open courtyard, away from the noise of the rest of the school, choosing the gazebo in the corner, shaded and private. A part of the school Roche had no idea existed. Seven bloody years and the school's had a secret garden this whole time; a pond – with goldfish for Christ's sakes. 'I never knew any of this was even here.'

'I don't think you're the only one. It keeps things tranquil.' Tucking her skirt flat behind her legs, Willow sits. 'I keep a distance from the school; it ensures my work stays clear. Teaching's not my world. Listening is. Helping. So, Roche.' Roche likes it that Willow knows she's Roche and not Rochelle. Likes how she puts on her glasses, which make her look like a little bird. No, more like a tiny owl. Willow studies Roche kindly. 'This is an informal chat, which is of course confidential, just so I can see if I can offer you any support at this final stage of your school journey. Now, I know you're not living with Mum . . .'

'We've not fallen out or anything,' Roche chips in, quick to improve the sound of her situation. 'I wasn't getting on with her boyfriend, that's all.'

'And that's,' Willow looks to her notebook, tucking her blonde bob behind her ears, 'Geoffrey.'

'Itsy if you know him.' Roche fills Willow in on the origins of Itsy's nickname, taking huge delight when she gets a laugh that sounds more like it belongs to a Chubb than a Willow as it reverberates round the courtyard. 'Yeah, the friendly neighbourhood spider man is actually a total prick, though.' Why not be honest and open? Because, if she doesn't want to pack a suitcase of secrets and carry it round like her mum and her nan have for their whole existences, then Roche has no choice but to share and start talking. And besides, keeping things hidden hasn't helped so far; in fact, it's only been in confronting the shit, however horrible and scary – her slap included – that's led them to any true progress. Maybe the shit does need to happen

EVA VERDE

before the dark clouds move on. The Shit Before The Sunshine. Which would look smart as hell on a t-shirt.

'What makes him a total prick?'

'Oh, Willow, where d'you want me to start?'

But Roche does start talking. She details everything she's witnessed; the way, for as far back as she can remember, Itsy's marked her mother out of ten – and what's more demeaning than being judged by a lazy, thick old fool, who's somehow assumed superiority because he was born with a dinkle. 'What I'd love to know,' Roche says, in conclusion to her verbal savagery, 'is what made his first wife simply pack up and vanish? Because it would be nice if she could come back and show my mum how she did it.' Roche drops her eyes, and the black humour. 'I'm always worried about my mum. Truth, I don't know how else to be but worried. It's like my default setting. Which has got a little bit better, living with my nan now. But I'd give anything to make her see sense. For her to open her eyes and see what the rest of us see.' Because it's true. Everybody who loves her mother loathes Itsy. Even Eden, who doesn't loathe anyone.

Eden. Roche pushes her from her thoughts. Ain't she enough emotional shit to deal with as it is? Things remain frosty between them. And it's fucking horrible. 'And I ... I worry about going away to uni, that I won't be there, should she need me.'

'Which is a lot on your shoulders at your young age,' Willow says, concerned. 'What is it that you worry about happening to your mum?'

'I don't know.' By Roche's age, her mum was safe with her dad. The two of them in love. The solidarity of that, despite never knowing him, is warming, a comfort against the loneliness she's never been able to rescue her mother from. Absently, Roche twists the rings on the chain around her neck. She worries that Itsy could hurt her mum. He has before. Roche remembers the words, the excuses; how it was only once, that it was her mother's fault. How it was best not to mention it to anybody because they might think bad of Itsy, which would be . . .

Or that her mother might hurt herself.

But Roche can't say those words. If she says them out loud, then that might make it a real thing, and she doesn't want to think about how that could possibly feel. She'd be frozen by pain. Forever. And isn't that what Mum's felt like too? All Roche's life.

Willow must sense her discomfort, for she changes the subject. 'So, Edinburgh. Brilliant choice. But you've not applied for any scholarships. They're always worth a shot, could change your whole experience. You can focus on studying instead of worrying about a job. Much as people love to tell you differently, being a student is expensive.'

'My student loan application's in though, and we're visiting for the open day in two weekends' time.' Roche breaks into a smile. 'I can't wait.'

It's strange to re-enter the school building, how forty minutes can feel like five, and Roche blinks to readjust. Doesn't really want to. 'So, d'you think I need to see you again?'

'Needing a bit of extra support from time to time isn't a weakness. And if you feel like you want to, then absolutely, but there's no pressure. It's a privilege being here, on hand to help. And most of you are lovely.' She looks over her glasses, giving Roche a cheeky wink. 'Most of you.'

'Do we need to set a time?'

'We can. What I'd really like, should I see you next week, is to hear you've made some scholarship applications. And I want to know all about Edinburgh. I think you're going to really love it. How could you not?' She smiles, putting her hands on her chest and her shoulders back. 'Scots are the best people.'

'Are you from Edinburgh?'

'Not far. My big sister went to Edinburgh. She lives in Canada now, deeply involved in environmental research.'

Canada. Imagine. A few scary forward steps and look what can happen?

Roche leaves Pastoral with a spring in her step, till she spots Eden, who actually avoids her this time, dressed as basic as the girls she's now hanging around with. Roche won't beg for her company, but it hurts, this sudden parting of ways, this excommunication. Knows it's her own fault too; her proud little bastard heart. Roche pictures war scenes, injured soldiers biting on sticks as some empathetic comrade digs a penknife in the bullet hole to find the metal culprit. Roche, similarly awash in agony, longs to eject her heartache. Wants it out, rather than buried, and hopes that soon, despite this pain, the bullet of love will be found and pinged out. A slosh of booze on the wound to stop the hurt spreading and becoming toxic, so she can scar over. And the healing can begin.

But for now, the best distraction from heartache is to keep Edinburgh in mind. To keep working, staying focused, perhaps even do as Willow Chubb says and pen that scholarship application before she misses out – Willow Chubb who is, thinking about it, very pretty too – and isn't that progress, to notice?

Progress is coming. In other ways too.

Roche will be glad, so glad, to see her mother later.

'Mum.' There are no games, no hesitation, as Roche flings herself into her mother's arms. 'You look so different,' she adds shyly, admiringly, thinking of stage magicians, who with a three, two, one and a click of their fingers can snap you out of a trance. And then, there you are again.

That's how Mum looks. Officially back in the room.

'She looks like herself,' Moon calls over her shoulder, sitting on the sofa in front of the telly, soaking her feet in the washing-up bowl. 'Hello, darlin' – I would get up, but I've not stopped in that garden today. I'm in agony.'

'What are you watching, Mum?' Delph asks, coming in and squeezing her mother's shoulder.

'Some old shit. I've seen it before. Sit down. Let me look at you without breaking my neck.' Delph sits, as Moon turns to her. 'There you are – my beautiful girl.' Moon takes her hand, leans closer, smiling widely when Delph's eyes drop to her lap, Roche wishing she was privy to the silent conversation that seems to pass between them. 'Good colour you've got in them cheeks there too,' Nan comments.

'I'm doing a veggie pasta bake,' says Roche, a tea towel over her shoulder. 'Shouldn't be long. D'you want a cuppa?' She skips out the door to the kitchen, like some eager to please kid again. But it still feels nice, hearing them in the background, all getting on under the same roof, Mum saying something like, 'Since when did my baby make tea?' and Nan saying something that sounds a lot like, 'Well fucking done, love.'

But, typically for them, the happy moment's over at the sound of glass smashing, an explosion of some sort coming from inside the oven, as Delph and even Moon, her feet soaking, arrive panicked in the kitchen to discover the source.

Moon buries her hands in her hair, before letting out an almighty wail. 'Fuck my life!' On her knees, she flings open the oven door. 'Fuck my fucking life!' The kitchen fills with the reekiest stench, which must surely render them instantly high. And all the neighbours too. 'Ninety quid up in smoke. Literally.'

Roche catches her mum's eye, can't help but keel over, roaring with laughter as Moon fights against the ferocious heat with a dustpan and brush, trying to rescue the sad remains of her weed stash.

'Oh, Mum, you can't be serious? Look at all the glass.' Delph takes charge, reacting unthinkingly to the situation, becoming mother to her mother. Roche studies Nan's catastrophizing against her mother's natural soothing, the quick order she establishes, along with the clear disappointment that her mother's up to her old tricks. It isn't hard to imagine her as a small child, doing the same. Roche's laughter becomes nothing but sadness.

'Don't you dare chuck it. I'm smoking it not eating it, Delphine Magenta,' she says crossly, as Delph drags Roche's pasta bake out of the oven, and plonks it on the hob, a glittery glass crumble on top of what would've been a very decent late lunch. Moon's face drops. 'But we can't go near that. Sorry, love,' she says, sounding a little more like herself. 'I've got some takeaway menus knocking about.' From behind the bread bin, she dislodges them. 'My treat.'

'Nan. Jesus, these are so unnecessary.'

'You're telling me you don't like pizza?'

'I'm saying, get a bloody smart phone and dump these nasty bacteria pages. What's that, even?' Roche points to the hardened crustation, darkening on the back of a Chinese takeaway menu, as a brittle noodle falls from the back of Pizza Pronto. 'It's got to be said, Nan. You're proper filth.'

'Sod it. I'll chance my luck.' Moon begins searching for her purse, finding it in the front pouch of her Jazzi shopper. 'I'm sure Kimberly didn't really mean it about calling the police if she sees me again this week. I mightn't get such a soft touch rozzer as you did, Roche.' Moon bites her teeth together, stopping herself from saying anymore, as Roche stares daggers at her, glad when she disappears to M&S.

'Police?' Mum's sad and worried. 'Oh, Roche – why?'

But Roche doesn't think she's ready to tell her mother about

Itsy. She might look, feel, even sound different, but who's to say anything's really changed. As much as she loves her mum, it really is very hard believing in her.

Yet, that Itsy's not told mum himself is unbelievable too; he loves nothing more than dropping Roche in the shit. The fact he hasn't mentioned it, that she could make such a fuckery of his vehicle and him be totally silent, is disturbing.

She thinks of what Willow said only this morning. About trying to encourage conversation, instead of burying things that only build and come out later as anger. If Roche stops letting things build, maybe she'll be less volatile.

And maybe she'd still have a girlfriend.

'I got caught keying Itsy's car.'

Delph's mouth falls open. 'That was you?'

'I'd just got a load of stick off some teacher, then I saw his car, that he was back and home with you, and I wasn't.' Such basic truth. 'I wasn't, Mum. And that's not right. It's never been right.'

Mum's face is a picture of shame. 'This is my fault.'

'And there you go, covering for him. Making excuses. I'd sell my soul if you'd only open your eyes. Then I could feel better. About leaving you.' Roche breathes in. 'I'm going to Edinburgh.'

Four words. That her mother takes far better than Roche ever imagined. 'Good.' She takes Roche's hands before pulling her close, holding her so tightly Roche can feel the pride emanating into her, the most beautiful, truly missed feeling. 'Good.'

'I love you, Mum.'

'Oh, Roche,' Mum's eyes fill with tears, her lashes damp, sparky, yet do not smudge a smidge. 'I love you. So much.' She holds her close again, then at arm's length to look at her properly. 'You mustn't worry about me. Things are changing. I know there's no love lost between you and Itsy, and to be honest, I'm feeling much the same. But it's hard unpicking, making sense of all the years I've lost.'

'Because of Dad?' So rarely mentioned between them, yet always, always there.

Mum is quiet for a moment. 'Not exactly. Certainly not in the way I thought. Just please tell me this police and school stuff isn't going to spoil these uni plans – you know you could lose your martial arts licence.' She slides effortlessly into concerned Mum mode, which feels really fucking good too. 'Don't throw away all your amazingness because of Itsy.'

Roche leads her mum into the garden. Glorious flowers are everywhere, some waist-high, their gentle scent held in the warm air. Such order outside, so contrasting with the house, to the front of the house, which screams Keep Out. Stay Away. But maybe that's the point. The back garden is Nan's island. Same as Mum's balcony. The neat tranquillity, delivered from the green fingers of them both.

'Beautiful,' Delph says quietly, as she follows her down to the shed. With a quick glance back at the house, Roche points through the window to the location of Moon's last box, now very well hidden, Mum's eyes widening when she goes in to investigate. 'What the ...' She shakes her head. 'Don't look at it, don't open it, in fact, pretend you've never even seen it.' Unwilling to even touch it, Delph kicks the box back into the corner and covers it back up – making a far better job than Eden's attempts at hiding things, and when will Roche stop thinking about her? 'That's a binding spell. Leave it be.'

'Do you know much about Nan as a kid?' Roche asks, feeling suddenly cold as she thinks of her nan's little paintings, the odd scraps of indication gone up in smoke. 'There was another box, but it's a long story. She's getting way, way too much out of the reefer lately,' Roche admits. More and more she feels it's a mask, a coping mechanism. Maybe it doesn't take anything away from who Nan is, but it does stop her feeling, so very, very deeply.

And buried things don't ever heal. Roche is learning.

'A little. I remember my nan vaguely. The odd visit. Not often. Just like at birthdays, you know?' Mum falls quiet, as if something internal has occurred to her, making sense. 'And I know none of them had it easy. She had a sister, who died very young. Auntie Janie, she'd say, with the most brilliant wings of all. Not so much a mystery. More, just a sad life best forgotten.'

'So why does everything always feel such a secret?' Why does her mother not have the mad, bad curiosity gene? Why can't Roche stop picking at scabs? Because she can't. And isn't it time for the whole picture to come into sight? All Roche wants is to put all the pieces together and take a good look. Then she'll be satisfied. And then, most definitely, she can move on.

'Not quite barbecue season,' Delph says, nodding to the old Weber, the charred curls of paper still moving about Nan's small patio area.

'She burnt some stuff the other night. Old memories, I think,' Roche explains, unwilling to drop herself in it, to admit her vast overstepping into Nan's privacy. 'Not all of them, by the looks.' Because tucked just beneath the leg of the barbecue is a piece of scrapbook, untainted. On one side, is a newspaper obituary.

The Smallman family announce the sad passing of Kingsley Thomas Smallman after a short illness.

A Service will be held at The Redeemed Christian Church, Northside Quay on 20th December 1986 at 2.00 p.m.

(Light Refreshments)

Feeling sick, Roche's mind races; chooses not to show the paper to her mother. Needs to think what to do. Whatever that is.

All the same, Roche has a name. And Mum has a dad.

A dead one. Just like hers.

A name changes everything. And like Roche has any real say in matters, against the temptations of Ancestry.com and 23andMe now bursting through the floodgates of her thoughts. Roche's a modern-day Alice: Curiouser and Curiouser. A dog with a proper moreish bone.

This is who she is.

20

IT COULD ALL BE SO LOVELY

Esplanade Point, 2023

Delph's thinking how nice it was to be back in that fuggy little house with the pair of them. How light; without the nagging worry of Itsy clock-watching, free from his hovering shadow, leaving at a time specified by him. And it made a change to sit in utter chaos and borderline dirt instead of the sterileness of home. It's been the worst kind of difficult, living apart from Roche, but even Delph acknowledges in looking back, how timely, necessary, the space has been for all of them. And it's a beautiful bond that's formed between her mother and her daughter, Delph less grudgingly can see now too. It warms, thinking of the two of them, raging against the state of the world, shouting at the telly during *Question Time*. And though none of their fierceness exists within herself, Delph's happy they all share the same genes, and had felt safe, and home, sandwiched between them.

But it would be nice to be as vocal, as passionate as them. Delph wonders if she might be the product of a generational skip. Or maybe, she should've been born first. The barriers Mother Moon's spent a lifetime rebelling against have always seemed unnecessary to Delph, who has never sought to challenge.

It is only when Itsy begins to start on Roche that Delph finds even she has a tipping point.

'Ain't it about time she visited me? Shocking disrespect. It's not like that in Jamaica, respect is *key*.'

Yes, Roche is all the things Itsy accuses her of being: disrespectful, argumentative, foul-mouthed. 'But it's you that brings it out in her.' Itsy's tricks are transparent now, his hold too loose. But worse than that, worse than anything else, is that Delph just doesn't trust him.

'And I can't do this anymore!' She winces the moment she says it, down into her shoulders like a petrified prawn. Pathetic.

Because what happens next – and where does she go? And is it even safe, to challenge someone you suspect has been manipulating, potentially drugging you for who knows how long. It makes Delph catch herself, like she's saved herself from falling. Which is ironic, considering her years of intrusive thoughts and almost actions.

Is she safe? Properly safe? Their imminent, still mostly unmentioned separation feels a homegrown ticking time-bomb. The big fuck-off elephant in every conversation.

'Do what anymore? The way I see it you don't do much.'

He gestures around the gleaming flat, the only drudge task in sight is the washing on the airer, dry and needing redistribution. 'Except tart yourself up. For whose benefit?' He stares at Roche's bedroom door as if he hates it. 'Certainly not mine while you're pretending to be a teenager again.'

'I wouldn't be a teenager again if you paid me.' Delph hesitates, licks her lips. 'You think I'd want to relive ... any of this?' It's the first time she's ever vocalized her unhappiness to him – to anyone in fact, since Geena, who never really counts because she never really gets it.

'I thought you'd be desperate to go again. Turn back time and get the first love back – right all the sad wrongs.' Though he sniffs, Itsy doesn't sound remotely hurt. He just sounds like a fucking knob.

'Sol.' It fills the room. And Delph's glad. 'His name's Sol.' How did he become a name she couldn't mention, when once he was her sole source of sunshine. Her friend when there were few, who'd made life at last so stable. Her heart. Her Sol.

'I swear that job's sent you crazy,' Itsy says, calm as, with his slick, gaslight trickery. 'I've got an airport run. Won't be back till late.' He looks Delph up and down, leaning into her face to retrieve his keys from the hook behind her. 'Try not to get lost in your time machine.'

Delph waits an age, watching from the balcony for Itsy to go through the fire exit to his car. And when he bursts through the doors with a bounce, even at a distance, Delph can tell by his step that he's pleased as fuck with himself.

*

Lenny's wearing his Deliveroo jacket, stood in the entrance of Delph's living room, a perfect square; three walls and a wall-sized window; overlooking the playing fields and a car park, rather than the sea, which would've been quite the view. Up on the fourteenth floor, privacy's unnecessary, but there's still a vertical bamboo blind, which matches the nest of tables in the corner, the largest one set with a faded school photograph of two boys with buzz cuts. Sombre-looking boys.

'Should I take my shoes off?' Lenny asks, and they both look at his feet, the giant white Nikes, arctic contrast to the charcoal shagpile.

'Best not,' Delph says, playing jumpy, before she squeezes his shoulders. 'I'm kidding. He's doing a drop-off at Heathrow, I took the booking myself. We're safe. Now, let me show you this garage.'

They take the staircase right down to the lower ground and out through the fire exit, following the same route as Itsy, which brings them out to the back of the garages, a grot-looking narrow strip of low-rise lock ups. Number 40.

'This one?' Lenny asks, on finding it, to double-check.

'That's it.' Delph hands her keys over. He looks at her incredulously, as the key slips in with such ease it's embarrassing, Lenny barely having to shove the door to send it swinging up and over their heads. 'Lightweight,' he jokes. 'What is it we're looking for, anyway – though, second thoughts, I don't think you're gonna find it.'

'What do you . . .' Delph steps around him into the empty

garage. Not a stick of old furniture, or any stopgap rubbish for a tip-run to be seen. Utterly, entirely, empty.

No bumper stash of little pink pills, either.

It's all a bit too spick and span for Delph's liking, the oiled key that comes out of the lock only adding to the feeling that Itsy's never been the protector, the solution for keeping her and Roche safe, but the opposite. Didn't her mother always talk about dangers within the home?

'Don't think for one bloody second that any of this is my taste,' says Delph when they're back upstairs, rewarding Lenny with a giant rum and a bag of Doritos for putting a lock on Roche's – now Delph's – bedroom door.

'How long you been here?' Lenny asks, accepting the drink and looking around again. When she replies fifteen years, Delph watches him baulk. Above the electric fire hangs a large picture of her and Roche, standing back-to-back with their arms folded. They are smiling so hard Lenny grits his teeth, looks to the mantelpiece below, and sips his drink. Lenny studies another picture, the one in the gold frame, from what was the early days. Delph all cleavage and haunted; Itsy draped huge and territorial around her shoulders. Dark clamping hands rest stark on her light brown shoulders, the smooth whites of his fingernails catching the camera's flash.

'Tenerife, 2006,' Delph tells Lenny, pointing at the picture. 'Look at the grin on him. Someone at the bar asked if he was the entertainment. He's always, always fancied himself as a singer.' Her stomach turns. It doesn't feel right, making fun of Itsy, especially in his home, which she knows is ridiculous, considering his far, far worse misdemeanours.

'There's no light.' He picks the picture up, holding it out to show her. 'In your eyes. Nothing.' And though Delph looks, she's unwilling to put herself back in the mind of the young woman looking out of it. Robotic on the surface, annihilated within. Just fucking terrified, really. Delph takes the picture, and setting it back, hears Lenny sit in the squeak of Itsy's armchair behind her, the one that plugs in, reclines and massages. A chair for a man who's got himself so comfortable he no longer needs to try.

Lenny spreads his legs, adjusting himself into the soft beige leather. Three remote controls sit to the left of him, the radiator to the right. He sets his hands on the curves of the armrests and gives them a squeeze.

'D'you want some music, or shall I put the telly on?'

'Na.' He curls his finger, motioning Delph over. 'Just you.' She sits on his lap, and he moves his hands from the leather to her hips. Their closeness makes her head reel, makes Delph close her eyes for a moment. 'You're so daydreamy,' he says, against her hair. 'It's proper lovely.'

'Well, I'm new to this. Don't laugh, I didn't mean it like that.' She cups his face, a little woozy from the rum, kissing her way across his jaw. Then she looks him in the eyes. 'I'm not used to wanting this.'

Delph's words spark something frantic and necessary, her breathing changing as his hands roam her body, the softest parts of her beginning to firm. Hooking an arm around his neck, she too reaches to open herself, for more contact, more frenzy, and Lenny doesn't stop until her thighs turn rigid around his hips. Kissing her mouth, pressing his forehead against hers, he looks right at her. And it feels like he sees everything.

Delph made flesh. Less of an ornament.

'Thank you.' Delph says it so quietly, she doesn't expect him to hear it.

'What d'you mean, thank you.' Lenny squeezes her. 'When you've given me heaven?'

'I saw these in the market, thought I'd drop 'em by.' Moon shows off a blue bag, sticking her head around the door Delph's just answered, Delph truly grateful she's now dressed.

'That's thoughtful.' Delph takes her mother's bags before opening the door fully, hoping to God Lenny's—

On his haunches, pretending to finish off the new lock, like the gift he is.

'Oh, hello.' Mother Moon looks between them, as Lenny stands to greet her. 'I'm Moon,' Moon says, a wicked glint in her eye.

'Lenny. Good to meet you.' Lenny offers his hand, but Moon takes both, running her fingers over his palms, turning them over to study them.

'A brave Leo,' she says, but not unkindly, giving his hands back to him. 'Thank God.'

'Just helping out your girl.'

'Yeah,' Moon says, looking at the empty rum glasses and his lack of footwear. 'That's what I thought.' She turns her attention back to Delph. 'Three for a fiver; there are big trays of marigolds and begonias down there too – and other bedding bits that'd fair better south-facing.' She nods to the carrier bags. 'Now, more importantly, Roche and uni. We're off to Edinburgh next Thursday. Wondered if you fancied tagging along. Now you're footloose,' Moon adds.

'Not exactly footloose.' Delph tries to think of an appropriate phrase. 'Decoupling,' she settles on, not wanting to look at Lenny as she says it. 'Things take time.'

And then all manner of shit suddenly happens, tiny things avalanching into huge life shifts. Because to even consider the prospect of leaving here, *really leaving* . . .

It's then that Mother Moon begins behaving in the way she always does with an audience. 'Terrible vibes, this place.' She walks around, her arms raised to the sky as if searching for supernatural signals. 'Always did have. Mister Cat knew it, didn't he? And Roche.'

'Mum,' Delph warns. 'Don't make things harder.'

'What exactly is hard, Delphine Magenta? Either it's done. Or it's not.'

Can her mother not read, in all her clever mysticism, that 'done', the finality, the fear it brings to stand alone in the world after so long by his side, is not an easy thing to even think, let alone say aloud. And are there not, still, too many questions that need answering first? For some sort of closure to this cesspit of doubt.

And then, then she's out—

'You know, you could just pack, come home with me right now and we never need see him again. Because seriously, love, doesn't *that* send out every warning you need?' Moon points at the new lock, wringing her hands, getting a bit too noisy now, which sets Delph wondering if she's on something more than just her old friend, Mr Pot. 'Look at it. Look. At. It.' Moon turns to Lenny. 'Could that bolt stop you, if you really wanted to get in there?'

'Your mum has a point.' Lenny frowns. 'And I'm not liking none of this one bit. You never said this was to protect you from him. I just thought a lock was for a bit of privacy, while you're still under the same roof – till you get your own digs . . .' He shakes his head, more distressed by the situation than Delph would like. 'I felt it, the minute I saw him.'

Moon nods emphatically. 'See? Vibes! My stomach dropped the moment I clapped eyes on him, because I felt it too. There he was, looming, like a big depressive beast that swallowed her. And now look. Padlocks. Protection. A child gone AWOL . . .'

Glancing at Lenny, Delph catches his eye, with a look that says I told you what she's like, knowing she's got her mum spot on. 'Please don't feed her. Or she'll never stop.'

'Or you could just come with us on Thursday. Get away that way. We're staying spitting distance from the castle; found a room with a double and a pull-out just in case.' Her hand flies up, blocking a reply. 'We can sure all that up nearer the time, but for now, if you won't see sense and come with

298

me, please would you at least hunker down with this hunk of . . .' Moon looks Lenny over, like she's performing a quality check on behalf of her daughter – which seems to shift the clouds of Itsy panic, just a smidgen. 'Brave Leo.' Out she bustles, in her gypsy skirt and flip flops, the t-shirt that says Eat The Rich, in writing like dripping blood.

'Whoa,' is all Lenny says, breathing all his breath out. 'She does not like him.'

'She's been convinced he was a demon from the second they met.' For a moment, Delph feels headachy, swimmy and strange. Mother Moon's intuition's a bit too accurate for comfort. Was her mother wrong? 'She'll be over the real bloody moon if you signal the back of him.'

'Hey.' Lenny scratches his head before taking Delph's hand, like he's something to get off his chest. 'A few nights ago, heading home, I saw him, chatting with this . . .' he shakes his head, like there's no other way to put it, '. . . girl.'

There's no green-eyed flare of feeling. Nothing, except waist-height revulsion.

'His tongue was on the floor. And she was young, man. Even for me, you know?'

'Perhaps this is how things go. He moves on to a younger version, like he did before.' It comes out so matter of fact, Delph doesn't even realize she's said it aloud, until Lenny replies.

'And what about you?'

'I don't know. Worst-case scenario is back round my mother's till the council sort me out, which likely means I'll be there forever. I'm hardly a woman of means.'

Except she is. And at the thought of her bingo thousands, sitting in her own little bank account, big, beautiful patio doors fling themselves open in her thoughts, fresh air and freedom and the lightest of most perfect, perfect days beckoning her through.

There is another side to all this, Delph's sure of it. Of a life that could be ... not magic, as in resurrecting the dead and living like Itsy never was, but as a grown-up. A grown woman, secure in her wants and her autonomy; a woman who will never be kept in the shadows again.

A woman, who, after all this time, is choosing herself.

21

THANKLESS TASKS

Wellsend, 2023

Roche knows, just from the odd hunch of Eden's neck and her sunken shoulders, that something's not right. She leans forward over the desk to poke her in the back with a pencil. Eden shifts in her seat but doesn't turn around. Suit herself, then. Can't say Roche didn't try.

Edinburgh's next Thursday. Roche was hoping their trip would be the focus, but Nan's gone off-key, miffed again, armed with a vendetta – Itsy firmly on her hit list. With the astral reports appearing to meet their sticky end, Nan's taken to trailing through Google instead, researching common plants and their properties, giving herself 'a refresher course', apparently having replenished her sacred weed stash after Roche burnt her last lot, filling her time smoking and investigating the toxic properties of her garden foxgloves.

EVA VERDE

Which, funnily enough, coincided with Nan coming back all cagey after visiting Mum. More secrets which, of course, are Itsy-related, contaminating; returning all the strange anxiousness over Mum again. More family weirdness hidden and festering, forever making things worse and never any better.

Wouldn't it do them good to just get rid of it, once and for all? Roche remembers the bonfire, the drama – but also the strange resolution after. What Willow might refer to as 'ripping the plaster off'. Roche won't open the other box, won't do that to her nan again. But she does remember the address on the burnt box, Danes Lane, knows that old pub still stands on the very same road. Wouldn't even Nan herself consider that a cosmic sign? Because what harm would it do, to hop on a bus, and see what might fall into the open. It's not like there's anything else to do.

Roche thinks of the scholarship application, still incomplete. One specifically for those from 'Underrepresented Backgrounds' or from 'Limited Circumstances' that might create barriers to accessing further education. Sixteen thousand pounds. Imagine. Like, *imagine*. And though writing a thousand words on why her life is shit won't exactly be hard, it also feels totally impossible to begin.

'Turn to page six,' says old Treason, just as Eden asks to go to the toilet.

What the fuck. She's crying.

And when Treason gives her a toilet pass, the second she's out the door Roche's hand is in the air. 'Sir,' she says. 'Please, sir.'

302

'Absolutely not.'

'But sir, it's my right—'

'Stop, would you? For one lesson, just please—'

'All I'm saying, calmly and politely, is if my saturated tampon explodes, don't blame me.'

'Just go!' he shouts, spitting as he says it. Refusing to look at her, he holds a toilet tag for her to take.

Moments later, Roche taps on the only cubicle that's locked. 'Oi.'

'Go away,' Eden snivels from the other side.

'Can't do that, bitch.'

'Huh,' Eden laughs, through her upset. 'Thought you were, what was it again? Ah yeah – sick of me.'

'Yeah, well. Maybe I was being a prick,' Roche sniffs. 'I'm sorry, innit.'

Eden sighs. She sounds so sad. 'It's too late.'

'Don't be daft. Open the door, would you.'

'What do you know? You don't know anything anymore.'

'What's it been? A week?' Roche says, knows to the hour it's been double that – but pride, innit? 'You're the one sounding daft right now, fam.'

'You think you're so smart. Bet you don't know about Dee's new boyfriend.'

Roche snaps her neck back, losing her chin. 'Shut up.'

'Mum heard 'em, all flirty-flirty on the balcony. Reckons she knows who it is n'all.' Eden, a little less upset, stops talking.

Roche kicks at the door, remembering Nan's 'colour in

your cheeks' compliment. Seriously, the fucking violation. 'Tell me then!'

'Lennox Anderson. D'you remember him? He was like in sixth form when we started . . .'

'Yeah, yeah, I know. I mean,' Roche shakes her head, 'I know that he works with her. What the actual.' Roche is bug-eyed, her face screwed up. 'That means, that means he's like . . .'

'Twenty-four, hun.' Eden opens the door, smiling sweetly as she sweeps past Roche. 'At a push.'

22

THE COVEN

Moon wonders if it's Eden-related, when Roche gets home all het up and ferocious looking; thinks it's best to keep out of her way. She stays in the garden encouraging her seedlings along in the makeshift glasshouse she's fashioned from old picture frames. It looks utter shit, but it does the job; Moon's new foxgloves are on the fast-track growing experience of their lives. The seeds were bought over the internet, everything on Klarna, seeing as she's broke; no time to earn through readings, and of course, no thanks to the sorry demise of the astral reports. There's too much else to think about than other people's destinies right now.

Roche's still in her room when Itsy turns up, puffing and panting, smashing on the door. Moon flings it open, right in his face, her shoulders back and chin up, like the bad bitch she is.

Itsy scrunches his nose. With a smile, he sniffs knowingly. 'Old habits eh, Moony?'

'If you're coming here to look for her then she's well and truly out of your grasp.' Moon laughs. 'The sad lengths people will go to.'

'Honestly, what is it with you? Obsessed with me. Always have been. Should have been you I had my eye on, should it? Jog your memory of how your girl got here.'

'If only you could fathom how everybody else sees you, you'd never go out again.' He tries jabbing his foot inside, but Moon's having none of it. 'Now, fuck off.'

'I know she's in there! Delph!' Itsy shouts, through the gap. And as they push and pull, a dangerous game with their fingers around the door, Roche appears, one side of her head French-plaited and the other wild and free, wearing an enormous Wu-Tang Is For The Children t-shirt and orange leggings.

With everything she has, Roche manoeuvres him into hold, before shoving him onto the lawn. He yelps in surprise, looking to his hands that broke the fall, now full of bits of glass. Tiny cuts. Nothing much. An enormous dealio to a baby man.

'You little ...' Itsy turns on Roche, but like her nan, she does not budge a drop. 'You ...' he rages. Scrambling to his feet, he snaps his fingers in her face. 'I could fuck all your grand plans up, just like that. Best you don't give me any more opportunities. Nine hundred quid to repair that damage. When *you* should actually be thanking *me*. For keeping all your little secrets.' He watches her, making her flush all sorts of emotion, which he seems to take great pleasure from.

And it is in the watching of him that confirms exactly where Moon's foxgloves are headed ...

... When they flower, and she dries the blooms to pestle and mortar them – and then what ...

By the time her foxgloves are ready, it'll be too late. She knows it. Can't bear it. Thanks the universe Roche's here, and Delph's found the light and ain't in that flat. 'There's no winning her back with your greasy ways, now. Anyone would think she'd got a job in Specsavers instead of a DIY superstore. And that's where you went wrong,' Moon says smugly. 'She found fresh air. Amongst other things.' Moon looks at him, making sure to plant the seed, as jealousy ignites behind his eyes.

'You'll be sorry. Both of you.' He points at them, like he's performing his own hex. 'Just you wait.'

'No. You wait.' Moon won't take her eyes or her own finger off him, holds it till he's uncomfortable, noting the weight of his hate, outweighed only by his fear. 'In the dark stillness of night, when you're tucked up in your own head, in your own bed, are you happy?' Moon says it like she knows of the ghost that shares a flat with him, rattling his bolshiness. 'Being you.'

'If you won't tell me where she is, then at least ... at least tell me where he lives.' His desperation is so incredibly ... desperate.

'As if. Off you scamper, you tool.'

They watch the sad sag of his shoulders, the way he winces when he touches the steering wheel to drive away, both women feeling momentarily powerful. Their first win.

A team effort.

'Tit,' says Moon, noticing that the oaf managed to upturn her cacti when he fell. The soil's tipped out, light and desiccated of any nutrient. Amazing, how it continues to thrive in the most neglectful and barren of circumstances. Turning the plant back into the pot, it pricks her fingers, leaving pin-like deposits in the pads of her fingertips that she tweezes out with a pincer grip. 'We should all be like cacti,' Moon mutters. 'Any unwanted touching and bam, out come the needles. There'd be perforated perverts from here to kingdom come.'

Roche turns to head back inside. Then she stops. 'Is Mum having it off with Lennox Anderson from work?' she asks, and not as judgily as Moon expects.

She is saved by the bell. Moon's phone comes to life with a sales call from Ipswich that she'll never for the life of her answer – Public Enemy's, Fight the Power, leaping loud from the device, and neither Roche nor she can resist. Life's suspended as they thrash their arms around, caught in the beat. Grabbing her nan by the neck, Roche kisses her face.

Teenagers. There's majesty in their impulsiveness, that disregard for consequence. It's a madness Moon's beyond blessed to be part of again. She squeezes Roche back for a little too long. Grateful for the love.

For being needed.

Moon spots Lin, Delph's manager, collaring her quick before she disappears into one of the sheds in the garden section.

'Sorry love, I don't suppose you can tell me where I can find Delph Tennyson? Thought I'd pop in, surprise her.'

'Day off,' says Lin. 'A real shame, too. Three off sick this morning.' She looks down at the two big watering cans she's carrying. 'Spreading ourselves into areas I've no bloody clue about. Of course, that's not your problem. Can I pass on a message?'

'That's all right. I'll try her at home,' says Moon, not fancying the flat, or repeating the odd ick of a feeling she took home with her the last time she dropped by. Weird how Itsy losing his power also feels ominous, like a gaping hole that needs sealing up fast. Dragging other people down along with him would be apt for the likes of him. Moon only hopes Delph's strong enough to swim against his current. But she does seem it. She's made an incredible comeback. More than Moon ever imagined.

'State of it.' Moon looks around despairingly. 'Is there anyone actually green-fingered who works here?' she asks, following Lin as she waters the reduced row of plants, so many neglected babies in need of rescuing. 'You can't just drown 'em once a week and think that's enough. And it's too dark in this corner.'

'But they can't go anywhere else. They're ugly.'

'They're dying.'

'Look, I'm covering plywood and plasterboard during my break and missing out on my own half day off. I ain't got time to rearrange a few pots full of twigs.'

'I do.' Moon doesn't know what makes her say it, shifting her statement into a joke by 'ho-ho-ho'-ing out loud.

But Lin doesn't join in. 'Everyone thinks they want the garden jobs – till it's winter – or mixing paint, till they realize how excruciatingly boring it gets after the novelty of using the machine goes AWOL. Excuse me.' Lin huffs herself between the mini conifers, setting the rows straight and at the same time scanning for her next job, like a retail Robocop. 'Kev's been signed off, ain't been himself for months, wouldn't let anyone else help. So, if you've got a CV, I'd kill to find a quick replacement.' Lin scans Moon up and down too. 'You'd fit the demographic.'

'I was joking,' Moon says.

'That's a shame,' says Lin.

It isn't even the steady money that Moon thinks of first. But the different headscarves she'd wear each day in a different floral print. No, she's not sat exams or got any paper proof to prove it, but that doesn't discredit her expert horticultural knowledge.

Magnolia Mondays, Shrub Saturdays – where she'd accessorise in greens, earth tones, her favourite colours, offering tips and planting suggestions. Fruity Thursdays: how to get the best from your container-grown soft fruit. She looks at Lin, teetering off balance again with those giant watering cans, despite those good, strong calves. Moon's strong as hell too.

Perhaps she could do it if she B&Q'd it. Just like Delph has.

'And Lenny, is he in?'

'Day off.'

Moon puts two and two together, coming up with

fireworks. At least them being wrapped around each other means Delph's safe. She looks at the plants longingly. Thinks of her glorious garden at home. Can't fucking afford to save Miss Salvia and Mrs Hydrangea today. Can't afford very much at all. Can't even score, seeing as treating Roche to those bastard Edinburgh train tickets has left her dry as the poor desiccated Lady Lobelias here.

There are addicts and there are addicts. Moon's rarely been at the by-any-means-necessary-crossroads. Even in this latest unfortunate blip, there's been no alcohol. No matter that she's thought about it. Only a lot.

But, if she sounded Delph out about giving her a reference, Moon's sure Roche could whip up a CV online for her, no sweat; work might just be the answer. A distraction. She'd be the right role model too.

A different Queen of the Green. At last.

23

REALITY BURNS

Wellsend Grove, 2023

Delph's eyes open to a furious woman in a power suit. 'You know, Len, you could've just bloody asked instead of – oh!'

It's a frantic, very obvious dash for decency, as Delph and Lenny cover their bodies.

'Nice. Very nice,' the woman says, eyeing Delph up and down. Unimpressed. Of course, she'd be unimpressed.

'Jenna.' Lenny's already back in his jeans, following her down the hall, and as much as Delph strains, it's impossible to hear anything more than the odd word among the muffle of conversation between them. Delph makes out, 'grown woman', 'disrespectful', 'chancing little shit'. And, possibly the worst: 'What would Mum say?'

Dressed, Delph pulls her trainers on slowly, stalling, unsure whether to join Lenny, sit tight, or just flipping leg it. Reminding herself she is forty-two years old, she heads to the kitchen. 'I can't apologize enough,' she says straight away, cutting through their bickering. 'I'm Delphine. Delph.' Delph sticks out her hand.

'Hello, Delphine,' the woman says, with a sideways look at her brother. She shakes Delph's hand. Loosely. 'Jenna.'

'Lenny's talked a lot about you, Jenna.'

She rolls her eyes, beginning to open and close her cupboards, checking the fridge. 'You got brothers?'

'I've no siblings.'

'Then you've an excuse.' She gets out four mugs, switching the kettle on. 'Ain't you got a home of your own to seduce young men in?'

'Sis, this is my fault. Not Delph's.'

Jenna gives him a tired look. 'You better set my lounge straight, cos, er ...' She looks at her wrist, as if for the time, but there's no watch on it, 'you've got about ninety seconds before your mummy knocks.'

As Delph reaches for the handbag she's left so carelessly on the dining table, Jenna adds with a smile, 'She'll be keen to meet you.'

'Come on, Jen,' Lenny tries. 'This is such a new thing ...'

'Should've thought of that, you chancing little shit.' She looks at Delph, properly this time. 'On the bedside, in my room. There's a comb.' Softening slightly, she points across the hall to a room with the door closed. Taking her bag, Delph flees and closing the door behind her leans against it, her heart still pounding.

'Christ, how old is she?' Jenna's voice. Unmistakeably clear.

Delph can do little but cringe at her refection in Jenna's mirrored wardrobe: daylight reality is wicked. What fool gets here? Because Jenna, Lenny's older sister – older being the operative word – is still at least a decade younger than she is, typecasting Delph as some decrepit old cougar preying on her baby brother, more than likely.

Now it's meeting the family – after hours on a weird futon that she got not a proper second's sleep on; without her night bonnet and without cleansing, toning and moisturising. Without preservation, with no safe routine, this behaviour's unlike Delph. She loosens her ponytail, flicking the comb through the ends. Setting her top straight, she rubs at the trace of lipstick that's bled into her skin. All the zest from their coupling, gone.

Delph looks exactly what she is. Past it. Past this. Tired and Done. As the joy of Lenny avalanches into shame. Itsy was right about one thing: this behaviour is embarrassing. She listens to their low-key rowing, as she pencils her brows back in, dabbing on some beauty flash balm, a hopeful bid for self-improvement, and pops a Polo mint.

It is not jealousy. Nor envy. Delph doesn't want to rewind, wouldn't put her heart through any of it again. She strokes her throat. How could Lenny want her, really – and more to the point, why? Words like grateful taunt her thoughts. She's simply a distraction after his massively crucial dissertation. How could she be anything else, when there's an aura of has-been all around her. She gives herself a tight little smile. It's like a fat line's been drawn a foot behind her, and some-one's only just pointed it out. She's troughed.

Having sex with a twenty-five-year-old magnifies the trough by a billion.

If she wasn't in his sister's bedroom, she'd likely give into the tears. But, with the timebomb of his mother about to knock, Delp fights for composure. Shit. With a touch of powder, removing the shine from their sweaty connection, Delph resets herself to something respectable. And feeling far more age-appropriate, she rejoins them in the kitchen.

'Apologies again, Jenna.' Delph uses her name, does as Itsy would, with his status games, his assumed authority, as she tries rebalancing things a little. 'Last night really wasn't planned, and absolutely no disrespect was intended. I'll leave you to your family time.'

'Family time. We get enough of all that. Who're you?' a voice says behind Delph. Lord, Lenny's mother. Delph recognizes her straight away from the picture he showed her before. But there isn't the same hostility about her as she smiles at Delph curiously. Kindly.

Lenny takes Delph's arm. Stands tall. 'Mum, this is Delph. My girlfriend.' Looking at Delph, he shrugs – everything out in the open, his face says, relieved in a way. Certainly happy.

Everything out. Apart from the fact Delph's been some-body else's common-law wife for the past fifteen-odd years. Someone clinging on by the skin of his teeth.

How on earth is this even happening?

315

'It's so nice to meet you,' Delph says. 'And apologies for the circumstances, but I really must go.'

'I remember you, child.'

Child. Delph feels even more like crying.

'This the poor gal whose man got killed. Way back.' She fills in her children, both suddenly rocked in their socks. 'Twas a terrible sadness.' She looks to Delph, who's doing everything she can not to crumble at this stranger's unexpected knowledge. How the remembering rushes into her brain like a burst pipe, a spilt memory all over again. 'A little daughter you had, if I recollect.'

'Not so little these days. She's seventeen. And perfect.'

Delph's words make Lenny's mother smile, before she turns on her son. Watching him with a wonky eye, she kisses her teeth as though she's not entirely surprised by any of this. She's hardly seen him lately. 'Now, you know the rules, and there ain't never been many.'

'I know, Mum,' Lenny assures her. 'Nothing's changed.'

'I . . .' Walking backwards out of the kitchen, Delph waves off Lenny's attempts to come with her. 'Best go.' She smiles, has done enough apologizing, and heads for the front door, as the conversation continues without her.

'Bring her home properly, son . . . . What you thinking, putting her through this embarrassment . . . . 'Twas a tragedy . . . Got so skinny . . . A skeleton child pushing that buggy around the estate . . .'

Delph pulls the door shut behind her.

Approaching home, filled with the same old feelings of

inevitability and pointlessness, Delph readies herself to face Itsy. On her landing, almost at the front door, she gets a text.

LENNY: You OK?
LENNY: Sorry to put you through that.

Delph reads them but she doesn't reply. She ignores his phone call too.

LENNY: Are we OK?
LENNY: Hope so x

She's about to switch the whole thing off, the pocket-sized evidence of the very different life she's living now to the one beyond the door of 40 Esplanade Point, when she hesitates, Roche entering her head to change Delph's mind.

Just as her phone starts to ring again.

'I'm so sorry, Delph. Jenna wasn't meant to be back till tomorrow night. It was awkward, yeah, but they liked you. Especially Mum.' Lenny rushes on, 'Why did you never tell me about Roche's dad? I can't imagine how that must've felt. How it still must feel,' he adds carefully.

'Because having the same conversation, the same questions, over and over is hard. Bloody exhausting, actually. Yet it never comes as any less of a surprise when he's mentioned.' Delph doesn't think she's admitted this to anybody before. Even now, seventeen years later, it lands with the same bombshell type of agony. 'And it's all I became.

317

Just like your mother said. The poor girl whose man got murdered.'

'It makes sense. You make sense,' Lenny says, quieter now. 'I'm really sorry.'

'Why? You didn't do it.' Delph's voice changes too, returning to its usual placidity. 'Lenny, Roche's trying to ring me, I better go.'

'That's cool. Do what you gotta. So long as we're all right, yeah?'

It's one of the loveliest things about Delph, the easy way a cross word gets dealt with. Never any grudge, no sulky silences; a sincere apology and it's sorted. 'Of course we are.'

24

GREAT-GRANDFATHER TENNYSON

Tanners Grove, 2023

Roche has decided today's the day. It's a snap decision, and she doesn't even get through the school gates before she's turned on her heels and got herself on a bus, heading for Tanners Grove. Google Maps tells her if she gets off at the top of Hamish Avenue, it's a six-minute walk to the Feather and Broomstick.

Disembarking with a 'thank you', Roche walks up and down the road a few times, before coming to a small windowless newsagent, its frontage caged by security bars. Inside they don't take cards, so Roche rummages in the foulery of her rucksack for suitable tender as the shopkeeper taps his little tin tray, dragging her coins across the metal like something from *Oliver Twist*. It's very back in time basic, but a can of coke is a can of coke, and it's not exactly hardship opting for a Cadbury's whole nut. It's just when she's scraped up her change that she notices the skinny old man buying a pouch of Golden Virginia tobacco. He steps out of the queue to stare at her, before covering his face with trembling hands, like she's some god-awful ghost.

Weird old creep. Roche heads out, back onto the road, which is like something out of that soap *Coronation Street* – but south. Narrow terraces with yards, all dulled with the feeling of nothing quite changing. The pub near the corner looks almost part of them, blending in as if it's almost another house, and accounts for the small, small feeling Roche got when she saw it in Nan's pictures. There's also an alarming number of St George's flags draped outside, and though she gives patriotism the benefit of the doubt on account of the football, it totally changes her mind about even going in, let alone asking anyone any questions.

Roche hovers for a bit, finishing her chocolate bar. What she's hoping to find she can't even tell herself; this isn't an episode of *Long Lost Family*, where everything magically slips into place with a well-timed emotional reunion. Plus, Roche ain't even looking for emotion. All she wants, all she's come here for, is knowledge; bare facts without the pollution, without the mystery that comes from all the secrets and lies. In her heart, Roche believes it will help Nan too.

Stuffing the wrapper in her pocket, Roche stares across the road as it dawns on her that it's the same house from Nan's photo. Number 76, on a slice of wood tacked level with the letterbox. The picture where the dad's slumped posing over the front of a new Cortina, with two waist-height girls in pigtails wrapped around each thigh.

Roche crosses the road like she's drawn, runs her hand over the gate, which sings into her palm; vibrations, a power chasing through her like she's made of magnets. Who the hell needs questions when truth itself comes ringing out of her own body?

She edges closer to the house, with its lead-framed windows and condensation, sagging nets damp round the edges, touched with the beginnings of black mould. She catches the edge of an armchair through the window, floral with wooden arms, an ash tray perched on it, like Nan would do. And it's like she's with her now, suddenly, all around her, filling Roche's senses, not as a ghost might, nor even that Nan's aware it's happening, likely high as a kite in her garden with the jug of ginger tea, plotting and planning absolutely nothing, because it'll take more than a few plants to fuck up Itsy.

And he does so need fucking up. Bad.

'You.' The old man from the shop queue stands on the pavement, cowering when Roche turns to face him. 'Don't hurt me!' His tiny mouth collapses around his words. So very feeble. 'Don't you touch me.'

'I wouldn't hurt . . . I'm not going to hurt—'

He tries jabbing his stick in Roche's direction, but it skids, not properly disconnecting from the pavement. Despite her better judgment, Roche moves back through the gate to assist him, but he shakes her away, clutching his heart now, calling 'Help!' beseechingly, with actual tears in his eyes – those eyes – the only part of him not thoroughly old, still fresh-looking, like polished marbles, a few shades lighter than the amazing amber of Nan's. Of her own.

Fucking hell.

Roche keeps her distance as he begins to wheeze, wasting his precious breath by saying, 'I know your kind; I know what you're after.' His sheer terror from her presence is like he's spent the past year glued to GB News. He makes a sudden grab for her hand. 'You ... look like ... her.' Reaching for her, a sickening invades Roche as he connects, resisting – but only just – her gut truth reaction to push this frail man the hell away. To repel. Repel – just like she did with Itsy. 'I was ill,' the old man tells her. 'I'm still ill!' His knees give, his upper body too weak to use his walking stick for much more than letting his descent to the pavement happen more slowly. He is not hurt, but Roche's grateful when the shopkeeper races over, taking control by calling an ambulance – and what should Roche do now but pretend she's a stranger, not part of things, not connected to this moment as she sees a bus edging into the road just ahead and thinks that it is probably very much for the best that she slips off and leaves them to it.

But as soon as she sits in an aisle-facing seat, the worry hits Roche like a brick. What if he died? What if there's CCTV? What if it all looks like her fault? She was in his front garden for fuck's sakes. Was it his garden, even – though she is more than sure of it. Sure also, that this all holds some sort of fateful timeliness.

Roche presses the bell before the bus even turns the corner, dings till it stops, the driver clucking something unpleasant at her departing back, but she can't hear as she's out before the doors even properly open, sprinting back, asking the shopkeeper loudly if there's anything she can do. There's not, so she keeps her distance, and a hovering lookout for the ambulance. She ain't no hit and run. Even when it's some bigoted boomer that she thinks is her great-grandfather.

Roche reminds herself that she didn't hit him. She didn't even touch him.

But no one will believe her.

Roche chooses instead to believe her gut dread. Watching as the flashing lights of the ambulance enters the road up ahead, she presses her phone to her ear. 'Mum?'

Cos like, who else is there?

It feels good to let her mother take over, starting with assuring Roche that she did absolutely the right thing in staying put. 'But we don't need to stay now. Hospital's the best place for him. Everyone saw how concerned you were. Old boys have falls every day.' Mum's arm goes round Roche, who's had her fill of pulling away, trying to prove a point. 'What on earth were you doing in Tanners, anyway? Not chasing ghosts, I hope.'

But Roche can't leave. 'Please, Mum, let's just sit tight, at least till they get hold of his family.' She stays tucked under her arm, willing with everything for some relative to turn up and absolve her, praying, just like when she willed for her mother to ... to what? Be a proper adult; to put herself together? To say with her whole chest that she deserves better. Because it looks like she's done that. Mum's living again. A tired-looking but nonetheless beautiful woman, still with worries, but without the usual fear. Is it really Roche's years of hoping that's made Mum whole again? Adult, and together? And if it is, Roche hopes with all her heart that there's a chance her willing might work on Eden too. Not for the first time today, Roche wishes she could confide in her, share what's going on. But how can she text, after the delight Eden took from dropping the Mum's-got-a-toy-boy atom bomb. Their Snapchat streaks have died and after all their drama, it feels more and more likely that they have too. Even crossing paths in the bloody school corridors, it is almost impossible for Roche to hide how much Eden's missed. How her loss feels like a fucking amputation, like actual missing limb syndrome. It is just like that; a terrible pain from her absence. Always.

'Where's your sidekick?' Mum asks, picking up on the Eden vibe.

Everything leads back to Eden. How could it ever be different?

Roche rolls her eyes. 'Can we not?'

'Like that, is it?' Before Mum arrived, Roche had filled her time in the waiting room by snooping on Eden's socials. So much for all her tears and spitefulness, her latest pics show Eden in some shitty local nightclub with some girls from school, the girls Roche doesn't like, namely Winnie

Russell and Leila Turner, because all they do is groom themselves for men's likes, their Insta accounts like baby porn hubs. It doesn't suit Eden – and zooming in, which Roche has, on every fucking picture, Eden looks like she knows it too.

'Nan said you've been changing the locks.' Roche changes the subject, takes a sip of water, giving her mother a sideways glance.

'That's right.' Mum hesitates. 'Padlocks, actually. Lenny . . . you know, the guy at work . . .'

'Guy?' Roche bunches her nose. 'Guy?'

'What should I say, then? What do I call him?'

'I dunno. Toy boy, maybe.'

Mum turns to look at her. Realizes. 'Why didn't you say you knew – put me out of my bloody misery?'

'Nan's colour in your cheeks bullshit got me proper reaching, though,' Roche says, because it is hard acknowledging that somebody other than her is responsible for Mum's happiness. 'Good for you,' she adds, as Mum looks relieved, like, proper relieved. 'Because in all my life, Mum, I've never seen you so joyful. Serious.'

Joy. From this small heart-to-heart. And so might the healing continue.

'Reckon you'd get on.' Mum leans back in her chair, as if the reality of her relationship is only just sinking in for her too. 'Both beautiful creatures. Inside and out, which is rare these days.'

'Do you love him?'

'God. I don't know. Not yet.' She pauses. Thinks. 'I could. I've not thought about it. Love is ... bloody hard, actually. Sometimes, I—hey.' She cups Roche's face tenderly. 'Honestly, don't cry – this old boy will be absolutely fine, I'm sure ...'

'I'm gay, Mum.' It is said. Roche's tears give way to smiles, relieved this matters not, that Mum's still Mum, who gives zero fucks. 'And I love Eden. So much.'

'Well, then. Everything's beautiful.' It certainly sounds beautiful, pure on her mother's lips.

If only it were still true.

'You were after an update – on the falling man's condition?' Surprised their most intimate bubble's burst, Delph and Roche nod mutely at the nurse, who doesn't stop to let them speak, anyway. 'We've confirmed his address, but no next of kin yet. We're keeping him in.'

'Will he be okay?' Roche asks.

'We're waiting for his records. Between you and me, I'm imagining this little fall is the least of his problems.' The nurse softens a little. 'Why don't you leave a number? When there's more info on Mr Tennyson, I'll give you a tinkle, how's that?'

Roche watches her mother's colour leave her face, as she blinks quickly, asking for a first name, closing her eyes when she hears: Mr Peter Tennyson of Danes Lane, Tanner's Grove.

With a sigh, Mum says, 'I best ring your nan, explain what's happened.'

'No.' Roche stops her, instead gets out her own phone. 'I've got to be the one to tell her.'

Because accountability, innit?

Moon can't say she's at all sorry to see it.

Lion Dad's watery eyes, weak and wandering, really fucking helpless, is unlike all she's held in her head, stored in the dream dream memory bank, that's allowed him such a hold, this fragile nothing of a man, legs and arms like McDonald's straws, hard believing they were ever once strong enough to lift a pint glass, let alone his fist to send old Mouse Mum flying.

His deterioration reminds Moon of how Mouse Mum vanished, swallowing herself in a matter of weeks, her giant mouth and teeth and the huge hands of bone, which were once the tiniest, flutteriest things. How strange that the weakest, most insignificant parts of Ma in her ill health became the most prominent. How she'd wanted so much to hold Moon with those hands, straining out sorries from her skeletal jaw, like a horror film, like a zombie, like all the video nasties Moon could never stomach watching as entertainment.

Aren't there enough monsters in real life?

Immediately, Moon's glad she came. The power of this man in her head has not let her live a good life.

It could've been such a good, clean life.

But there was always so much to battle through first.

'Liver disease. Heart disease. Diabetes. Emphysema.' Moon chuckles, standing at the foot of his bedside, his notes in her surprisingly steady hands. In fact, it's the sound of her voice that sets him doing the shaking, the monitor he's attached to hitching up in speed. Role reversal. All these years later. Yet no less satisfying than the time with her old ouija. And Moon still doesn't know if that was down to her gifts, or just cracking good timing.

She could have twenty, thirty more years if she knocked the fags on the head. Took herself back to the doctor's, pressed reset and took her meds properly. But the thought of never knowing the beauty of feeling utterly bollocksed brings proper sorrow. And she'd be lying to herself if she promised it would never happen again.

Would she even have needed pills, all her many props, if it hadn't been for this man. Not that she's ever been the type to mope. All she can do now is try. Little by little. Day to day manageability. She could change. Some people can. And some people ...

Moon looks at him again – puny, full of tubes. This weakling, clinging-on no-mark of a no one.

'He's dying, Nan,' Roche tells her at his bedside, knowing not one thing.

'Well, I hope he hurries up,' Moon says, annoyed by the silly collective gasps from the pair of them, angels at this beast's bedside.

But they don't know who he really is.

Watching her mother carefully, Delph stands. 'We can go, Mum. We don't need to stay.'

'I don't mind staying. Like I say, it's all part of life.'

'Don't be wicked,' Roche says.

'Wicked?' Moon swoops at her, just as Delph moves between them. 'You instigate this revolting situation, and I'm the wicked one?' She tuts. 'I had such high hopes, but your judging's worse than your bloody mother's. Why don't you just sod off to Scotland now.' Yes, it flies from her mouth, but she means none of it. Always the way, disguising the truth with her acid words.

Roche looks so incredibly guilty that Moon feels almost vindicated. 'Please, Nan, let's not do this again.'

'Do what again?' asks Delph, as Moon snaps that she has nothing to do with this.

'This.' How does 'this' feel? Really, 'this' is only him, dying before her, small and hopeless. Moon doesn't need to be cruel – not to Roche, because you can't understand what you don't know – and there's no rule that states she even needs to be cruel to him, Dad, in 'this' – the timely coincidence of his demise, which feels a little like retribution.

Whether he remains unconscious or not, there is nothing good coming for him.

'Nan,' Roche tries again, but Moon is hard and unreceptive as Roche talks to her back, using therapy buzzword terminology, like 'ripping the plaster off'. And 'confronting the past to move forwards'. And the same as ever, because she's never, ever been able to say it, Moon turns sour, shutting herself in, impenetrable. But then. 'You can try and push us away, Nan. But we love you.'

'We do.' Delph's own light fluttery hand moves up Moon's

back, administering warmth right to the core of her mother. Her hand comes to a stop, radiating comfort. A balm. 'And we're not going anywhere.'

Everything about Moon, everything that's ever held her up, the mental scaffold she installed within herself that's somehow kept her going, suddenly evaporates, becoming as if she's made of nothing but tissue, or some other insignificant useless material that means she's weak, and fragile and ripe for hurting. Like her heart's too exposed. Too easily manipulated. Too fucking taken advantage of.

Like she's Joy again.

Who always spoke best through a picture, or a poem – or a story. Perhaps Moon could try telling it, speaking of it that way.

Telling. Like she's the snitch who can't keep a secret.

A secret is just the beginning. A secret brings with it a hold, which grows and emboldens the ill behaviours, and sows such powerful silence. A half-century of silence, if we're being precise.

'I used to be dead good, you know, one of the brightest at school. Always loved writing, and poetry – *you* might know that already,' Moon adds, for Roche's benefit, but doesn't look at her, keeping her back to them both, focusing on the bleep from the small screen, which traces that blip of a heartbeat.

'He liked breaking dreams. Making you small. He watched his own dad do it to my nan, who was really bloody gifted, but wasn't allowed to paint because there were real things to be getting on with. So repressed that all her creativity curdled into madness. Don't it always? Anyway, him, my dad, he just carried on the tradition.' Out comes her vape. The window's half open. Who's going to tell her no?

'I won this prize once. For the poetry. It really bothered him, got right under his skin, seeing me praised. Other kids' dads were so proud. But mine ...' Moon swallows thickly. Forgets the vape, begins to tremble. 'I'd always sleep with my curtains open; loved watching the moon as I fell asleep. And this one night, instead of the sky, there was the shadow of him. D'you remember?' Moon asks the old bones in white sheets, but gets nothing, not even a jumpier line on the screen. 'Stumbling pissed into my room.' Closing the door behind him. Moon holds her breath, there again, his beery rot mouth on her face. 'I knew it was going to happen. Could tell, felt it coming. That intention. That I'd stopped being someone to look after, and turned instead into someone ... that he was ... fascinated by.

'The thing, the thing that made it worse, was how he'd be so much nicer to me. To everyone. He'd even give me money.' A small sound comes from the back of her throat. 'I'd give it to Ma. Slip it in her purse without her knowing. Save her having to go crawling round him for a bit of extra keep. And you know, every time his ... fascinated hands touched me, climbed my legs to get what he wanted, all I'd do is think of the day I'd walk out for good. Because I thought, I really believed, I was going places. That I'd go and never look back.' Moon adds, so very sadly, 'Fifty-nine years, and the furthest I got was half an hour up the road.'

Roche is blanched, ghostlike, unable to hold in her steady weeping. 'He raped you?'

'For years and years. And that's not even the worst of it. On my life, this ...' Moon leans across the bed, watching his eyelids flicker in his otherwise motionless face, thinks of all the words, she still cannot say. '... does not deserve any kindness.'

'But my sister did. Janie.' Names sound different when spoken aloud, instead of whispering round in your head. 'She was sweet and gentle and really fucking funny before she was scared. Before she started hurting herself, before you had the chance to.' It's as if Moon is speaking to him now, in clear unhidden fact. 'It wasn't a known-out-loud thing then, self-harming. Self-inflicted violence. No one knew anything about it. And it killed her.' She leans closer, assessing the papery state of him; scaly, sore. 'You killed her. And you almost, almost killed me too!' Moon gasps, her knees suddenly wobbly, as Delph and Roche rush to support her, catch her crumble, each taking a hand of hers, which brings nothing but tears. And better words. 'But look what I've got. Look who I am without you.' Leaning closer to him, Moon squeezes their hands and does not stop. 'Love saved me. D'you hear that, Mother Fucker? Love saved me.'

People always get stuck in the past. And what's the good in that? Living a self-contained never-ending torture. A mental form of self-harm. But never Moon. She's here. Her own beautiful reinvention. Queen of nothing but the present.

Surviving.

This moment was needed. Emotionally explosive, yet restorative. But it is hard not to cry. 'I hope it's painful, you old cunt.'

Because this is painful. Too much. Moon can't shake the image of Janie. The only person who truly knew her, until she didn't, and she was gone. Now she feels her close again – observing, never disturbing. Same way she led her background life. Same way she took those scissors and—

Fuck this shit. Fuck it right up the wrong'un.

'Nan.' Roche's voice is full of worry, as Moon shakes them off. 'Stop. At least say where you're going.'

'Where am I going?' Moon sniffs. 'I'm knocking on sixty you nosey cow, and it's none of your bloody business.' She slams the door, leaving behind her cape.

Just her rage keeping her warm.

Vodka greets Moon's throat like an old friend. Half a bottle down, and she's extracted the dregs of her funds from a cashpoint, posting the money through Hungry Harvey's letterbox. He pushes out a small envelope that she pushes back. 'Roll me one for the road?' she asks, gesturing into the night. 'I can't see for shit.' Grunting behind the door, Hungry Harvey, or indeed whoever it is running shop tonight, does as they're told. 'Genius,' says Moon, all admiration as it comes back through the letterbox and into her happy hand. 'Thanks a million.'

She's a lot of catching up to do. The triple whammy of codeine, marijuana and alcohol sends her into the stratosphere, embracing the high that begins the dissipation, obliterating every ounce of sadness.

Moon walks along the promenade. The sea's slippery and silvery and the noise enticing, but she's still enough wits not to venture down to the water, knowing people by name, by addled friendship, who made similar errors. Where are they, now they cease to exist, having entered some measureless euphoria, becoming part of the stars and unknown otherworldliness; just an element of the universe for the blissful infinite.

Life on earth, their identity, and their mistakes.

Irrelevant.

There's the old seafront. The pier, jutting from the prom. Where all the joy used to happen. The bygone holiday time that seems a fucking nonsense: Miss Lovely Legs, Mr Knobbly Knees. A place people came by choice. And people still try – even Six Dinner Sheila next door, who tried renting her spare room on Airbnb; only forty minutes from London, Wellsend one of Britain's sunniest seaside towns. A bit of staycation exploitation, but there's no mistaking the feeling that the place is stuck.

Like her. Like her whole life.

More booze. More of the green. It is dark when Moon finally reaches the parade of shops that means she's not far from home. She's hungry. Thirsty for more – for a litre of Co-op vodka, cheap as chips lemonade, and pie and actual chips from next door. She sits on the bench outside, eating with her hands as some dumpy cow takes the piss. Well. Fuck the lot of them.

Fuck. The. World.

Moon thinks she can remember. The never-ending space pre-dating her birth, a forever blackness lit by the tiniest of stars. Mind emptied. Or no mind at all. But still definitely her. Moon's soul a hologram, a transparent golden disk, ethereal, weightless.

In her utter annihilation, Moon wonders if she's happy. Christ, she feels sick. A smashed old trash bat, a walking cat-acomb for the demons of her past. Each dead memory a pain that's stretched across her lifetime. And if she's truly honest, it's been exhausting.

'I'm tired, you hear me?' she informs a pair of youths she shuffles past, heading off home.

'You good, love?' one of them asks. The short one, with a kind face. Though he's very, very out of focus.

'Who knows, you charmer,' Moon nods, graciously. 'Don't fret, pet. I only live round the corner. I don't suppose you have a light?' The youth holds one out for her, his kind face flabbergasted when she blazes up with a very polite, 'Thanks, babycakes.'

Full-bellied and proper bollocksed, Moon approaches her turning, a hand on the wall to steady herself. She takes a moment to look around; ain't so obliterated not to sense the pending danger of finding herself alone in a quiet spot. Cutting through the shadowy rows of cars and ancient oil spills, past the old multi-storey on the corner, Moon senses his approach before he grabs her; a hand on her back, the other on the back of her neck. Coordinated handfuls that do more than just hurt. It's not raining, but the wall Moon is slammed against feels wet to the touch, her hair catching on gritstone and cement. 'So strong,' she says, 'but you don't frighten me.' She fucking means it too. 'You never have.'

Delph pictures Itsy's waiting face; his questions, his endless, endless observation . . . But the flat's empty.

The relief of it. Delph closes the door, closes her eyes.

And weeps.

For has this not been the longest, longest of days? Running a bath, Delph reaches for her toothbrush, noticing Itsy's is missing. His washbag's vanished too – and his razor. What the— In the bedroom his underwear's gone, along with his clean pile of laundry, jewellery, colognes . . .

The weirdest of things. Delph checks for his passport – that's not here either and it crosses her mind that he may've returned to Jamaica. But surely, even in their awkward sorry state of things, he'd have left a note, sent her a bloody text, at least.

Before Delph calls him, she logs into Facebook, trying to glean in advance what fresh family tragedy might've sent him packing, not having looked since the panic to get him those bargain flights. And Delph must be losing her mind, because Itsy's sister Claudette's is the first post on her feed, a picture from less than an hour ago. Of their mother.

'Happy birthday, Mum. So grateful you got to see your 90th. Here's to many more!'

A message underneath from another sibling, Roberta: 'Keep getting better, Mum! We love you.'

Has Itsy lied about his own mother dying? Delph rolls her eyes at her own stupid question. Then feels foolish because she's pleased his mum's living and breathing, that it's good news, misguided maybe, but probably stems from her being stuck half the day in that bloody hospital.

That long man made of bones had been her grandfather. Who broke her mother's happiness and innocence. Rape. A rush of sadness enters her heart. Mother Moon's secret, that she tried burying so deeply she even changed her name. Like Roche had, most of the journey back, Delph weeps with abandon, having no skills to make any of it better.

It's out of character, but Delph doesn't care about the stigma of drinking alone. Thinking fuck to it, she pours a big rum to accompany her cigarette on the balcony. All looks neglected but her asparagus, which hasn't suffered from the recent lack of her attention, as fine as any spear you'd find in a supermarket. Delph admires its sturdy girth, how it pretty much takes care of itself, taking nourishment from its own roots. It feels like a good example.

'So you're telling me, all I do is press that button, and I get a coffee shop coffee?' Itsy, his smooth unmistakeable tone, fills Delph's ears, making her jump like someone's firing bullets at her feet.

But he's not behind her. Not in the flat at all. Only when she hears him again, laughing along with somebody else, does Delph realize his voice is coming from above her.

In seconds, she's banging on Geena's door. 'I told you things,' Delph gasps at her perfect friend, feeling relief, like a clean line, because this undoubtedly declares Delph and Itsy's relationship dead. But it's the betrayal of the more important kind, which has so very little to do with Itsy, that hits her hardest, the most gutting part of all. 'I told you things I'd never admitted out loud.'

'Yes.' Wearing a brilliant white tracksuit, like some snow leopard, Geena folds her arms. '*You* said you'd rather B&Q than your man. But you've nothing to be jealous about. I'm just doing him a favour. Was you who kicked him out, weren't it?'

'Me?'

'Look, maybe try talking in the morning. Like I say, I am neutral, happy to mediate.' Behind Geena, Itsy makes noises, like some satisfied king of the castle.

'How you turn your telly over, baby?' Itsy asks, Geena knowing how he's watching her backside as she gives him that slow smile over her shoulder, the same smile that sent most of St Martin's hot-blooded pupils into cardiac, back in the day.

Baby.

'You know what, Geena?'

But Delph doesn't know what.

Geena leans out into the hall, whispering in Delph's ear. 'True love never was your motivation for being with him, anyway. Be honest.' Staring at Delph, she raises her brows. 'Ain't I done you a massive favour?'

But Delph can only hear her mother. '*I always said, you*

338

wouldn't want her in your lifeboat.' Crazy old bitch. Accurate as fuck. And it is then Delph remembers. 'Your mum's looking well, Itsy. If only she knew what a pig of a son she had.' She calls around the door. 'Wonder what your sisters would think if I filled them in about you faking her death?'

That gets him moving. He leans into the frame, taking up all the space, exactly like this is his kingdom now.

'What you hasslin' me for? You got what you wanted. Our delicious mutual friend's giving us some space. Thought you'd need it.' He looks at Delph like she's dipped in shit. 'The girl must be disgusted.'

'Disgusted?'

'With her pervert cougar of a mother. Couldn't you be his mother too? Shame of it.'

'As far as I'm concerned, you can stay up here forever.' An unrepentant energy rises in Delph's belly as she pushes a finger into Itsy's chest. 'But bother me or my family again, and I'll be speaking to yours.'

Itsy ignores the threat. 'Boy'll get bored with the MILF shit. You're nothing but a fetish.' He spits at her back as she heads for the stairs.

'It's so much better than being yours,' Delph says, thinking fuck you too as he slams the door on her, just as Eden is heading up, who quietly turns back down the stairs, avoiding having to pass her. 'Eden,' Delph calls down the stairwell, but there's no answer, just the sound of the fire doors far below opening then shutting, as Delph hopes with every exhausted bone in her body that she can begin to put things right.

Now she's back on her own time again.
Properly and permanently.
For ever, amen.

25

EDINBURGH

Self-Explanatory, 2023

Roche takes a lot of convincing to go to Edinburgh at all, because Nan's still MIA. Gone since she flew from the hospital. Her coat's on its peg back at home, and every time Roche notices the dark green cape hanging there without its owner, she feels sick.

It's been four days.

'Don't keep worrying,' Mum assures her on the phone, as Roche heads to the train station. 'This is what she does.' She says it matter of factly, but Roche hears the worry in the strain of her voice. Even with Nan's previous inexplicable vanishing, four days is a long time. 'You know, I never doubt her love, I'd even trust her with my life, knowing all the while what an utterly grave mistake that likely is. Funny, really. But that, I suppose, is what it's like having an addict as a parent. All the love in the world but never any truly solid ground.'

This is the uncertainty Mum warned Roche of, right at the beginning. Nan, made of love and fun in one minute, then transformed into a stranger the next, pushing everyone away because she wants to be left to just get off her tits. Never any hint of dealing or acknowledging her problems or her past – which are serious. And plenty. But even Roche must admit that Nan's behaviour is a total return to type.

'Now, are you sure you don't want me to come too?'

But something in Roche tells her that going alone is meant to be. Like maybe it's some final barrier she must break through to move onwards unsupported. Mum, of course, is happy she's off and flourishing; Nan too had been an incredible champion, before she disappeared. And Eden. Well, Eden will probably be glad to see the back of her. 'No, Mum. But thank you. And I promise I'll ring as soon as I get there.' Roche pauses. 'Has ... has there been any news?'

'The demon clings on.' It is the addition of him that's multiplied the normal type of worry; Nan's absence different from the stubborn fury when they had beef before. Faced with her demon, Nan had cracked open before their eyes, found the strength to let them in, to take off the Moon mask. And all Roche has wanted to do since, is hold her. Comfort her.

Love her.

'Well, let me know if that changes.' Pulled down instead of full of excitement, Roche changes the subject. Because hasn't she been counting the minutes till this moment? 'So, what are you doing on your day off?'

'Channelling a bit of Mother Moon, this morning, actually. I'm about to eat my girthy asparagus.'

'Sounds deeply phallic. Go on.'

'With great ceremony.' Mum ignores her. 'With a soft-boiled egg. Then, I'll try very hard not to keep checking my phone for you. And I've got a lunch date.'

'TMI. But have a nice time and all that.'

'Not with Lenny, cheeky. I bumped into a lady I know at the hospital. She's not been well, and I thought it'd be nice for her ...'

'You're proper kind, Mum.'

'I could be kinder.' Mum sighs. 'I saw Eden briefly, but she shot off before I could speak to her. Should've gone after her, but after the day we'd had ...' Mum drifts off. 'I just didn't have it in me for anything else. I got a feeling she was upset. I hope she's all right.'

'Well ... Well, you're my mum. Not her's, innit.' Inside, Roche is desolate. 'I love you.'

'Stay safe. Keep in touch. I love you too.'

'I will, Mum.'

'Remember Roche – you're fantastic.'

It's a good job Roche likes trains.

Before she alights, stiff and feeling very, very far away, Roche tries once more to ring Nan, her phone again going straight to voicemail. She never was very good at remembering to charge her battery, anyway. The hope of Nan coming last minute ain't dead yet, but neither is Roche frightened to be here exploring on her ownsome. It's light, the sun hitting the layered buildings that seem to stagger down from on high towards her, feeling disorientated and tiny beneath the Edinburgh Waverley station sign, noting its British Rail font, like a friendly nod to the old familiar. Roche's never been anywhere like it; this place of such defining geography. A city, set into the hilly surround, like a stone pushed into the green fabric of a jewellery cushion – a visual balance of nature against human progress. Of order and wilderness, which tells her there's more out there. There is always more. Yes, this is her first encounter, but it's beautiful. Perhaps even love at first sight.

Weird, how being somewhere totally different heightens your senses. Edinburgh feels proper olden times – more like London than she thought it would. The streets share those same feelings of the past that emanates off the old brick walls, that look proper grimy, a place that's lived life and has all the stories to tell. Roche takes a scattergun of pictures she can study properly later, cos is there anything worse than looking like you've not got a clue what you're doing? The hills in the very far distance appear again through her lens – and no, this is not like London, Roche realizes, because here a different kind of energy to the solely urban wraps itself around her. God, Nan would bloody love it. Suddenly cold, adding a jumper to her layers, Roche checks her weather app – it's thirteen degrees and showers tomorrow; twenty-two and light cloud back at home. Thinks she'd still rather be here.

Nan would be pleased to know there's a Gregg's too. Cheaply fed and with a bellyful of tea, Roche feels less of a tourist, finds her hotel no sweat and, so far, thinks everyone's friendly, apart from the pair of basics giving her evils outside a KFC. Sunshine or showers, wherever you are, the bitches will always be bitches.

Checked in and showered, after a quick text to Mum, Roche sets out exploring. It's almost 8.30 p.m. in her busy pocket of the city centre, and one bold drink is the plan. To toast herself – not as a scaredy cat in her little en-suite, but as a grown woman in a new city. Her new home. Maybe.

'What you having?' The barperson asks and Roche says a beer, ignoring the sparkles she imagined celebrating with. But sparkling drinks were Eden's thing – and truth, Prosecco's never not given Roche chronic wind, anyway.

And it's while she's thinking how she's saved her guts that a bloke about her age approaches her, and when he opens his mouth to talk, he sounds incredibly just like she does, and it's nice, familiar, rather than remembering she's a visiting species every time she opens her mouth. 'Essex?' he says, with a high five. And what are the odds? 'Yes, my sister!'

'Wellsend, to be precise. You?'

'Just a Billericay boy spreading my wings. Here for uni?'

'Yes!' says Roche, as they cheers bottles and talk open days, courses, and three drinks later it's almost ten o'clock.

She's doing it. Letting herself go in the throb of lights and it's fun to dance but she's not stupid. Knows as soon as he offers to buy whatever the hell she likes from the extortionate drinks menu that he likes-her-likes-her. It's nice to be admired, though, a comfort against the loneliness she's been fighting since her and Eden's parting of ways.

'*Don't accept anything,*' comes Nan's voice in her gut, like a personal message announcement from Jesus, '*cos chances are they'll want something in return.*' It doesn't take half a second for Roche to fill in as to who Nan was talking about when she first heard that advice.

He, George, bounces closer to her on the dancefloor, all sweat and pretty eyes. She can't hear what he says as she pushes her hair back, shakes her head for him to repeat it. 'You're fucking stunning,' she thinks he says, blushing all the same. And when he puts a hand on her waist, and she lifts it off and places it confidently back at his side, he looks at her for a long moment as if something's clicked. 'You gay?' he asks, and this time she hears him perfectly.

'Yeah,' Roche says, 'I am.'

'That's cool,' he says, easily. And it totally, totally, *totally* is.

Moon listens to it all: 'You are seven shades of special to get this far.' She enters the lecture hall, an actual lecture hall that she's seen so many times in films: slumped scholars in staggered rows; a presentation delivered to the brainiacs by charming, slightly scruffy academics.

'Freedom comes from the courage of your own convictions. From the decisions you make. And you deserve opportunity, encouragement. You deserve everything your greatness can offer you. Here, with our guidance, you will reach your potential. Go into the world and into careers some can only aspire to . . .'

Here is the world's future. And it feels like its own community. A place of special otherness. A selectivity. Moon knows, sure as eggs, that even if she'd got herself to uni when she should've, she'd still never have been the right shape for it. Wasn't her brashness already too much of a curse, being told perpetually to moderate herself? It would've only got worse somewhere like here, as she evolved into something more socially fitting, likely fighting it all the way. Moon thinks it was better to choose herself, where her poor fit never mattered.

But it could've all been hers; she was certainly bright enough. Didn't Ma always say how she was born blessed, for fuck's sakes, because looks can get you everywhere. Looks open all the doors. And looks did. First at home and then everywhere she went. But Ma never meant coming somewhere like here, for a career, building a life of perfect self-sufficiency; she meant men can get you everywhere if you're a pretty girl, especially if you're built beyond the ordinary. But Moon never wanted to be measured by goddess standards. Nope, she rejected the bullshit and embraced her own version of beauty – doing it braless for a while, too, her swinging mammaries that gave her ferocious indigestion to be so unsupported but became a battle of wills against all she'd so daftly swallowed, sick of looking and living any sort of life the way men and silly society thought she should.

Fuck men.

Moon touches her head, feels the bruise, the only consequence of that vicious arsehole the other night. What night
exactly, she can't do the maths, all nights since the hospital
having blurred into one. Till last night. Her internal clock
reminding her the bender's gone on long enough, which to be
fair had its breakthroughs and benefits too. But she's sweaty;
feels the vodka escaping her skin, hot and clammy above her
collar. Booze is shit when you're old and can't get over it the
next day. Her five-day hangover feels like she's recovering
from some terrible cranial surgery.

But she is here. And really, what else matters?

Moon's shit doesn't apply to Roche. Her granddaughter's
brilliance and all her glorious potential makes Moon swell
with pride.

She spots her, third row back, defined by that glorious hair.
Call her biased, but Moon sees her shine, bright beyond the
others, sat there, listening to everything, surrounded by stars.
Shuffling down a side gangway, hauling herself in the row
behind her, she jabs Roche in the shoulder. 'Listen.' She leans in,
noting how Roche flinches at the breath Moon's under no illu-
sion she could likely light a match to. 'Just get yourself here and
don't ever fucking look back.' Before Roche can do much more
than gasp at the relief of seeing her, Moon orders her to face the
front. 'Now pay attention. I'll catch up with you later, I promise.'

Roche spots her little mother, perched on the wall outside
her hotel. In her skinny jeans and messy high bun, she could

be a student herself. She looks ... Normal. Like how she always should've.

'That's your mum?' says George, with a low whistle. He side-eyes Roche. 'Is she gay too?'

Roche shoves him, laughing, says she'll catch him on Snaps and thanks him for walking her back. Carefree. Care-Fucking-Free. 'Mum.' Roche hugs her tightly. 'What are you even doing here?'

'I had a point to prove, didn't I? That nobody has the slightest say over how I live my life.' Mum smiles, and Roche knows suddenly what Nan means when she says how somebody's full of lights. What a perfect thing to witness – more so, to view such a dazzling transformation within her own quiet mother. 'So, I chose to buy a train ticket to Edinburgh. And I am choosing to take my brave beautiful daughter out for dinner. Your choice – and after,' she winks, 'I've got a little treat for your nan.'

Roche's choice is a Lebanese restaurant. In a small shisha lounge, they eat amidst embroidered floor cushions, tassels, gorgeousness – and hookah pipes. Nan's in her element, eating for ten, better for the rest – and glad she wore the maxi skirt, which rocks so well with the décor, even if it is a bit chilly.

That they came to support her independently means more to Roche than she's able to say. The manifestations are working. Roche hopes they keep providing to get her back here, because Edinburgh does seem the right fit. How she knew it would be, though, is beyond her. It was only a daydream.

A vague aim. And now look. Look where daydreaming can get you.

'Roche, they can't be tears – what on earth's the matter?' Nan says, bundling her close against her fleshy breasts. 'What is it?' she cocks an ear to a squashed Roche. 'You missed me? Bless your cottons.' Releasing her, Moon smothers more aubergine dip on her bread. 'I had things to do. To sort out. Don't worry. Everything's going to be fine.'

'I bloody loved today,' says Roche. 'And I do get good vibes here. I'm so very glad you came. Things feel good.'

'Things will be good, I promise,' says Nan.

'You're not God, Mum,' says Mum, in a way Roche once would've thought made her a chronic dry lunch.

Once would've.

Nan wags her finger at Mum. 'Why not? Why can't I know things, solve things? Does it make me any less gifted because my brain likes naughty substances? Because I'm a noisy unreliable old flake—'

'Your words, not mine. But you might be right, after all.' A smile begins around Mum's lips. 'I've got the keys to move into my new place. It's ready from next week. So that's that.' Mum watches them for reaction. 'Itsy keeping everything in his name proved beneficial, after all.' Nan's mouth hangs open, her look of delight building with every word Mum says. 'How did you wangle that? Bulldog June opposite's firstborn was almost in secondary school before they had even a whiff of a council house. Imagine that, all them years on a waiting list . . .'

'No, not council. Thanks to the bingo win, I'll be renting privately. My friend Nora's letting out her upstairs, turning it into a flat, now her legs aren't so good. She's lived there since God was born, I think. Right on the seafront ...' Mum drops her lovely eyes to her plate. 'And Lenny said he'd help renovate.'

'Lenny.' Roche raises her brows, looking to Nan conspiratorially.

'Lenny with his do-it-yourself skills,' Nan adds. 'Lenny the scotch bonnet.'

'Not to live together. None of that.' Roche likes how Mum makes sure they know this is her plan and nobody else's. 'This is my time now. Our time.' She raises her shoulders, lifting her glass. 'So, cheers.'

'Halle-fucking-lujah, baby. Christ,' Nan says, 'my face aches with joy. Why don't you come back with us, stay till next week?'

'I can't, Mum, I need to pack, get things straight. Plus, there's work. I'll need that job more than ever now, won't I?'

'He'd have been so proud.' Nan looks out of the window, up at the night sky, just as Mum's doing.

'I reckon, too,' Mum smiles, and though the pain remains in it, Roche sees very clearly that it's real. 'I like this place. Like how distant I feel from ... As if something, somewhere, is finally healing.'

Edinburgh. Who'd've thought it? For all of them.

'Come on, Mother Moon.' Mum's voice is soft, full of love. 'I've got a surprise for you.'

*

Moon, after the witches walking tour – Delph's blessing of an idea that came from asking a tour guide for directions earlier – sits on a bench with her small tin of rollies, and sparks the wrong one up.

'A tad disrespectful, Mum?' Delph says, more from habit than being truly miffed.

'Love, I don't think the witches would mind.' What's more magic than smoking a plant that kisses your brain, anyway? 'Terrible, to think they'd have been put to death for less.'

'I never knew hag was a Scots word for a witch,' says Roche.

'I've been called both many a time, back home,' Moon chuckles. 'Like it's an insult. Stupid Brits.'

'You're a Brit.'

'I'm a Citizen of Nowhere. A Friend of the fucking Earth. Always have been.' Rising to get a good look at it one more time, Moon kisses the brass plaque above the Witches Well, now a drinking fountain, feeling the raised pattern of the image of a foxglove on her lips.

One last time she reads the plaque, still feeling at odds with the words, which are not half the apology Moon expected to find here:

... This fountain, designed by John Duncan, RSA, is near the site on which many witches were burned at the stake. The wicked head and serene head signify that some used their exceptional knowledge for evil purposes while others were

misunderstood and wished their kind nothing but good. The serpent has the dual significance of evil and wisdom. The foxglove spray further emphasises the dual purpose of many common objects ...

Imagine the fear, arriving at this very spot, so long before her time. But Moon knows it would've been her too, had she been about then – and maybe, along the way, she grudgingly admits, there's been a scratch of progress.

Not enough, though. Not by any means. And will the imbalance ever resolve itself, truly? Will anyone ever be able to live without fear, without the worry of anticipating threat? Moon traces the foxgloves again. Wonders maybe.

'Give me your hands. The both of you. Quick.' Moon doesn't know what compels her to ask them to, but there's something in the way she says it that makes them do as they're told. 'Bloody hell,' Delph says with a smile, closing her eyes. 'Do I even want to know.'

Moon ignores her. Embraces the moment anyway. Because the good omens and the God winks are in all the little moments we can miss in the world. And we owe it to our souls to remain vigilant. 'Now my girls, it's down to us to forge our own paths, once we're grown. Can't keep laying the blame of our desires and mistakes on all that's wrong and gone, letting grudges get in the way of the future. Remember, the universe is your biggest cheerleader, when you choose to acknowledge and embrace it.'

'But how do we do that?' asks Roche.

'Ah, love,' Moon says, so very glad she asked. 'Just hold your arms out and claim it.' She gathers her most precious into her own arms, wrapping them both in love. 'It's all yours.'

26

Scholarships:
AKA Flora and Folk Tales

Wellsend, 2023

'Roche,' greets Willow, pleased to see her. Her smile grows when she spots what's in Roche's hand. 'Edinburgh was all you hoped for, I take it?'

'More.' Roche hands out the sheet of paper protected by a plastic pocket. 'I've already sent it, just wanted you to read it. Felt weird, writing something truthful, for once. You don't get much chance in lessons, being taught what they've already decided is correct, long before my take on it.'

'That'll change for the better at university. Your skills will prove invaluable there, I've no doubt.' Willow gives Roche's arm a little squeeze that makes her fizz with pleasure. 'I'll save this for my tea break. I really look forward to reading it.'

355

27

INSPECTOR EDEN – AND
A SECOND FLOURISH

Esplanade Point, Wellsend South, 2023

Delph says 'yes' because she can. Packing up Esplanade Point can wait, and she does so want to show Lenny her new abode, especially while it's empty. She has missed him. Next week she'll go each day after work, cleaning the little place up in preparation for Nora's return home from hospital. Nora, the lovely old duck from that day at the bingo with Geena, the day Delph's world began turning again. Which really wasn't so long ago, but God, what a blast back into living it's been.

'Geena Maneater,' was the first thing Mother Moon said, when Delph spoke of Geena's deception. Her school nickname's still as apt, and Delph's still as oddly grateful for her betrayal. She'd watched them the other morning, linking arms, heading off to work, Geena in her silky 70 deniers, dressed in the neatest, blackest, most corporate two-piece suit, which hit every curve for maximum impact, and Itsy, all smugly satisfied, like he's bagged the arm-candy of the century. But forgiveness is different from forgetting. And keeping Geena at arm's length requires so much less energy than enemy status. Delph's had enough of grudges.

And though 40 Esplanade Point no longer contains him, even without Itsy, Delph's absolutely no desire for the flat to contain her either.

What a comfort knowing she has money, a lump of her very own, which has secured Nora's deposit, and which will keep Delph going too, now she's changing jobs, in the dry gap between wages. Because the moment Mother Moon spoke of joining her in B&Q was the God wink Delph needed to find something else.

More healthy change.

Without doubt, Lenny is heaven sent; in mind, spirit and – oh Delph's days – body too. His stomach and chest, taut pouches of peak condition. Lenny, who adores her. He does, undoubtedly, by the soft look about him, the way he strokes her face like they're on the telly, as if they're head over heels. And normal. Delph feels luscious in his arms, beautiful, and it elevates to the clouds and back, puts a goodness, a warmth, back in her bones. A real, living connected feeling. Heat. Comfort. The very real sense of being in the absolute right place.

Another feeling of coming home.

'I could get used to this,' he says, after they've trembled their way through two climaxes, without any risk of interruption. 'Us together. Properly.'

'How together?' Delph asks with a smile, gesturing to his arms, already looping them tightly together in nakedness.

'I've a second interview Monday next. It's thirty-eight-K a year. Starting.' He turns, making sure she's listening properly. 'I know what you need now, more than anything, is freedom, and I don't expect . . . I never want to do anything but help you fly. Honestly, you mean everything to me. I've never felt nothing like it. Do you think this, this thing we've got, is good?'

Oh God, she does.

Such a deep, gentle soul. Striking how Itsy was not. How Delph's mind shrank in step with her world. And she felt nothing but relief.

But that is behind her now.

'I love you,' Lenny says, and when he heads to the bathroom, beckoning her to follow and turning on the shower, doubt punches her in the guts so visibly he notices. 'Please, don't do that.' He holds her face like she's treasure. 'Don't not feel because it's easier. Heat. Steam. Your own little fixer-upper. How perfect is this? Me and you, Delphine.' Leading her into the cubicle, Lenny begins to soap her neck, his hands travelling across her wet skin, as Delph does what all the dazzling celebs do, and lives in the moment. Hasn't fear and doubt eaten up enough of her life? Letting go, she frees herself, as all the tricky shit flies out the window, and he presses her gently against the tiles, and loves her again.

Delph has an adrenaline spring in her steps as she heads back to Esplanade Point. That's what she's calling her nerves, anyway. All she's got to do is pick up her bags, because she decided, just then, when locking up her little fixer-upper, that there will be No More Flat. Even before Mother Moon said it, the place had felt ominous, and there's really no need to suffer it any longer. Until she's got Nora's clean and in order, she'll just get her stuff and head home to Wellsend Grove.

Yes. Home.

The air is delicious on her face, keeping the blessed feels of being free. Delph walks along, hands in her pockets, and apart from her holdall, realizes she doesn't own very much of anything at all. Baggage. Possessions. She's accumulated no more of them really than she had at twenty-odd years old. Yes, there was the lightweight purchasing, the odd photo frame, a new cushion or two when she first moved in. But nothing that couldn't fill a suitcase, even if she had one. Which doesn't really matter, because she wouldn't want to fill it anyway.

There is nothing from this life lived on standby that Delph wants to take.

But then Eden.

She sits, hugging her knees to her chest outside Delph's front door. Without a word, she helps Eden to her feet and lets her in. Eden might as well be her baby too; her upset breaking Delph's heart in the same way. The apologies pouring from her makes Delph dread what she's about to say.

'It was actually Winnie who made me believe it,' Eden begins, shoving kitchen roll into her nostrils. 'Remember

Winnie? With them big brows – Roche's nemesis, who's actually all right once you get – anyway. We were out. Proper caned if I'm honest. And we come out the club onto the cab rank and there's this guy in the line that I'd been dancing with and ...' She drops her eyes. 'I don't know how it happened, but we were kissing, and I'm not gonna lie, it was all good till Winnie started kicking off out of nowhere. Shouting stuff like, how she'd rather walk than get in his cab. And that's when I see him. Watching, like he always does.' She shudders. 'I can't tell you what it's been like, having him in the next room to me at home. How much I've wanted to talk to Roche – not that she'd want to see me.'

'I'm not so sure about that,' Delph says, watching the hope bloom across Eden's face, just as she remembers how adamant Lenny had been about witnessing Itsy with a young girl too.

'He gave Winnie a lift from the club a few months back, and she ain't been right since. Seeing him jogged her memory or something. Anyway, the way she was talking reminded me of ...' Eden hides her face with her hands. 'I hate to tell you this, but Itsy's a drink-spiking perv, Dee.'

Retching, Delph stands, turning her stomach into the kitchen sink.

Spiking. Because why limit it to her?

'So, long story short.' Eden takes a big breath. 'I took his keys.'

How did Delph ever doubt her gut instinct, which screamed he'd been drugging her? The doubt, that had her deciding that moving on should mean forgetting all about it because she could never truly prove it. And now, too busy self-flagellating to almost miss Eden's admission. 'What keys?'

'There ain't nothing much going on between them.' Eden casts her eyes to the ceiling. 'Not that he ain't trying and Mum ain't liking the attention. There's been a lot of music and late nights, though.' Delph does know, having suffered Itsy's greatest hits till silly o'clock, BLACKstreet and Babyface, doing it on purpose, ever since he moved upstairs. 'I'm invisible, anyway, we know that. So, I took advantage, slipped off with his keys. And you know, there was nothing in his car. Nothing. Apart from these.'

From her bag Eden pulls free a bottle of water. Setting it central on the table with a bump, Delph remembers the bottle herself, Itsy's insistence she took one after picking her up from . . . Turning, she heaves into the sink again. But there is nothing left to come out.

'None of them properly sealed,' states Eden, spitting facts, less upset by the second. 'Not a manufacturing problem, not knocks at the cash and carry. Tampering. By him.'

They sit with the bottle in front of them. Until Delph says, 'We need a guinea pig.'

'Yes we do, Dee.' Delph notes again, truly melancholic, how Eden's dropped the Mama. 'And a plan. But first.' Eden pauses. Closes her eyes. 'I want to tell you before he does. That Roche and I . . .'

'Are a thing. Yes, love, she told me. And it's no surprise things have been fraught between you.'

Eden smiles, so relieved she loses inches as her shoulders

relax. 'But it's not just that. I've been so worried what Mum will say. She's not like you. And God, my gran especially will have a hard time, accepting, you know what I mean? Still, that don't explain my kissing someone else.' She looks away, not wanting to meet Delph's eye. 'I think it's knowing that she's going. I'm scared to be on my own. I like being Roche's, you know. We've always been together.'

'You, my lovely, must listen to me.' Delph holds Eden's chin, looking into her eyes. 'I swear on my poor wounded heart that if your love's true, then no distance on earth will make any bloody difference.'

'You look so different,' Eden says, grateful. 'You even sound different. Why?'

Delph thinks, searching for the right words. 'It was time.'

'I don't know why I'm up there when this is all mine, anyway.' Itsy casts his arm across the living room that's never looked nor felt more depressing. 'It's boiling in here. You know I'm still paying the electric.' Turning down the thermostat, he chucks open the back door onto the balcony, ignoring the drink Delph offers. 'Never thought you'd be asking me for help again.' But he looks her up and down with the same old hunger, before kissing his teeth. 'Let me see this sink then. Can't have it flooding if nobody's here.'

It takes a simple undoing of the U-bend for Itsy to discover it's Delph's Elizabeth Duke cubic zirconia causing the blockage. 'Which you might as well have back,' Delph tells him, but only once he's accepted and guzzled his drink.

'You should keep it,' Itsy mumbles, pocketing it anyway.

'I don't want it. What I do want is to know why you've spent so long making the girls feel like their relationship was wrong? What exactly were you hoping to gain from that?' Delph jabs him in the chest, and from his face it's clear that Itsy can't quite believe it. 'The nights I lay next to you wondering how I could end this. How I could end my life. How it would be a blessing. When all I really needed to do was clock whatever it was you've been slipping me. Yeah,' Delph says triumphantly, acknowledging his fear. 'I know. I know everything. And so will the police.'

'With what proof?'

'Winnie Russell proof.'

From indignant to nasty, faster than light. But other than Eden hiding in Roche's room with her finger poised on emergency services, there is no instant back-up. Itsy's fifteen stone; they're ten a piece, tops. Would the amount of drugs in that bottle even touch a heavyweight of man like Itsy, anyway?

He shakes her, but nothing more. 'I've never hurt you, Delph. Never.' Yet his hands are on her just the same as before. Pulling abruptly from his grasp, Delph's shirt tears, flinging her into a cupboard that twists her wrist and grazes the side of her face, as Itsy looks down at his hands, surprised.

'Was it years? Tell me, how long it was, exactly, that you were drugging me for?'

'You're talking rubbish.'

'To control me, even more than you did already? What was it you needed me unconscious for? All that fuss you made.

EVA VERDE

Why I kept being sick. I detoxified, though, didn't I? In more fucking ways than one.'

'You're as bat shit as your fuck-up of a mother.' But Itsy's lost his grip, like a bear, catching a fish with his paws, the success of it short-lived, as with a twist the fish escapes his slithery grasp. Just like Delph has. 'Won't be long before she's back in your head, giving you all sorts of grief,' he tries, giving Moon, even if he does so unwittingly, a run for her money with his cauldron-stirring. 'Then you'll be no better off than before.'

'Though still much better than you'll be when I tell everyone – the police, the girl's school ... *your mum,* what an abusive controlling deviant you are.'

His hands are on her throat, yet Delph doesn't seem to care. 'Fancy joining your poor dead soulmate, is that it? You want me to give you your big reunion? Is that what you want?'

'Help!' Emerges more like a croak, as a calamity of sound comes from Roche's bedroom. The sudden fear on Itsy's face that someone's coming to her rescue is most enjoyable. The marks on Delph already pointing to his guilt. Along with eyewitness Eden.

Delph closes her eyes against the strain, will not give him the satisfaction of any sort of protest. A pressure builds in her head, like it wants to burst from his hands, which are still round her throat, feeling no less strong.

Shouldn't the water have kicked in by now, weakened him, if it was spiked?

Or was this Delph's mind? Her invention. Turning into her mother. Putting her faith in everything that's not real. White light fizzes behind her eyelids, a swelling popping strangeness taking over her body.

'Things were good, Delph. Things were good. All you had to do was stay the same.' As fast as they were there, Itsy's hands leave her neck, leaving Delph collapsed, gasping, as he stumbles to his feet, clutching his head. 'You ...' He reels around, coming face to face with Eden, who aims that heavyweight framed picture of his kids at him again. Itsy looks at his hand, like he's expecting blood, but there's nothing, which only freshly emboldens him.

'You said you been cheating on her batty baby, yet?'

'Like anything I do holds any weight against your multitudes of terrible actions,' Eden says, aiming for him again, both her and Delph catching the bewildered look that crosses his expression. 'It's a real proper cruelty, what you did to me and Roche. We was pure, man. Before you and your spying – and spiking ...'

'Pure? You're just a nasty, confused likkle girl, who ain't nothing to no one.' Itsy chases Eden to the front door, just as she flings it open shouting for help. 'Throwaway baggage.' He follows her onto the landing; a beast cornering its next dinner. 'Ask your mother.'

'It's you who ain't nothing.' Out of options, Eden shoves him. Stumbling at the top of the stairwell, he makes a grab for the banister, and finding a grip, catches himself steady. Pulling upright, he grins at Eden, like he's won.

And it's in slow motion, when the water kicks in and the plan begins to work, which calculates correctly in Itsy's head too, as he fathoms what they've done, how it's his eyes this time that roll backwards into his head, the strength from his legs extracted as they fold beneath him. Missing the hand-rail as he leans over, he falls through the central well, which swallows him.

The sense of an ending. Weird, how one second you're present, and then you're not. We think we're so important. So valuable. Foolish. Because there's no coming back from a fall like that.

As Delph has always known.

28

THE DAZZLING FUTURE

Butterfield Estate, Wellsend Grove, 2023

Delph moves as if drunk, bandy-legged as she grips the doorframe. But this is real, and it is true, as she hears her own terrible voice, her small smooth face beaming up at his. At Sol's. Pub karaoke. The pair of them doing Delph's fave, Saint George Michael and Queen Mary J Blige's cover of 'As'.

'Just as all is born is new. You know what I say is true. That I'll be loving you always.'

'What on earth?'

Roche is exactly her. How Delph was back in the day, on this resurrected videotape. The posture, attitude, the sheer abundance of youth. Vibrant fearless buds in bloom.

'Dad's seriously handsome,' says Roche.

Of course he was.

'Been here all this time,' Moon chips in, gesturing to the

telly, all sweaty and bowled over by how happy the pair of them are. 'Was in the wrong VHS sleeve.'

'In the other mystery box,' adds Roche. 'You want to watch from the beginning?' Beckoning her mum wildly, Delph slumps onto the sofa beside her as though her bones have been stolen. Sol fills the screen before the camera pans out, scanning the crowds in the pub, which is heaving with high-waist jeans, bodysuits and brown lipstick, blokes in puffa coats with either French crops or curtains. Nineties nostalgia in a nutshell. But not Sol. All those heavenly angles and hair lighter than his skin. And the glasses. Little black rectangles. There was nothing wrong with his eyes. If you lifted him out of the video and placed him in the pub present day, he wouldn't have the same hazy, jaded feel about him like the rest of them. He'd slip back in. Like he never left.

Delph's not seen Sol for years. Not years and years.

Time's such a truth-twister. The past, before the pain of that night that never left, past all that useless sorrow and love raging as strong but with nowhere to go. Love forever stuck, behind a thick throat and a lead heart. Take time past all that, back to the good, and it's clear that everything was just that. Perfect. Together, cast in their best light. Matched only by the golden hour Delph finds herself living in now. Her second flourishing.

Surrounded by love. Mother Moon with a job and back on prescription meds (Delph turns a blind eye to the rest, acknowledges progress for progress's sake); Roche with a girlfriend again, Eden apparently showing up and ordering

368

her usual from FreshFry just on closing, with the offer, 'D'you wanna share my chips, bitch?' which of course Roche found irresistible. But long-distance love it'll be; Roche's stack of uni purchases takes up most of her nan's hall. If her grades land as anticipated, it is officially Edinburgh in October. And though Delph's asked Roche plenty, she'll be staying with Moon until uni begins – which Delph's accepted without animosity.

'Did me the world of good. Ripping the plaster off,' Moon says, with a nod of acknowledgement in Roche's direction. 'We found all sorts in the good box. There's always got to be balance. See?' She places a trowel in the left pocket of her new work gilet and a small fork in her right. 'See?' she says, pointing to them both. 'Balance.'

'Mum.' Roche looks a little awkward as she pulls the gold chain off from around her neck. 'It's definitely time you had these back.'

Delph gasps at the sight of the rings, dropping into her palm like a wish come true. There's a soaring sensation in her chest, as she hands them back, chain and all to Roche. 'They're meant to be yours.' Planting a kiss on her daughter's shoulder, Delph snuggles in, resting her head. 'When you wear them, we're all together. Always.'

How she loves being here again, exactly as they all belong, no matter how far away Roche might find herself. Because love has no earthly boundaries. And Delph can't help but remember their start, how her whole body had swollen in step with her pregnancy, her ring cut off before an emergency caesarean. Waking to the broken band, feeling feelings only tempered by Roche's distracting snuffles in the hospital cot beside her. Her daughter: enormous, alert, so obviously overdue, those long fingernails, peeling at the edges of the tiniest of fingers. Gripping hers. A living, breathing product of love. Of them.

Now grown. With the world at her feet.

'Gimme your phone, Mum.' Delph hands it over and Roche aims it at the screen. 'We need copies – can you copy video?'

'We'll need to do something.' Delph's mesmerised all over again. And it does still hurt like hell, only with a little less of the old devastation. Another weight that's lifting, like the fetid binbags that broke Itsy's fall, putting him in intensive care instead of a coffin. When he's strong enough, he too has a new home waiting for him, about the same size as Roche's old room back at Esplanade Point – only under His Majesty's pleasure. Winnie speaking and breaking the silence had a domino effect; similar stories that have saved Eden and Delph from little more than a caution to never entrap a significant danger to the public again. And as for the other coffin dodger, Mother Moon's father is safely back home, with his demons and ailments for company, till the end of his wicked days.

Delph and Roche are only just beginning to learn the complex, difficult truth, as Mother Moon very slowly articulates her early life. But there's no rush. Not with her big B&Q garden messiah plans doing a brilliant job of keeping her mind full of positives.

'There you go.' Rochelle hands the phone back. 'Press it then.'

Delph presses the button, and the screen fills with a picture of her and Sol celebrating New Year's Eve 1999. Millennium Night. The cusp of it all. Twenty-three years have passed since that night in the pub. Eighteen without him, without those arms that were always around her. Such love. Would it be the same now? Would he be the same?

People change.

And some, some people just remember who they are.

'Looks a bit like your scotch bonnet there,' says Moon, over her shoulder. 'Never thought it before.'

Full circle. Even bagging a job in John Lewis, back in her red suit working for Clarins, with a hot new love interest and the world at her feet too.

Happy.

'That's my girl,' Mother Moon says, visualizing the lot along with her. 'Manifest it all.'

Whether her gifts are real or just a purpose-built protection, perhaps it's time Delph believed at last. Opened her heart and embraced the universe.

For joy's such a fleeting commodity.

Rochelle Soleste Barclay

Date of Birth: 22/06/2004

The Edna Roberts Scholarship Application –

Journalism and Political Studies BA

Factors in support of your application (in 600 words or less):

Flora and Folk Tales

I count five flower women in my maternal row. Linked mother to mother to mother until me, for nearly two hundred years, by DNA and family ties. Five buds, who without the right set of circumstances to grow, missed any chance to flourish and live the brilliant lives they deserved. Their barriers came from many sources – a lack of sunlight, being smothered by bigger plants, or picked prematurely, some too delicate for the harsh climate of a harsh world, where each of them failed to thrive.

Why is it so important for me to come to Edinburgh? Will I miss the people who are my world? What is it like to stop worrying for somebody else's safety? To live without permanent anxiety? Because for some time now I've been pot-bound – with a real need to find out if I can flourish elsewhere.

There was a silence that strangled my family. My hunger to uncover our secrets broke my nan's trust, who saw my curiosity as prying. But my discoveries were only ever to colour in the background of all that went before. It's helped us all, despite the trouble it caused, equipping me with a better sense of myself. Of who I am. This maternal story is all that'll ever be possible, because the other half of me remains a mystery, and likely always will. Yet I'm learning that two sides to every story is only really the beginning anyway, which has encouraged me to think about how much I enjoy digging, discovering, researching – and okay, being

372

nosy too – all my reasons for choosing this degree. The family roots I chased led to so much sadness; tragedy, suicide, addiction, rejection. Lives full of pesticides and pollution, preventing flowers of any real magnificence. My nan was an especially beautiful flower. Made of Joy, yet smothered since childhood by such insidious bindweed, she stayed a closed bud forever, unable to open her heart.

Love. Even the word still hunches my mother's shoulders. Had my mum received warmth and encouragement to take root again, if our home had been a cold frame instead of being full of cold feeling, a place of protection to get over her shock, maybe she would've moved past the grief of my murdered father, when she was twenty-four years old. A devastation that left her scared of the world. Scared of life. Scared, with me in her belly.

Grief put my mum in a concrete tower, high in the sky, like a fairy tale princess, locked away for her own protection, guarded by a creature posing as a good man – and everyone knew it but she. Without Mum's natural sun from Sol, my dad, her wilting and trauma lasted almost forever. For years, she simply went through the motions, living without really living, disconnected from the universe. Absent, the same as our own Sun in the future, when on one non-day, in one non-moment, billions of years from now, it too will become nothing.

I believe that the act of returning to the dirt, crumbling back into the earth, sometimes needs to happen. My only fear is that my roots will then entwine with the links of my lineage – not the fault of the plant, but the soil it came from. Or can I rise beyond the cracks of our bleak past, and all which failed to nurture those before, to find another future, the guiding light to grow a different way?

This is my family story. From all we've sown together, through all I couldn't ask.

I want to be the bud who makes it.

ACKNOWLEDGEMENTS

With love and special thanks:

To my brilliant editor Clare, for trusting me to write this quietly, then knowing all the right things to improve that very raw first draft! And to all the fabulous folk at Simon & Schuster; Sabah, Judith, SJ – you truly are the best people.

My agent Abi, for your continued belief in me, which means more than I can say on our journey of growing together.

My husband Matt, for providing the most wholesome and nurturing life balance. And my amazing little women Zoe, Joanie and Eliza – I hope the world is kind and good to you always.

The blessing, Steve the dog; best friend and golden child.

My ever-expanding OG family; Mum, Dad, Jen, Rose and Fi, Martin, Reg, Blousey, Alvin, Sooz and Robin.

My fabulous mates. Your stories of courage and heartbreak, your endless support in gluing together all the pointless creatures we've ever suffered to create the monster that became Itsy. And Emily, who told me a story containing the line 'I had so much more to say,' which made everything click as to what this story was about.

Especial thanks to the graffiti near home which says: 'Don't Die Wondering,' inspiring my bravery to be truly creative, that set my own life In Bloom.

And to my readers – that we've found each other is still so bloody astonishing. I thank you with all my heart.